OILIES

A NOVEL BY

Richard Landerman

ISBN 978-1-7354468-0-6
Printed in the United States of America.
Editor: Cecily Condie, Inglestone Publishing: www.InglestonePublishing.com
Layout & Design: Leslie Thompson, LT Graphics: www.ltgraphics.me

---

DEDICATION

For Rusty and Tammy Snow, for their friendship, support, and agility in surviving the Great Oil Bubble of the 1980s.

And, as always, for my wife, Janet, and our children.

Oilies: n.; plural of oily; slang term for a person or persons associated with or working or employed in the oil extraction industry.

ONE

The Petroleum Club, Denver, Colorado
Spring 1979

"He's late."

"As usual."

"Where is he?"

A uniformed server wearing white gloves hovered nearby as the men fiddled with their knives, wheat rolls, and butter. One glanced at his watch. Someone coughed.

The men assembled in the richly decorated private room were not accustomed to waiting. For anyone. The cream of Denver's business elite: manufacturing, technology, real estate development, trucking, finance, retail, agribusiness. Multi-millionaires to a man. Members of exclusive country clubs and influential churches. Philanthropists. Generous contributors to the arts, universities, hospitals, various worthy charities, and celebrity golf events.

Seth Summers swept into the Petroleum Club private dining room. He appeared neither hurried nor worried. Tall, military straight, tan, manicured, barbered. He was tailored in a bespoke, navy-pinstriped, Savile Row suit and a silver tie. His shoes were also custom-made. By John Lobb of London. He smiled confidently.

Seth took the seat reserved for him at the head of the table. Pride of place.

His movements were carefully calculated. He slowly shook out his linen napkin, creased it neatly on his lap, nodded to the server.

"Gentlemen," Seth greeted them.

"What's so all-fired important that you had to keep us waiting?" Ted Malmo challenged.

Seth waved away the barb with a graceful hand motion. On his left wrist he wore a showy diamond and platinum timepiece that had set him back just north of $50 thousand.

"You'll all be glad you came—even you, Ted," Seth replied. "But first, let's eat!"

A rare white Zinfandel was presented to Summers, who tested it and approved. The wine was poured. Luncheon commenced: Atlantic wild-caught, poached salmon (flown in that morning), with baby potatoes and spring asparagus. Topped off with crème brûlée, cognac, or Kahlua-laced coffee.

When the dishes were cleared away, Seth stood and motioned to his shapely female assistant. Every male eye in the room followed her runway stroll to a side table where she gathered up an armful of heavy-stock navy folders embossed with gold lettering. She handed each of the seven men one of the folios. Not one of them took his eyes off her disarming smile long enough to look down at what she had given them. They continued to watch as she excused herself and all eyes, except Seth's, followed her starlet exit.

Still standing, Seth spoke. "Gentlemen, what you have in your hands is a highly confidential executive summary of a business plan. For a completely new venture. With a totally new concept for doing business."

A few of the men started to open their folders. Summers frowned, waved them off.

"Before we examine this document, I want to make a short speech."

Some groaned, some chuckled at this. Seth was not known for being brief; he loved the microphone.

"I know what you're thinking: 'Old man Summers has never made a short speech in his life!'" Good humored laughter all around.

"Well, I can assure you this one will be short. There *is* one document I need you to take a look at before I start. Go ahead and open your files." The men proceeded to open their folders as invited. "You can scan the contents while I talk."

"The first page you see on top is a legal document that I need all of you to sign before we proceed any further. It's a nondisclosure agreement that I had my lawyers draw up. I'm sure you are all familiar with this document. Normal business practice, and all that."

The men reached into their coat pockets and produced expensive fountain pens. They quickly scribbled signatures with barely a glance at the dense legal wording. Then, they passed the papers to Summers.

"Thank you. Now, for the speech. I'm proposing we start a new bank. Right here in Denver. I know some of you are thinking we already have too many banks in this market. But, stop and ponder for a minute: How many Denver banks do you know that specialize in petroleum lending? I'm talking about the oil business. Hmmm?"

He looked around the circle of prominent businessmen.

"I don't see any hands. That proves my point."

Heads nodded, knowing glances were exchanged.

"Now, you're probably wondering what this has to do with you. The bank will need capital, several million, to get started. Twenty million to be precise. And management. Members for the board of directors. Advisory committees. So on. That's why I invited you all here today. I need your help."

Summers paused and let this sink in.

"If you will now take a look at the executive summary, let's walk through the major points."

All heads bowed, several of the men produced half-moon reading glasses, and they each began to scan the five-page executive summary before them.

"First, you will note that the bank is tentatively named Larimer Square Bank."

TWO

Colorado State Banking Commission, Denver

"Commissioner Morgan will see you now."

Seth Summers was ushered into a small gray office in a nondescript government building occupying space in the Colorado state government complex.

Dennis Morgan, early fifties, squat, balding, cheap plastic horn-rimmed glasses, short-sleeve white shirt with a white plastic pocket protector full of pens, and an ugly, wide necktie, extended his hand to the taller, white-haired businessman. They shook hands briefly.

Morgan motioned to a cheap, Naugahyde-covered side chair. "Please. Sit."

Seth settled himself while Morgan cleared away a stack of papers, tented his fingers and peered over the horn-rimmed glasses that had slipped down his thin nose. What did this man want now? Morgan knew that Seth Summers had a reputation as a successful penny stock promoter. That he was wealthy there was no doubt. Just one look proves it: bankers gray, hand-tailored Saville Row suit and shirt, with an expensive maroon silk tie perfectly knotted. His handmade cordovan brogues. Also London? Where did he get his money?

Nobody requested private meetings with the Colorado State Banking Commissioner, Dennis Morgan, without wanting something. Well, let's see what he wants. This rich, successful, penny stock promoter.

"How can I help you?" Morgan opened lamely. Summers noted a bit of sarcasm.

Seth Summers handed across a copy of the executive summary, CONFIDENTIAL rubber-stamped in red ink across the tops and bottoms of each of the five pages.

“And what’s this?” Morgan asked, not looking at the folio in his hand.

“A group of friends and I want to start a new bank. Here in Denver. One that specializes in banking for the oil and gas industry. A fairly new concept, I admit. But …”

Morgan didn’t bother to read the document. He laid it on a tall pile of files and papers teetering on the corner of his metal desk. He would get to it later. He had more important things to deal with just now.

“What do you know about banking? I’m sure you appreciate that banking is a totally different business than the stock, uh, investing, uh, than finance?” He almost slipped and said penny stocks.

Summers nodded, stayed cool. “We have a slate of directors who collectively have decades of experience dealing with banks. One or two have even served on bank boards. In the past.”

Morgan nodded. “But the most critical position in a bank, as I’m sure you already have learned, is the chief loan officer. I don’t give much stock in the CEO. It’s the loans that make or break a bank these days. So critical …” He trailed off. Glanced at the stack of papers. Thinking of several troubled banks in that pile, large and small. A couple failing banks that he might have to close down soon. Those headaches were more urgent than yet another start-up bank.

“We have several excellent candidates in mind. For job security reasons—as I’m sure you can appreciate in your line of work—we can supply their names and resumes later. At the appropriate time. I’m confident you’ll find any one of them eminently qualified for the loan officer position.”

Seth’s mind wandered back to the discussion on that very subject around the Petroleum Club table a few days earlier.

Seth had rejected the names of several Denver bankers. Well known to the inner circle. Red herrings. All. What he had in mind, what he needed, was a fresh face, an unknown, who would be carefully hand-picked for the job.

Right now, he didn’t really have a clue who that man might be. But he wasn’t worried. He would find the right man; it might take some time, but it would happen.

What he did know was the name and reputation of his pick for CEO. He had been personally and carefully chosen by Summers after much research. Summers had looked for someone hungry and willing to take a new approach, someone aggressive and brash. The man he had in mind had no fear. And he would have been struggling for years under the load on his back only too well-known to many generations of middle-level bankers: stuck in middle management. Passed over for promotion. Never enjoying the fruits of the top job and all the perks, salary, and adulation. And the power of being top dog.

Seth needed a CEO who would bend to his will, a man who could be manipulated, yet would remain loyal and discreet. Loyal to Summers and his own plans. Discreet and able to keep secrets. Maybe even a dirty little secret when the situation warranted.

But now was not the time to reveal the big picture or disclose his private plans to Morgan. That would come when the time was right. It would be a last-minute announcement, timed when Morgan was buried in the fruitless rescue operation of yet another failed small-town bank.

For now, Seth Summers was intent on riding the swell of the storm. It was the perfect storm, one he'd seen brooding, gathering on the horizon, promising an unquenchable deluge of money and power for someone like him, someone who had recognized and taken advantage of the inevitable signs.

THREE

Easy Money

For many decades, natural gas didn't signal even a wisp of a cloud of opportunity. A byproduct of crude oil production, the "oilies" in the Great Basin petroleum-producing states of Texas, Oklahoma, Colorado and Kansas (and as widely scattered as Wyoming, Montana and Utah) treated natural gas as mostly a nuisance. Because it was so plentiful and cheap and there was little demand for it as a fuel, natural gas was usually flared off, just burned from the wellhead into the atmosphere.

Following the Middle East oil embargoes of the mid-1970s, energy policy thinking changed dramatically. Politicians were eager to prove to voters that they were *doing* something about the fuel shortages—and the resulting long lines at the gas pumps. Armed with masses of data to support their cause, a group of clever petroleum engineers and oilmen from Oklahoma launched an assault on Washington. Their goal: deregulation of natural gas, which would then allow them to promote a cheaper (and cleaner) alternative to crude oil products.

Because the price of natural gas had been kept artificially low through outdated regulations for such a long time, the public utilities were eager to hop on board. And by having more abundant fuel, the big utilities—monopolies—would be able to make long-term contracts with the producers for a predictable supply far into the future.

The producers would be happy because the increased demand would raise the price they got for the gas. The utilities would be happy because they could average the higher-priced new gas into the rates they were charging consumers and pass the increased prices on to the public.

The utilities embarked on a massive PR campaign targeted at consumers. The goal: convince consumers that they were getting a better deal with natural gas. The ads repeatedly emphasized the catch words "cleaner and cheaper." It worked beautifully.

Part of the Washington lobbying team pushing for deregulation was a small band of petroleum geologists, engineers, and specialists trained to find and quantify fields of petroleum—fields that sometimes lay more than two miles below the earth's surface.

Of particular interest to these petroleum gurus was a potential field in west-central Oklahoma known as the Anadarko Basin. The Anadarko had been extensively mapped using seismological technology.

Natural gas production is measured in terms of *mcf*, or thousand cubic feet. The Anadarko, it was speculated, probably held billions—*billions*—of cubic feet of gas.

If anyone could reach it.

Conventional wells of the day maybe ran as deep as 10,000 feet. And, even then, drilling that deep was risky. Drill bits were prone to disintegrate. Temperatures could reach over 600 degrees Fahrenheit. Drill pipe could shear off. Tools could be lost down hole. Bore holes could collapse. Gas could cause explosions. So many unknowns.

Nobody had dared (or had the risk money) to drill as deep as the Anadarko gas was thought to be located: below 20,000 feet. Or more.

Big risk.

Bigger than anyone had ever taken.

But big rewards.

For the gamblers, the wildcatters. If …

If they could find the money.

The Natural Gas Policy Act was signed into law by President Jimmy Carter on November 9, 1978, and the natural gas boom was on, together with renewed enthusiasm for petroleum exploration, generally.

But where to get the money to buy leases, to pay for exploration, for drilling and completing wells? Where could someone find the money to purchase or lease more drill rigs? For drilling pipe, chemicals? To hire more labor? Where would the needed money come from to build new gas processing plants? New gas transmission pipelines?

Money would not be a problem for the majors: Exxon, Standard Oil, Shell, British Petroleum. But what about the smaller companies? The Little Guys? The lone wildcatter operating on a shoestring?

One option was to try to get a loan from a local bank. Pretty tough to do.

There were a few bigger, regional banks in the money centers of Dallas, Houston, Oklahoma City, Tulsa—and a few in Chicago or New York—that specialized in providing funds to established independent oil companies, using their proven oil and gas reserves in the ground as collateral. But nobody loaned for exploratory—wildcat—wells. And certainly, never on just oil leases as collateral. No matter how proven the field was. And, don't even ask for a loan using your drill rigs as collateral. In a downturn, that stuff became a pile of scrap iron. They had all seen many a boom followed by bust in the oil business.

Here's where Seth Summers saw a chance to seed the mounting clouds. The current tax laws encouraged investment into oil and gas ventures. Investors could write off a percentage of their investment against their tax bill. This advantage helped the oilies find the money to help offset the risky nature of oil drilling. And there was always the thrill of those investors telling friends at country club cocktail parties that they owned a piece of the oil business.

So limited partnerships became the favored way to raise drilling funds. But oilmen would rather spend their time and energy finding the black stuff, not raising money. They looked to hired guns to do the money-raising for them: a specialized class of entrepreneurs to gather the money. Tax shelter promoters. Money-raisers. Hustlers.

About the same time Congress passed another act that would prove to have a decisive impact on the way business was done in the oil patch. It was delivered as a gift in the form of the Garn-St. Germain Depository Institutions Act, a bill co-sponsored by Senator Jake Garn (R-Utah) and Congressman Fernand St. Germain (D-RI).

The desired effect of the bill was to allow savings and loan institutions to compete directly with banks for deposits and loans. The S&Ls now had individual deposits insured up to $100,000 each, and

S&L loans no longer had to be tied to real estate as the purpose of the loan or for collateralization.

The financial industry free-for-all was on! S&Ls began offering "jumbo" certificates for $100,000 deposits with absolutely absurd interest rates attached as an incentive to depositors. Interest rates as high as 25 percent for long term CDs. The banks immediately jumped on this bandwagon and began offering their own competing CDs with their own absurd rates of interest attached.

Funds that were previously tied up in other savings or investments were swiftly moving toward the hot new jumbo CDs—an effect that bankers and economists labeled disintermediation. Banks that had shied away from energy loans in the past (and even some S&Ls), now had money to lend on riskier deals. Such as oil and gas. And they took a fresh look at the potential profits to be had from these loans. And a fresh look at loans for wildcatters, land leases, and oilfield equipment.

Financial institutions could now tack on higher interest rates, and they did. They could charge origination fees, known as "points," for the risk they were assuming. And they did. They could also collect huge "service fees" for preparing the paperwork, record-keeping, filing titles, reporting to regulators, and collecting payments from the borrower. And they did.

Banks that were previously averse were now eager to get their share of huge profits to be made in the energy boom.

The borrower didn't care too much that lenders were cashing in on higher interest rates and service fees. Not when they could get the needed money to expand their business, buy new leases or rigs, drill new wells. Their thoughts were: Who cares about a few more interest points or fees when a couple of new producing wells will solve those minor worries? Shoot, throw in another $10 thousand on that loan, and I can get that new Ford F-150 truck! I just need to know what the quarterly interest payment is gonna be so I can factor that into my cash flow projections.

And they signed on the dotted line. Many looking toward the ultimate dream: We're gonna get us some of that Anadarko deep gas!

Everybody was happy with this New Energy Age.
It had all the makings of a perfect storm. Seth Summers knew it.

FOUR

Elkhead Creek, a Trout Stream near Craig, Colorado

Dill Robertson was deeply engrossed. He had just felt a slight bump at the end of his fly line, not a real strike, but a teasing bump from a trout. It was just what he had come to expect in spring when the mercury was hovering in the low 40s.

Twenty yards away, on the opposite grassy bank, a pair of Canada geese muttered and hissed at him for interrupting their nest making. Mist rose off the stream as the morning sun warmed.

He retrieved his line and made another roll cast. His rig of a weighted San Juan worm with a chartreuse Glo Bug suspended ten inches below did the trick. The trout took the Glo Bug, Dill struck with practiced skill, and the fight was on.

Within seconds, Dill gently handled a two-pound Colorado cutthroat trout, admiring its beautiful coloring, garnet gill plates, the orange-red slashes under its throat, the prominent black spotting on its sides and flanks. He never ceased to marvel at the perfection of God's creations, even in his hand, in the form of a trout.

He treasured these moments alone on the stream when he could wrestle with so-called deep thoughts. At least that's what he told his family and his bank employees, when he stole a few hours on the stream. He usually was focused only on his fishing and the task in front of him, so rarely had deep thoughts. But fishing was his personal therapy, deep thoughts or no.

Dill gently lowered the trout back into the cold stream, reeled in his slack line. He rinsed off his hands, wiped them on the seat of his Wranglers, and climbed up the steep bank to his truck. He chucked his fly rod into the back and headed for town.

Satisfied. A couple hours of stolen pleasure. A short parole from the usual daily worries of helping run a small country bank, balancing his time between the bank's demands and constant details of managing the family ranch he inherited, while still carving out time for family, church and civic obligations. A welcome break, indeed, but not a complete reprieve from the unending niggling about his wife, JoEllen.

He was anxious to hear what Jo had learned from her doctor's appointment in Steamboat Springs. The recent fatigue, a little scratch that wouldn't heal. Her doctor had taken blood samples and forwarded them to the hospital in Steamboat Springs for analysis. He thought it was acute anemia, but he wasn't sure. He'd let her know when the results came back. In the meantime, the doctor told her, "Get plenty of rest, and try to get more iron in your diet."

Or. It could possibly be something more serious. They'd had this same concern two years before. Turned out then it really was just anemia. Still …

As Dill made his way from Elkhead Creek into the town of Craig, the scattering of late spring snow blowing horizontally across the road matched his cold, unsettled feeling. He shivered as he suddenly happened on a herd of pronghorn antelope crossing the road and almost didn't see the animals in time.

He pulled into the parking spot at the bank marked with his name: Dilworth Robertson, Vice President, the spot he had objected to vigorously. "I don't need a special parking spot. What kind of signal does that send to our customers? That I'm somehow somebody special? Above them? I need to blend in with the locals, my neighbors."

Actually, Dill Robertson *was* somebody special in Craig. His family had ranched there for three generations before him. The men in his family were hard working and their efforts paid off. They had endured through ups and downs of bad weather, bad markets, massive bank loans, and crippling government rules and regulations.

In addition to an aversion to debt and government regulation, the Robertson family was known for two other remarkable traits: education was as important as was service to their fellowmen. Dill had the advantage of getting a fine college education at the University of

Colorado, followed by two grueling years at the Amos Tuck School of Business at Dartmouth, where he earned an MBA. He had resisted the MBA, but his grandpa and his own father had ganged up on him and insisted. "You never know when you just might use that degree, sonny boy," his grandpa had said. As it turned out, grandpa had been right.

Dill's grandfather had started the bank with a couple of friends in the middle of the Great Depression, the Wall Street crash that had triggered so much misery. But, against the odds, this bank had survived, thanks to grandpa's deep pockets and his willingness to continue pumping capital in to keep the bank from going under.

That, and his willingness to trust his rancher neighbors and their honesty in repaying their mortgages and crop loans. His patience and trust were proven well-placed when, time and again, his neighbors somehow managed to come up with at least interest payments and a little bit here and there on the loan principal.

Over time, with the help of President Franklin D. Roosevelt and his government subsidies and recovery programs, the Robertsons and their neighbors came out of the deep misery of the Depression slightly better off. Then World War II came and, with it, a new era of prosperity for farmers and ranchers as prices for their crops climbed to higher, sustainable levels.

The bank ownership had been passed down from father to oldest son twice. Dill was the second son. So his older brother, Ephraim, had inherited the title of bank president plus 51 percent of the stock.

Dill was invited to be vice president, with 29 percent of the stock passing into his hands. Ten percent was owned by his older sister; the rest of the shares were owned by a few bank directors. In actual practice, Dill ran the bank much of the time, while Ephraim, who had political ambitions, was off politicking.

Dill stopped for a minute in front of the bank, located at the intersection of Yampa Avenue and West Victory Highway, a choice location in the center of town. He looked at the new yellow paint marking off the parking spaces.

His objections had been overridden when his secretary, his cashier/ operations officer, and his board of directors—which included Ephraim,

Ephraim's son Heber, and their aged sister, Aunt Ida—all insisted. So up came the sign. And the yellow parking stripes were slapped down onto the pavement. He reluctantly pulled his truck into his reserved space next to the rarely used one marked: Ephraim Robertson, President and CEO.

Still dressed in his Wranglers, sheepskin vest and the red flannel shirt that his muscled, wide-shouldered frame filled nicely, Dill left his fly rod, waders, and gear in the back of his truck and strolled into the bank. His roughout cowboy boot made a pounding staccato against the Vermont marble tiles of the lobby.

At the door to his office, Dill's secretary, Trudy Rawlings, intercepted his forward progress and handed him a stack of pink phone messages. "How was the fishing? Catch anything of any size?" she asked.

Dill just nodded, took his messages and placed them on the corner of his desk, then removed his tan, sweat-stained Stetson, and ran a hand through his unruly, thick brown hair.

"You have three really urgent ones from some gentleman in Denver. A Mr. Seth Summers, who insists it's really critical that he speak to you. Preferably today."

"Three? Who is he? I don't recognize ..."

"He wouldn't say what it was about. I tried to get it out of him."

"Thank you, Trudy. I'll call him and see what could possibly warrant three calls." Dill closed the door to his office, something he rarely did. His first call would be to Jo. He needed to know.

"Hi, sweetheart. How'd it go? Yeah, I snuck off for a couple hours to play with the trout. I figured fishing would help pass the time. I knew I wouldn't be any good here until I heard from you."

After a few seconds that seemed like minutes, she cleared her throat on the other end of the line. He could tell she was trying to hold back tears. Dill finally broke the silence. "And ...?"

He listened, waited, held his breath. For the longest time it seemed. When she broke the news, he exhaled slowly, fighting to keep his voice strong, calm.

"Are they sure? I mean, last time it was just anemia. Did they take, uh, tissue samples? Biopsies? Have them analyzed by experts? Oh yeah, I forget, that Steamboat specialist is kinda new. Yeah, oncologists, that's the word I was looking for."

He choked on the title.

Neither spoke for several minutes. The Regulator clock on his wall loudly clicked off the seconds. Life slowly unwinding. He could tell she was now quietly crying on the other end of the line.

"Look, dearest, I'm so sorry. But let's get a second opinion. We can call someone in Denver. Make an appointment. I can take the time off and drive you there."

He hung up and stared at the phone. Dill didn't much care for phones: so often the bringer of bad news.

The Regulator ticked off several more minutes before Dill was composed enough to place a return call to a Mr. Seth Summers in Denver.

FIVE

A Country Club in Summit Township, New Jersey

Jerry Jordan smiled. Broadly. He had this group of suckers right where he wanted them.

Jerry was lucky that his roommate from Cornell happened to be a member of the posh, exclusive Patriots Country Club in upscale Summit County, New Jersey.

Bo Bentley was Old Money.

Bo Bentley lived amongst Old Money.

Bo Bentley went to church with Old Money.

Old Money voted together, usually Republican. So did Bo.

Old Money made donations to the favored charities together.

Old Money ran together in the same pack.

Old Money gathered at the same watering holes—like this elegant country club.

Old Money tended to trade investment tips.

Old Money bragged about their successful investments at cocktail parties. Or wherever they gathered to drink and gossip about each other.

Bo Bentley was just as greedy as the rest of the Old Money crowd. So, when Jerry had contacted him and pitched Bo on the latest deal Jerry was involved in, no big surprise there when Bo quickly jumped in for half of whatever Jerry would make on commissions.

But Jerry neglected to tell Bo about the bonus kickbacks from the drillers and operators. Didn't tell Bo about the carried interests and overriding royalties that could figure into the longer-term profits for the guys who raised the money to drill, complete, and equip the wells.

Just think: what if one of Ginger Foss's wells actually did come in a gusher, say 250 barrels a day? And at the current price of crude just nearing $50 a barrel? And with the petroleum engineers that Foss had on his payroll predicting—*in written scientific reports*—that West Texas Sweet Crude would top $100 a barrel by the end of this year?

Jerry had told the group of well-heeled potential limited partners gathered in the packed private room at the Club, "Shoot! You'd be stupid as a post not to get in on this bonanza! Like shooting fish in a barrel!" Jerry was on a roll, setting aside all sense of decency—all sense completely—as his sales pitch continued, strung together with his signature coarseness and favorite four-letter words.

They weren't offended by his crudeness. He was a guys' guy among this rough-around-the-edges audience. They ate it up. Right out of his hand. Just like the group yesterday that Bo had organized in Manhattan at the Cornell Club.

And, hopefully, like the group tomorrow Bo had set up for Jerry to pitch in Philadelphia. Doctors. Dentists. Lawyers. Accountants.

And the New Money guys Jerry loved even more: Professional athletes. Rock stars. Rich sons-of-guns, all! Look at the cars they drive up in, will you! Mercedes. Cadillacs. Porsches. Jaguars. Land Rovers. Even a couple of Rolls Royces!

They can afford to invest. They can't afford not to!

He spelled it out, saying, "Think of the tax breaks you're going to get in this deal: three-to-one. Plus, you'll get investment tax credits as a bonus. That comes off the bottom line of your final tax bill, folks!

And don't forget the sweetest part of this deal: It's leveraged! By using a letter of credit from your bank you only have to come up with 25 percent in cash. The other 75 percent is provided by your friendly banker.

In other words, you're using OPM. Other People's Money! Isn't that sweet?

All your lines of credit are lumped together. Then the driller delivers those LCs to his bank. Which, in turn, creates a line of credit for the driller to draw down as he needs it to drill, complete, and equip the well. *If* it's deemed to be a producer from the drill logs that are kept as he drills down hole. Remember, I said, "*If*."

No one knew this Jerry Jordan guy.

But everyone liked Bo.

Everyone trusted Bo.

His word was good enough.

He's one of us, they reasoned.

If Bo is in this deal, then we're in it, too.

"This stage coach is leavin' town, folks. So, you all better step up and put your names on the subscription agreements my lovely assistant, Patti, has ready for you on that desk in the back of the room."

They couldn't sign up fast enough.

Jerry gave another glowing report that night from his first-class hotel back to the powers that be of Stagecoach Energy Corp. in Dallas, the sponsor of the oil and gas limited partnership Jerry was selling.

There would be a half dozen other similar phone calls that night to Stagecoach Energy in Dallas from various other parts of the country, from other salesmen just like Jerry. With those reports in hand, Lorne Bagley, CEO of Stagecoach, then made a call to Ginger Foss to keep him apprised of the progress on the fundraising. Ginger grinned and did a little dance as he rang off and sipped his Old Turkey. His third one that evening.

Seth Summers, too, had a drink in his hand. He propped his elegant, handmade brogues up on the divan and sipped a well-aged single malt. He scanned his checklist. The phone call with Dilworth Robertson (funny name, Dilworth. Family name?) earlier that afternoon had gone well. Seth had outlined a few details, and Robertson had been somewhat interested. Said they might be able to meet in the Petroleum Club in Denver in the near future.

Seth scanned over the Robertson background report Lucky had compiled for him. He was confident that Robertson would be his first choice for Larimer Square Bank's chief loan officer. It might take some selling to convince him, but Seth was certain he could bring him in.

Seth had one problem to contend with: Why would a man like Robertson want to leave his position as head of an old, established, family bank and his somewhat profitable ranching operation to move to Denver and step in as the chief loan officer of a startup bank? What could he use to convince him to say yes? What was this Dilworth character's hot button? Seth was a consummate salesman; he knew how to read people, find their soft spots and close the deal. He also possessed the greatest weapon for a negotiator: He was patient. He believed in the idea that all good things come to those who wait. Even still, he trusted even more in helping things along, in finding a chink, and then pushing what he wanted forward as soon as he had skillfully sniffed out the slightest opening.

Seth stared at the folder in front of him. How was he going to get to this guy with the strange sounding name? He had no prior arrests, no run-ins with the law, no skeletons in the proverbial closet. Nothing.

Seth took another sip of his scotch and remembered something Robertson had said that morning. About meeting in Denver in the near future. Denver, now why would this squeaky-clean guy be planning a trip to the big city?

For Seth, the next few weeks were packed with a flurry of activity. He had a million things to think about and plan, but no matter how full he filled his plate, one thing kept nagging at him.

Summers liked to compare himself with the African crocodile: silent, still, patient and hard to spot until too late. Still, try as he might, this one was getting to him. Unable to concentrate on the work in front of him, he slammed shut the file he was working on and grabbed another off the corner of his desk.

He had read these notes about Dilworth Robertson a hundred times, but there had to be something he was missing. As if on cue, Seth's phone rang, and he picked it up on the first ring. He didn't even get a chance to say hello before, on the other end, the voice he recognized as Lucky's, blurted out. "She's sick, Seth. Jo-stinkin'-Ellen-stinkin'-Robertson. She's sick. Possibly bad sick. Leukemia. I'm bringing you the details. Stay put."

Seth set down the receiver and slowly exhaled. That's it. Dilworth Robertson's wife was sick. So sick that the existing medical care facilities in Craig and Steamboat were far less than adequate. Okay for minor injuries and simple cases. But not for leukemia. That's why he has to come to Denver, Seth concluded. Only in Denver could they find the oncologists, surgeons, procedures, and state-of-the-art medical equipment they could need. Only here could they get the treatment that could include chemotherapy, radiation, and bone marrow transplants.

Not only did Dilworth need to be in Denver to get the treatment she needed, the cost could be enormous.

Dilworth needed to be right where Seth wanted him. Plus, he needed the kind of medical insurance package Summers was prepared to offer him.

Seth rubbed his hands together and smiled. He poured a drink and waited for his private detective and informant to arrive with the details, but he knew he'd already found the hot button for Dill Robertson.

SIX

Tulsa Guaranty Bank, Tulsa, Oklahoma

Ricky Bob Peabody was in a high state of anxiety. Extremely high, near to catatonic. His request to extend his line of credit had just been turned down. Refused—by his best friend, Kyle. Put him on the used-to-be-best-friend-no-Christmas-card-this-year list, you jerk! Ricky spat.

He jammed his truck into gear and almost hit an old lady as he screeched out of the Tulsa Guaranty Bank parking lot. A flashing yellow light on the dash warned him he was low on gas. He peeled off the main road into a gas station. He slammed the door, stomped inside, and thrust his credit card at the pimple-faced kid behind the counter. The attendant swiped his card once, twice, then informed Ricky Bob that his credit card was denied.

Rats! Ricky Bob climbed back into the truck, seething in a cold fury. "Arrogant idiots!" Then cold panic began to grip him. Ricky Bob prayed he had enough gas to make it from Tulsa to his home in Okmulgee. If he shut off the engine and coasted down the hills …

On the slow drive, he went back over the meeting in his mind.

He had reminded Kyle of their friendship that went all the way back to high school. Of all the firsts they experienced together: first drink of real booze. If you could call sloe gin real booze. First time to make out with girls. First deer they each shot and gutted in the woods, coming home all bloody and drunk. First touchdown pass Kyle threw to Ricky Bob. How they had double dated. How they had sat in the early dawn after a game night at Oklahoma University laying out their big plans for life while sharing a bottle of Old Turkey.

Kyle would follow in the tradition of joining his family's bank, The Tulsa Guaranty Bank. Old, old money. Ricky Bob would someday inherit his Daddy's oil and gas drilling and service business—after a reasonable period of apprenticeship learning the ropes, with another drilling company, owned by a friend of his Daddy.

He and Kyle had rehashed how they had made a lot of money together by Kyle's bank providing drilling funds to Ricky Bob. And how Ricky Bob had been successful at drilling little 1,200-foot gas wells at first in the many patches of "blanket sands" around Okmulgee County. "Three-Day Wonders," he called them. Open hole completion, no down hole pipe to buy, just drilling mud to pack and line the bore hole. Tiny little pump jacks called "Poppin' Johnnies" in the industry. Keep the costs low. Each well produced maybe ten barrels a day and about one mcf of gas that they just blew off into the atmosphere for lack of a decent pipeline nearby. But as the number of wells added up over time. Shoot, the math was easy …

Then, reaching farther afield and deeper. Drilling serious wells of 5,000 feet or more. Most had been successful completions for Ricky Bob. Sure, there had been a few dry holes. A few wells, the highly fractured formations around Okmulgee County, had filled with salt water after coming in so strong at first, so promising. But … shrimp farms, he called these water-filled failures.

Ricky Bob fumed at how Kyle had sat there nodding. In his banker's suit of gray pinstripes, starched white button-down shirt and his OU fraternity necktie. His banker hands steepled together, their favorite defense pose. Leaning back in his big leather banker's chair. Smiling. Nodding.

Then, the mood had changed from good-old-boys friendly to serious business. Ricky Bob could feel it. He felt like a fool. He'd been played. Again.

"Yeah. We had good times together, Ricky Bob." Kyle had cleared his throat, leaned forward.

Here it comes, Ricky Bob had thought. The big turndown.

Kyle had rummaged through the pages in a thick manila file before him. Finding what he'd wanted among the papers, he'd stopped. Scanned. Frowned. "Hmmm."

Then he'd grinned. The stupid jerk had grinned!

"I see from the latest report on your wells that production has dropped off. Considerably."

Like that's anything to grin about?

"That's the Oil and Gas Commission. Regulations limiting production and pressures," Ricky Bob had insisted. He had been sinking slowly. He'd been desperate for a lifeline, anything.

Kyle had held up his hand, palm out. "Yeah, well, maybe. But …" Long pause, eyes averted. "We … I mean, the bank, just can't extend any more credit at this time. You're already behind. Even your agreement to keep your interest payments current. It's way past due."

Ricky Bob had started sinking faster and not just in the massive debt he owed the bank. He'd been drowning in humiliation and despair. He had nothing to come back with. He really could use a drink.

"Wish I could help you. Just can't at this time," Kyle had said. He'd folded up the manila file, stood. Meeting over. Nice try.

Ricky Bob had sat there. Too stunned to move. Kyle had reached out a hand. Ricky Bob had ignored the gesture.

"Have you considered, uh … cutting back?"

"Cutting back? On what? I'm already bare bones as it is." Ricky had wanted to hit him. He'd relaxed his balled-up fists. Sweat, acid sweat, had been trickling down from his armpits, staining his one good shirt.

Kyle had returned to his desk, shuffled through a stack of business cards, and handed one to Ricky Bob.

"What's this?"

"This company is a professional business turnaround consulting firm. They specialize in oil and gas companies. Small companies like yours." He'd proffered the card.

Ricky Bob had ignored the insult, hesitated taking the card. "Why would I need them? What do they know about actual operating problems in the oil patch?"

Engine off, he coasted into the yard of Peabody Oil Company, stopping beside the bulk gasoline tank. As he refilled his truck, he thought: This fight ain't over yet. I'll just have to find me another banker. One who ain't so uptight about loaning on good leases and rigs instead of just proven reserves.

SEVEN

Craig, Colorado

JoEllen only spoke once during the five-hour drive to Denver. Dill had tried to get her to talk, but she ignored his questions and finally, "I just wish I could see our future," was all she said. Dill wished she would open up and say what she was really thinking. She ought to say more, about their four sons, about her parents, about him—anything but this heavy silence.

Dill dropped her off at the oncology wing of the hospital. He kissed her on the cheek and said, "You sure you don't want me to come in with you?" She shook her head, turned and squared her shoulders, started for the entrance. She carried with her a simple bag of personals. In case they needed her to stay overnight. Dill slowly drove away. He was in no hurry to get to the appointment he had set up with Seth Summers.

Summers had promised he would be waiting at the front door of The Petroleum Club. Robertson pulled into the parking lot, slowly slid out of his truck and walked toward the building, trying to size up the man standing there. Summers offered his hand; it was as dry as parchment, cool to the touch and uncomfortably gentle. Dill looked him in the eye and saw an intent stare in return. He felt like a cottontail rabbit being sized up by a coyote just before the powerful jaws closed on its neck. The feeling passed. After the formal preliminaries, they sat down to lunch. The Petroleum Club was ostentatious, cavernous and quiet. The serving staff stood around at attention like soldiers in a parade with their white gloves and stiffly starched livery. Dill would have preferred to just meet at a Burger King, or at Summers' office.

They ate in uncomfortable silence. Dill's thoughts were on his wife at the oncology center.

Seth ordered coffee. Dill politely declined. Seth was not surprised. Mormons don't drink coffee, and Lucky's confidential report had noted this man was a devout Mormon and had been a Mormon bishop. Twice. Seth thought briefly of the old joke, "Why do you bring two Mormons fishing with you?" Answer: "Because if you only bring one, he'll drink all your beer."

But that hadn't really been Seth's experience. For the most part, his dealings with Mormons had been pleasant. Whether other Mormons were watching or not, they were mostly all true to their beliefs, strange as they seemed to Seth. He came back to the present.

"I prepared a formal offer for you to read." Seth handed over a single sheet.

Dill scanned through it, raised his eyebrows more than once. As a banker, he had naturally become suspicious of anything on paper containing inflated figures. This was almost beyond ridiculous. He glanced up to see if Summers was smiling, but he sat there deadpan. He nodded for Dill to read the last paragraph. Dill finished reading, folded the paper and laid it beside his crisp linen napkin.

"Any questions?"

"Well … yes." Dill started with the job title: Senior Vice President. What did that mean, what was involved in the job description? He would be giving up the title of CEO and the only vice president with his own bank. If he was senior VP, obviously other vice presidents were planned for? How many? What was so special about being a senior vice president in a startup?

"I'd be coming from title of CEO down to a senior vice president in a startup bank."

Seth nodded. "We'll get back to that. And technically, we're very close to getting our charter. I'm hoping you decide to help us with the opening of the bank." He waited.

Dill said nothing.

"Next …?"

"Well, I'm frankly baffled by the salary. I mean, to start out in a new bank at $350,000 a year for a guaranteed three years, well, that seems a little rich." He thought about the modest-by-comparison $65,000 annual salary he drew from his little country bank back in Craig.

"I'm concerned that maybe you folks don't have a real grip on the realities of the costs associated with banking. And the profit margin, as I'm sure you know, is very slim in banking. Are you sure about this?"

"We did extensive research on the market for bank executives, not just in Denver, but across the major cities in the country. It's in the ballpark."

"For established concerns, maybe, but…"

Seth held up his hands, palms out. "I admit we plan to be aggressive in capturing the bulk of the petroleum business in this region. We think—no, we are *convinced*—our aggressive strategy will yield above-average profits. Which we intend to share with management, as you may have read further down the page."

Dill nodded.

"You don't have a problem with the concept of profit-sharing, do you?"

Dill admitted he didn't.

"Who do you have in mind for president/CEO? Is he—or she—anyone I know?" Dill asked.

"Now you probably know I really can't disclose that just yet. But I'm sure you two will get along just fine."

"Experienced?" Dill wanted to know.

"Fifteen years, mostly in lending and business development. A good combination. That's why we want him." Dill just gazed at Summers for a minute, trying to detect any deception in the older man's eyes. Summers met his steady gaze. He's either a consummate liar or he's being truthful, Dill thought. Time would tell.

Dill then asked, "What's my lending authority when I start out? And how long before it gets raised?"

Seth took out an expensive gold and lacquer fountain pen, wrote a figure on the offer sheet. Dill whistled softly at the low-seven figures on the sheet. Summers smiled. "As for how soon you will be raising that figure is entirely up to you." He let that hang in the air, then asked, "What else?"

Seth was using his well-honed skills, holding back just enough to have the advantage. Dill, too, was playing the game, refusing to appear desperate by revealing too much about his own situation.

"No, nothing," Dill said. "Not for now. I think all the perks were covered. Pretty standard stuff." He gestured at the paper lying there.

Still, Dill sensed Seth had a hidden agenda that needed to be laid out on the table. Plus, Dill wanted full disclosure, especially when it came to medical insurance—the perk that he needed most.

He knew from his many hundreds of meetings with bank clients, borrowers, and debtors that the unspoken things usually gave rise to the problems which popped up down the road. There were ways to slant the paperwork, by putting out skewed figures or information, or simply by leaving out some of the facts. Trying to unearth that agenda, Dill asked, "Was there anything else you wanted to discuss with me?"

"Since you mention it, there is one thing."

Dill waited.

"You won't find this in that offer sheet." Summers gestured. "All the same, it's part of the package, and, if you are in agreement, will be spelled out in a separate agreement that the lawyers will draw up. It has to do with your bank stock. Your bank in Craig, that is. We want to make an offer to buy it. That way, you won't have any conflicts of interest with us."

"First of all, I only own 29 percent."

Summers nodded.

"And if your bank fails, or I'm let go for any reason, what will I have to fall back on, should I need it?" Dill looked directly into Seth's cool gray eyes, not flinching. "You're like Napoleon asking me to burn all my boats on the beaches so I can't retreat."

"We are confident that your stock and options in Larimer Square Bank will make you exceedingly rich, over time." Summers smiled.

Dill was skeptical about this latest claim. This guy smiles far too easily, he thought.

“Anything else, Mr. Robertson?” Summers waited as Dill picked up his Carhartt jacket, roughout sheepskin gloves, and his Stetson.

Dill straightened, clamped on his Stetson and looked Seth in the eye. “Your offer sheet didn’t say a lot about health insurance and what kind of insurance you would be providing.”

“You have my word that it will be all spelled out in your final contract. I assure you, it will be the best we can find for you and your family—your wife.”

Surprised that Seth had singled JoEllen out, Dill averted his eyes and fought the lump rising in his throat at the mention of JoEllen.

“I’ll direct the lawyers again to include the medical coverage,” Seth said. He smiled as he met Dill’s brown eyes. He had his unknowing prey right where he wanted him.

Summers stood. The meeting was over. All part of his masterful manipulation. He knew he had the bait Dill would jump for soon enough. He smiled again and extended his hand. “Take a few days, Mr. Robertson—Dill. Think it over and get back to me. Take your time. Take all the time you need. My offer will stand open indefinitely. It’s up to you to make the next move. This is a big decision for you, we appreciate that.”

Dill folded the offer sheet and tucked it in the breast pocket of his navy blazer. “Mr. Summers.”

Seth turned.

“You didn’t put a price per share on my bank stock.”

Seth asked for the offer sheet back, took out his fountain pen and wrote a figure. Dill whistled softly.

They agreed to keep the lines of communication open. It was still several weeks before the infant bank would get its charter and open for business.

What Dill would learn was that Seth was an expert liar. He was good at keeping dirty secrets. He would have been a perfect spy.

EIGHT

Anchorage, Alaska

It took something spectacular to impress Jerry Jordan. And Jerry Jordan was truly impressed as he looked out the plane's window. The setting sun's slanting rays were hitting the peaks of the tall, craggy mountains below, bathing them in a softly glowing, golden orange. To the east, the horizon was taking on the inky blue of imminent darkness. So many mountains. They seemed to go on forever, their white tips standing out in the descending blackness. He was a Southern California, beach-town kid, always had been. He'd never seen so many mountains.

The big Delta jet began to drop in altitude, slowing, on the final approach over open water for the landing in Anchorage. The plane bounced around in a strong headwind, jostling passengers, knocking them off balance as they scrambled for last-minute trips to the restrooms or searched in the overhead bins and under the seats for personal effects. Flight attendants crossly reminded passengers to return to their seats and buckle up for final approach. Jerry was glad this long flight from Dallas was nearing an end. The flight attendants were also glad.

The jet skimmed low over choppy, wind-whipped water, gray-green with white caps. As it flew over the grassy verge and nosed down to the runway below, the big plane lifted on a stiff cross-current of turbulence, lurched dangerously on its right wing, and, at the last second, when it seemed they were doomed to crash, righted to screams from several passengers. The plane finally banged down hard on the ice-sheathed runway, bounced a second time, reversed engines, and screeched to a rough stop. The pilots taxied the big aircraft up to the jetway, the door opened, and the deplaning scramble began. Welcome to Anchorage.

Only last night Jerry had sat up late being briefed by Lorne Bagley, CEO, and Ted Malmo, chief financial officer, of Stagecoach Energy, in their luxurious North Dallas offices. They had discussed plans to take their limited partnership investment program to the far north.

"There are lots of workers in the North Slope operations with huge tax problems," Ted had told him. "These guys are making upwards of 300 thou a year with no tax breaks. We've been invited to come up there and give a presentation to a bunch of tax clients of one of our friends. You're the obvious guy to go because of your easy way of gaining peoples' confidence."

Lorne had snickered.

Jerry had frowned and protested, "But these are small guys. Three hundred a year doesn't even come close to qualifying them for our program."

But here he was on the plane landing in Anchorage. The end of the civilized world.

Jerry reached into his genuine alligator-skin attaché and pulled out a well-thumbed prospectus for Stagecoach Energy Partners Drilling Program. He flipped to the relevant page and read out loud, "Stagecoach will only allow qualified and otherwise sophisticated investors who fully understand the risks they are assuming to subscribe. As used elsewhere herein, the terms *qualified and otherwise sophisticated* shall mean …"

Lorne had cut him short. "Ted has an idea. Ted?"

"Jerry, don't be difficult. Look, all you have to do is lump four or five of these guys together into a sort of little sub-partnership. Then that sub-partnership will qualify under the annual income provision of the program requirements."

"I don't know," Jerry had frowned. "That seems like a lot of paperwork. Who's supposed to document these so-called investment sub-partnerships? Have the legal brains passed on this idea?"

He had looked squarely at Ted. Then at Lorne. They didn't flinch.

"Jerry, Jerry. Of course, they have," Ted hedged. "Now, stop creating problems where they don't exist and pack your bags. I just want you to go to sleep in first class on that redeye flight tonight dreaming of the big commissions you're being handed on a plate. These guys are just waiting for you to get up there to Anchorage and show them where to sign their names."

So, here he was, nearly crash-landing in Anchorage.

Elmer Presley met Jerry in the terminal and offered to take his one suitcase for him. Even though it was late April, a bitter cold wind slapped against their faces as they walked to Elmer's car. It was the kind of wind that froze your nostrils, bonded your eyelids together, made it almost impossible to breathe.

Jerry's heart sank. Elmer's car was an old Dodge sedan, rusted and falling apart, windows crusted with hoar frost. Jerry prayed it had a heater. He hoped it would even start.

Jerry heard the mournful honking of a lone goose somewhere above the icy water he'd just flown over. It fit his mood perfectly.

After several fitful attempts, the old Dodge coughed into life and Elmer crunched it into reverse, lurched backward out of his parking spot and into another parked vehicle. Elmer didn't stop, but pitched forward, sliding out of the parking lot.

They drove to downtown Anchorage in silence. The heater didn't work. Nor did the wipers. They almost wrecked twice before Elmer maneuvered into a sorry-looking strip mall. Jerry relaxed his death grip on the door rest.

"Here we are."

"This is the hotel?"

"My office. There's a room in the back where you can sleep. I don't believe in running up costs."

Jerry's spirits sagged. He followed Elmer inside.

It was as cold as a meat storage facility and just as spare and drab. The twenty-by-twenty room had a big chalkboard, a single table, and a couple dozen old folding chairs with ripped upholstery. Jerry's heart sank even more as he realized this was the venue for the so-called presentation.

"Any chance of getting something to eat?" Jerry asked.

Elmer shrugged out of his cheap, faux fur-trimmed parka, peeled off his gloves, and pulled off his worn, fur-trapper hat.

Jerry jumped back as something looking like a dead rat fell at his feet. Elmer unceremoniously bent over and picked it up, set it on his head, straightened it somewhat. Jerry laughed as he realized it was a very cheap hairpiece Elmer wore to cover his baldness.

Elmer fished through a cardboard box, found a handful of outdated menus, and handed them to Jerry. "You can use the phone and order something from these. What do you like?"

"Mexican?"

Elmer snorted. "In Anchorage? Don't think so. Lots of Chinese places though."

They ate in silence. The Chinese takeout that had been tardily delivered was now cold and left a nasty coating on Jerry's tongue. He didn't finish. Jerry thought about the fine restaurants he had enjoyed on his other trips, the first-class hotels, the room service.

"Look, if it's all the same to you, Elvan…"

"Elmer."

"Whatever. I think I'll book a room at the Marriott and pay for it myself. Since you were kind enough to pay my airfare up here." Yeah, economy class, middle seat, Jerry thought. Cheapskate!

"Suit yerself. We have our first presentation here tomorrow starting at eight o'clock in the morning. Then it's every hour after that through the day. These guys work really oddball shifts up on The Slope. We catch them when we can."

"So, I'm just curious, Mr. Presley, how do you fit in with all these, er, people? What is it you do for them? Accounting, taxes, financial adviser? Lorne and Ted weren't too clear on the details."

"I do their taxes. And you're gonna show them how to get a six-to-one tax write-off."

Jerry was stunned. "Wait a minute! Our program is only set up to offer a three-to-one. Didn't Ted explain that to you?"

"We discussed it, and he said he was setting up a special program just for my people with a six-to-one. He faxed me the subscription agreement. I'll make enough copies for everyone. Your job is to briefly explain how letters of credit work and answer any questions. Don't get too deep into the tax stuff. That's my job. Then you just help them fill out the subscription and take their checks. They all come with their checkbooks, some with cash in large bills. They don't have time to screw around with fine-print legal stuff and details."

"Ted said you would be grouping some of these investors into what he called investment clubs."

Elmer nodded. "And ...?"

"You have any paperwork set up for that little, er, *detail*?" Jerry asked, though he was fairly certain he didn't.

"Just get the subscriptions signed for now. You can have your lawyers do that stuff and send me the paperwork for their sub-partnerships. I'll get their signatures and send it all back to you later. Everything's gonna be fine. Don't make things complicated. We like to keep things simple around here."

Jerry gathered his things and used the phone to call a taxi to take him to the Marriott.

"Suit yerself," Elmer muttered to himself yet again, as he crawled into the sleeping couch in the back room. He took off his hairpiece and set it on the lampstand. He fell asleep in his clothes.

NINE

Peabody Oil Company, Okmulgee, Oklahoma

Ricky Bob Peabody watched grimly as the constable drove away. He'd just been served with more papers. Again. A writ commanding his presence in court on a date specified, thereby to answer in person regarding his assets, income, and his ability to satisfy the default judgment that has heretofore been entered against him in the matter of …

"Dang it!" He threw his hard hat against the wall, smashing the glass in a framed picture of his first real producing well: The Steiner No. 141-A4. That was a real beauty of a well, no water problems, no completion difficulties. A real beaut. Still producing.

The phone rang. He didn't answer. Probably just another creditor. Or Kyle demanding an interest payment. Shysters!

The ringing stopped. Ricky Bob rummaged in his desk, dying of thirst. Now where's that bottle? Empty! He threw it at the wall. It bounced off, didn't shatter. He kicked it across the room. It came to rest against the door.

The phone rang again. He hesitated, let it ring four more times before giving in to curiosity and picking it up.

"Yeah, Peabody here!" he barked.

"Mr. Peabody? You don't know me, but my name is Ginger Foss. From Dallas. I work with a substantial oil and gas limited partnership group by the name of Stagecoach Energy Corp. Ever hear of us?"

Ricky hadn't.

"Well, here's the deal: We have drilling funds available and need to line up some prospects for my client. I'm already booked, that is, my leases and crews and rigs are all committed, and I've been referred to you as a successful oilman."

Ricky Bob nearly wet his jeans.

A Hospital Room, Denver

Dill sat beside JoEllen's bed in her private hospital room, holding her hand. She slept.

The initial tests had been inconclusive as to whether the leukemia was the aggressive kind, so they were keeping her here for more testing, always more testing. They couldn't say how long, maybe two-three days, maybe more. Just depends.

Based on her past medical history, Dill wondered whether they would confirm what he and JoEllen already suspected. It didn't look good for Jo. But they still continued to pray, to hold out hope.

Doctors. Oncologists. Experts.

Dill was an expert only in a couple things: banking and ranching. So he had to respect their opinions as one expert relying on another.

Jo slept the deep sleep of tranquilizers. How long would it be before they knew? Her lack of fear was amazing. On the way to Denver, she had only wondered aloud about the future, but real fear wasn't in the discussion.

But as the days would stretch into weeks and the test results and the reports and the consultations came in, her lack of fear would be replaced by a stoic acceptance.

Jo's stoicism was a mask she put on for her family, her loved ones, Dill, her four young sons, Matthew, Mark, Luke and John. Her Four Apostles, she called them. More like the Four Horsemen of the Apocalypse, as Dill and the townspeople of Craig knew them.

Matthew, the oldest, was away as a missionary for the Mormon church. Two years in Thailand. He was already halfway through his two years. How would he take this news of his mother's problems? Jo had often smiled at the pictures he sent home: her tall, very pale-skinned son in a white short-sleeved shirt and tie towering over those happy, smiling, much smaller, darker-skinned Thai people.

Then, there was Mark. Stout, solid, dependable Mark. Their football player. Mark was almost finished with his freshman year at University of Wyoming in Laramie. A full-ride football scholarship. A skilled linebacker, he started every game last fall and had done very well. Lots of tackles for a loss, which is how linebackers kept score. He was tough on the outside, but she knew he had a soft heart. Very soft.

Luke wasn't far behind when it came to athletic prowess. Just finishing his junior year in high school, he was a running back, more wiry, shorter than the first two brothers. He wanted to be a teacher—high school English—and a football coach. He was the one Jo worried about the most. He was a romantic in so many ways, with the heart of a poet. How could she help toughen his heart for the final outcome? If … if there was a final outcome. Or should she even try? It was so difficult, and she was so tired. She was frustrated the results were taking so long.

And then last was young John—JJ—always resentful of being considered the baby of the family. Jo had fought the impulse to treat him like the youngest, like the daughter she never had, never could have. In ninth grade this year, he would start high school next year. JJ was the curious one, the scholar in the family. He loved long walks in the woods and fields examining and collecting plants, rocks, trees, animals. His earliest acquisition had been a telescope that he used to chart stars and planets. They often had to drive him back to bed at early hours in the morning when he was up, gazing, charting. He was so excited when he made a new discovery, he couldn't wait to share with anyone who would listen.

Dill held her hand in the semi-darkness. The wall clock ticked softly. He dozed off. A nurse came in to check Jo's vitals. What an ironic term: vitals. He needed her to keep her vitals, keep strong for them—her boys and him. She moved slightly, asked for water which the nurse helped her drink through a straw by gently raising Jo's head with one hand, holding the beaker with the other.

The nurse left. It was quiet again except for muffled hospital sounds from far off. Dill thought of Paul's letter to the Thessalonians: *And that ye study to be quiet.* Quiet is highly underrated, he thought. Does it really take an effort, must we study how to be quiet in this busy world of working and playing, going and coming? Maybe that's not such a bad idea, quiet.

He thought back to the times he had spent alone fly-fishing on a remote alpine stream, deep in the forested far reaches of the ranch—or on his favorite, Elkhead Creek. He thought of the many cutthroat trout he had caught and released. The jewel-like little brook trout he had held in his hand and admired for their perfection.

Or those times on an elk stand. Again, in the high mountains. No sounds but birds, the wind, an occasional marmot scolding, protecting its space. But alone, always alone, with just his own thoughts. How he had worked out many knotty problems at the bank, on the ranch, at home, in his local church as their bishop, their leader. Study to be quiet.

The real problem was the future. Ongoing treatment for Jo's cancer, her leukemia. They had determined it was acute myeloid leukemia, the aggressive, fast-growing species. They were prescribing chemotherapy, most likely followed by a bone marrow transplant. That would then be followed by chemotherapy, again. And she was pretty well assured there would be radiation after. Jo had a history of hemoglobin deficiency, low red blood count. Sometimes dangerously low. Like when she had delivered each of their four sons. They'd have to raise her count, get her stronger if—if—she made it through the first round of chemo and the marrow transplant.

Right now, Dill was mostly worried about Jo's attitude. She seemed resigned, happy almost, at the thoughts of leaving this world of trouble and gloom for a better. But why? He couldn't figure it. She had always been a fighter, spunky and full of life and enthusiasm.

He also had another matter that demanded his attention: how to tell the boys? They were almost out for summer break and would need some degree of normalcy to get them through this. Should he find a place in Denver where they could be with him for the summer, and close to their mom? Would it be better for them to live at home on the ranch where there was familiarity? He could commute between Denver and home to check on them weekends. What would JoEllen want? She would want what's best for them.

People had often told Dill the thing they loved most about her was her attitude, her smile, and how she looked outward toward others. It was true; she always built people up. He'd never heard a negative comment about anyone escape her lips. She almost slipped once calling her detractor "a poor, dumb thing. I'll just have to pray for her." Dill chuckled as he remembered that isolated incident. But that was JoEllen, that was her faith—in God and in the goodness of others.

As for spunk and fight, one of the first things that attracted Dill to her had been when they were at a church youth conference and had played on opposite volleyball teams. She was a competitor, leading both teams with kills. In church ball! She could also be a real mamma grizzly where her sons were concerned. Sometimes embarrassingly so. That's why he was so puzzled about her resignation now. Maybe she is just really and truly tired and doesn't have the energy to fight this thing right now, he thought, as he kissed her goodbye. Let her sleep, let her rest.

The morning sun slanting through the window, the hospital rousing into activity, woke Dill. A new day. He had fallen asleep sitting in the chair next to Jo's bed. He kissed her forehead and crept quietly out of the room, praying for Jo in his heart as he took the elevator down.

He needed to decide whether to make that phone call to Seth Summers. But first, he needed to be alone in the mountains, where he could be quiet and let some answers come. And he needed to sit down with the boys and talk. He would need to get permission to make an overseas phone call to Matthew in Thailand and include him in the family council.

Dill slipped out of the hospital to his truck. He checked to make sure his fly rod was in the back, then pulled his truck out of the hospital parking lot and headed for I-70 west, and the Frying Pan River, towards Aspen and Vail. A couple hours fly-fishing to sort out his thoughts, then he'd head for Craig and a meeting with the boys.

As he got underway, he glanced in the bed of his truck to make sure nobody had taken his waders. They were still there. Old and patched many times. Sometimes he felt that way, too.

TEN

Marriott Hotel, Anchorage, Alaska

Jerry drained the Bloody Mary, set the heavy glass down on the bar, wiped his mouth with a napkin, and sprayed some minty atomizer in his mouth. "Put it on my room," he said and signed the chit.

As he slowly made his way to the conference room in the Marriott, he wished he could be someplace else. "Anywhere but Anchorage freezing Alaska!" he barked to the walls and ornate carpets. "Late spring and still blasted freezing! What a place."

Back in his room, locked in his overnight bag, was a pile of subscriptions—over seventy, in fact—with personal checks of $10,000 attached to each. Except one. It had a stack of $100 bills paperclipped to it. The subscriptions had been filled out and signed by the roughnecks, drillers, engineers, truck drivers, and cooks who spent more than half their lives working in sub-zero temperatures in the creepy semi-darkness of the North Slope.

The North Slope, Alaska

The place had such a romantic cachet to it. Turned out it was anything but. It was really just flat and dismal. On Elmer Presley's insistence, Jerry had a quick trip on the daily shuttle plane to the North Slope drilling sites where they met with several of Elmer's clients between shifts.

The 737 Boeing commuter banked sharply right and dropped quickly, just above the dirty, gray-brown Bering Sea waves constantly slapping against landfall. The landscape was mostly flat, barren, void of any defining landmarks except for many brightly lit oil and gas drilling rigs and a virtual artificial jungle of piping, massive valves, and towering metal tanks.

Everything was dismal and gray—perpetual darkness. The only light came from the numerous massive oil drilling derricks and corrugated metal buildings, and from the twin headlights of the occasional service vehicles crawling slowly through the wind-whipped ice storm.

They deplaned and leaned into the howling wind which serrated through Jerry's new parka like a hot knife through butter. His poorly shod feet slipped on the crusted snow as he fought his way into the dingy terminal that was North Slope, Alaska. The sharp cold seeped upward through the thin soles of his Guccis. He now understood why everyone wore those ugly, heavy fur-trimmed mukluks.

Once inside, Jerry searched for something resembling a radiator, anything that could give him some warmth. How did these guys stand to work in these awful conditions? No wonder roughnecks made so much money. You'd have to get paid a lot to work in this freezing wasteland.

Jerry and Elmer worked around the clock for nearly twenty hours presenting the Stagecoach Energy limited partnership drilling program, answering questions, tap dancing around objections, holding hands, twisting arms, making outlandish promises that both he and Elmer and the clients knew deep down were outright lies. Okay, call it fraud if you want. Anything to close the sale and get back to the warmth and sun of southern California.

Jerry swallowed and thought of the sleek red Ferrari that he planned to reward himself with when this selling season was over. He'd lease it, of course. This limited partnership stuff being so transitory, nothing you could count on in the future. Their own prospectus had warned potential investors of the uncertain risks of oil and gas investments, our nation's tax code, etc. Buried deep in fusty prospectus language hopefully nobody ever bothered to read carefully.

That is, until they learned their well was a dry hole and they lost all their investment, including the letter of credit that would be called in by their own bankers, a full 75 percent of the investment. Leverage.

And the lawyers would round up a bunch of investors and convince them they were victims and had all been well and truly fleeced.

Then the lynching party would begin.

Then the investor would say under oath that they never read that thing. Who reads all that mumbo-jumbo legal stuff anyway? Just language to cover the promoters' fannies! And the jury would buy the victims' sob stories and sock it to the promoters.

Where was the guy's brain when he drooled at the huge tax write-off, wrote the check and talked his skeptical banker into issuing a huge letter of credit—a loan, a promissory note in effect? But all loans come due someday.

All these guppies were thinking about when they signed was the huge tax refund they were going to get, thanks to Elmer Parsley, or whatever, dummying up their tax returns. Six-to-one!

The investors, if you could call them that with a straight face and clear conscience, wasted no time booking trips with their wives or girlfriends to Hawaii or the Gulf Coast. Good grief, Jerry thought, what am I doing here?

Jerry's thoughts turned to a badly needed vacation for himself. He was really getting burned out. Not enough sleep, too much to eat and way too much alcohol. No way to exercise. Constant stress and pressure. Bahamas here we come! Away from the rotten cold of Alaska for a few glorious weeks. All thanks to kindly old Uncle Sam and his generous oil and gas investment loopholes!

But Jerry would gladly go along with their dreams and fantasies. Shoot, he had his, too.

Tell them, promise them anything to close the sale and get the check! He pictured himself and Connie, his latest girlfriend, top down on the Ferrari, taking the curves on the Coast Highway somewhere near Malibu. Sun on their faces, Connie's blonde hair streaked with red highlights blowing wildly in the breeze, as they passed the vast rolling green campus of Pepperdine University on one side, the beautiful blue Pacific on the other side.

Marriott Hotel, Anchorage

The conference room was small-ish. Jerry had booked that room on purpose. He knew from experience the advantage of having too many people in a small room versus just a few scattered around in a big one. Bad psychology all around. Small, but crowded, was much better.

He glanced around to make sure everything was ready: podium, projector and screen, coffee and sweet rolls on rolling carts, uniformed servers standing by. Piles of brochures containing numbered prospectuses in royal blue jackets with gold-script lettering piled neatly beside his podium, in plain sight for all to look at and focus on.

The only thing missing in his planning were the sub-partnership documents, the belated ones the Stagecoach lawyers in Dallas had promised but not delivered. These would make everything legal, the lawyers assured him on the phone.

Jerry straightened his tie, looked down at his Gucci loafers now dry and freshly shined, crease in his navy suit pants. He tugged at his French cuffs and strode for the podium.

"Showtime, everyone!" was his hearty greeting. Scattered applause. About fifty tough-looking oilfield workers in plaid flannel shirts, Carhartt denims, and lace-up Wolverine boots looked up at him with suspicious stares, eyes bloodshot from sleep deprivation from too many long hours on the Slope.

A few of the men had brought their women. (Wives? Lovers? Girlfriends? Elmer warned Jerry never to ask. Unless he was willing to risk a fist in the mouth with a "Just you mind your own business!")

Stagecoach Energy, Dallas

"How'd it go, Jerry?" It was Lorne from Stagecoach. Still at his office at this late hour. Must be way past midnight in Dallas.

"Fine. I'm glad I'm leaving this hole tomorrow. Where'd Ted come up with this character, Elmer Gantry?"

"Presley, actually …"

"Gantry, Presley, Parsley, whatever. He's a real piece of work. Never met a more disgusting person. His personal hygiene, I mean. Which doesn't exist in his world. I swear nobody ever showers up here."

"Must be too cold," Lorne laughed.

"When will the legal guys get those sub-partnership documents up here? They promised them three days ago. Typical!"

"They tell me they're working on it. I'll light a fire under them tomorrow. Anything else before I tuck you in for the night?"

"Yeah. I can't get this one guy out of my head tonight. He was the only one clean shaven, no beard, know what I mean? Seems they all wear beards up here…"

"Too cold to shave, I guess?"

"Maybe. Anyway, he was dressed different, too. Harris tweed jacket, bowtie. Really stood out, know what I mean? Nobody but undertakers and preachers wear ties up here. But a bowtie? Really stood out. Kept asking me hard, specific questions."

Lorne became wary. "What kind of questions, Jerry? Give me an example, if you can remember."

"Oh, yeah, I can remember. He asked if our lawyers had covered the issue of *integration* in the prospectus? I didn't have a clue what he was on to, so I just nodded my head and said, 'Yeah, we have the finest law firm in Texas looking at this stuff and they passed off on it and it's all right there in the prospectus.' That kind of stuff. Then I just went on to something else. Did I screw up, or something?"

"Naw, don't worry too much about it. Probably doesn't mean anything in the long run. So, how much money you bringing back for us?"

A loud knock at Jerry's hotel room door interrupted their conversation.

"Just a minute, Lorne. Someone at the door. I didn't order room service or anything. Hold on. Don't go away."

He set the phone down and opened the door a crack.

"Yes? I didn't order room service."

"Mr. Jordan? Jerry Jordan? Of Stagecoach Energy Oil and Gas Drilling Partnership?"

Jerry then recognized the midnight visitor as one of the uniformed servers from the conference room. He had been busy serving coffee and donuts and circulating among Jerry's invited guests, pushing his linen-covered cart, filling cups, handing out napkins and spoons, sugar and cream. Being solicitous. As he should have been.

And there standing behind him, partially hidden by the dim hallway lighting, was the bald, Harris-tweed, bow-tie guy. Neither of them was smiling.

"Yeah, that's me. Who wants to know?"

The server produced a badge that identified him as a special agent for the Alaska State Securities Division. Jerry didn't catch his name. He almost fainted.

"Mr. Jordan, I have here a subpoena and a cease-and-desist order from the Alaska State Securities Division. You are summoned to a hearing at our offices in Juneau in 20 days. Or you may respond to the subpoena in writing."

He handed the subpoena to Jerry.

"You may bring your lawyer and any documents you deem relevant to your case. In the meantime, you are enjoined from any further sales efforts of your unregistered program. Is that clear?"

Jerry swallowed, nodded.

Any questions?

Jerry started to close the door, shaken. Then stopped partway back inside.

"Who's that guy?" Jerry pointed to the lean, clean-shaven balding man in the shadows outside his door. The man in the Harris-tweed jacket and bowtie.

"That's my boss."

Harris tweed grinned wolfishly.

Jerry slammed the door. "Idiot, Elmer!"

Lorne's tinny voice bled through the phone into the room. "Jerry? Jerry? What's going on, Jerry? I heard somebody. Who was the guy at the door? Talk to me!"

Jerry grabbed the phone and shouted into it, "Lorne, I just got served a cease-and-desist order!"

"No! Really? Did they ask to see any of the subscriptions or checks in your possession?"

"No. And I didn't volunteer I had any on me, either."

"Good boy. I wonder how they knew…?

"He had to have a recorder. The serving guy. I'd bet it was probably hidden under that rolling cart he was pushing around. Must've got every word on tape that I said in that presentation. What sneaky lowlifes!"

"You need to get to the airport. Fast! There's a Delta redeye that leaves at 12:30. You have a little over an hour. Get on that plane and come straight home. Now!"

Airport, Anchorage

"First class to Dallas. One way, please." Jerry peeled off several of the hundred-dollar bills from his roll and paid for his ticket with cash.

"This flight terminates in Salt Lake City where you'll need to change planes, sir."

"Yeah, yeah, whatever," Jerry uncharacteristically snapped.

Jerry left the new parka and gloves hanging in the airport men's room.

ELEVEN

Colorado Banking Commission, Denver

"This hearing is now in session. I am Colorado State Banking Commissioner Dennis Morgan. I will be conducting this hearing in the matter of an application for a banking license for Larimer Square Bank, in organization. Will the parties please identify themselves?"

"I'm Stephen Anglesey, counsel representing the applicant, Larimer Square Bank. Seated with me to my right is Mr. Seth Summers, who represents the applicant group."

"Thank you, Mr. Anglesey. The record will also show that the application is opposed by a consortium of Denver financial institutions represented by …?"

A smartly dressed young lawyer stood to introduce himself.

"You don't need to stand, Mr. …?" Morgan smiled helpfully.

"And I am J. William Eager, attorney for Farmers & Mechanics' Cooperative Bank of Denver, representing the opposition to this application. We want to show …"

Morgan cut him off. "Save that for your opening statement, Mr. Eager. And while I'm with you I have a question, just curious …"

Eager waited.

"Has your client ever considered a shorter name? What a mouthful!" Laughter from the small group filled the room. Mr. Eager didn't know what to say. An attorney at a loss for words.

Morgan continued with, "Does the applicant wish to enter a statement for the record?"

And the hearing commenced.

This hearing was a formality that Morgan had decided to put in place to cover his backside with the powerful established Denver banking interests who predictably opposed this young upstart institution.

Morgan and his employees had carefully researched the application and found nothing lacking. Other than a nagging distrust he had for that Seth Summers. Too slick by half.

The economic study of the market area proposed to be served by the new institution was sound and thorough and was introduced into the record.

The business plan was sensible: target oil and gas companies as the base for the new bank's customers to be served. Also entered into the record.

The proposed board of directors read like a Who's Who of Colorado business elite, all solid and financially deep-pocketed. No skeletons discovered.

Again, the only concern had been Summers himself. A well-known penny stock promoter, who had had numerous scrapes with both state and federal securities regulators. But he always came out mostly clean; nothing really ever stuck to him. Summers was named as the Chairman of the Board. No real banking functions or decision-making authority. Still ...

The actual operating team looked good. Background checks had found nothing of concern. Morgan especially was impressed by the man they had put forth as the chief loan officer, Dilworth Robertson, a banker from Craig, with a lot of actual experience running a small bank. He looked good. He'd make good loans.

And this wasn't wishful thinking on Morgan's part. His people had researched Robertson's loan record with the people at Federal Deposit Insurance Corporation and found no blackmarks, no adverse comments from past audits.

The only other question mark for management was the CEO. That was still a blank space yet to be filled. He had better be good.

The applicant's only expert witness, one Herbert Feiss, PhD, economics professor from the University of Pennsylvania, took the witness chair, was sworn, gave his CV, and proceeded to fumble his way through his presentation.

Feiss had set up a slide projector to summarize the lengthy economic study he had prepared and submitted into evidence. He proceeded to flash through the slides of charts, graphs, and many photos of businesses in the six-square block area surrounding the proposed site.

"He's sweating. And he's repeating himself," Seth whispered to Stephen Anglesey. "Where'd you guys find this bozo?"

"One of the senior partners knew him, used him in other hearings. Swears he knows his stuff," Stephen whispered back.

"Maybe he looks good on paper, but he's a clown in person. He's killing us!" Seth whispered back.

The Commissioner glanced up at Summers; he'd been thumbing through pages of the application file, not really following the presentation. "Something you wish to say, Mr. Summers?"

"Maybe this would be a good time to take a break, if you don't mind? Mr. Morgan?"

Morgan agreed.

Robertson Ranch

The family council with his two boys still at home went smoothly, Dill thought. Too smoothly, in fact. Luke and JJ were mostly quiet, subdued. The atmosphere felt like someone in the family had just died. Then they got on the phone and called Mark in Laramie. He voted to stay at home and hope and pray for the best. He had planned on helping out around the ranch for the summer. He looked forward to hay-baling time when he could wrestle with the big bales and toss them around like feather pillows. The work helped build his already huge muscles.

U-Tapao, Thailand

U-Tapao, Thailand, where Matthew was serving as a missionary, was fourteen hours ahead of Mountain Time, so Dill figured they needed to wait until about ten o'clock that night to call. That would be noon the next day for Matthew, and they were hoping to catch him during his lunchtime.

While they waited, the three Robertson men wandered around the house, looking for things to do to kill time. The hours and minutes passed like molasses in winter. Finally, they called and the phone rang on the other end for an excruciatingly long time with no answer. They waited fifteen minutes and called again. This time Matthew answered.

"Dad? Anything wrong? How's mom?" He sounded much older to Dill. Older, worried and deeply concerned. They talked for less than ten minutes and Matthew's counsel was for his three brothers to stay at home. He felt they would get into trouble hanging around Denver with nothing to do for three months except worry themselves to death. There were things to do in and around Craig, the ranch, and they had friends and family there to look after them.

JJ cut in with, "I've grown up since you left, big brother, and I don't need nobody to look after me. I'm pretty good at looking after myself."

Matthew wisely responded with, "I didn't mean anything by that. I meant to say you would be with loved ones."

"Mom's the loved one I care most about," Luke quietly said.

"Who was that? Was that you, Luke?"

Luke nodded and turned away so the others couldn't see the tears welling in his eyes. Matthew couldn't see him but felt through the long distance that Luke was hurting, too. They all were.

Then Matthew did something that surprised them all: He offered to say a prayer for their mother, right there, over the phone, thousands of miles away.

After their brief family prayer, they said their goodbyes and rang off. Dill looked at his two sons and said, "I'll arrange for your aunt Ida to stay with you guys." They nodded. "I'll call Mark and let him know what we've decided." The two boys nodded and Luke squared his shoulders. He and JJ were the closest and Luke would bear the burden of being the one to help his younger brother get through this. No matter how it turned out.

Dill finished up by saying, "I'll call the hospital and tell your mother. You guys want to be on the call with me?" They nodded. "I'll try to be home every weekend when I'm there with your mother. Otherwise, I'll be here, too. Waiting and praying. Remember this: I'll only be a phone call away, so if you need me …"

Dill hugged his two sons and they hung onto him for a long time. In his mind he was already making checklists. Item number two, right after he discussed their decision with JoEllen, was to try and find a place to hang his Stetson in Denver.

Colorado Banking Commission Hearing, Denver

During the break, Summers, Anglesey and Feiss conferred. In the huddle, with heads close together, Seth could smell booze on Feiss's breath. "You've been drinking."

"I only had one small brandy to calm my nerves before we started. It honestly doesn't affect my …"

"Idiot! Seth hissed. Then to Anglesey, "I say we cut this short and get out of here. It's obvious to me Morgan's made up his mind long ago. He's going to grant it and this hearing is just a dog and pony show to cover his fanny.

The hearing reconvened; Anglesey stood and made a short speech. "Mr. Commissioner, we have nothing further to add, and we'd like to submit the witness's study and statement into the record. And we respectfully ask that applicant's request be granted. Thank you, sir."

Morgan nodded. "Mr. Eager, is there anything else of substance you wish to add?"

"Yes, sir, we'd like to cross-examine the witness."

Morgan cut him short. "May I remind you that this is an administrative hearing and, as such, I am not bound by the usual rules of evidence and procedure that you may be accustomed to invoking in a court of law. Meaning …" He let the thought hang for a pregnant moment. "Meaning, that I'm allowed a lot of leeway for the finer points of evidence and procedure in these hearings. It's apparent to me that Professor Feiss is more comfortable with the written word. And owing to the long trip he has had, and the fact that he looks quite fatigued, I'm inclined to deny your request for leave to cross-examine."

Professor Feiss smiled gratefully,

"Anything further, gentlemen?"

Nobody offered any more remarks.

"I will take the matter under advisement. This hearing is concluded."

By the time Stephen Anglesey got back to his office there was a telephone message waiting for him from Commissioner Morgan. It simply read: "Prepare findings and order granting license to organize the new Larimer Square Bank. Congrats."

Anglesey phoned Seth Summers.

"I told you he'd already made up his mind in our favor," Seth said.

"How'd you know?" Stephen asked.

"Better you not ask," Seth replied, then he bid goodbye to his attorney, poured himself a stiff double of his special reserve malt, and raised his glass in the direction of the new Larimer Square Bank.

Seth picked up the phone and made a call.

"Mr. Eager? I'd like to have you make an appointment with Brad Capener at Farmers and Mechanics Bank. Yeah, your client."

"I guess we both know he's going to grant your application?" Eager said. "So, I guess it's not too early to congratulate you folks?"

"Thanks. I need to talk to Brad about a large loan to our group. Based on our business plan, we'll need about $10 million in capital. Think you can arrange that for us? Good boy. And thanks."

Within two months' time, Larimer Square Bank had officially opened for business in a rented double-wide trailer set up in a large public parking lot two blocks off the Square. Not pretty, but it would serve until they could get into permanent digs, actually on Larimer Square.

TWELVE

Tulsa Guaranty Bank, Tulsa, Oklahoma

Calvin "Buck" Buckley tossed the last of his personal effects into the two Bankers Boxes and smiled with deep satisfaction. It was the last he would see of this dingy interior office. Now he was headed for the Big Time. An opportunity he had been working on for a long time.

Buck strolled into Kyle's big corner office, the sort mandated for all vice presidents or above by the Tulsa Guaranty Bank and Trust employee manual.

He didn't knock. Buck never knocked. And that was just one of the many annoyances that rubbed his colleagues and his seniors at TGB the wrong way. He didn't give a flying drunk armadillo what they thought. Never had, never would.

Well, they could think about this now: He was on his way to Denver to become the new CEO of that upstart bank that everyone in the banking world was buzzing about—Larimer Square Bank. Whose mission, it was announced, was to become the biggest oil and gas lending bank on the planet!

Let them chew on that around the water cooler or over lunch at the Bankers Club!

Kyle looked up, startled. "I didn't hear …"

"So long, buddy!" Buck shouted, as he plopped himself on the edge of Kyle's big desk. Buck said it loud enough to be sure it carried out into the bullpen adjacent to Kyle's office. Certain that the secretaries and other flunkies would hear.

"You don't have to be nasty, Cal."

"Just statin' the facts, old buddy." Buck reached out his hand. Kyle hesitated, then shook it limply. He didn't meet Buck's steady, ice-blue eyes.

"Well, good luck anyway," Kyle offered. "I'll be sort of sorry to see you go. You always provided some entertainment for our dull lives."

"Oh, cut it out, Kyle. You know I've been a pain in the collective backsides of you and your family for years. Now you don't have to worry about me anymore. Is he crazy, bringing us this loan? Is he out of his mind talking to our biggest customer that way?"

"It wasn't always as bad as you make it sound."

"No. It was worse and you know it! Well ..."

"No hard feelings?" Kyle asked.

"Not on my account. I'm glad to be movin' on. I still can't believe the package they're givin' me. Did I tell you, high six-figure salary to start? Plus bonuses and incentives?" Buck rubbed it in. He knew that Kyle labored under the burden of an upwardly mobile young wife who constantly bugged him about asking his daddy for a raise. Kyle would never be a good enough provider for that woman.

Oh, well, that was Kyle's problem. Buck stopped at the door, turned and rubbed in some salt: "Did I tell you they're making me a 10 percent shareholder with options for more?" He grinned at Kyle's stupefied look and walked out.

In the parking lot, Buck gave a sarcastic salute to good old TGB. So long, suckers!

Buck drove straight to the Tulsa airport where he boarded a jet bound for Seattle.

Next stop: Mt. Rainier Trust, a major bank in the northwest, where Buck would pitch the top executives there on the simplicity of getting a slice of the oil and gas lending pie.

And just how easy it was for Larimer Square Bank to fulfill the greedy wishes of these profit-hungry bankers.

Breckenridge County, Texas

"What are ya thinkin'?" Ginger Foss asked Ricky Bob.

They were standing atop a rise just north of the dusty town of Weatherford, on the edge of Lake Breckenridge, in West Texas, a couple hours' drive west of Stagecoach Energy Corporation's Dallas offices.

Mid-May. Dry, hot breezes. The last of the dried-out bluebonnets nodding in the breeze, scattering their seeds on the wind. Open country, live oak and locust groves. Groups of grazing cattle as far as they could see. The landscape was dotted with pump jacks moving up and down sucking crude oil from 5,000 feet below the earth's surface to the waiting batteries of holding tanks above.

Here and there Ricky could see drill rigs working, workover rigs and crews laboring in the hard, dirty job of harvesting the black gold.

Crude. Ricky loved it—the smell, the feel, the look of it as it flowed to the surface. He loved the business, had grown up as fourth generation oil man. Had wanted to be an oil man—an Oilie—since he could remember. It was in his blood.

He loved reading over the fine print in leases, operating agreements, and drilling logs. He loved the equipment, the tough men called roughnecks who worked the rigs. But most of all, he loved the money. He loved the freedom and independence that came as a reward for the risk and hard work. And there was plenty of both.

He loved taking his childhood sweetheart, Nan, now his wife, to exotic places like New Orleans and Nashville. He loved to lavish little surprise gifts on her and the kids. He went all out at Christmas and Valentine's Day. No expense spared.

But lately things were tight.

He grinned, turned slowly to face Ginger. "What do I think? Let's do it! Why are we standin' here wastin' time when we could be drillin'?" The two young oilmen wiped their dusty hands on their Wranglers and shook on it. Peabody Oil was on board the Stagecoach Express.

Back at Ginger's truck, they paused as Ginger Foss pulled out a brown paper bag from under the front seat. Ginger produced a fifth of Old Turkey. "We need to baptize this little patch," he said as he unscrewed the top. He poured out a stream onto the dry ground, some splashing onto their mud-caked Tony Llama boots. Ricky nodded and licked his lips. They both removed their cowboy hats, bowed their heads.

"Lord, we thank you for thy generous bounties and especially for this little patch of thy vineyard which we now dedicate to the harvest of some of thy blessed crude. Sweet Texas crude! Amen."

"Thank you, Lord. Lord, Jesus, yes! Amen!" echoed Ricky Bob.

After they shared a drink from the bottle, Ricky asked about the well spacing.

"The primary well spacing on completed wells will be forty acres," said Foss.

"Then, of course, there are the logs on nearby wells. They show several zones up hole that could be produced from smaller spacings. Say twenty, maybe even ten, acres? We could step out and drill a lot more on this lease. Keep you going for a couple years just on this lease alone," opined Ginger.

Ricky nodded knowingly. "Sounds good to me. Count me in!"

Ginger reached into his denim shirt pocket and produced a fat roll of bills, new crisp hundreds, which he passed over to Ricky Bob. "A little walkin' around money to get you home, a welcome gift from the guys at Stagecoach Energy," he said with a grin.

"Well, that's really nice of y'all. Tell them thanks from me. I really mean it." Ricky averted his eyes as he accepted the cash. "You need a receipt?" Ginger shook his head, smiled slyly.

Ricky made a quick detour. This won't take long, he thought, as he stopped at a mall just off Preston Road, North Dallas, on his way home. He quickly made his way to the jewelry store, where he bought Nan a pair of half-carat solitaire diamond earrings. He proudly peeled off twenty of the hundreds, casually handed them over to the cute young salesgirl.

"And here's one for you," he said as he winked and generously tipped the amazed girl.

I'm feelin' lucky tonight, thought Ricky, as he drove home to Okmulgee. Every few miles he patted the roll of cash in his shirt pocket. Must still be $20 thousand there. At least.

“Lorne? Ricky’s on board. You can put this lease into that latest drilling program you’re sellin’,” Ginger had reported to his boss at Stagecoach.

Ricky couldn’t wait to get home and give the good news to his eagerly waiting crew boss, Todd, and to his wife, too. He scribbled a list of To Do’s on a dog-eared yellow pad on the seat beside him as he wound homeward on US 75, through the hilly country of north Texas.

“So much to do!” he shouted as he crossed the Red River, the symbolic boundary that separated Oklahoma and Texas. “Sweet home Oklahoma!” he shouted. Lots to do to get ready to ramp up the operation again, he thought, scribbling furiously on the pad lying next to him.

He patted the new operating agreement folded up in his other pocket. Money in the bank. Tomorrow he’d put on a white shirt and tie, his one good navy blazer (shoot, he’d even shave!), and pay a visit to good ole Kyle up in Tulsa.

This new operating agreement was good for not only a re-write of his present outstanding line of credit (with accrued and past-due interest), but a whole new loan agreement. Fresh cash!

He still couldn’t believe his good fortune. This agreement would provide an income stream to Peabody of around a half-million.

And that was projected just for the first two wells they would drill with Ginger Foss and Stagecoach Energy. With more step-out wells if the first one was completed as a producer. His money worries were over.

Ricky bowed his head and said a little prayer of thanks.

He kept one eye open for stray armadillos and possums.

THIRTEEN

Hospital Oncology Ward, Denver

A ringing telephone woke Dill out of a troubled sleep. JoEllen stirred, shifted in bed.

"I'll get it, dear. Go back to sleep," Dill whispered to her.

"Yes?"

"Dad, it's Luke. How's Mom doing?"

"She's sleeping right now, Pal. How are you guys? I really miss you two."

"We really miss you. Especially Mom. What's really happening, Dad? Is she … Is Mom going to … you know … die?" They hadn't even discussed this as a possibility in their family council or in the days since.

Dill struggled to hold back tears, fought with the big lump sticking in his throat. There was a long minute of silence. Dill could hear his son's heavy breathing on the other end, fighting to keep back the tears.

"You know your Mom. She's … she's always been a fighter. This cancer, this leukemia thing, is a tough one."

"But what did they find?"

"It was leukemia all right, and it's one of the aggressive forms. It's called—heck, I can't remember. Anyways, it isn't the good news you were hoping for."

Silence on the other end.

"So, here's the plan …"

Dill then briefly laid out the course of treatment the doctors had discussed with JoEllen and Dill: They would start with chemotherapy to kill any bacteria in her system so they could move to the next phase, which would be a bone marrow transplant. If that was successful, there would be more chemo followed by radiation.

"Is she going to get better? Or is she going to die?"

"Luke, I can't really tell you that. But I don't think she will die. The doctors are quite positive about her chances for recovery."

"They always say that. What do doctors know, anyway!" Dill could hear his son's voice catch, followed by big, gulping sobs. His big tough son.

"Luke …" Dill had no idea what to say, but, somehow, Luke regained some control and picked up the conversation again.

"Dad, the ward members … well, all of us, me and JJ and everyone from church, we're all gonna fast and pray for her to get better and come home. We want her back home. Especially JJ. He really needs her."

"I know, son. That's really swell that you're all going to fast for her. Mom will be happy to hear that, too. I'll let her know when they come in and wake her to take her vitals." Dill fought the lump in his throat and changed the subject. "Back to JJ; how is JJ doing?"

"Not good. How long do you think Mom will be there?"

"From three to six months. Like I said, she has to have the chemo and bone marrow transplant procedure first. Then when she's recovered enough from that, from the surgery, she will have to get her red cell count up and all that. Then probably chemo. And, most likely radiation to follow. It's going to be a long, hard battle for her."

"Please tell her we miss her and to get better and come home, okay?"

"Sure, Pal …"

Dill reluctantly said goodbye and hung up. He felt so torn, needing to be in two places at once.

A nurse came in and, for the tenth time that day, Jo had her vitals taken and received her meds. When the nurse left, she motioned for Dill to sit next to her on the bed.

"I need to tell you about the dream I had," she said. He braced himself to hear she'd died or had had some vision or glimpse into the afterlife.

"Jo, shh, go back to sleep."

"No. You need to hear this." She motioned for him to adjust the bed so she could sit up. "I dreamed that we were in church, and Matthew was back from his mission and was married and he was blessing a new baby. All of us were there, you, me, all the boys. It was lovely. I'm not sure what it means for sure, but I woke up determined to fight this thing. I'm going to fight it, Dill. And we're going to beat it."

Dill started to put his finger to her lips, to suppress this sudden surge of hope. Was she being unrealistic? Was it destined to be devastating for them all in the long run?

She gently brushed his hand away. "No! I really mean it. I'm going to do the bone marrow transplant, the treatments, radiation, the chemo. The whole deal. That is, if the doctors will agree, and I'm sure they will because that's what *I* want."

He nodded.

Jo kept talking, "So I think you should take that job offer for the fat salary and the medical benefits, and then find yourself some kind of a temporary place here where you and the boys can be close by me and help me and I can be here and get the treatments I need to lick this thing. Promise me, Dill!" She squeezed his hand with surprising strength.

"You're really sure that's what you want us to do?"

She nodded, tears running down her cheeks.

"I promise, then. We'll do this together. As a family. Like we always have. I'll be here for you every step of the way. The boys, too."

"Hug me?"

While he held her, he whispered in her ear, "Luke called to say the whole ward back home is fasting and praying for your recovery. Your sons with them, too."

"That's so lovely. I love my family. Love you guys more than anything else I could ever want in this world."

Stagecoach Energy, Dallas

Jerry Jordan was off on another selling trip to Omaha when Lorne finished his extended conference call with the law firm he'd retained in Juneau.

The lawyers had worked out a consent decree with the Alaska state securities division. That meant that Stagecoach Energy, all of its officers and directors, and Jerry Jordan, were permanently barred from ever selling unregistered securities again in the state of Alaska.

Stagecoach was also ordered to offer to all of the Alaska investors a full rescission (a formal written offer to buy back their limited partnership interests they had previously invested in). Stagecoach would then verify the results of the rescission offer back to the regulators.

Stagecoach would also be required to disclose the negative Alaska regulatory action in any of its current (and future) offering prospectuses.

Lorne would let the Dallas lawyers figure out how to do the wording in the amended prospectus and sales literature.

Of greater concern to Lorne would be the disclosures Stagecoach Energy would have to make in the Initial Public Offering (IPO) of its stock, a deal that Lorne had just worked out with Seth Summers and his brokerage firm in Denver. A new underwriting of $25 million, capital that Lorne and Ted had plans to leverage to their own benefit down the road.

But again, all the high-priced lawyers in Dallas and Denver and Juneau could work out those disclosure details. They were clever at burying the wording deep in dense prose or footnotes to financials that nobody ever read anyway. That's why he paid them the big bucks.

Oh, and Stagecoach would also pay a fine of $50 thousand to the state of Alaska "victim" restitution fund. "Peanuts," Lorne muttered.

Overall, the Juneau attorneys felt pretty pleased and smug about the deal they'd worked out. Sure, they would have liked to go to a full hearing, with the obvious fees to them that a three-day hearing would represent. But Lorne was too shrewd to incur the time, effort, and expense of traveling to Juneau just to look the regulators in the eye and have his so-called day in court. He had no desire to be anywhere near that place.

No. The lawyers had done a good job getting them out of this mess with just a few civil penalties. They could have been facing criminal charges as well, the lawyers had told them.

Peabody Oil, Okmulgee, Oklahoma

All of Ricky Bob's boys at Peabody were euphoric. Two new wells to start drilling right away, with plenty of money in the bank to cover costs. And the promise by their new partner, Stagecoach Energy, of more to come in the near future. Ginger Foss had even hinted at a possible wildcat well sometime soon in the Anadarko. That gave Ricky a warm glow.

Ricky was still puzzled over his earlier meeting with Kyle. The banker informed Ricky that the loan to Peabody Oil was now owned by a bank in Denver called Larimer Square Bank.

"Whadda ya mean my loan is owned by another bank?"

"We sold a large part of our oil and gas portfolio to this new bank in Denver."

What Kyle failed to mention was that Ricky's line of credit, woefully past due, was part of a loan portfolio owned by TGB that was now out of the "non-performing" column. Based upon the latest audit by the Feds who regulated all banks in this region, including Tulsa Guaranty Bank. TGB was only too glad to offload this liability from their books. Let some other sucker bank worry about collecting from these deadbeats.

The Comptroller of the Currency, the federal bank regulators, were happy because those problem loans of TGB were now being supervised by the FDIC, yet another agency in the massive federal bureaucracy. Now it's another agency's headache!

"Larimer bought the whole darn package from us. You included. We're only keeping energy-related customers we consider gilt-edged. Don't get offended, Ricky. We'll still be friends."

Ricky stifled a snicker.

“And we’d welcome you, we’d really be pleased, if you would keep your deposits with us. And your equipment loans. And your credit card accounts.”

Ricky started to say, “Fat chance, and good luck,” but thought better of it. Don’t burn your bridges, boy. Things change quickly in the oil patch. He may come back to you some day and you might need a favor to call in.

Ricky just smiled and thanked Kyle. He even gave him a brotherly hug.

“So, who am I supposed to call and talk to in Denver? This new bank, Square Something …?” Ricky paused at the door.

“You remember Calvin Buckley? Bucky? Used to work here?” Ricky nodded. “Oh, yeah, I remember good ole Bucky.”

“He’s the new CEO at Larimer Square Bank. He’s waitin’ for your call, I’m sure.”

Ricky’s eyes widened. He just could not believe his luck. The energy gods were smiling down on Ricky Bob Peabody today for sure!

FOURTEEN

Seth Summers' Office, Denver

Seth sat with Ted Malmo who had flown up from Dallas at his request to close out the private stock subscription for the new bank's initial capital. The application for a banking license had boldly indicated an initial capitalization of $20 million, half in stock subscriptions from about 25 subscribers, and the other half in the form of "a loan of $10 million to be arranged with another bank on reasonable terms acceptable to the banking commissioner and the new bank's board of directors."

The new stock in Larimer Square Bank was to be issued by a newly formed bank holding company that would, in turn, own all of the shares issued by Larimer Square Bank, making the new bank a wholly owned subsidiary of the parent holding company.

The $10 million loan that Seth arranged with Farmers and Mechanics Cooperative Bank of Denver, was collateralized—secured—by all of the outstanding shares issued by the holding company.

All the holding company shareholders agreed to subordinate their shares and any future dividends to FMC until said loan was fully paid.

The anticipated dividends on the bank shares, paid to the shareholders of the holding company, would be in turn paid to FMC to service the debt on the $10 million loan.

Seth explained all this to the stock subscribers, adding that this was common practice in the banking industry. Banks may fight each other for market share. They always fought hard to keep the new bank out of the competition when an application for a new bank charter was filed.

But when the banking license was granted, they all closed ranks and welcomed you as the newest member into the closely knit brotherhood of bankers. And they were all too eager to help you with your capital requirements with a loan. At a preferable rate of interest. Of course. Case in point, FMC.

Seth also quietly lined up personal loans for most of the new bank stock subscribers, who would use bank loans to pay for their stock subscriptions. These lending banks, scattered around the southwest, in turn took a subordinated interest in the subscribers' new bank stock as collateral.

So, in fact, the whole deal was almost entirely leveraged. Nobody really had any of their own money in the deal, no skin in the game. If the bank failed, they could write off the lost stock against their tax bill. An added bonus.

Seth Summers and Ted Malmo carefully reviewed all the paperwork, added up the figures three times. Then, satisfied, Seth dictated a letter to Commissioner Dennis Morgan certifying that the new bank holding company had, in fact, fulfilled its capital requirements as set out in the Commissioner's previous Findings and Order.

"I think we deserve a toast to celebrate," Seth said, as he opened his authentic French antique maple liquor cabinet and poured drams of his special reserve of rare single malt into two expensive heavy cut crystal glasses.

"To the future."

"To the future," Ted echoed.

"Ted, I'd like you to sign on as our Chief Financial Officer for both the bank and the holding company," Seth said.

"How long do I have to think about it?"

"About as long as it takes for me to pour you a refill," Seth grinned.

Ted grinned back and nodded his head affirmatively.

Banking Commissioner Morgan faxed an official notification to Seth Summers that Larimer Square Bank now had full authority to conduct all phases of commercial banking under the statutes and regulations of the state of Colorado. Meaning it was authorized to take deposits and make loans. Starting immediately.

The new bank's management—meaning, for now, its Chief Operations Officer/Cashier—made arrangements to move a leased double-wide trailer onto a spacious public parking lot two blocks off the Square. The temporary bank quarters were wedged alongside a tall brick building on the far side of the lot, away from the entrance. It had no drive-up window and the interior of the mobile home was crowded from the first day they opened for business.

At least they had adequate parking. And a toilet that worked. Until the holding tank filled up and began overflowing. A pumping service was called to suck out the smelly effluent.

But the wobbly box—as the employees dubbed it—would have to do for several months until they could move into larger leased space closer to the Square. There was no vault, only a portable safe. Cash was counted and transferred by Diebold in an armored vehicle twice a day to FMC Bank across town.

Newport Beach, California

"Gentlemen, I'll cut to the chase," Calvin Buckley drawled. He looked out over the blue Pacific from the seaside headquarters of Newport Security Bank in Newport Beach, California. It was one of the largest banks in Southern California, and they had gained a reputation for being very aggressive bankers. They practically owned the market.

This was the part of banking he loved most: "Rain-making," Buck called it. Bringing in new clients. Not just clients, but really big, important ones. The kind of client that could make a big difference to his bank's bottom line. And his own bonus package and secret retirement fund.

Like Newport Security. And, just like Mt. Rainier Trust, the big northwest bank he'd brought into Larimer Square's fold just day before yesterday.

Tomorrow morning it would be Midland First in west Texas.

Same day, afternoon, on to Dallas. Three big banks to corral and bring into the fold.

Two days after that, Houston. Two banks.

Then Chicago. One of the biggest, oldest banks in America!

Then the Big Apple, where Buck would launch an attack on the staid New York banking fraternity. He reckoned he would see at least a half-dozen banks while there. That would be three days, maybe more, in that wreck of a city. He could stand it. Heck, for the money he was making, he could stand just about any inconvenience. Short of making him stay in a Holiday Inn in New York, instead of the Plaza Hotel.

Buck's folksy pitch was beguilingly simple*: Guys, we're in the middle of an oil boom. The country is thirsty for crude oil and its products—gasoline, diesel, so on. To drill for oil, the oil men, the drillers, they need capital. Where they gonna get that capital? From Larimer Square Bank. With the help of you-all. There's lots of money to be made here, folks.*

Here's how it works: Larimer Square originates the loans. We keep a small part of the loan, maybe 5, 10 percent at most. We're not greedy, we're happy to share. Then we upstream the bulk to you-all, our major correspondent banks. Larimer services the loans for you. For a fee, of course.

We tack on a few interest points to cover your risk. Which the borrowers are more than willing to pay. Oh, yeah, they'll pay it. Otherwise, where the heck they gonna get the cash they need to drill? Hmmm?

Of course, we have expert oil and gas people on staff (not remotely true) *to look over all the supporting loan documentation, such as ...*

Such as leases, operating agreements, financial statements, drilling logs, title abstracts, credit reports, reserve depletion studies by petroleum engineers and so forth. All the usual paperwork you'd expect to see in a loan package. Just like you, we believe in prudent and normal banking practices. (This would turn out to be just one of many empty promises. The upstream bankers would remember and shake their heads in sorrow.)

And you, our correspondent banks, can pick and choose among the loans, which ones you want to participate in, and how much you want to take. We'll do the bundling and pass the info on to you to look at before you commit. Really reduces the risk, don't it?

Now, our lawyers have prepared sample loan participation agreements which you just need to have your board of directors ratify, and then we're in business!

Buckley sat down, crossed his Tony Llama ostrich-booted legs, and lit up a contraband Cuban cigar, grinning steadily at his quarry before him. He hooked his thumbs in his saucer-sized silver and turquoise belt buckle and leaned easily back. He hadn't removed his $300 Stetson during the entire presentation.

It was almost too easy. They fell all over themselves to sign on, promising to send a platoon of their young trainees to the new bank in Denver to help handle the paper flow. Larimer Square Bank would make room for these fresh-faced kids with a promise to train them in the finer points of loan packaging. (Another empty promise.)

Board ratification of the master loan participation agreements by their boards of directors? A mere formality.

Here come the profits. They couldn't wait to put out press releases. They were in the oil business! Couldn't wait to send out interim reports to their shareholders, to financial analysts, stockbrokers and investment banking firms.

We're in the oil business!

Larimer Square Bank, Denver

They were finally moving out of the wobbly box! The bank's skeleton staff were ecstatic. They were already tired of working in the cramped temporary digs where their lungs were polluted by rank, indoor oxygen, and where the lighting was poor and the air-conditioning non-existent. And where every time you turned around you were in somebody's face.

Or, even worse, female employees recounted in whispers numerous instances of unwanted groping at close quarters. Always followed by an insincere, "Oops, sorry. Accidental touching!" Nobody filed charges; nothing would come of it anyway. They just went back to the routine of trying to conduct banking business out of a mobile home parked in a scummy parking lot off an alley where winos slept in the daytime, and where you had to watch where you were stepping so as to avoid the cast-off syringes and needles. Or, worse yet, certain used birth control devices. Yuck!

The new offices were just a couple blocks away, but it might as well have been in another city; it was a vast improvement. The female employees might still be subject to some harassment from coworkers and may need after-hours escorts to their parked cars in the early darkness of winter, but that was a very slight inconvenience they could put up with.

A temporary sign immediately went up on the plate glass windows of a pod in a strip shopping mall one block from Larimer Square announcing that Larimer Square Bank would be open for business the next week.

Workmen moved in and began the round-the-clock work of outfitting the premises for the bank's new permanent home. Teller line and vault on the main floor; executive and loan offices on the upper floor. The vault was giving the workmen special problems.

New, stronger floor joists had to be rigged to carry the heavy weight of the monster apparatus. The Diebold people, who made the vault, had to be brought in to supervise. More delays. But it had to be done to comply with state and federal banking regulations.

Full page ads appeared in the local newspapers and all the local television channels and radio stations. A full-page ad—a tombstone—was placed in the Wall Street Journal emphasizing that the new bank intended to become the market leader for oil and gas lending, the biggest such financial institution in the country.

"A brash, gutsy claim coming from such a small startup bank," the Journal wrote.

Seth had persuaded an old crony, TJ Brimhall, a retired banker, to come out of retirement and assume the position of bank president. It was largely an honorary title for TJ, as Seth intended to have a very firm but unseen hand in things.

He'd let his protégé, Calvin "Buck" Buckley, Chief Executive Officer, front their operation. With Ted as the titular Chairman of the Board of directors.

Seth, TJ, Ted, Bucky, and a couple other hand-picked cronies would comprise the initial board of directors. Seth held out seats on various bank committees as inducements to the biggest investors to come on board to lend their names and reputations to the new venture: compensation, compliance, recruitment. Eight-by-ten glossies, glamorous head shots, Seth called these men and women. The most important committee, loan approvals, where *real* banking happened, was the exclusive province of Seth, Ted, and Buckley. Maybe they would add this Dill Robertson fellow later on. If he ever decided to join them.

The Chief Operations Officer/Cashier they hired from an obscure branch bank down south in Montrose, a most un-dynamic man, whose wife was only too happy to leave the boredom of small-town life and return with glory to the big city of Denver.

The new COO/Cashier had the thankless task of hiring the little people who would run the day-to-day banking operations: clerks, tellers, secretaries, accountants, receptionists, collectors, etc.

Seth's nagging concern was with the man who still hadn't agreed to be the new chief loan officer, Dill Robertson. Seth had many friends, many former clients who were practicing Mormons, for whom he had the greatest respect. They were all solid, upstanding, family-oriented, civic-minded people. Mostly well-educated and hard working. As a people, they were admirable.

He knew the Mormons of his acquaintance to also be morally straight. He'd never known any Mormon to be in trouble with the law, no hint of scandal, no gossip of extramarital affairs.

His concern with Robertson was just this: Would he be too straight? How would he react to a borderline case, a questionable loan or line of credit, where maybe a member of the board or management wanted a friend given special treatment by the bank?

Seth thought of Calvin Buckley who was out there rounding up the correspondent banks. Buckley was yelling at the board of directors, and most especially targeting Seth, to get him some badly needed help so he could book more, and bigger, loans. The upstream banks were demanding more loan packages.

How would Robertson get along with this gunslinger, Buckley? If … if Robertson would ever make up his mind and commit to come on board.

And what about the entertainment aspects of the business, the trips to Atlantic City or Las Vegas to cultivate their best upstream banking partners, their biggest clients? How would Robertson deal with that?

Only time would tell. Seth figured it was only a minor hurdle, something that could easily be managed when the time came to sign a contract with him. And he was sure Robertson would soon come calling. The latest reports Seth had received on Mrs. Robertson were not good: Leukemia. An aggressive, often deadly form. But, in a morbid way, Seth knew that her condition was good for him and his plans. The costs were going to bury Dill Robertson if he wasn't handed a lifeline. And Seth Summers was just the person to do that.

Dill Robertson would sign on with Larimer Square Bank all right. What other option did he have? It was only a matter of *when*?

FIFTEEN

Larimer Square Bank, Denver

The bank opened in its new, permanent quarters almost on time. Almost. They should have opened the doors at ten o'clock, but there was a one-hour delay while technical workers finished some final tweaking of the sensitive, computerized teller equipment. The harried cleaning crew worked around the technicians, picking up piles of wiring scraps, sweeping, vacuuming and polishing.

Finally, at eleven o'clock of opening day, TJ Brimhall, always one for the flair, ceremoniously unlocked the doors for business. The calm and serenity of deposits and opening checking accounts on the main floor belied the chaos and bedlam above. On the second floor, workers were still moving dozens of desks and mountains of equipment into offices through the rear fire escape.

"Where do you want these filing cabinets, sir," they asked the cashier.

"Uh, I guess you can put them over there on that long wall," he said, checking the blueprints. He looked out over a large, 40-foot by 100-foot office area. This was designated as Loan Operations, and plans showed more than 40 cubicles to be filled. And filled they would be: by the fresh-faced kids their correspondent banks would soon be packing off to the Gem of the Rocky Mountains: Denver.

As that first day wore on, more desks, chairs, and typewriters arrived and were set up. Cubicles began to take form and a fair number of nicely dressed young men and women materialized, taking up residence behind the choicest desks, opening new bundles of tools of their trade: pens, pencils, staplers, calculators, liquid correcting fluid.

Their personal items—such as photos, coffee cups, and plants—would materialize a day or so later.

The cashier had no idea who was in charge of all these eager faces; it wasn't his department. He found his corner office, which, he was thankful to see, had an outside window. Stacked floor to ceiling were dozens of Bankers Boxes which he assumed were loans the new bank had purchased from other banks. He went off in search of a worker who could help him set up sufficient filing cabinets to house all the paper. Then he retreated to the safety of his own office.

Mid-afternoon, Buck showed his face and called everyone together for an impromptu meeting in the large bullpen.

"Welcome, everyone," he said, puffing on his ever-present cigar. "I'm Cal Buckley, CEO of this here bank. Everyone calls me Buck or Bucky. We don't stand on ceremony here."

The new young bankers looked at each other and nodded. This was going to be fun, much different than the stodgy places they had worked in before. Who wouldn't be put at ease by a paunchy guy wearing Tony Llama boots, a Stetson, and a big silver and turquoise belt buckle the size of a Thanksgiving platter?

"Our job in this part of the bank is to process loans. Mostly oil and gas loans. I say mostly because that's the business we want to serve. Once in a while we may be asked to do a loan for somethin' like real estate, or a small business, or whatever." Heads nodded.

"Otherwise … The huge majority of our customers are in the oil business, drillers, lease hounds, land people, engineers, lawyers, chemical and equipment suppliers, rig builders, you name it, they all relate back to the oil business somehow. The reason we're here is to provide them a service: We loan them money so's they can carry on their business. They pay your wages, so it makes sense for you-all to hustle and give them the fast service they—and I—expect. And deserve."

A smartly dressed young man in the back raised his hand.

"Yes, son?"

"But Mr. Buckley, many of us work for other banks. We're not employed by your bank. Technically …"

"And your point is, son? Buckley shot back.

"Well, who do we take our marching orders from? You people or our own banks back home, so to speak?"

"Well, I guess you have a point there. But not to split hairs, we're all on the same team, so in the spirit of teamwork, I'd like to see everyone under this roof pulling on the same oar. It all works out for the best. In the long run. So to speak. Know what I mean?" Buck flashed a nasty smile at the young man, who nodded and retreated behind a wall of other kids.

"Good. Now, I'd like to say a few more words." Buck launched into a long-winded monologue: "I've been a banker most of my life. I only know how to produce results, and that's with hard work. Sometimes you have problems or questions. It's a foolish man, or woman, who doesn't ask questions, doesn't ask for help. I place a lot of stock on details, accuracy. A good loan portfolio requires a lot of detailed back up, so if I send you back to fill in some missing details, don't take it personally. At some point our work will be scrutinized, probably by a crusty old bank examiner. Some day. Down the road …"

The youngsters laughed, put at ease by his folksy humor.

"So, let's do our jobs the best we can. And at the end of the day, let's lay our tools down, knock off, and go play. Welcome aboard." They applauded him politely.

"Thanks," Buck said. "Now, let's get to work."

Oncology Wing, Denver Hospital

"How was your day, dear?" Dill asked. JoEllen's condition had worsened. Only slightly, the doctors assured her, but the leukemia was accelerating its nasty effects and her body was feeling it. They needed to do more tests before they could plan the chemo and marrow procedure. And there was still the problem of finding a compatible donor. In the meantime, all they could do was wait. She was tired, but hid her fatigue well with her upbeat attitude.

"I'm not too bad. All I need is a big hug."

He embraced her, feeling her ribs through her hospital gown. She had already begun to lose weight. And she was just getting started. After the testing today, there was another round planned for tomorrow.

"You up for tomorrow?" he asked. She said she was. More tissue samples. Another biopsy.

"Have you had time to find a place to stay yet?" Jo asked. "You can't keep sleeping here. Maybe you should get a motel room. You'd rest better."

"I'm okay. Depending on how things go with you tomorrow, I was thinking of leaving early on Friday to visit the boys, maybe bring them back here for a couple days. I think it would do a lot of good for you. And them."

She closed her eyes and nodded. "I'd like that. In the meantime, what are you planning to do about the job offer from the bank?"

Dill verbalized what they were both thinking. "Depends on how things go here with you."

"Dill, I have decided you better swallow your ego and take the job. You heard what the doctors said about the costs, how they are typically so high that some people lose all their savings, their homes. Have to take out bankruptcy, even. In the meantime, the costs, they're so …" She let that thought hang out there unspoken.

He looked at her, took her hand in his, and said evenly, "We're not going to lose our home. I promise you that much. We may have to sell off part of the ranch, or …"

"We can't sell the ranch, it's your legacy, our legacy, you, me, the boys, future generations, even. We owe it to your family, your great-grand dad, all the ones who worked so hard to build it and make it what it is today."

He nodded. He clamped on his Stetson and said, "Then that's settled. I better call Mr. Summers and tell him I need the job; if it's still open, that is." She agreed. Her worried eyes told him what words couldn't.

Weatherford, Texas

Ricky Bob stayed late in his office, poring over well logs. He had asked Ginger for as many logs as he could supply of wells adjacent to the new drilling site in Stephens County, Texas. The new one overlooking Lake Breckenridge.

He laid all six logs side-by-side and closely examined them for depths, pressures, formations, and other data that would give him comfort that they had a better-than-even chance of making a well.

He identified four wells, two to the southeast and two more to the northwest, all on forty-acre spacing. All had been drilled to a depth of approximately five thousand feet. Of the four, only the two to the northwest had been completed and operated for any length of time.

His working hypothesis was that there was a trend with the target formation sloping upwards from southeast to northwest. And their proposed well site was right in line with those two producers.

Ricky pulled an old, dog-eared textbook off the shelf and thumbed through it until he found the chapter he was seeking. The text had been written by his favorite professor at OU and it had become Ricky's bible. He read and re-read the chapter about the type of formation he'd soon be drilling, scribbling notes in the margins of the logs for the two wells he'd identified as most productive.

It was two in the morning when he turned off the lights and headed home. He was satisfied that he had a winner in this next well. It was important to him that he bring in a producer.

Still, he was also a little concerned. Looking over the logs of the wells that had been closed as dry holes, he'd noticed many formations showing sizeable "kicks"—spots, geological formations—where it was pretty obvious to any experienced oil man that they should be at least tested for oil or gas. Why had they been shut in as dry holes?

He sure as heck would have at least tested one or more of those potential formations. Didn't make sense. Oh, well. He'd look again when he wasn't so tired.

On his drive home, he fought sleep all the way. He turned off the bedroom light and quietly crawled into bed beside Nan. He moved toward her and cuddled against her curved, warm body.

Ricky lay there for a few minutes wondering if he should wake her. The euphoria of his eventful day was draining away. A profound weariness began to overtake him. Nan moved in her sleep, snuggled her face against his neck. He breathed in the calming fragrance of Shalimar and fell into a deep sleep.

More Tests

JoEllen's family—her immediate siblings, her parents—all agreed to be tested for bone marrow compatibility. The tests were successful: Two siblings were found to be compatible; but one of those, her older brother, was eliminated because he was type 1 diabetic. Her younger sister, however, was quite strong and healthy in every respect and she readily agreed to be Jo's bone marrow donor.

And the good news—if you could call it that—was that the procedure could be scheduled for two weeks. They would be flying in a specialist from the Mayo Clinic, in Rochester, Minnesota, to oversee the procedure. He had a two-day window in his busy schedule before he had to fly off to deliver a paper at an international conference in Vienna.

Everything had to be timed to perfection to make this happen. Her red blood count was deemed high enough to start the chemo. Jo lay there and thanked God for the miracles of modern medicine. She could do this!

Dill headed home to bring the two youngest boys back for a quick visit. The doctors asked the family to keep it short. Dill assured them it would be brief. He checked the back of his truck; the fly rod was still there, a good sign. He drove home slowly, thinking a lot about Larimer Square Bank.

As Dill walked through the door at home, he heard the phone ringing. It was Seth Summers wanting an update. Dill explained Jo's situation and told Seth that, with her support and after sleeping on it over the weekend, he was ready to take the position Summers had offered.

"That's very good news. Very, very good news," Seth said. "When can you start?"

At Seth's obvious insensitivity, Dill suddenly felt sick to his stomach. He needed to be available for the bone marrow procedure. He also would need some time to put things in order at home, with the two boys soon getting out of school, arranging care for them. Then there were some matters at his own bank, as well as the ranch, to be taken care of. Plus, he needed to find a place to stay in Denver. He ventured a hopeful, "How does four weeks sound?"

"Three sounds better, or even two. We really needed you yesterday."

"I understand, but I …"

Seth cut him off. "Look, man, I know it's not a great time for you, but we can't wait many more days to have someone functioning in this position. I would hate to think we need to look elsewhere."

Dill clenched his jaw, angry at Seth's underlying threat. "I'll do what I can," he whispered.

"Good," was all Seth said. Then, added a less-than heartfelt: "I am hoping for the best for your wife."

SIXTEEN

Stagecoach Energy Offices, Dallas

To say Jerry was disgruntled would be an understatement. Furious, more like.

Lorne and Ted had called him into the Stagecoach Energy corporate offices in the high-rise building overlooking the LBJ loop in North Dallas. For late spring it was a very warm, humid day in Dallas. It seemed like it was always warm and humid in Dallas, Jerry thought. Dried cicada carcasses littered the pavement and sidewalks, crunching under his heavy feet.

Something didn't seem right about this meeting. Jerry felt tension, a knot in his gut, as he entered the building and turned toward the elevators.

He got off on the tenth floor. Gold letters above a massive door proclaimed: STAGECOACH ENERGY CORP.

There had been rumors that, because Stagecoach was going public soon, they would have millions in cash and would no longer need to rely on the riskier oil and gas limited partnerships they had been offering. That could possibly mean Jerry was no longer needed as a salesman for those ventures.

There were also hints that Jerry had become a liability to the company because of his scrape with the Alaska securities regulators. But that all had been settled favorably and swept under the rug. Ted assured him it was no longer an issue.

Lorne and Ted, in shirtsleeves, were huddled over a mass of paperwork. It sprawled over the small conference table in the corner of Lorne's huge corner office and spilled onto the floor. This office provided a sweeping view to the south over the LBJ and the urban sprawl beyond. To the north was the Red River forming the Texas-Oklahoma border. Beyond that, was the hilly country of Oklahoma.

Jerry waited nervously while the two men continued their whispered conversation. Finally, he could wait no longer.

"You guys brought me here to fire me, didn't you?"

The two executives looked at each other. Lorne gestured to a seat. "Why don't you sit down and we can discuss this rationally, Jerry, like gentlemen."

"I'd rather stand like a man. Thanks anyway." He was angry. He could feel the bile beginning to rise in his throat. He could use a gin and tonic right now.

"Have it your way." Lorne straightened up, shrugged his shoulders to relieve some of the strain in his neck and back. "Yes, we, the company, we've adopted a new paradigm for our business model. We're getting out of the limited partnership business. After consulting with our legal team, we determined that it's just too risky. It's a risk we no longer care to assume. So … we're out of that business. You and the other salesmen have become redundant."

Are you kidding? Redundant? Really? Why don't they call it what it is? Jerry felt the heat rising under his collar.

"So, cutting through all the corporate speak, what you're saying is I'm fired. That's about it, isn't it? Nothing more to say."

Ted opened a drawer in the desk and extracted a manila envelope. He fished inside and handed a thick sheaf of papers to Jerry.

"What's this?" Jerry asked. He didn't accept the papers.

"It's normal corporate practice for corporations to have former business associates, contractors, sign a separation agreement. We need you to sign this before we release your final commission payment to you."

Jerry eyed the documents, made no move to accept them. "And if I don't sign?"

"Now, Jerry, don't be difficult. There's nothing in there that puts you at any disadvantage. We're just following the advice of our lawyers, and they …"

Jerry stopped him. "So, maybe I should have my lawyers look at these, advise me too? That's fair, isn't it?"

Ted nodded. "Of course, Jerry, take all the time you need. Just remember, your final commissions check is being held up until you do sign off."

"Held hostage is more like!" Jerry grabbed the papers and stormed out. No handshakes were offered.

Jerry was seething. But he kept to a reasonable speed as he drove to DFW to turn in his rental car. He struggled to keep his anger under control. No need getting a speeding ticket. He checked into the Delta Airlines Crown Room and found a private phone.

Jerry had anticipated they would pull this. He had been thinking of his next moves, who he should call in the event they sacked him. He placed the call.

"Hello, is this Phil Connoff? Yeah, this is Jerry Jordan calling. Don't know if you remember me. We met at an oil and gas investment symposium this last winter in Calgary. You gave me your card. You said you might be interested in doing some business with me someday … Yeah, so you do remember our conversation? Good. Well, listen Phil … Is it okay if I call you Phil? Oh, you prefer Phillip. Good. Phillip, I think I see an exciting opportunity for us to do some business together. It just so happens that I have a couple days free on my calendar. I was wondering if I could stop by to see you on my way back to Los Angeles? Fine, tomorrow? Good. See you then, Phil, er, Phillip."

Jerry went to the concierge desk and asked to have his return ticket changed to Salt Lake City. "And could you also book me a room at the Marriott in Salt Lake? Thanks, I appreciate it."

Life was already looking up again.

Jerry always landed on his feet.

Jerry's next call from the Crown Room was to his friend, Darren Magelby, a lawyer with a solo practice. Magelby operated out of an old barn converted into a combination home, legal office, and workout room. It was situated on eighty pristine acres among the verdant rolling hills of Skiatook, Oklahoma, a small town about a half hour's drive north of Tulsa.

Darren and Jerry had roomed in the same dorm at Cornell. Darren had gone on to law school, then started his own practice in his home town. He was a little eccentric. But he was the smartest, cleverest lawyer Jerry had ever encountered. Darren was well-known in northern Oklahoma for his aw-shucks, gee-whiz, I'm-just-a-country-lawyer manner. It was beguiling to juries. It also went down well with the laid-back style of the ranchers, oil men and small-town merchants he counted as clients.

He also had several high-powered clients who frequented the exclusive watering holes of the rich and famous. Among these select clients were a few small independent oil companies scattered across the southwest and the plains of Kansas. Notable among them was Ricky Bob Peabody. Peabody Oil. Of Okmulgee, Oklahoma.

Darren gloried in his little oddities. He was fond of Birkenstocks, didn't wear cowboy boots, except when he had to appear in court in some rural county. And then he wore an old pair of roughouts, badly scuffed in the toes, and generously smeared with cow dung.

He drove an old Ferrari he had picked up during his junior year of college abroad in Italy. He proudly drove it everywhere, lovingly cared for it. He named it Mama Ferrari.

"Shoot, anyone can drive a Cadillac," Darren reasoned. "It takes real panache to drive a Ferrari in these here parts."

His business card was also unique. Engraved on cream cardstock by the finest stationers in Tulsa, it read:

DARREN MAGELBY, LAWYER

Skiatook, Oklahoma

But the back provided the best clue into this unique legal mind. It bore the claim:

Full-Service Lawyer: I'll Incorporate You – Take You Public – Preside Over Your Bankruptcy – Help You Through Your Divorce & Defend Your Criminal Fraud Charges.

Darren was fearless. He had taken on some of the biggest, most-politically connected foes in Oklahoma and elsewhere. He had both friends and admirers. He probably had more enemies. His life had been threatened more than once. He had a concealed weapons permit and always carried. He was relentless when pursuing what he considered a just cause—if it was Darren's client's cause, it was Darren's cause.

He had been hauled before the state bar ethics committee more than once to defend trumped-up complaints from people who had never been his clients, but claimed some vague connection to someone Darren had crossed swords with. The complaints were all dismissed.

He had also had to face charges before the state securities division. The charge sheet said that he had supposedly aided and abetted his clients in some allegedly fraudulent money-raising scheme or other. The most notable being one client who had raised a lot of capital from small investors. They were the kind known in the industry as brother-in-law investors—family, friends, fellow churchgoers. The very individuals who had no business investing in the first place. And because they had no good sense, the state securities regulatory people were duty bound under the law to protect them. Mostly from themselves.

This particular client had developed a fond taste for fresh shrimp. And because Oklahoma was far inland and had no adjoining oceans, our genius hatched the idea of starting a shrimp farm. He had lots of land and plenty of water. All he needed was capital for the tanks, equipment, and brood stock of shrimp. All of which didn't come cheap.

So, the shrimp farmer went about hitting up family, friends, fellow church members for the money he needed. He wasn't much of a businessman (or a shrimp farmer either). He hadn't bothered to spend much time with research or even a formal business plan, cash flow projections, budgets, and the like. His next mistake was also foolish. He just accepted investors' checks and deposited them into his personal checking account.

The shrimp farm finally was up and running, but not really what you'd call a going concern. The farmer needed more capital. So he widened his field of possible investors. Things were looking up. He was raising more money. He was happy.

Until … until he ran into a potential investor who insisted that he be provided with a prospectus, complete with business plan, financial projections, estimated payback—all the basic financial data. He wanted to have his lawyer and accountant take a look and advise him, as they always did before he invested in any startup ventures.

The shrimp farmer put together a poorly written document that he tried to pass off as a prospectus. The investor then innocently asked if Shrimp Farmer had registered these securities with the Oklahoma state securities division?

Shrimp Farmer, not having the least clue, panicked and made another classic rookie mistake. He lied and said he had. Or, at least, his lawyer had taken care of all that legal mumbo jumbo.

The would-be investor thanked him, said he'd think about it, and placed a phone call to the state securities guys. They arrived at the shrimp farm the next day with a subpoena and a cease-and-desist order.

Shrimp Farmer placed a call to his minister (who had also invested and had referred several of his flock to invest). He advised his terrified parishioner to call Darren Magelby, who was also an upstanding member of his congregation.

Darren worked it out beautifully. But not before he had had to defend himself of the spurious aiding and abetting charges filed by the state securities people. He did so by producing a retainer agreement dated long after the shrimp farmer's encounters with the whistleblower.

But the state securities folks have long memories and continued to keep Darren in their crosshairs.

"Mr. Magelby, maybe you don't remember me, but this is your old college roommate, Jerry Jordan."

"Well Jerry, you sly ole snake charmer, for what do I deserve the honor of this phone call? You're not in any trouble, I hope? Or, should I say, I hope you are in trouble!"

"I'm seriously considering starting up my own operation, oil and gas drilling funds. You familiar with how they work?

"My boy, I invented them!" He lit a cigar, kicked off his Birkenstocks and propped his stockinged feet on the desk. "You've come to the right place. How can I help?"

"Well, first of all, I need a good driller with a good track record. One who won't cheat my investors blind with carried interests, overriding royalties, operating costs, that sort of stuff. One I hope has some really sweet prospects just waiting to be drilled. Say 5,000-foot jobs?"

"I know just the man. You ever hear of Ricky Bob Peabody? Has a small family business down in Okmulgee. He's been working with an outfit out of Dallas, calls themselves Stagecoach Energy. Ever hear of them?"

After a long pause, Jerry said, "Yeah. Somewhat familiar," he hedged. "Why does this Ricky Bob guy want to leave them, anyway? If you don't mind my asking?"

"What I tell you is in strictest confidence?"

"Sure."

"He's been noticing some things about their well logs from surrounding wells that were shut in as dry holes. Says they ain't dry holes but that Stagecoach is playing games. Are you familiar with how the dry hole game is played?"

Jerry's mouth went as dry as a dry hole. He grunted, took a deep breath to calm his mounting anger, the pounding in his chest, He wondered if any of those dry holes were in the limited partnerships he'd been instrumental in selling. Most likely they were. Had to be at least one or two. His mind flashed back to the sinking feeling he'd had when that Alaska securities cop had laid that cease-and-desist order and subpoena on him at the Anchorage Marriott. His mouth felt like the Gobi in a dust storm.

"Enlighten me," he managed to croak.

"Well, you drill a hole then shut it in as a dry hole. You say to investors, 'Sorry, but it looks like it's a dry one. So sorry about that. But that's the risk you signed off on. But at least you can still keep your tax benefits.' That kind of song and dance."

Jerry grunted.

"You show them dummied up drilling logs. If any of them are smart enough to bring in a petroleum engineer to look at the logs. You wait a decent spell, then go back into the lease after a reasonable period using a dummy company totally not connected with you or the partnership what drilled the well in the first place. You open up the shut-in well and test the formations, the ones what showed up as kicks in the real drill logs that you hid from the investors. You complete the well for yourself. You don't have to share with any investors. Bob's your uncle! See what I mean?"

"I see. Has he said anything to Stagecoach? This Ricky guy?"

"Nope. Ain't about to, neither. He's—we're—just gathering facts and sitting on it. If they try to screw with him, he has a big hammer over their head for insurance later on down the road. Just in case."

"What are his plans? What's he want to do? And why did you mention him?"

"Well, seems like the stars have aligned. He wants to set up a new company, outside of Peabody, and outside of his current commitment to drill two wells with Stagecoach, see. And possibly do some exploratory drilling in some prospects he might get to participate in as a farmout by a consortium of majors. We're talking deep gas. Anadarko. Twenty-thousand-foot babies!"

Jerry whistled softly. He'd heard about the Anadarko deep gas, and how just the thought of it gave many an oilman a real warm glow.

"What else can I help you with?"

"I need you to cut me a deal on the private placement documents I'll be needing for my own limited partnership: prospectus, subscription agreement, formation of general partner corporation, limited partnership agreement, all that stuff. I have a good template. All you have to do is cut and paste. You know, keep the fees reasonable?" Darren blew a puff of smoke at the ceiling and gave a noncommittal grunt.

"I'll also need a new corporation. I'd say in Nevada, closer to where I live, more management-friendly than Delaware, I hear. I'll FedEx the stuff to you tonight, you'll get it tomorrow."

Darren nodded, taking notes on a yellow legal pad. Outside his open window a meadowlark sang beautifully in the newly green hay fields. "Sure. No problem. What you gonna call this new company?"

"Haven't gotten that far. I'll let you know."

"Anything else?"

"I was just cut loose by Stagecoach Energy Corp. They want me to sign a separation agreement. I looked it over and there's a lot of good stuff about holding them harmless. But there's no reciprocal clause covering me."

"That's standard corporate cutthroat practice." Darren exhaled another cloud of smoke toward the lofty barn rafters.

"Yeah, well, it's a bluff and they know it. They're holding my last check hostage until I sign. Another thing, I didn't see any reference to my keeping the carried interests and overriding royalties in the wells. That's in my employment contract. That's my retirement, Darren!"

EIGHTEEN

Oncology Ward, Denver Hospital

JoEllen hung onto the rim of the toilet bowl with her face just inches from the water. She retched again from deep inside. Every inch of her body in pain like she had never experienced, even during four childbirths. And they had all been very large babies. Those big sons of hers. Those Four Apostles.

She almost passed out as she crawled back to her bed, trembling violently from the effort. She was afraid her stitches would rupture from the awful vomiting. Every joint ached beyond belief. The painkillers helped for a little while. But, they also made her unbelievably nauseous.

The leukemia had progressed even more. Rapidly. And with a fury that surprised her and the doctors. Her own marrow procedure had been a success. Or so they said. Now she was in the waiting period until her sister could have her marrow harvested under the watchful eyes of the Mayo Clinic specialist.

The doctors had told her that the chances of beating this thing weren't all that good. Cautiously, they said maybe fifty-fifty. But Jo had chosen to take the fight to the monster anyway. For JoEllen, there was no other choice. She wanted too badly to see her sons married. To hold grandchildren in her arms. To grow old with Dill.

She lay back on the cool sheets, nestled her pounding head carefully into the soft pillow. She was so tired. Sleep was a luxury. How she missed sleep. If it wasn't pain, or nausea, or nurses coming in every hour to check her vitals, it was someone from home calling on the phone. Or "just dropping in to say hi."

Poor company I am, she mused.

Another thing: She found it almost impossible to eat, and then to keep anything down. Her mouth, gums, and throat were developing sores, which made for very difficult chewing and swallowing. But she forced herself to eat. Something, anything. She had to keep up her strength to fight this thing. To win. Jo drifted into a sleep, dreaming about her first grandchild. A girl. It had to be a girl. For the daughter she never had.

Larimer Square Bank

One good thing in all this, she thought, was Dill's decision to take the job at Larimer Square Bank. For that, she was greatly relieved. It had ultimately boiled down to a case of necessity. JoEllen needed the best medical care available. And that meant Denver. And Dill felt he needed to be close to Jo for the duration. And it was going to be outrageously costly, more than they could afford on their own. So, they needed the generous financial and insurance umbrella—or parachute? They needed the coverage Seth Summers had offered.

Dill had briefly considered a mortgage on the ranch but nixed that idea. The thought of working for somebody other than his immediate family galled him. But, for now anyway, it wasn't about what he wanted but what would be best for Jo.

He took a couple weeks to wrap up a few things at the bank in Craig, and to tidy up some details on the ranch. Things were settled for the boys: Dill's older sister would move into their home for the summer and keep an eye on things there. Not that he was worried. Those boys were fast becoming good young men, reliable and good through and through.

After that he was ready, reluctantly, he admitted, to sign the employment agreement. He put on a blazer and tie, sucked up his courage, and reported for duty. He parked in the lot behind the bank. He checked to make sure his fly rod was secured under the spare tire before making his way up the rear fire escape stairs.

Oncology Ward, Denver Hospital

Dill quietly slipped into the dimly lit room. Jo was sleeping, a rarity. He was aware of how little sleep she got and did his best not to disturb. It had been a rough day at the bank. There had been an unseasonal, early summer snowstorm that had surprised everyone and had virtually shut down the city. Employees were hopelessly late to work. Or called in saying they were stuck in some huge snowdrift and would be hours getting unstuck. Probably wouldn't be coming in. Some didn't even bother to call.

Dill had a long list of questions about loans that had been approved by Buckley. Each of the loans had either been made by him or under his say-so. They were all uniformly terribly lacking in backup documentation. Dill needed to talk face-to-face with Buckley to sort it out. But, Buckley was out of town, somewhere in the upper Midwest.

Today, in Chicago, probably. Schmoozing new clients. Meaning rounding up more big, upstream banks to lay off participating loans to. Or harvesting deposits from fat cat depositors. The new jumbo deposit thing everyone was going crazy over.

He'd only been on board a week and already Dill was starting to form an opinion of his new boss's sloppy banking. Make that bosses. Seth Summers, Cal Buckley, all of them were at fault. Too many loans being authorized without proper backup. Inadequate documentation in the files. Lack of collateralization. His list of concerns went on.

Dill had a stack of files—over two dozen—that were waiting for title reports on oil leases. Or current financial statements. Or lists of hard assets (equipment, rolling stock, drill rigs, etc.) that needed to have UCC-1s filed and recorded properly. Again, the list went on. That stack of files represented a staggering $83 million. It was all happening too fast. Dill's staff was too small, too overworked. All operating under a cloud of unreasonable stress and discouragement. It was depressing to say the least, but Dill was determined to make this thing work. For Jo's sake.

He considered going over Buckley's head and speaking to TJ Brimhall, the titular president, about the many problems. But he didn't have a lot of faith in the kindly old gentleman. As Dill now knew, TJ was mostly a figurehead for the bank—window dressing.

TJ was the upfront guy who was there merely to give the established Denver banking community and the regulators, confidence that the new bank was in safe and prudent hands.

Prudent hands. That title was way short of falling on Buckley's shoulders, Dill concluded. That guy was a cowboy banker. Made snap decisions based on good-old-boy connections. Or worse yet, on Buck's guesstimate of the customer's ability to do favors for Buckley. Or for some of his other favored clients. Buckley laughed at the concept of safe and prudent.

Take, for example, the one fat file Dill had at the top of the stack. A Buckley-approved loan. His huge initials were prominently scrawled at the top of the loan application in green ink. Why did Buckley favor green ink? Did he fancy himself as *C* in some James Bond movie? Weird. The stated purpose of the loan was for "*acquisition of drilling pipe, chemicals, and various operating expenses.*" The loan was for $2 million.

But when Dill made a spot check of the customer's recent checking account disbursements, his practiced eye discovered an item that caught his attention. An $800,000 check had been written the same day the loan proceeds had been deposited to the customer's account. Not for drill pipe, drilling chemicals, or anything remotely related to oilfield drilling or operations. Not even for a lease payment.

The check had been written to Archway Farms in Ardmore, Oklahoma. It had not yet found its way back to Larimer Square Bank, but was still working its way through the antiquated check-clearing system. It would be a few more days before Dill could physically examine the check to see if any memo had been noted for the proceeds.

He looked up Archway Farms. They purported to be an established horse farm known for buying, selling and trading champion quarter horses—sometimes Arabians—to high rolling customers. In their glossy brochure and newspaper ads, Archway even boasted a couple of Saudi princes as their recent clients.

A typical price tag for one of their champion animals, a quarter horse stud with documented bloodlines for breeding? $800,000!

Dill correctly reasoned that if there was one loan that was being used as a cover for other purposes than stated in the loan application, there were probably others buried in that stack. The day had been a bust due to the blizzard anyway, so Dill rolled up his sleeves and took a hard look at some of the other loans in his growing "problem" pile.

He wasn't too surprised at what he began to uncover:

$2.5 million—for independent movie production.

$1.9 million—for private club and restaurant, Oklahoma City. A pole-dancing club.

$3 million—for used Lear Jet, leased by a bank in the northwest.

$2.7 million—to re-write past due loan purchased from Midland First Bank.

$1.25 million—ditto, from Tulsa Guaranty Bank (debtor: Peabody Oil Co., Okmulgee, Oklahoma).

$1.6 million—for two Arabian horses, no gender indicated. Same borrower as the other Archway Farms purchase, but using a different corporation, one that had been set up in Nevada using nominee directors the day before the loan was made.

$5.9 million—for first phase development costs for condo development in Florida, with $1 million peeled off for option on developable land in Jackson, Wyoming.

This was the kind of stuff that made bank regulators go ballistic! It was also the stuff of class action lawsuits by stockholders. If they knew.

But, what was Dill prepared to do about it?

Nothing for now. Sit, wait, watch, listen. Gather facts. Make copies. Document his findings.

NINETEEN

Salt Lake City, Utah

Jerry Jordan flew into Salt Lake City the same day as the freak late-spring blizzard had hit Denver. The same storm front had passed through Salt Lake, dropping almost a foot of new powdery snow, snarling traffic, and slowing down operations at Salt Lake International. They sat out on the tarmac for an hour before he could finally deplane.

Jerry rented a car and drove himself downtown to the new Marriott, checked in, and poured himself a drink from a little bottle in the mini bar, a pre-mixed Bloody Mary. He kicked off his Guccis and sprawled on the king bed thinking about his upcoming meeting with Phillip Connoff.

He'd done some checking around with friends in the industry, asking discreetly about Connoff, his reputation, background, how much business he did, what kinds of ventures he'd raised capital for.

The reports were mostly positive. The only negative: The guy will really grind you on fees and commissions. He likes to live the high life—wears expensive clothes and eats out at the most expensive restaurants. Drives a vintage, right-hand drive Bentley.

Oh, yes, Conoff is also a Mormon.

The day warmed up quickly and by late afternoon the snow was mostly gone, running in chuckling little rivers in the city's unique square gutters. Phillip Connoff was due to pick Jerry up for their dinner meeting at 5 p.m. Jerry tried to take a nap but couldn't sleep. Too many things rolling around in his brain. He finally gave up, fixed himself another Bloody Mary from the mini bar, and got out a yellow legal pad.

He played with names for his new corporation. Darren would need that to form the new Nevada company. Darren could work out number of shares, par value, all that stuff. Didn't matter anyway, Jerry would be the majority shareholder. His own boss this time.

He wrote down several company names. None sounded right to him. Had to have the right cachet to attract investors' attention, give them confidence. Needed to sound solid, old money, very financial.

Jerry put that aside and flipped through his Black Book. He found the number for Ricky Bob Peabody, dialed it, waited. He got a recorded message. He left a short message, saying he had been referred by a mutual friend, Darren Magelby. And, asked Mr. Peabody to please call him. "Thank you. Here's where you can reach me." He left his number on the recording and hung up the phone.

The next matter was, what to wear? It was just past four o'clock. Phil had suggested a favorite place of his up some canyon that Jerry couldn't remember. But it sounded rustic. A suit and tie were out of the question. He didn't have many clothes with him, so he went with what he had: Ralph Lauren wool slacks in a muted taupe plaid, a button-down pink shirt, topped with a dark green vee-neck sweater. And the Guccis, of course.

He considered another drink from the mini bar, but decided against it. Mormons don't drink. Jerry could have a nightcap by himself later. Then it hit him.

The name of his company should be discussed with Phillip Connoff since the idea was for them to become partners. Of course, Phil should be involved in naming the new company.

"Mr. Jordan? Your ride is waiting for you downstairs," the young woman from the front desk announced on his house phone.

Phillip Connoff was behind the wheel of his silver and blue Bentley waiting in the port-cochere for Jerry. He stepped out of the majestic car as Jerry came through the front door. Phillip was dressed in a dark blue, pinstriped double-breasted business suit, crisp white shirt with French cuffs, and an expensive tie from Burberry's, London. And, against the cold, a Vicuna top coat and gray kid gloves.

He removed a glove and offered his hand to Jerry. "Hi. Phillip Connoff. So pleased to meet you," he softly said. They shook.

Phillip was somewhat short and stocky, had thinning dark hair and black, very bushy, expressive eyebrows that seemed to waggle up and down as he spoke. And he spoke animatedly.

"Please. Hop in. Hope you're hungry. We're going to one of my favorite places. It's out of the way, kind of secluded. I chose it precisely for the reason that we have some serious stuff to discuss, and I don't want us to be interrupted."

They pulled into traffic, and Phillip continued, "I find I'm quite well known in this city and, when I'm out dining, people come up to me all the time wanting to visit."

Jerry nodded. He wished he'd put on his suit and tie.

It was a beautiful drive up a nearby canyon. The roads had been mostly cleared. Fresh puffs of powdery snow clung like cotton bolls to the branches of spruce and fir trees. They followed a winding, two-lane, paved road. Close by ran a clear stream lined with aspens, birch, red-twig dogwood. Ancient cottonwood trees were just budding out in spring colors. A lime-green glow hovered over the canyon. It contrasted perfectly with the darker spruce green that crept up the mountain peaks. Then the conifers gave out and the snow caps took over, touched with the glow of the setting sun.

As they drove, Phillip opened up, telling Jerry about himself and his past. He said he'd been born poor, in the poorest part of Boston. Growing up, he'd never had anything resembling a normal life. His father was a day laborer who gambled and drank most of his earnings. There was no financial security, no stability. They were constantly being evicted from rented digs. Never enough to eat. Always wearing hand-me-downs, ashamed to show up at school in old, worn-out clothes. He never had a decent warm coat for the harsh winters.

All his life, Phillip had been a fighter. He'd found his salvation in boxing. He'd been taken in by a crusty old trainer at the Boys' Club gym who taught him how to box. Phil had gotten beat up a lot but kept at it, entering matches that paid $10 to the winner, $5 to the loser.

He'd started winning and was soon stepping into better-paid rings, bigger purses. Before long, Phillip had become the provider for the family. He'd been paying the rent and putting food on the table. Life had settled down enough that Phillip could finish high school.

Phillip had barely managed to scrape by with his grades to graduate high school. He'd quickly joined the Navy and found success in their competitive boxing program. Most of his meager seaman's pay had been sent home to his mother.

Jerry was intrigued. No wonder he flaunts his success the way he does, Jerry thought.

Phillip tapped the brakes and slowed the car almost to a stop, as he continued with his story.

"There was this guy—my bunkmate, actually, who was a Mormon kid from Star Valley, Wyoming. He would kneel down—actually kneel down in our barracks—*every* night and say his prayers before crawling in his bunk.

Phillip had been intrigued. He'd been sort of raised in a Jewish family. Sort of. They'd never gone to synagogue. Never observed any of the traditional Jewish holidays. He'd never had his own Bar Mitzvah. The closest he had to any religious training was from the many folk sayings of his angel mother. She'd seemed to have a wise saying for just about any situation, good or bad.

Apparently a few had stuck, had a positive effect, for Phillip ultimately gained some self-esteem, began seeing himself as a fairly good human being with some value. He'd been sending money home each month to his family. Didn't that prove he was good for something?

He'd asked his bunkmate what motivated him to pray every night? Why didn't he smoke or drink? Or gamble? Or use foul language?

His reply had simply been: "Ever hear of the Mormons?" That question had changed Phillip's life.

Phillip pulled the vintage car into a parking lot of a roadside inn that bore the signage: Silver Fork Lodge. "Well, this is it," he said cheerfully. They entered the rustic lodge. The crisp mountain air was rich with wood-smoke fragrance.

The lodge was constructed of large logs and had mullioned windows of leaded glass in a single front door. They stepped inside onto a well-worn wooden plank floor. The main dining room was host to pine tables and rattan-backed chairs. They all looked to be handcrafted, old. A friendly, pine-wood fire popped and roared in the stone fireplace that was tall enough for a man to walk into and that radiated heat throughout the dining room.

Most of the diners were dressed in outdoor wear straight out of Eddie Bauer, Cabela's, and Orvis catalogs: Woolrich jackets, khakis, Pendleton plaid shirts, leather-topped lace-up boots with gummy rubber treads. A few diners turned to look at this odd new pair.

Phillip definitely stood out with his dark suit and tie. He paid the gawkers no attention as he swaggered with his boxer's rolling gait to an open table in the center of the room. It was far enough away from the huge blaze to be comfortable, yet still warm. Phillip was greeted with the familiarity reserved for regulars and he returned the greetings.

They were seated, offered menus. "I highly recommend their burger," Phillip said. "Best in town. But if you don't prefer that, their meatloaf is their specialty dish. Or if you want something lighter, warm spinach salad or the smoked trout salad are great, too."

"You sound like our server," Jerry said.

Phillip laughed. "Actually, I waited tables here many years ago when I first arrived in town. I was dead broke and it was a paying job. Better than boxing for my dinner," he shrugged.

They were offered a wine menu but only mini-bottles or "splits" were available. "Welcome to Utah," Phillip said. Jerry ordered a white wine to start with and Phillip ordered Perrier with a slice of fresh lime. The men scanned their menus, placed their orders, helped themselves to fresh sourdough rolls and butter. Then they got down to the serious business of their meeting.

By the time Jerry got back to his room at the Marriott, it was nearly midnight. Jerry and Phillip had virtually shut the Silver Fork Lodge down for the night. They had hit it off immediately. Jerry really liked this guy, his easy going, positive manner. He also appreciated Phillip's practical approach to doing business. Everything was on the table for discussion. There were no games, no hidden agendas.

Jerry undressed to his boxer shorts, put on a plush bathrobe courtesy of the Marriotts, then fixed himself a brandy and soda from the mini bar. The evening had gone well.

Jerry would be the head guy, putting together the paperwork for their new limited partnership, handling the banking, client relations, administrative duties. He would also help out with the marketing, turning over his precious Black Book of previous clients.

Phillip would be in charge of marketing, almost exclusively, for that seemed to be his strong suit, his first love. Oh, he was a schmoozer all right! He monopolized the evening with war stories of the many conquests he'd made selling various investments over the years. In every story he was the Lone Ranger, riding in at the last minute to save the beleaguered settlers. And, of course, he had made tons of money in the process.

Jerry dialed Phillip's number. He hoped his new partner would still be awake. "Phillip? I think we should call our company Old Bay Financial Group."

TWENTY

Denver

The blizzard quickly melted away. Denver was visited by warm Chinook winds. Dill would have loved to do some fly-fishing. The latest reports indicated the rivers were quickly rising, turned muddy from the storm. Very soon the real runoff would hit the streams.

His thoughts turned to phoning some of the extended-stay places off Interstate-70, close to the hospital. But his heart wasn't into looking for a suite just yet. He'd been virtually living in Jo's room, sleeping on a courtesy roll-out bed and only using his cheap motel room to shower and change clothes.

The boys were now out of school, and he ought to have a place for them when they came to visit. They needed stability amid all the uncertainty.

Dill could feel a cold or flu coming on. This was a real worry because he would have to stay away from his wife for a while. The doctors had warned that she could easily catch a bug.

The bone marrow transplant had apparently been successful. The doctors wouldn't be sure for a few days. In the meantime, they had started the next phase of her treatments: chemotherapy. First, they filled you full of rat poison, took you to the brink of death. Then, if you survived, they did it all over again. That was the cure, however medieval it seemed.

Life at Larimer Square Bank was starting to settle down into a somewhat normal routine. Most of the desks in the bullpen were now filled by young, eager interns and trainees. They came from Larimer Square's growing cadre of upstream correspondent banks. Dill had no real responsibility over these young people, but they naturally looked up to him as a calm, steadying influence. He was becoming a mentor who could help answer their questions. And, every day, every hour, they came to him with questions:

"What's a carried interest?"

"What's a working interest?"

"What's a division order?"

"What's an overriding royalty?"

"Okay, what's a UCC-1? And, why does it have to be recorded?"

"What does recorded mean?"

"Where do I record a UCC-1?"

"Why do you have to file a lien on title?"

"What's a lien, anyway?"

"What's a drill log?" "… a reservoir analysis?" "… a decline curve?"

"This customer wants his proceeds checks, yes, checks, made out to a third-party corporation. Is it okay to do that?

"Mr. Buckley wants me to renew this loan and it's already delinquent and past due and no interest payments have even been made. I'm not sure my bank can agree to that. What should I do?"

From a young woman: "What's fracking? That sounds sort of yucky!"

"What's drill mud?"

"Why would someone buy mud? Why not just mix up dirt and water?"

"What's a kick? That sounds like Brazilian boxing."

"What's a tight formation? Is it something to do with football?"

Dill decided that since he had to stay away from Jo for a few days he'd fill the lonely nights by holding a seminar for these young folks. Attendance advisable, but not compulsory.

He ordered a whiteboard be brought in and plenty of Magic Markers in various colors. He filled the board for three nightly sessions with charts, definitions, graphs, and hypothetical cases for them to discuss and solve.

He prepared some basic handouts covering terminology, proper procedures for documenting loans, steps in filing liens. Most critical, what red flags to watch for.

The communication between them was not just one way. Dill asked a lot of strategic questions and kept mostly silent and let these kids do the talking. By being low key, he was able to gather a lot of information about the way Buckley worked. Or putting it another way, just exactly how Buckley managed to book so many loans in such a short time.

At first only a few brave souls showed up. But word soon spread and, by the third night, all but one of the interns were there eagerly taking notes. The feedback he got was mostly positive from his appreciative audience.

He considered suggesting in the next senior executive management meeting that the bank seriously consider hiring an assistant operations person to be assigned specifically to creating an operations manual and training all employees from the top down to the lowliest door-keeper. He was surprised nobody had thought of that yet.

Los Angeles, California

Jerry got back home to L.A. Before he called his girlfriend, he listened to the many messages on his answering machine. There were two calls from Ricky Bob Peabody. Jerry dialed the number, waited.

"Mr. Peabody? Jerry Jordan here. Darren Magelby suggested we talk. I'm in the business of raising limited partnership drilling funds. I understand you have a pretty good track record drilling wells. Think you could drive up to Darren's place in Skiatook? Meet with me and my partner? Good. When would be a convenient time for you? Suits me fine. See you at ten o'clock next Thursday."

"Phillip? This is Jerry. What are you doing next Thursday? We have a meeting with Ricky Bob Peabody at Darren Magelby's office. It's in Skiatook. That's in Oklahoma. You'll need to fly into Tulsa. I can make the arrangements for you and meet you there. And I'd suggest casual attire. No suits needed. We may be stomping around some oil patch somewhere and it can be hard on your nice Guccis out there."

"Darren? Jerry here. Yeah, good to hear your voice, too. Yeah, I'm fine. Fine, fine. Listen, we need to get together next Thursday at your place. Ricky Bob Peabody is driving up from Okmulgee and Phillip Connoff, my new partner and I will be flying in for a meeting. It would also be a good time to wrap up the paperwork on our new drilling partnership. We want to call the company Old Bay Financial Group, Ltd. Yeah, that's the new Nevada corporation. And you can call the limited partnership Old Bay Drilling Fund. Thanks. See you then."

All set, Jerry thought. He quickly put work out of his mind and dialed the girl he knew was waiting.

Larimer Square Bank, Denver.

Larimer Square Bank lurched into the summer months. Instead of operations smoothing out things, they got more chaotic daily. Dill laid this on the bank's nominal CEO, Calvin Buckley.

Buck had already proven he was a real rogue. A gunslinger, with a shoot-from-the-hip style of management. If Buck had a friend who needed a loan, it was as good as done. And Buck had lots of friends. Where did he find these guys?

Except for the fact that JoEllen needed the medical care Denver could provide, and she needed him near her, Dill would have quit this bank and gone back to their quieter life in Craig.

Dill missed the wide-open spaces of his ranch, aptly named Robertson's West Slope Ranch. He ached for the peace he felt when driving his truck or when he was on a horse, slowly roaming along his fence lines.

He missed his time spent casting flies for beautiful cutthroat trout on Elkhead Creek that ran through much of his property. He missed the Green and Yampa Rivers and their many small tributary streams. He missed being in control of his life, like he was at his own little country bank.

Those times fly-fishing on the stream or grouse hunting in the mountains were his touchstones with life and with the world around him. It was his sanctuary. There, he could just lazily cast a fly. Or, sometimes, just sit, think, and figure things out. He usually came down from the mountain with his answers.

But this Denver banking thing was crazy. Things moved too fast at Larimer Square Bank. There were no controls. He was like a man who slipped into a stream at highest snow melt and was swept off his feet, swirling in fast water. He had to find bottom soon. He was losing sleep. His gut was in a constant knot. Management meetings—the few times they were held—were a joke. Loan committee meetings were even more deplorable, almost nonexistent.

He quickly concluded that he and the other executives and board members were window dressing. They were just there to provide a rubber stamp for Buckley and his cronies. And, more subtly, for Seth Summers and his most favored clients.

Seth appeared to not mind Buckley's way of doing business. Seth seemed to look upon Buckley as a son and he was the father figure. Summers looked the other way a lot.

Right now, Summers was absent from the bank a good deal. He spent large blocks of time across the Square at his swank investment banking office in a restored red brick building.

TWENTY-ONE

Stagecoach Energy, Dallas, Texas

In fact, at the moment, Seth was deeply involved in shepherding Stagecoach through its initial public offering of stock. On Wall Street, it's known as an IPO.

Long hours had to be spent with management, accountants and lawyers. Time spent poring over the fine print, the disclosures in a prospectus required by the Securities and Exchange Commission for a public stock registration and offering.

Then there were countless conference calls with other brokers who later would become part of the underwriting syndicate or "team."

Egos had to be massaged. Investment bankers fought viciously over silly little things. Like the order of firm name placement in the tombstone ads. On the prospectus cover. Even obscure little things in the underwriting documents!

Arrangements had to be made for the "dog and pony show." Stagecoach management would have to literally go on the road to pitch the draft prospectus to stock analysts, financial journalists, and stockbrokers for the first time. From that, they would make their own calculations of earnings ratios, earnings prospects, likelihood of success (or failure) of this upstart oil company. They had to know: How safe would the dollars be that their clients were asked to invest?

The other daily cat fights consisted of investment bankers wrangling over Stagecoach's valuation, or what the value, or opening price per share assigned to it, should be. The long knives were unsheathed.

As was typical of any IPO, the syndicate would hammer on the company—in this case, on Stagecoach—arguing that their per-share price was overstated. There would be tremendous pressure on them to drop the offering price per share.

Some of the arguments were based on the fundamentals of the company: how long they had been in business; management experience; earnings per share, if any; assets versus debt ratios; on and on.

And then there were other, more subtle arguments, more psychological in nature and more specific to Stagecoach. These centered on the vagaries of the market; the number of the many other oil and gas companies that were also going public at the same time; the price of crude per barrel and other market factors. There were so many unknowns about OPEC, about United States tax laws changing, about possible environmental regulations, and so on.

All designed to pound Stagecoach management into submission, forcing them to lower their offering price per share. A sane person would ask why? Doesn't it make more sense to get the highest price per share you can sell for? The object here is to get more money into the company, isn't it?

Yes, that's the sensible argument. But here's why: Because the real incentives for the underwriters were not the commissions that they could make on the initial round of stock sales on opening day. Oh, no. It had everything to do with options.

In addition to receiving a healthy sales commission and all legal, accounting, printing, and mailing expenses, plus a healthy chunk of cash for "due diligence" and "unaccountables," the underwriters' compensation package also granted options to buy future shares at a price below market.

This bonus package of options would be set aside for later issuance should the brokers exercise their options. And the issuing company would then get the privilege of registering the optioned shares with the Securities and Exchange Commission at its own expense for the benefit of the underwriters. Seems a bit one-sided, unfair? Maybe. But the underwriters' fallback was the Golden Rule: They had the gold, so they got to make the rules.

It may look like splitting hairs. Because, technically, the investment bankers really didn't invest their own money in these ventures. They were too smart for that sort of risk. Oh, no, they invested other people's money: Their clients took all the risk. Love that OPM!

The plus side for Stagecoach Energy? The world was suddenly crazy about crude oil. And the stock markets were hot for oil issues, especially new oil companies. Like Stagecoach Energy.

Especially hot were the penny stock markets. The markets off-Wall Street. Stocks not listed on the NYSE or the American Stock Exchange. That's where the smaller-priced, riskier stocks were listed on NASDAQ. If … if they were lucky, and could qualify under the easier rules for listing. That was the target market for listing Stagecoach's new shares.

But if a new company's shares were more risky still, small companies seeking smaller chunks of cash, maybe only a couple million dollars, then they went the over-the-counter route. Or the OTC, as it was called. Shares for these smaller offerings were quoted in a quotation service called the "Pink Sheets."

This was the fertile territory where Seth Summers had operated for years and made his storied fortune. Penny stocks. Seth knew this market very well.

Starting out in Salt Lake City in the 1950s, in the days of the uranium mining penny stocks, a much-younger Seth and a couple of carefully selected lawyers and accountants had a virtual mill, churning out as many as three offerings a week at $50,000 a clip.

Most of these little companies spent a few bucks on trying to drill test grids on so-called uranium claims, only to find nothing and quickly go out of business. But not before the company officers and directors (and always Seth as guest) had spent the rest of the money on weekend trips to Las Vegas or Lake Tahoe, living it up at stockholder expense.

And the stockholders? The ones who invested in these yellow dog companies? Well, for a few days they were happy. The smart ones knew when to cash in, sell their shares and get out. You bought one of Seth's deals on Monday at one-cent a share. By Monday afternoon, the price had risen to two cents a share (thanks to strategically placed rumors and press releases put out by Seth and his cronies). Tuesday morning the shares would open at four cents. Hot diggity dog! Tuesday afternoon and two more rumors later, five cents.

Wednesday morning began to see a sell-off of shares at five cents. The smart guys were bailing. After all, why be greedy? If you invested $1,000 on Monday and could reap a windfall of $4,000 a couple days later, take it and run. That's enough of a profit for this week. Good ole Seth will have another offering or two out next week and you can do a repeat.

And, of course, Seth's rumor mill would go to work to assure the scaredy cats to stay the course. All will be well. This is only a slight correction. The price will come back up in a couple days. Hang on. But the price never did come back. The losers had some lovely colorful stock certificates to use as wall decorations.

The Utah state securities people investigated numerous complaints against Seth's brokerage firm. But they never could find enough evidence or witnesses to make anything stick to him. Conveniently, the guys who had started the rumors that drove the stock price were lying low until the storm blew over. Or they simply did a runner and skipped town.

There's an infallible economic dictum at work in the market: After every boom, there's a bust. Uranium ran its course and fizzled by the end of the decade. Seth turned his attention to condos and time shares in Park City, Utah, the next new investment craze. That lasted a few years, followed by conglomerate mergers into the early 1970s.

What next? Opportunity beckoned in the form of The Shell Game. In Denver.

Seth moved his operations to Denver where he sensed he deserved (needed?) a fresh new start, a new perspective. Meaning: He needed to get out from under the microscope of the Utah securities people. He also needed new investors and he found plenty in the former frontier mining and cattle town.

Denver was just starting to boom. It also boasted a major league football team: the Denver Broncos! And an NBA team, the Nuggets. Soon there would be the Rockies. Denver was an excellent place to entertain clients. Salt Lake was well known for its antiquated liquor laws. Denver was just the place for Seth.

Reverse mergers, or The Shell Game. It was a virtually non-regulated mechanism for a small company to become publicly traded without the expense or hassle of a registration with the U.S. Securities and Exchange Commission (SEC). Here's how Seth Summers made it work. And how he manipulated the process to his advantage:

Seth had quietly gathered up the controlling shares of over 120 penny stock uranium companies gone bust back in Utah. The same companies he had helped launch with seed money from his gaggle of favored investors. The same investors who somehow knew just when to sell their shares and who got out before the market collapsed.

Seth had kept the shareholder lists and corporate records of all these defunct shells. The former officers and directors were long gone. Using new nominee officers and directors, usually the same two or three people, Seth paid the fees to reinstate these formerly moribund companies and brought them back to life.

The shares were technically still considered to be "publicly traded," since there were no securities laws or rules on the books prohibiting the shares from trading again. Providing …

Providing you could have a real business purpose in the corporation plus financial statements that could be published in news reports.

Providing you had a broker who would once again "make market," i.e., quote your company's shares on the Pink Sheets. This quaint moniker came from England in World War II, when paper was in short supply and financial reports were published on newsprint that hadn't been bleached white. They were truly pink-colored sheets. The Financial Times continued to publish on pink newsprint for decades after.

The Pink Sheets was essentially a quotation service that listed stocks on a weekly—not daily, hourly or certainly not real-time—basis. This was the OTC market. Definitely not your NYSE-quality companies. But, at least the broker could assure a potential customer that the stock was, in fact, being quoted. "Go look it up," the broker would say with a straight face. "It's in the Pink Sheets."

The hardest part to doing a reverse merger into one of old, revived shell companies of Seth's was finding a candidate company that had an actual ongoing business: a business plan, a track record, officers, directors, assets. And financials, a real balance sheet to attach to the thing. Something an investor or his broker could hopefully analyze, touch and feel.

Seth set up a network of bird dogs, retainers who would comb the countryside looking for hot little companies that wanted to raise money by going public the easy way, i.e., through the process of a reverse merger. The favored ones were in the fast-growing new computer industry or medical services companies.

Company A, a former burnt-out uranium mining shell from Utah, resurrected by Seth, was available to make an "acquisition" of 100 percent of Company B—the hot little startup that was looking to go public.

Seth would engineer the merger, hold a shareholder "meeting" of all the shares he had in his desk drawer of Company A, which would approve the acquisition of all of Company B's shares. The shareholder meeting minutes would reflect a name change for the shell, which was the survivor of this engineered "merger." The new company name would be that of the hot new deal. The owners of Company B would be elected as the new management.

Seth's nominees would resign, and the new guys would sign a deal, whereby Seth's investment banking company would be paid a nice fee to arrange to float a "new" issue of shares to raise capital for the new venture. With much press coverage and hype, of course.

The campaign revved into high gear. The sponsoring broker-dealer carefully chosen by Seth Summers would start quoting the shares on the Pink Sheets, with all sales personnel excited to have a new stock to flog to their unsuspecting clients.

And Seth's firm would collect a consulting fee of at least $50,000 for each shell he sold. Sometimes more. Whatever the market could bear. Plus, he had a pile of the old, free-trading shares in the "new" company. All these shares were in nominee names offshore in Cayman Island, Antigua, Bahama, or Hong Kong brokerages and bank accounts, just waiting for the price to peak so Seth could begin selling nominee shares into the market.

Not just hundreds but usually a half million shares. With a current bid-ask of $2 to $3.50 a share. If all his shares could be sold at $2 a share over a reasonable period of time so as to not upset the market price, well that translated into a million dollars!

All tax-free because all those shares were sold *legally* by an offshore company or companies which owned the shares, not Seth personally. This clever arrangement of shells, cutout companies, nominees, numbered offshore accounts had been masterminded and set up by a very high-priced, exclusive London firm of solicitors with several offices in key cities around the world. Seth strategically kept this firm on retainer.

Meanwhile, the eager, young trusting entrepreneurs at XYZ Computers, newly merged into Company A, one of the old uranium mining shells Seth had provided them, had no clue where all that stock was coming from. It just seemed to magically materialize one day.

On its face, all appeared to be legitimate. The names on the stock certificates matched up neatly with the names on the shareholder list, all right. This illegal practice was called pump-and-dump. And Seth's nominee shares just kept being dumped into the market, coming at the new company's naive, unsuspecting management team like worms out of the woodwork.

All the while, Seth Summers just sat back and monitored the action while secretly depositing tons of cash into offshore bank accounts.

In nominee names, of course.

TWENTY-TWO

Modern drill rigs are outfitted with a lot of very expensive, very sensitive instruments to measure various phases of the drilling process. The rig's big diesel engine, for example, has its own set of instruments to measure its functions, fuel, down-hole temperatures, oil pressure, amps for the electrical circuitry, etc. But the actual drilling job is measured by other instruments, the most closely watched of which is the drill log. The drill log is closely related and similar in appearance to a seismograph. Special graph paper is stretched over a slowly rotating drum, and, over that is suspended a slender arm, which has a very fine tip or needle that acts like the nib of a fine pen. This tip is supplied with ink and scratches wiggly lines across the surface of the graph paper as drilling progresses.

As the drill bit chews through a rock formation, electric impulses or signals are sent through a wire, up the hole, and back to the drill log. The log is designed to record the presence of any hydrocarbons—crude oil, natural gas, or other valuable "condensates." These would appear on the graph paper as heavier lines or sometimes even dense blobs of ink. These are called the kicks. The driller watches the log almost constantly for any of these kicks. An experienced driller will know how to interpret these kicks and compare them to logs of other wells that may have been drilled nearby, if any. In Texas, for example, copies of logs are required to be filed with the Texas Railroad Commission.

In the case of a wildcatter, finding oil, even with the aid of drill logs is mostly educated guesswork. With a lot of voodoo, prayers, and luck thrown in. Frankly? Your chances are far better in Las Vegas. Ricky Bob Peabody shied safely far away from wildcatting. Far away.

Weatherford, Texas

Ricky Bob had driven all night from his home in Okmulgee to the drill site near Lake Breckenridge a few miles north of Weatherford, Texas. He had to be there early Monday morning when they would spud in the first well his company had contracted to drill for Stagecoach. He had gone to church with his wife and kids on Sunday, enjoyed a lazy unhurried dinner of fried chicken, potato salad, beer, and key lime pie, followed by a long nap to prepare his tired body for the all-night dash to Weatherford.

Ginger Foss gathered Ricky's crew around the tail end of the drill rig for the ceremony. Circulation pits had been dozed. Temporary electricity lines had been wired into the site. Auxiliary tanks for diesel fuel to drive the big drilling rig were in place. Permits were in hand. All was ready to start the drilling or what they referred to as ready to "spud in." But first, the ceremony.

"Boys," said Ginger gravely, "I welcome you all here for this occasion. Let's pray the Good Lord blesses us with success and we find oil. And may he keep us all from harm and warn us of danger as we all look out for the safety of one another."

Amens all around. The men put their hard hats back in place, pulled heavy worn leather gloves on, and waited for the official word to begin work. This was a happy crew. These boys appreciated how blessed they were to have this good, honest, back-breaking work. They all had a good feeling about this well. In a burst of good ole Texas fun, they had named the new well after a famous female country singer, the lady with a substantial anatomical endowment. It was to be emblematic of their hopes for substantial crude oil endowment, too.

"So, let the work on the Dolly P-Number 1A begin." Yeah!

The engine on the big drill rig roared into life, belching a cloud of diesel smoke that was quickly carried away by the constant West Texas wind. The men knew their jobs and scrambled up the steel ladder into their positions on the platform. The Dolly P was now a reality, as the drill bit was lowered and began spinning, chewing rapidly through cactus and bluebonnets and dirt on its way downward into hard rock formations. That's where the crude oil was trapped—hopefully. Those oil-bearing formations lying many hundreds of feet under this slice of virgin Texas soil. Waiting to be tapped.

When Ginger Foss had named the well for his favorite female country singer, the Texas Railroad Commission, which was the state agency authorized to issue drilling permits, hadn't even lifted an eyebrow. They'd seen hundreds of bizarre names for wells. Some for old lost loves. Some for wives, daughters, girlfriends. Favorite hunting dogs. Horses long dead. Some for spouses (or mistresses) of fat cat investors. Some for the owner of the lease because of a clause in the fine print. Some for politicians, both living and dead. The Commission didn't have to ask Ginger what Dolly P stood for.

Drilling progressed at the satisfying rate of a couple hundred feet a day. Ricky Bob was happy with just how smoothly things were going. After two days they hadn't lost any equipment, or fingers, or time due to machinery breakdowns. But, in the back of his mind, he kept thinking about the Thursday meeting up in Skiatook with Darren, Jerry, and Phillip-something, Jerry Jordan's new partner from Salt Lake City.

Ricky wondered if the new guy was a Mormon. He'd been warned often enough by the pastor of his Baptist church in Okmulgee to stay away from the Mormons and their false "gold bible." The pastor had warned, "Don't read their book, because that's how they lure you into their church."

Based on his experience in college, though, all the Mormons he knew were pretty good old boys. A little straight. Wouldn't drink coffee or liquor with the rest of their school chums or frat brothers. But, overall, pretty decent, clean-cut guys. He'd just have to meet this new guy, Phillip, and see for himself if he was a Mormon or not. And just what kind of guy he was. As a businessman, that is.

Ricky was more interested in his prospects of getting in on a piece of that deep Anadarko gas well Darren promised him as part of the deal with these guys. Man, would he love to be in charge of the actual drilling and not just a second on that rig! In his mind's eye he could see the massive machine, the miles of pipe being stockpiled. He could feel the excitement tickle his senses.

But Ricky's problem was that he didn't own or even have a leased drill rig that was capable of exploring to that depth. Still, his mouth watered at the prospect of getting his hands on such a big rig. A rig, that to oilmen, dreams are made of.

Maybe those new bankers in Denver, the ones that claimed they now owned his loans, his new credit line, could set him up with the big rig. That is, if he was lucky enough to persuade the decision-makers that he should be the driller. Chances were pretty good they had their own driller who probably had his own jumbo rig.

But then again … You never know. Luck plays a funny part in the life of an oil man. Lady Luck. She could either love you or hate you. You could never be sure what she was thinking. If he owned the jumbo rig, he'd be in a position to call the shots …

His reverie was shattered when one of the roustabouts yelled at him. "Ricky, you better come take a gander at these rocks we just cut through."

"How deep are we?"

"Nineteen two-fifty."

"What're you seein', Todd?"

"More like what we're smellin', Ricky."

"Crude?"

"Yep."

"I'm comin'."

The kick on the log and the rock cuttings he examined were comparable to the several logs from nearby so-called "dry holes" he had pored over weeks ago. Those logs had clearly revealed to Ricky that somebody had been playing dirty games.

He had found this same formation and its telltale kick on the log at almost the same depth as the other logs had uniformly indicated. It was a crude-rich strata, one that any savvy oil man would have completed and been happy to make a producing well at such a shallow depth before he kept on drilling down deeper.

Ricky went into the shack to check the gauges. He wanted to smell (and taste) the cuttings for himself. He sniffed and tasted. Crude, all right. Todd waited.

"What do you want us to do, Ricky?"

Ricky looked off in the distance, north and eastward toward the lure of the Anadarko. He could hear her talking to him, calling his name. "Keep drillin'. Too early to pull out and test."

"But Ricky, that's one heckuva kick. Never seen one that big. Must be 30 to 50 feet of saturated formation! And we only got 1,900 feet of pipe to pull …" Todd pleaded his case.

Ricky stood firm. "Keep drillin'."

Todd was genuinely puzzled. And confused. This wasn't like Ricky Bob. The Ricky Bob he knew and had worked with for many years through all kinds of weather and the ups and downs (mostly the downs). That Ricky Bob would test this formation before moving on. Todd stared at Ricky. He coldly stared back. Todd shrugged his bulky muscled shoulders, looked away and said, "Okay, Ricky. You're the boss. But if'n it was me …"

"Yeah, yeah, okay. But it ain't you whose butt will get canned if we're wrong so just keep on drillin'. Anyway, Ginger said this well was sold to the investors as a 5,000-footer."

Ricky scratched at his stubbled chin, thought a minute, then, "I'm gonna discuss it with him tonight. Meantime, keep on rotating that danged bit, okay?"

"Sure thing, Ricky."

When Todd cleared out, Ricky went to the tool shack to make a call. "Larimer Square Bank? This is Ricky Bob Peabody here. Y'all don't know me. Is there somebody there I could talk to? I was wondering if I could discuss a loan with you. A big loan. For a new drill rig. One with at least 20,000-foot capacity. Price tag? About $7 million. Yes ma'am, that's what I said. Seven million US dollars all in."

Oncology Ward, Denver Hospital

JoEllen walked with a cane carefully, slowly, down the darkened corridor. It was the first time she had left her own hospital room unassisted since she arrived many long weeks ago. The place was quiet except for muffled sounds from life-support machines coming from rooms of other patients. She stopped at a room just three doors down from hers. The door was partially open and a soft light seeped through the opening. She tapped softly and pushed the door fully open. A young girl sat upright in her bed clutching a big teddy bear.

"May I come in?" The girl nodded. All her hair was gone. Her eyebrows, now missing, made her dark eyes look very large and shadowed in the dim light. The clock on her wall showed nearly three o'clock in the early morning.

"Hi, my name is JoEllen. What's yours?"

"Corrie," came her soft answer.

"How old are you, Corrie?"

"Ten. Almost eleven."

"What are you in here for, Corrie?"

"I have ovarian cancer."

"Aren't you a little young for that? I thought only older women ever had to worry about that," JoEllen said, stepping close to Corrie's bed. "Mind if I sit with you?" She patted the edge of the bed. Corrie nodded.

"The doctors all say it's really rare for a girl my age to get it. But I did." JoEllen nodded.

"What do you have?" Corrie asked.

"A kind of cancer called leukemia. Have you heard about it?"

Corrie nodded.

"It gets into your bone marrow and upsets the body's ability to make red blood cells. It also upsets your white blood cells terribly, the ones that fight infections."

Corrie nodded again.

"But I think I'm going to beat it," JoEllen said bravely.

Corrie nodded.

"How are you holding up?" JoEllen asked, placing her hand softly on Corrie's arm.

"At first I was really scared I was going to die. But then after they operated and said they got it all and I started the chemo treatments, I didn't think much about dying any more after that. Were you scared you were going to die?"

JoEllen nodded. “At first? Yes. I was mostly sad about leaving my family behind, my husband, my four sons.” JoEllen sighed and looked away, fought tears. “My four big boys.” She laughed at the thought of how fast they’d grown up. Just yesterday they were Corrie’s age. “I was a little afraid that I’d miss out on ever living long enough to see my sons marry and have children. That I wouldn’t ever get to see my grandchildren. But I’m okay now.” JoEllen raised her chin.

“So, you don’t have any girls, no daughters?” JoEllen shook her head.

“I wasn’t lucky enough to ever have a girl. But I have four really great boys that I love a lot.” JoEllen lifted Corrie’s chin, looked into her large dark eyes. “I have an idea: maybe while we’re in here together, getting better, you can be my daughter. Could we do that? I’d love to do your hair… Oh, I’m sorry, I didn’t mean to say that!”

They laughed together at JoEllen’s awkward mistake. The first time for both of them in many long weeks.

TWENTY-THREE

Weatherford, Texas

Tuesday night at his motel room in Weatherford, Ricky got a phone call from Ginger Foss. He looked at his watch. It was almost midnight. "What's up?" he asked.

"The boys at Stagecoach want to have a dog and pony show tomorrow for a bunch of their investors, the limited partners. Plus, a couple of financial analyst types from New York. They're bussing a group of these guys into Dallas tonight."

"Tomorrow?" Ricky cursed softly to himself. Thanks for the short notice.

"They have a bus lined up to drive them out to the well site in the morning. You need to make sure the place is sort of spiffed up. No junk lyin' around. Need to show them a good time. Understand?"

"I've never done one of these, what'd you call it? Dog and pony shows …"

"Just be polite and try to answer their questions matter-of-factly. Don't need to go into any deep science about what you do. And by all means, keep your roughnecks as far away from them as possible. Don't want any of them screwin' things up!"

"Got it. Anything else I should know?"

"The tour of the drill site shouldn't last more than about an hour. That's if they get there by around ten or so. Then we have them scheduled to bus on over to have lunch at Oscar's BBQ smoker in Cisco. You're familiar with it?"

"Yeah, I been there plenty of times."

"Good. Sorry again about the short notice, but Ted sometimes flies by the seat of his pants."

Ricky rang off. He pulled his jeans back on, turned out the lights and drove back out to the well site to look things over for tomorrow.

At least it was tomorrow, Wednesday, and not Thursday. Thursday he had to high tail it up to Skiatook for the all-important meeting with Darren and the two guys who wanted to do a drilling program with him. The deep gas well in the Anadarko. Now that was important. This, this … dog and pony show. Just a major pain in the butt.

It would be a long night.

A Restaurant, Oklahoma City

Buck was having a very late dinner with one of his pushover clients, a wildcatter who called Stillwater, Oklahoma, home base. Buzz Bixby was around 50 years old, a former running back for Oklahoma State, but was now getting a little paunchy around the middle. Buzz had weather-beaten arms with ropy muscles from years of hard work. He could still be a threat to anyone who crossed him.

Buzz was what Buck called one of his debt junkies. Buzz loved to borrow. It was easier than hustling investors. Buzz got most of his money for drilling his risky wildcat prospects around Stillwater through Buck and the various banks he'd worked for. Sure, Buck was a little loose with the facts he presented to loan committees, leaving out the very important detail about wildcat drilling.

Banks just didn't lend for wildcat drilling. When Buckley was at TGB, he had not been above doctoring up the paperwork to make it look like the loan was for equipment. Or payroll. Or anything else he thought would pass muster with the loan committee. But, he never mentioned wildcatting.

Buzz had actually been lucky and hit a couple of really good producers in between the many near-misses and the salt water wells, what oilies call "shrimp farms." The production from these few good wells was just enough to service the loans and keep him barely in the good graces of the bankers. Barely …

Buckley had called Buzz yesterday and indicated he'd like to meet him at his favorite restaurant in Oklahoma City to discuss a sweet business deal that he was sure Buzz was going to like. The wildcatter said he'd check his calendar and get back to Buck. Buzz let several minutes pass before he picked up the phone, called back and agreed to meet. He lied and said he'd canceled another engagement just for Mr. Buckley.

Because of the late hour, they were just about the only diners left in the place. Their waiter poured their water and handed each a wine list that they carefully studied even though neither one had the first clue about wine. Other than it was a drink that tasted like grape soda pop. With an alcohol kick.

The waiter returned after a respectable interlude, discreetly coughed and asked what they had decided. "What would be your recommendation?" Buck asked.

"Well gentlemen, it depends largely on what you intend to order, then we can provide just the right vintage to complement your choice." He waited.

"I don't know about you, but I'm having a filet medium rare," Buck said.

"Same for me," Buzz admitted. The waiter nodded and silently returned a few minutes later with a bottle of rare vintage Napa sauvignon cabernet. He poured a small amount into a wine glass and handed it to Buck. He gulped it down with one swallow. He didn't swirl, swish or sniff, the hallmarks of a true oenophile. Buck handed the glass back to the bemused waiter. He'd seen this hick routine many times before, so he nodded and filled both their glasses and left. The $150 bottle would be marked up to $350 and added to the bill.

Buck held up his wine glass and, through the light, the expensive liquid was the color of blood.

Buzz couldn't wait until they had finished their meal, so he leaned forward and brushed his plate and silver aside with a loud clatter. "So, tell me what's so hush-hush that we had to meet here in Oke City in the dark of night?" His eyes were bright with excitement, his face florid from the wine warming his blood.

"I've got a deal for you like none other you've ever seen, Buzz, my boy. I guaran-darn-tee you're gonna love it. Now listen carefully …"

Buzz nodded. "Yeah, yeah, go on!" Buzz hadn't touched his steak; it was growing a slick of grease on the surface.

Their waiter arrived and asked if they wanted dessert, coffee? Buck ordered two espressos. The waiter shimmered away.

Buck borrowed a crisp linen napkin from a nearby table, took out a Sharpie from his shirt pocket and began writing on the linen. He outlined the deal for Buzz who had rediscovered his filet and was now steadily stuffing his face with cold steak and baked potato. Buck scribbled and slurped his own espresso. When it was gone, he started in on Buzz's.

Buck jotted figures on the borrowed linen. The last was a string of numbers Buzz understood to be a numbered account offshore somewhere. At some time in the future Buzz would be expected to wire a large sum of money to this account. Sounded like a million. Or was it two? He didn't bother to ask any questions.

The deal Buckley presented was this: A new bank up in Denver called Lariat or something would set up a line of credit for Buzz's new, yet-to-be-formed drilling company, in the amount of $10 million.

Buzz nearly choked on the big chunk of steak he was chewing. Never had he been remotely close to that kind of money. The biggest loan he had ever had outstanding was just south of $2 million.

"How many wells you think you could drill for that kind of war chest?" Buckley asked.

Buzz swallowed his meat. "What depth?"

"Five thousand. Feet."

Buzz thought for a minute and said, eight, maybe no more than ten. "Yeah, I guess it could be ten."

"But I ain't talkin' about your crappy Lincoln County wildcat wells. Nope. I'm going to set you up with a real good lease hound. He don't work for me. He don't work for the bank. He's independent. We … he's got some really nice prospects that I know you're gonna like. And they ain't no wildcat hokum! Those days for you are over. From now on it's gonna be like shootin' fish in a barrel for Buzz Bixby."

Buzz started to ask where this hot lease was but thought better of it. Shoot, if they were willing to put up 10-mil, they can call the shots.

He'd even go to Alaska if that's what they wanted. At least he thought he'd heard somebody say once there was oil in Alaska.

Buzz sat back, set down his napkin and picked at a piece of filet caught in his dental work. He asked, "Okay, what's the catch? There's always a catch. This deal is just too sweet to not have some hidden loophole."

"Well, now that you ask … there are a few conditions. Off the record of course." Buzz nodded, waited. With Buck there were always conditions. Always.

"First …"

For the next five minutes Calvin Buckley, banker, outlined in very broad terms what Buzz Bixby, wildcatter, would have to do for Buckley and friends to get his hands on that honeypot full of cash.

Buzz would contract with a few companies he'd never heard of or done business with to provide certain services typical to oilfield operations: pipe and chemical suppliers, trucking companies, water carriers, petroleum engineers. The list went on. Buzz nodded his approval, details to be worked out later.

"So, what's your cut, Buck?"

Buck looked around. "Keep your voice down." Buck fumbled in his pocket and found a scrap of paper. He wrote a figure with his Sharpie and pushed the paper toward Buzz, who gasped and shook his head.

"I dunno, Buck, that's a pretty steep cut. Two million? Looks like about 20 percent to me. Plus, your buddies providing services will get their payoffs."

"Shh. Keep yer voice down and don't ever say that word again! And there's a problem with what I'm proposing? Why? Listen, I'm setting you up for the rest of your life. You don't even have to show up for a loan closing. No credit checks. No audited financials—which your crummy little company probably doesn't even have. Am I right?"

Buzz nodded weakly, defeated.

"And it's all handled through me and FedEx. Don't blow this, Buzz," Buck warned ominously.

He got up as Buzz said, “With that kind of a haircut, let’s revise that figure. I can’t drill no 10 wells with that skinny a budget. Better make it seven wells.”

Buck didn’t reply but motioned to the waiter to bring the bill, leaving Buzz still sitting with his big fat stupid mouth making like a beached catfish. Buckley headed for the register to pay. With cash.

“Wait,” Buzz said. Buck grinned to himself. Gotcha! He owned Buzz Bixby.

TWENTY-FOUR

FDIC Regional Office, Kansas City

The Federal Deposit Insurance Corporation was the government agency tasked with providing insurance on deposits for banks not otherwise insured by other agencies, such as the Comptroller of the Currency. The FDIC regional office—which included Colorado, New Mexico, Texas and Oklahoma—was located in Kansas City.

It had been about six months since Larimer Square Bank had officially opened for business. The new bank was now due for their first visit from the regulators. This was not to be a full-blown audit. Just a friendly visit so the regulators could get a feel for how things were working out. Sort of a spot check on any problems that needed fixing. Give them a pat on the back. Do a general scoping out of the bank.

It was also a chance to sniff out any practices that were suspect or shoddy. Head any such practices off at the pass.

Gary Swope, in his late 20s, with a degree in accounting from Kansas State, was eager to prove to his bosses that he was up to the task—his first solo bank audit. Swope knew it wasn't a real audit, just a routine spot check onsite.

For the last year, Swope had worked under the mentorship of a senior auditor, a sleepy career government employee named Max Puckett. Max had long since lost interest in his work and was literally counting the days until he could start drawing his retirement checks.

Gary was excited as he packed his bags and kissed his wife goodbye. Due to austerity moves in Washington, Gary drove his own car to Denver. He would have enjoyed the luxury of a government-paid plane trip. He kept detailed track of his expenses, for reimbursement later.

The weather was unusually warm for late fall as Gary drove west on Interstate 70. Captain & Tennille were singing on his tinny car radio "Do That to Me One More Time," just as Gary was merging onto Interstate 70, headed west.

He had intended to get his car's air conditioning serviced before he left Kansas City but didn't think he'd need it. Now, his mind wandered and he fought drowsiness brought on by the warm, humid air blowing in his open window.

Gary went over the audit checklist in his head for the 10th time. A big 18-wheeler overtook him blowing diesel fumes into his window and creating an uneven turbulence. Gary slowed down.

A week prior to the on-site visit, Gary Swope had sent the usual letter to the bank informing them of his visit, together with a list of audit items that he would need to review with management. Nobody from the bank had responded.

Larimer Square Bank, Denver

Inside the bank, the task of dealing with Mr. Swope was passed from hand to hand until it landed on Dill Robertson's desk. He was puzzled why he should be the one. He was told it was because he had so much prior experience dealing with regulators as head of his own bank.

Dill read Swope's letter carefully and considered the many items in the checklist. Near the top of the list would be a review of loan files. Based on Dill's experience, the loan files would be selected at random. The examiners would want to see backup documentation in each file: loan application completely filled out and all the boxes checked off, applicant's financial statement, collateral, loan committee or lending officer's notes with reasons supporting the decision to approve or deny, sign-off initials from senior lending officer, loan agreement, promissory note, lien documents if collateral was involved, copy of check disbursement or debit memo to customer's account. Dill was familiar with the drill.

Out of curiosity, Dill asked his assistant, Marty, to pull a half dozen random loan files from a list he handed her so he could see for himself what was inside. After several hours of not hearing back from her, Dill buzzed her phone extension.

"Any luck finding those files I asked for?" There was an awkward silence. "Marty …?"

"A strange thing, Mr. Robinson …"

Dill didn't correct her mispronouncing his name; everyone was still fairly new around here.

"Mr. Buckley's secretary said all the bank's loan files were off-premises, moved to a storage facility."

Dill's head lifted in amazement. News to him. When were they moved? Over the weekend? "Did she say why?"

"I didn't ask. I assumed it was because we have no storage room here. As everybody knows … Should I ask her where they are and maybe I can help you retrieve them?"

Dill pondered for a minute. "No. Thanks, Marty, but I can follow up myself. You've got enough to do as it is. I'll find someone to track them down. Thanks for your help."

"Yes sir." She rang off.

Dill walked to the window and looked across the city skyline, thinking.

I-70, Somewhere in Western Kansas

Gary drove for nearly eight hours through a sleep-inducing autumn heat wave. Passing a dormant soybean field, he noticed dozens of big pump jacks stretching to the northern horizon, laid out in a line like soldiers, rhythmically working up and down, up and down.

It dawned on him that while he was working for the government at a salary that barely covered his growing family's living expenses, there was a lucky farmer somewhere who had leased this soybean patch to an oil operator who had found black gold several thousand feet down in the earth.

And while he, Gary Swope, was slaving for the government in a virtual dead-end job, that farmer was off pheasant hunting. Or sipping ice tea on the veranda of his rented cabana in Panama City, Florida.

Clipping coupons. Banking his monthly royalty checks from that oil under the ground that nature had deposited there millions of years ago. Just sheer dumb luck!

Gary shook his head sadly, took a sip of his watery Coke, wiped a trickle of sweat off his forehead and grimly continued his drive west.

Larimer Square Bank, Denver

Gary Swope reached the outskirts of Denver at approximately 4:30 p.m., Mountain Time. He made a mental note to change the time on his cheap Timex watch. Gary had never been this far west. He thrilled at his first view of the Rockies rising majestically out of the plains west of Denver. They appeared as a rugged hazy blue barrier reaching high into the sky. Masses of threatening storm clouds boiled thousands of feet above the distant peaks.

Gary pulled into the first truck stop he came to on the edge of Denver to stretch his legs, take a bathroom break and refill his soft drink container. Somewhat refreshed, he checked the Denver city map to orient himself for the fourth or fifth time for the bank's location.

He negotiated through the city streets choked with commuters heading home and at last found himself in the vicinity of Larimer Square Bank.

Swope's first pass by the bank was hampered by the street being blocked off by several trucks and large mobile homes lined up in front of the bank. It appeared to be a television show or movie in the process of being filmed. He made a right turn at the corner stoplight and, three blocks away, finally found a parking spot. He stuffed a few coins into the meter and began walking back to the bank.

Larimer Square Bank still displayed the front-window banner declaring its temporary location status. It was sandwiched between a Woolworth's on one side and a ladies' lingerie boutique on the other. It occupied approximately 5,000 square feet of space on each of two levels.

The ground floor was devoted to a cramped reception lobby, five or six teller cages, and, behind those, a gated vault and safe deposit boxes screened off by a barrier of floor-to-ceiling heavy metal bars. On the sidewalk in front of the plate glass windows were two long rectangular boxes of dying geraniums. They needed watering.

It was now after 5:30—nearly 6:00—and the bank was getting ready to close its doors for the day. A uniformed doorman, a small, soft-spoken man who looked to be of Asian descent, politely asked Swope if he could please complete his transaction quickly as the bank would be closing in five minutes.

Gary shook his head and said he was just looking, thanks, picked up a couple of brochures from a display rack and stepped back out into the late afternoon heat. His eyes had taken in what he needed to see for the moment, and he didn't want to announce his official visit. Not just yet.

As he made his exit, the doorman apologized for the trucks and mobile homes parked in front of the bank.

"They have been here for better part of three days makin' a movie. They shot some scenes inside the bank lobby. Supposed to be a bank holdup. That's in the story. They used a bunch of us as extras. We even got paid. I might be in a movie," he said proudly.

Gary nodded as he left. He would be back first thing in the morning when the doors opened again for business, with his briefcase, calculator, red pencils and checklists.

Gary walked around Larimer Square admiring the many flower baskets hanging from turn-of-the-century lamp posts. There were bunches of geraniums, Shasta daisies, and some kind of little frilly blue flowers he couldn't identify. He knew his wife Marcia would really like the flowers—in fact, she'd probably like everything about Denver.

He stopped in front of a Ralph Lauren Polo shop, feeling a little envious as he looked at the display of preppy-looking clothes on the models. They were in sharp contrast to his crotch-wrinkled khakis, his short-sleeved white shirt with the sweat crescents under the arms, and his cheap polyester necktie, and his geeky plastic pocket pen holder.

Back in his worn-out, robin-egg blue Chevy Nova, Gary checked the map again for the location of a Motel Eight.

It was nearly seven when Dill tidied his office, locked some papers in his desk, turned out the lights and walked toward the elevator. Mildly annoyed that he was already late getting to the hospital, he almost ignored Mr. Buckley when he saw him heading out the back door that led to the fire escape that went down to the rear alleyway.

But Dill needed to know. "Mr. Buckley," he called.

Buckley stopped in the doorway. Obviously piqued. He waved his arm in exasperation, the one holding the ever-present contraband Cuban cigar.

The open door let in a blast of hot air from the street. A trail of strong cigar smoke hit Dill in the face. He tried not to show his distaste.

"What?" Buckley waited, made a show of looking at his heavy gold watch. "Look, I'm running really late. What is it?"

Buckley was always "running late."

Wanting to keep it short so he could get over to see JoEllen, Dill simply said, "I was going to ask you about some files that have been moved to storage. It can wait until tomorrow. Have a pleasant evening."

Buckley was not used to people being nice to him. He was caught slightly off-guard. He grinned and said, "Sure, let's talk tomorrow." He turned to leave then turned back. "By the bye, did you get the invitation for the Las Vegas whing-a-ding-ding?" He seemed pleased at his clumsy attempt at coarse humor.

Dill had not. What Las Vegas trip? Why would people from this bank be traveling to Las Vegas? And what business did the bank have in Las Vegas? He shook his head no.

"I'll have Anita fill you in tomorrow," Buck said. And he was gone. It was Wednesday night.

Lake Breckenridge, Texas

Ricky Bob worked late on the Dolly P. They were close to their target depth and would probably reach it sometime day after tomorrow. By late tomorrow morning Ricky would be up in Skiatook having a lunch meeting with the money-raisers, those two boys from Salt Lake City. He turned over the rig operations to Todd, his next in command, stuffed some papers and logs into his battered old cowhide briefcase and climbed down the metal ladder to his waiting pickup.

Ricky Bob was sorely tempted to swing past his home in Okmulgee to have a little warm sendoff with his wife. After which he'd shower, shave, change into some clean clothes and head for Skiatook.

He ached as he thought about snuggling in Nan's warm welcoming arms. But, it was already midnight. And, even if he broke a few speed limits, he wouldn't get home until nearly six. By then, Nan would be up brewing coffee and fixing breakfast and school lunches for the kids.

As much as Ricky Bob loved his chosen career as an "Oilie," this was the part of the job he hated most: being away from his wife and kids for such long stretches. He couldn't tell you how many important events involving his family, his kids, he'd missed. Dance recitals, little league baseball, Christmas and Thanksgiving programs and Pop Warner football games.

Ricky Bob pulled into a Love Brothers truck stop on the edge of Fort Worth for a bathroom break, a coffee refill, and a quick snack of peanuts and greasy truck stop nachos. He'd eat as he drove. It was going to be a long slog and his gut already recoiled at the thought of the crap he was poisoning his body with.

There was a time when girls turned their heads to get a second look at this handsome young athlete, this golden-haired god. Now Ricky had to admit that his once-ripped body had started its inevitable decline into dissipation. Gravity had taken over. He no longer flexed and admired his biceps in the bathroom mirror. He couldn't remember the last time he and Nan had seen each other without clothes with the lights on. He sighed and started up his truck, merged into the late-night traffic heading east.

TWENTY-FIVE

Seth Summers's Office, Denver

Seth Summers picked up the phone and dialed a number in Ft. Lauderdale, Florida. It was a private line. Even though it was nearly two in the morning on the east coast, Seth knew the person on the other end would pick up.

"Yeah, Seth, what's up?" a gruff voice asked.

Seth chuckled and said, "Good evening to you too, Morty. Just wanted to break in on your latest dalliance and see how my favorite stock promoter was doing. I'm sorry if I interrupted any, shall we say, tete-a-tete with … what's the name of your latest cutie? They sort of all run together in my mind."

Morty Resnick laughed, hacked out a smoker's cough and said, "Unfortunately, nothing like that going on tonight. Just working late. What's the latest word about, uh, what is it …?" Seth heard papers rustling.

Morty was notorious for keeping poor records. His office was a pig's breakfast of old stock offering prospectuses, sales confirmation slips from brokers, outdated Pink Sheet quotes, canceled checks and adult magazines. If you excavated hard and long enough to find bottom, among all the detritus would also be found an odd assortment of half-eaten hot dogs or pizza, cigarette butts, and empty vodka bottles.

Morty was back on the call with, "Aha, found it! Stagecoach Energy, that's the latest scam. Looks like another piece of crap if you ask me."

Seth responded, "Nobody asked you, Morty. I never said it was Standard Oil or BP. These deals never are about blue-chip companies. You, of all people, should have learned by now that's how we operate.

Now, listen very carefully and don't take any notes. Can you focus that thick brain of yours for a few minutes?"

Morty Resnick. Early 40s, tall, fit, very tanned from hanging around Florida's sunny tennis clubs where he found a lot of success hustling rich retirees from New York, New Jersey, Toronto. Mostly Jewish.

Morty was Jewish, too. When it suited his purposes. Yes, he'd been raised Jewish, had done the Bar Mitzvah thing at age 12. Or was it 13? He couldn't really remember. He always carried a yarmulke in his pocket. He'd put it on when the occasion called for it.

Morty was actually handsome, with a full head of thick, brown hair streaked with sun-bleached blonde. His warm brown eyes inspired confidence, especially when they crinkled at the corners when he laughed at the stories his "clients" shared with him about their many near misses in the world of investing. That's when Morty was ready with a tale of how this next deal was going to put their fortunes back in the plus column. Although he never shared the dirty little secrets of his trade with them.

Morty liked to brag about his Ivy League credentials, which he knew nobody ever bothered to check up on. It's mostly true that he had once "attended" the highly revered Harvard Business School. In actual fact, he had merely shown up one day at the start of fall term to hand-deliver a totally false application to the admissions office. Morty guessed that counted as attending.

His application had listed at least two prestigious private colleges, where he had earned dual degrees in electrical engineering and finance. He graduated magna sum laude. It never happened.

The red flag that tipped off the Harvard admissions people was the reference to *sum* instead of *cum* laude. Because Morty had used the fake name of J. Martin Sykes III, and a false Greenwich, Connecticut, address, there was no way the Harvard people could track him down.

The folks at the Greenwich address were frankly puzzled when, in their mail one day, was a rejection letter with the impressive return address on a crimson-embossed Harvard Business School envelope, addressed to a Mr. J. Martin Sykes III.

By then, J. Martin Sykes III, aka Morty Resnick, was far away working at his first job in a Dublin, Ireland, boiler room cold-calling "guppies" off a client list stolen from a staid old London private merchant banking firm. He was doing what was known in the trade as "hard-selling."

The deal he was flogging was an offering of shares in a totally worthless, "hot" penny stock offering based on a barely existing hydroponic farming scam out of British Columbia, Canada. The hot, new startup company was growing hemp. For its "medicinal" properties.

Morty pocketed a cool 50,000 pounds from that scam, which he deposited in a secret Lichtenstein bank account. He quickly moved on to Barcelona to another boiler room. And so, it came to pass that the hemp deal totally cratered when the promoters hyped the stock to their desired level of profits through a fierce campaign of totally false press releases, pocketed their loot and vanished, leaving the shareholders holding reams of worthless stock certificates.

The puzzled shareholders were baffled at first. They went into full panic mode when their phone calls to the brokers who talked them into parting with a good portion of their retirement didn't answer their phones. Their next calls got a message: the phone number they were calling was no longer in service.

Next call was to the regulators at the Vancouver Stock Exchange. The regulators immediately halted trading in the now-worthless shares. A full-scale investigation ensued. Complete with a huge media event. "The perpetrators of this fraudulent scheme will be brought to justice where the full weight of the laws of British Columbia will be enforced to the fullest extent of the penalties on the statute books, etc., etc.

What they didn't say was: "As it is our duty to our dumb-as-fence-posts citizens to protect them from their own stupidity, here we go again with yet another offshore boiler room scam that by now is shut down and the rats have melted into the woodwork. We'll never find them, etc. etc."

Except … one of the investors in the hemp deal was a recent émigré to Vancouver from Hong Kong, who had figured that a clever way to get a bunch of his money out of The People's Republic of China, where he'd been illegally operating under the radar for years, was to buy penny stocks through a brass plate company he'd set up in the British Virgin Islands, a holding company, or shell corporation the officers and directors of which were all nominees.

This company in turn owned all of the bearer shares in another shell company domiciled in Panama, another known tax haven with its secretive banking laws, where it had opened several numbered bank accounts in other offshore locations with very tight bank secrecy laws of their own. Of course, this shell also had nominee officers and directors.

The actual investor behind this maze of shells and cutouts, was a Mr. Deng Yong, who went by the more acceptable, Anglicized David Young, businessman. Formerly of Hong Kong. Before that, the PRC. Now a Canadian citizen by purchasing his Canadian papers. Home address 5111 Connaught Drive in the posh Shaughnessy Heights neighborhood of Vancouver.

David Young did not have a sense of humor.

He had invested a cool $2 million Canadian into this hydroponic/hemp farming scam and now it all appeared to be lost. His eyes narrowed as he pointed his remote at the TV screen and clicked off the CBC, after just watching the press conference of the Vancouver Stock Exchange people, flanked on either side by the BC attorney general, and some big shot from the Royal Canadian Mounted Police–or RCMP, also known as the Mounties—complete in his red coat, shiny brown leather knee-high boots and Buster Brown hat.

Young picked up the phone and dialed an overseas number. It was already late at night in Yokohama, Japan. A phone rang in the sleazy back-street office of a nasty little man who had a reputation among certain elements as a member of the Yakuza, Japan's version of Mafia.

This dangerous little operative of assassinations, revenge killings, extortion, theft, and a host of other criminal activities had formerly been a member of Japan's secret police and had learned his craft by chasing, catching and prosecuting actual criminals. David Young didn't care a pickled sea urchin about any nefarious connections. On second thought, this wicked little man was exactly who he needed to help get his money back.

Barcelona, Spain

Meanwhile, a week later on a balmy evening in lovely Barcelona, Morty was off with his new boiler-room friends celebrating their latest hard-sell scam by spending lavishly on a party of rich red Spanish wine, tapias, paella, and the company of several black-eyed beauties Morty's new friends had invited to join in the fun.

When the party sort of ran out of steam Morty accompanied one of the girls back to his cheap rented hotel room. While fumbling for his key, he spotted a small man lounging in the shadows down the hallway. The man appeared to be Asian. Morty couldn't be sure.

Whatever he was, he had been staring hard for several seconds at Morty. Their eyes met briefly. The little man had an evil look in his eyes. Morty quickly looked away. He had a creepy feeling about this brief moment. There was definitely something sinister about this person.

The little man turned away. Morty shrugged it off and entered his darkened room with the giggling Spanish girl crawling all over him.

Next morning Morty awoke with a ferocious hangover. The girl was gone. His wallet was empty of cash and credit cards. No matter, they were maxed out anyway. He moved some clothing looking for a phone so he could ring for room service, for coffee, strong and black. Then he remembered: there was no room service in this hotel. There wasn't even a phone in his cheap room.

He pulled on designer jeans, an expensive vee-neck cashmere sweater in an outrageous purple and Gucci loafers without socks, the current European trend. He fumbled to light a Marlboro Light with shaky hands before he headed down to the street to find some strong coffee.

Morty took a deep drag and exhaled. Better. He put on his aviator-style dark glasses and started to leave his cheap hotel room for the street.

As Morty opened his door, he heard something rustle under his shoe. It sounded like paper. He looked down and saw what looked like the reverse side of a stock certificate. Strange. What would a stock certificate be doing slipped under his door?

He turned it over and recognized it as a certificate for 10,000 common voting shares of The Coquitlam Hemp & Hydroponic Farming Enterprises, Ltd., a British Columbia corporation. The owner's name was David Young. Didn't ring any bells.

But the certificate had been marked up by hand with red ink or a heavy crayon, he couldn't be sure. Maybe it was lipstick. Maybe that girl had left it as a prank. It said "Cancelled" and below that "This is a scam. You lost all my money. You are Dead! Dead, Dead, Dead!"

Morty forgot about the coffee. He quickly stuffed his few possessions into an old canvas Portuguese Navy duffel bag, settled his hotel bill by tossing some cash he had hidden in the soles of his Guccis at the hotel clerk.

He rushed outside and hailed the first cab in the queue. He piled in and told the driver to hurry: "Aeropuerto! Tengo prisa!" Morty spent the next stressful 25 minutes constantly glancing behind them for any more sign of the creepy little Asian.

Morty bought a one-way, first-class ticket with the last of his cash. He caught the next available flight back to the U.S. He breathed a huge sigh of relief as the plane lifted off the ground.

It would take several years before Morty could stop automatically looking over his shoulder to see if anyone was following him.

TWENTY-SIX

Oncology Ward, Denver Hospital

JoEllen slept through the night for the first time in weeks. She awoke freshened from a good sleep. She was physically and mentally ready to take on the next round of chemotherapy. Then she'd be almost done with the chemo treatments. The doctors said the leukemia had at least stopped spreading. They were encouraged—cautiously encouraged—about her future prognosis.

Maybe she'd be able to skip the radiation treatments. She'd just have to wait and see and trust in the Lord's tender mercies. But, every day she was allowed to live, she counted as a blessing from God, a sign of His grace.

She thought she'd check in on her little friend Corrie. She opened her door and started to walk the few steps across the hall. But something stopped her. Corrie's door was open and her bed was empty and all the linens had been removed. She felt a dark, bad thing knotting up in her stomach. A female orderly was mopping the room. She hurried over and asked the orderly, "Where's Corrie?"

The orderly, a Latina woman, shrugged, smiled and said, "Yo no se," *I don't know*, and continued her mopping.

JoEllen rushed down the hall as fast as she was able to move in her condition. She stopped to check at the nurse's station. She waited an agonizing minute while a young nurse with stylishly cut red hair finished a phone call. The nurse looked up at Jo and smiled. "Can I help you?"

"Where's Corrie? Where has she gone?"

"I'm afraid your little friend left us ..."

"Left?"

"She died during the night. Heart just stopped beating. So sad. She was such a brave little fighter."

Jo slumped down on the polished linoleum floor, her back against the nurse's desk and cried her heart out. Her sobs racked her body and rolled through the sterile hallways. The red-headed duty nurse pushed a red button signaling an emergency on her wing. Doctors, nurses and orderlies came running.

Larimer Square Bank, Denver

At 9:00 in the morning Gary Swope was standing on the sidewalk in front of the Larimer Square Bank, waiting for the doors to be opened by the uniformed doorkeeper who had been so polite to him the day before. The movie people, with their trucks and mobile homes, were gone. Gary carried his briefcase, calculator and checklists. He was ready to do his job.

Inside the bank was a veritable beehive of activity. Dozens of smartly dressed young executives from about 20 major and smaller banks around the country, including one each from Brazil, Italy and Spain, two each from Japan and France, and no less than three from London, had been on the premises since early morning.

They arrived with paper cups of steaming coffee and bags of donuts, and their smart attaché cases. Some came with armloads of paperwork. All of them looked harried, stressed, overworked (or, in many cases, over-partied). Some were certifiably hung over and in no condition to work. Several had eyes that looked like they were actually bleeding from consuming too much coke the night before. Or was it this morning on the way in? Dude, I forget.

Dill had gathered all the staff and young people from the correspondent banks the day before and briefed them on the upcoming audit. He had asked them to be polite. They were not to bother the auditor with questions, but to try and answer his questions. If they could. If they didn't know the answers, Dill had told them, "Please refer him to me."

Dill was mostly troubled about the fact that all the loan files were off-premises. He still didn't have a clue as to their whereabouts even though he'd asked around. Nobody seemed to know anything. What a way not to run a bank. He sensed trouble.

Archer Horse Farms, Ardmore, Oklahoma

Calvin Buckley had made sure he was nowhere near the bank premises where the FDIC auditor could collar him and ask embarrassing questions. Questions whose answers could prove to be very uncomfortable. Questions that would require more lies, more cover-up. So, on this morning, Buck was several hundred miles away in Ardmore, Oklahoma, inspecting and approving one of his latest purchases.

Buck had already put the rather unpleasant dinner with Buzz, the debt junkie behind him.

Right now, he was admiring a lovely Arabian filly named My Doll that Buck was about to snatch up from some unnamed Middle Eastern oil sheik who was entangled in a complicated internecine tribal squabble. The sheik was quite anxious to liquidate some of his assets so he could stockpile more weapons should his squabbles snowball into a war with his rivals. This fire sale had to be handled with the utmost discretion and secrecy. It wouldn't pay to let his enemies know he was weak or desperate.

There were quite a few questionable purchases the sheik had made while demanding unquestioned austerity from the people he ruled. He also had a lot of assets around the world that could prove to be embarrassing if ever associated with him. Such as that huge yacht. The chateau in Provence. The apartment in Manhattan that had a great view of Central Park. That lovely Victorian mansion in Belgravia Square …

My Doll was pregnant, a bonus for Buck. This deal would be a two-fer-the-price-of-one. The price tag was a good bargain, too, at a mere $500,000. If he decided to sell her he could probably get $800,000 in this hot market. Just for the mare. After she dropped the colt, of course.

He could sell the colt—if it was a colt—for around $250,000 because of its bloodlines, which had been carefully vetted by Archer Farms. Of course, if she had a filly, the price would be somewhat lower. Colts were in greater demand for their potential as studs.

He stroked and patted her soft velvety nose. Her breath smelled of oats and molasses. Buck nodded to the dealer. "She's a beauty. I'll take her. You know where to pick up your cash?"

The horse dealer nodded. "Thanks for your business, er, Mr. Holbrook. We'll take care of all the details for you. Same company to show as owner on the registration papers?"

Buck nodded. He couldn't wait to wrap this up and pay a visit to a certain attractive divorcee named Angie, who lived the other side of Ardmore, just 10 minutes away.

Meanwhile, Dill got an urgent call from the hospital informing him that his wife had had some sort of meltdown. He was badly needed to be at her bedside. Panic gripped his gut. "Meltdown? Could you be a little more specific?"

"I'm not at liberty to divulge any details as I'm sure you can appreciate …"

Dill cut her off. "I'm her husband for crying out loud!"

"I'm truly sorry."

"I'll be there as fast as I can," he barked and rang off.

Skiatook, Oklahoma

Jerry waited nervously in the arriving passenger reception area of Tulsa International. Phillip's flight from Salt Lake was late. Jerry checked with the Delta desk and was told that the first leg of Phillip's flight from Salt Lake to San Francisco had been fogged in. His plane had been rerouted through Phoenix.

"When do you expect his plane will get here?" Jerry asked.

The lovely customer service rep in her light blue uniform scanned her screen for a minute and smiled as she looked up. "The best we can hope for is around 1:30 this afternoon. Is there a phone number where we can call you when it's close to Mr. Connoff's arrival time?"

Jerry fumbled in his pocket for the scrap of paper with Darren's phone number. He'd already lost Darren's unique business card. She wrote down the number. Jerry noticed with interest that she was left-handed and wore no wedding or engagement ring that he could see.

What was he thinking? He had a girlfriend back home. He was practically engaged. At least he and Connie had discussed a possible engagement in the future. But still, a guy should let the world know he was available. Just in case things didn't work out with Connie. You never knew …

Jerry made a mental note of her name by trying to memorize the name tag: Terry. Terry and Jerry. They went together nicely. Cute. He thanked Terry by name and gave her his best smile as he headed out of the terminal for his solo meeting with Darren. Phillip could catch up later. If he, in fact, ever got here.

Stagecoach Energy, Dallas

When the financial markets at 9:30 a.m. opened for trading in New York, Stagecoach Energy's IPO, was officially launched, with an issue of 12.5 million shares priced at $2 a share for a total offering of $25 million. Out of that would come the fees, brokerage commissions, printing, lawyer and accountants' fees, and the "incidentals."

The company would net around $20 million. The $5 million—20 percent off the top—was described in the offering prospectus as "dilution," or the amount by which the investor's $2 per share was immediately diminished in book value before they ever got possession of their stock certificate. But that was part of the deal they agreed to before making the decision to purchase Stagecoach's shares.

The underwriting syndicate expected to sell at least 75 percent of the offering within the first few hours, based on the indications of interest received from the syndicate's network of institutional players, hedge funds, retirement funds (the biggest of which was the California State Employees Retirement Fund), foreign banks that represented wealthy "phantom" buyers. Buyers like our oil sheik, who had just unloaded one of his prize Arabian mares.

Last came the smaller brokerage firms—domestic and foreign—the ones not so lucky as to have been invited into the syndicate. They got the crumbs of the deal. If they were lucky. Often the little firms would be allowed just a few shares to buy. They would hold a drawing and the winning sales rep got to flog those few paltry shares to their "lucky" clients.

For these lower-tier firms there would be no deeply discounted stock options, only the chance to make a few bucks in commissions off their "best" clients. These smaller "bucket shops" located in far-flung cities and towns around the country and in a few foreign capitals would sell the other 25 percent of the offering over the next few days or so.

Lorne, Ted, and Seth held their collective breaths. The number Seth and his minions watched closely was the after-market quote, the price Stagecoach's shares would start trading for after the initial offering was sold and shares snatched up when speculators started trading.

Because of the recent avalanche of new oil and gas IPOs, the SEC had adopted a policy of requiring a "cooling off period" for these new issues, usually 24 hours, but sometimes longer, before the shares could start trading hands in open market trades. Once the SEC gave Stagecoach the green light, its shares opened at $2.50 bid, $3.05 ask. In the first hour of trading Stagecoach, with its newly minted trading symbol of SECT, 1.76 million shares changed hands.

This number would remain fairly constant for the next couple of days, until the PR firm stepped in, ramped up the campaign, and started beating the drum.

There would be strategically placed press releases of new leases acquired by Stagecoach, deals it was discussing with other oil exploration companies, a tantalizing piece that Stagecoach was already being considered for a "strategic" affiliation with a larger independent oil pipeline company out of El Paso.

By the end of the first week of trading, Stagecoach, with its trading symbol SECT, had steadily climbed toward the magical $10 a share mark. It was a number closely watched by the brokers, stock analysts, the SEC—and, of course, Seth Summers.

Hidden among the dozens of pages of dry accounting data in SECT's financial statements, attached to its IPO prospectus, was a rather obscure footnote that indicated a fairly large number of non-voting preferred shares owned by a company innocently listed in all that dead verbiage as Fidelity American Holdings, Ltd., a company incorporated in Antigua.

Antigua is a small island country in the Caribbean. It's a nice vacation destination with lovely white sand beaches, reasonably nice beach hotels and decent eating places whose signature dish was always conch salad.

But the main source of income for Antigua, like many other Caribbean island nations, was the hundreds and thousands of brass plate companies like Fidelity American that claimed Antigua as their country of domicile. These companies paid handsome fees to the national treasury each year for the privilege of incorporating there in order to maintain an impenetrable wall of secrecy and anonymity.

If you had the right connections, a mere phone call to a well-placed solicitor in Antigua would get you a brass plate company complete with faceless nominee officers and directors together with bearer certificates held in the lawyer's safe deposit box. All within 24 hours. The same lawyer, licensed to practice in most jurisdictions in the British Commonwealth, could discreetly arrange a private-numbered bank account for your company.

American Fidelity owned 250,000 shares of Class B preferred shares in SECT. At the time management of Stagecoach issued the shares to Seth Summers—actually to American Fidelity, as directed by Seth—for consulting services, SECT (nor their highly paid Wall Street legal counsel) had no idea what they were doing or what the consequences would be down the road.

But Seth Summers did.

Stagecoach was incorporated in the state of Nevada, a state whose corporation laws granted a lot of discretion to officers and directors to run the company pretty much free from stockholder scrutiny or interference.

Stagecoach's bylaws had been hastily drafted by its lawyers without truly giving thought to the consequences of the disservice they were doing to their client.

They did a hasty, extremely sloppy cut-and-paste job on the incorporation and the new company's bylaws, for which they billed $10,000. Little did the lawyers know they most likely had committed malpractice.

Actually, it wasn't the lawyers so much as Seth Summers who did SECT a huge disservice. He spotted the provision in the bylaws and cannily suggested to Stagecoach management that his fees be in the form of stock.

The handwritten memo went like this: *250,000 shares restricted under Rule 144,of the Company's non-voting preferred Class B shares to American Fidelity Holdings Ltd., an Antigua corporation, for consulting services, the adequacy, value and benefit of which to Stagecoach Energy has been received by the Company and duly approved by the board of directors, which shares will have attached a call to convert to common voting at the rate of ten shares of new voting unrestricted common for each share of the said restricted preferred shares tendered for removal of said restriction, the cost for which will be borne by Stagecoach Energy .*

Which is exactly what appeared in the board's minutes. And a copy of those minutes was forwarded to Stagecoach's stock transfer agency, Pacific Stock Transfer in Las Vegas, the independent entity hired to take care of issuing the share certificates for SECT and to keep track of all the company's shares, as those shares could swiftly change hands literally every few minutes in a hot market.

In the early 1970s, the SEC adopted Rule 144 to try and curb the abusive practice of stock promoters getting their hands on large blocks of "free trading" shares issued to them for various "services."

These large blocks of stock, normally issued to phantom nominee shareholders, but very well known to the promoters, would suddenly find their way into the market. When they did, it would usually cause a steep drop in share prices, thus disrupting an orderly trading market. An unruly trading market discourages investors from purchasing the more risky shares of an IPO, making it harder for small companies to raise badly needed capital.

SEC Rule 144 essentially placed a two-year restriction on the trading of shares issued to officers, directors, or "control" persons (interpreted as anyone owning, beneficially or of record, not less than 5 percent of the outstanding shares of the issuer company). The SEC extended that reach to shares issued to stock promoters, those people like Seth Summers, who had a hand helping in organizing a company, finding deals to merge into the new company, helping raise capital, or providing PR services in later promoting its shares.

Seth didn't have a problem with Rule 144 shares being issued for his services. He'd made a ton of money this way. He was patient. Patience wasn't just a virtue but Seth Summers's operational MO. From past experience, he knew that this MO would eventually pay off handsomely. So, he held his Stagecoach shares for just barely one day over the two-year restriction period and now he—American Fidelity—wanted the 144 legend removed from the preferred share certificates and the issuance of 2.5 million new free-trading common shares.

"Seth, what are you doing to us? You're trying to kill us! And what in the world is this notion that Stagecoach has to pay for registering your shares?"

"Lorne, Lorne … You have my word that these shares will dribble into the market slowly. There won't be any disruption to your trading scheme. Give me some credit for knowing what I'm doing. Why would I want to drive the price down by dumping a crapload of shares all at once? I've been in this game a lot longer than you have. Just do it, okay, and everything will be tickety-boo."

Lorne swore.

"And by the way, read the fine print. Your lawyers wrote all that legal language into your company and it's in the minutes that Stagecoach pays for registering my shares."

Lorne wasn't happy.

Seth's next call was to Morty Resnick. "It's started. You know what to do?"

Morty assured him he did. Seth rang off.

TWENTY-SEVEN

Oncology Ward, Denver Hospital

Dill careened into the hospital parking lot. He didn't bother to lock his door or check to see if his fly rod was still in the back. He jumped out and ran to his wife's room, his Tony Llama boots slamming loudlyon the polished linoleum. Arriving breathless at Jo's room, he found her sedated and resting. A small cluster of interns, nurses and PAs had gathered around and were conferring in hushed tones. Jo's eyes were closed. Her breathing was shallow. She looked tired and pale.

Dill, slightly frightened at her appearance, squared his shoulders, pushed his way through the small knot, and knelt down beside Jo. He took her hand and kissed her forehead. She must have recognized his presence for she smiled faintly. He caught his breath as his heart skipped.

"What happened?" Dill looked up at the young intern who was holding a clipboard of charts.

"She had quite a bad shock. Her little friend from across the hall …" he motioned, "she passed away last night. I guess the news of it just hit her wrong."

"Jo told me the little girl was so courageous and quite a fighter," Dill said. "What was her name again?"

The intern checked his notes. "Corrie."

"Yes, Corrie. She was one of the best," one of the nurses added through her own tears.

"We're recommending some counseling for your wife," the young intern said. Dill nodded.

Skiatook, Oklahoma

Before Jerry left Tulsa International for Skiatook, he made a quick call to Darren to let him know they were running late. Darren said that Ricky Bob had already arrived and they should just meet for coffee and hang out until Phillip showed up. He gave Jerry directions to a little roadside diner on the edge of Skiatook.

"It don't look like much, but they do serve a good cup and great homemade pies."

They killed a couple of hours drinking too much coffee and eating too much pie. To fill the time, they talked about OU football, the stock market, rising interest rates, and girls they had dated in college. Phillip finally showed and they moved the meeting back to Darren's office.

"My first question, and I can assure you boys it's the most critical hurdle you have to get over, is what's going to be the ratio of tax write-off you're offering your investors in this deal?"

Phillip and Jerry looked at each other. They had already discussed this issue several times and had argued fiercely. Phillip wanted to take a more aggressive approach with at least a four-and-a-half to one ratio.

Jerry had held firm on three-to-one. Jerry had been in the game long enough to have developed a healthy respect for the IRS and their auditing abilities.

Ricky Bob just looked on and shrugged like he didn't care one iota, which in fact he didn't. Just go get me the money.

"We've had this discussion," Jerry opened, "and are not yet in agreement. He wants 4:1 and I'm holding out for 3:1." Darren looked evenly at Phillip. Phillip nodded back. He looked at Ricky Bob who shrugged again. He could care less. Just get the money and my big rig.

"Can you give me a legal basis that supports your argument, Mr. Connoff? Or a tax code citation?"

Phillip snorted. "Are you kidding me? You're the lawyer. That's what we're paying you for, your very expensive legal and tax expertise."

Darren waited patiently. He knew Phillip was on shaky ground and he suspected Phillip knew it, too.

Phillip scratched his head thoughtfully, shrugged and said, "Okay, I'm not a tax expert; I'll admit that. But … I just know that what I'm suggesting is based on what my investors have wanted in the past."

"So, because the investors wanted it, that's what you gave them. Is that what I'm hearing?"

Phillip nodded confidently.

"How many of your prior deals have been audited? How has your 4-to-1 write-off been treated in those audits? Did it pass the IRS?"

Darren waited for Phillip's answer while his client maintained his composure. A minute passed with no response.

"That's what I thought," Darren said. "That's why I'm inclined to agree with your partner, Jerry. As your lawyer, I'm recommending a 3-to-1 write-off."

"Can you tell us what you base that on?" Phillip asked.

"Oh, I can cite all kinds of legal precedents. Which I will do in my opinion letter. But to me, it just boils down to two things: first, my experience with IRS auditors. They are starting to crack down on these so-called tax shelters for too many abuses. First thing they look at? Yep, high-ratio write-offs. And, second, I guess I'm kind of an old lady about these things. Go ahead and call me a chicken, but I'm really serious about wanting to protect you guys and your clients, your investors, from too much of their own greedy impulses. Just avoid the appearance of greed and you're on the safe side of the IRS."

Both his clients and Ricky nodded. Hadn't he heard his daddy and granddaddy say something just like that before?

"One other thing I should mention: I'm the one who has to put his name on the opinion letter as to the tax aspects of your offering. So as a practical matter my ample fanny is on the line just like yours."

Phillip grinned. "So that's why you charge us the big bucks?"

"Darn straight," Darren shot back, grinning.

"So, let's go get some barbecued ribs and celebrate," added Ricky Bob. They all agreed it was a good idea.

From Ricky Bob's perspective the meeting had been a huge success. Phillip was still smarting. He didn't like losing, and he felt he had just lost a fight. Phillip was already secretly scheming ways he could work around those two old women—the lawyer and Jerry—and get his clients their promised 4:1 write-off.

Ricky Bob was euphoric as he drove down US 75 toward Weatherford. He was sorely tempted to detour through Okmulgee for a little afternoon delight and to share the good news with Nan. He checked his watch. It was already past four o'clock. The kids would already be home. Those kids sure could interfere with his love life, as he knew from prior experience.

In the meantime, he badly needed to get back to the Dolly P and check on things. He was still creeped-out about the false drill logs he'd discovered. He decided those could wait. He vowed that someday they would see the light of day. Right now, they were low priority.

Darren had had Ricky sign a ton of paperwork, copies of which were stuffed in his old cowhide briefcase. He'd read that dry, boring legal print later. For now, he basked in the warm fuzzy feeling of a ton of cash waiting for him at that bank up in Denver. Not to mention the limited partnership drilling fund deal he'd just sealed with those two promoters from Salt Lake. Yes, Ricky was feeling pretty good.

He made a mental note to call that Dill Rogers guy at the bank and make an appointment when he had a quiet moment with no snooping eyes or ears to listen in.

Dill. What a funny name.

Weatherford, Texas

While Ricky was putting together his deal of a lifetime, the Stagecoach people had their dog and pony show at the Dolly P well site. Over the past few years Stagecoach had found pockets of investors scattered around the country, such as Jerry's groups he'd signed up in Summit, New Jersey, and Alaska.

Jerry, like other fund raisers for Stagecoach, had quickly learned two things about finding subscribers for oil and gas limited partnerships. First, qualified investors were most likely to be reliant upon the advice of an influential person that was trusted by the investor. This influential person was almost always their tax accountant or tax lawyer. So, the natural thing for Jerry and others like him was to curry the trust and confidence of those key influencers.

Second, investors loved to brag up their investments, especially if they ever hit a home run. Of course, they didn't talk much about their losses. Except to their lawyers when preparing to sue the persons and companies touting the investment. If those persons could be found to serve process on.

To keep the investors' confidence and calm their nervous doubts, their buyers' remorse—which always later set in—the promoters kept up a constant stream of news reports. They described how the drilling was progressing. The lovely potential formations they had found. How they would soon be hooking up pumping equipment. That things were looking rosy, so don't get nervous. Just think about how that flowing oil would soon be paying back your letter of credit. And so on.

The really resourceful promoters would take a few carefully selected investors (translated: the ones who seemed to be the influencers, the ones who could either keep the nervous ones in line, or who would be the first to form a lynch mob if things went wrong) and show them around the drill site, buy them lunch, send them on their way with a lot of photos and mementoes of their exciting trip in the oil patch.

This particular group was from the Omaha area. They were mostly referred by one solo practitioner of the mysterious art of creating huge tax write-offs for his clients. He never bothered to tell his clients that he was getting a generous referral fee from Stagecoach.

He accompanied them on this trip which originated at his office at 7:30 a.m. Everyone piled into the chartered Trailways bus in high spirits. Right off the get-go, things went haywire. The air conditioning broke down so everyone had to wait for another two hours before another bus could be located.

They finally got underway and someone started singing "Ninety-Nine Bottles of Beer on the Wall." The sing-along fizzled out by the time they reached 93 bottles of beer. It was going to be a long 12-hour trip to Dallas. The road stretched endlessly before them shimmering in the unusual autumn heat wave.

The Texas Oil Patch

They arrived in Dallas late, hot, tired and very grumpy. Stagecoach had arranged to have their party at a Marriott in North Dallas. After a midnight dinner of spaghetti and limp salad and a few short speeches nobody listened to, the investors went to bed exhausted.

Next morning, after a huge oilman's breakfast, they were hustled back on the bus. There was a stop at a shopping center in Fort Worth where everyone was treated to a free pair of Tony Llama cowboy boots. Courtesy of Stagecoach Energy.

The site visit went off without incident. Todd, Ricky's number two man, was assigned the job of answering the endless string of stupid questions. The investors nodded knowingly like they really knew what Todd was telling them as they toured the rig and the site.

Todd patiently explained to them that no, oil wasn't normally down there in great big pools just waiting to be released so it could shoot high into the sky like they'd been led to believe by Hollywood. No, the oil was, in fact, trapped as tiny little molecules in the layers of lime rock or sandstone hundreds of feet down. He explained how fracking would release the molecules of oil.

"Then how do you know where to frack, as you call it?"

Good question.

Todd showed them the drilling log, and they watched as the delicate needle scratched its squiggles on the slowly revolving drum of paper. He explained kicks to them.

"I still don't understand how you get the oil out if it's trapped in layers of rocks," a matronly female investor said. "I always heard there were huge pools of oil down there." Good point.

Todd took a piece of paper and drew a rectangle with lots of little circles on it. "Think of the rock as a sponge, a very porous sponge. You know how a sponge soaks up liquids?" They all nodded. "The many small oil molecules are trapped in the sandstone rock down there. Sandstone rock acts just like a sponge to the oil molecules."

"Then how do you get the oil out of the rock, up the pipe and over there?" one man asked. He pointed to the battery of shiny new storage tanks just waiting to be filled with crude to later be picked up by truck and carried to the refinery.

"Good question," Todd said and launched into an explanation. "There's a lot of pressure down hole. That pressure helps push the little drops of crude to the bore hole. And we also use a pump jack, one of those big machines you see over yonder moving up and down."

All heads turned to where Todd pointed at the mantis-looking machine.

He continued. "Well, those pumps create a huge amount of suction and, well, think of how you suck at a milkshake through a straw to pull that sweet stuff into your mouth. Same thing with crude. Sweet crude being sucked through a straw, so to speak."

Heads nodded and understanding lit up a few eyes.

"Speaking of sweet stuff, I'm hungry. How about you folks? We have a nice BBQ lunch all prepared for you, Texas-style." Todd waved his arm, motioning toward the bus. "If you'll follow me, we'll get back on the bus and eat!"

Most of them didn't have a clue what they had just heard and seen, but the schmoozing continued as the potential investors were then given a gift of a translucent paperweight with a dram of crude oil and a miniature copy of the cover page of their prospectus trapped inside.

They piled back on the bus and were driven a few miles west to the dreary little Texas town of Cisco. There they feasted on barbecue at Oscar's, a popular roadside smoker that had been converted from a 1940s vintage Signal Oil gas station.

The feast was set up under a canopy of live oak trees crawling with singing cicadas. On folding tables, covered with red and white checkered paper that flapped in the wind, were two Mason jars filled with reddish-colored liquid.

Oscar himself came out, wiping his hands on a dirty greasy apron. He brushed several dead cicadas off a table and welcomed them with a big smile. He explained that one jar held hot sauce and the other, the darker liquid, was triple hot! Everyone laughed, but again, Todd thought, none of them really knew what was going on. Oscar posed for pictures with the investors. The atmosphere was pure West Texas oil patch, and the guests were being drawn in, just as planned. The dog and pony show had been a success.

On the road somewhere

Calvin Buckley was always headed to or from somewhere. "Oh, he's on the road," was the stock answer when anyone inside the bank was asked about his whereabouts. Buck called his secretary on a private line reserved for secretive discussions that he didn't want prying ears to hear.

"All the arrangements been made?"

"Yes, sir. Four private jets, just as you requested. Reservations all made for the bungalows at the Aladdin Hotel in Las Vegas. Rooms for 20 people in all. All the other arrangements are set too, limousines, and the hospitality, uh, people …"

"And you made sure that Mr. Roberts is on the guest list?"

"Mr. Robertson. Yes sir."

Satisfied, Buck rang off.

Oncology Ward, Denver Hospital

Dill sat with his sedated wife as she slept. What am I doing here, he thought. Not here in this room, but here in this situation. He mind was careening with concern. Concern for Jo, of course, but for everything else too.

He was having some serious second thoughts about his decision to go to work for Larimer. Separated from his boys, his beloved ranch, his friends, and even the many customers back home who were actually more like family. He felt no close connection with any of the people he worked with at Larimer Square Bank. Dill was feeling very alone in a strange land.

Dill suddenly remembered that the FDIC auditor was still at the bank. He knew he should get back and check on things. Why he felt responsible, he couldn't figure. In reality, in spite of all the fine promises on the front end, he wasn't really in the management chain of command, the inner circle. That circle consisted of Buckley and Summers.

He had no real power or authority. His fancy titles and his so-called lending authority were a joke. Decisions about big loans were typically made behind his back or without his seeing any documentation. Decisions always made from above his head and for the wrong reasons and for all the wrong people.

Oh sure, there may be a few customers with legitimate capital needs that could be supported with collateral. But Dill would surely like to see the loan workup file on those. So would that auditor, he supposed, as he kissed Jo goodbye.

Dill checked and saw his fly rod was still in the back of his truck. He had been promised a new car of his choice as one of his perks, but that was another thing that hadn't happened yet. Calvin Buckley drove a shiny new Porsche, courtesy of the bank. Let him have it. He'd take his truck any day. A Porsche was worthless for climbing rough, rocky two-tracks off-road.

Dill looked at his fly rod and for a minute was sorely tempted to head west to a cool Rocky Mountain trout stream and leave Larimer Square Bank and all its growing messes behind.

Even this late in the fall there would be some kind of hatch going on. Blue winged olives maybe? Grasshoppers would work for sure.

TWENTY-EIGHT

Larimer Square Bank

Gary Swope wandered around the bank unimpeded, which he found really strange. It was like the bank people were avoiding him. Nobody made eye contact. Maybe this was normal. After all, he was a government regulator, an auditor, sent to check up on them. Of course, people would be somewhat closed, defensive.

So far, he had spent his first full day observing the bank's normal activities of accepting deposits, cashing checks, answering phones, dealing with customers' complaints. He asked a few questions of the employees and was treated politely.

But he noticed a pattern emerging. When he asked a question about the loan application process, none of the employees seemed to have the answer. For example, he kept getting the same reply, "I'm sorry but you'll have to ask Mr. Buckley about that." Gary made a note in his checklist.

His brief encounter with TJ Brimhall, the bank's president, was equally frustrating. A courtly, soft-spoken gentleman. A pipe smoker with smiling blue eyes, a full head of white hair, and gentle manner. He was what would be called an "old school" banker.

TJ had come up through the ranks the hard way, starting in a bank's mailroom as a parttime job after school. He slowly advanced to top management, where he was stuck until he got a call from the governor asking if he'd like to accept the job as state banking commissioner.

Mostly an honorary position, the governor had chosen TJ based more on his party affiliation rather than any particular administrative skills. The bulk of the heavy lifting in the commissioner's offices was routinely handled by TJ's second in command, Dennis Morgan, his successor as commissioner.

TJ had been enjoying a couple of years of quiet retirement when he was tapped by Seth Summers to assume the title and position of president of Larimer Square Bank. The salary and benefits were nice and TJ would have little more to do than show up occasionally. Morgan rubber-stamped TJ's appointment as Larimer's titular president.

After a few minutes of vapid chit-chat with the old gentleman, Swope thanked him for his time and made another note: *Pres. doesn't have a clue!!* The way things were going, Gary would be done by the end of his first day and on his way back home early tomorrow.

But first, he definitely needed to have a chat with Mr. Robertson, the Chief Loan Officer. And part of that visit would be looking inside a few of Robertson's loan files.

The same day that Gary Swope was touring Larimer Square Bank, a dozen carefully selected executives of America's banking establishments—old, staid, respected, trusted guardians of billions upon billions of the nation's dollars on deposit—received nicely worded invitations written in a graceful Spencerian-style hand on heavy cream stock, inviting them as guests for a weekend banking seminar (subtitle: Opportunities in Oil & Gas Lending) in Las Vegas, Nevada. Guests of Mr. Seth Summers, Chairman, and Calvin Buckley, CEO, of Larimer Square Bank of Denver, Colorado. Summers would also pull some strings to arrange for Morty Resnick to attend.

A fleet of private jets would fan out across the map to pick up all of these bank executives and whisk them off to this exclusive retreat. Dress would be casual. All expenses courtesy of Larimer Square Bank. RSVP. The invitations were followed up by personal calls from Anita, personal assistant to Mr. Calvin Buckley. Nobody said no to her dulcet voice.

One day before the junket was to depart from Denver's executive air terminal, Anita personally handed Dill his invitation. He looked at the cream-colored envelope and asked, "What's this?"

"Open it," she said, and waited for his response.

Dill read it and looked up. "I don't suppose there's any graceful way for me to get out of this thing? I'm really not much of a party guy."

Anita smiled, "Only if it's life or death. You know, blood and gore all over the carpet."

"Well, there is the small matter of my wife ..." Anita was embarrassed. "Oh, I didn't mean ..." She blushed deep red.

"It's okay. Tell Mr. Buckley I'll do my best to make it. Depending on how things are at the hospital." She smiled gratefully and turned to go back to her office. Dill added, "You ever been on one of these things before? Based on what I've heard about the last ones, they're pretty wild."

"You'll have to ask Mr. Buckley. I've never been," she said. Then she added, "As you may or may not know, I'm a devout Christian. Have been all my life, or at least since I was saved and turned my life over to Jesus. Well, anyway, I don't go in for those kinds of things. I prefer a good Bible study group." She reached up and fingered a small gold cross hanging from a slender chain around her neck.

"I think I understand. I really do," Dill said.

He understood all right, only too well. Dill had heard the rumors from some of the employees who volunteered their versions of what went on at Buckley's "corporate retreats." Lots of drinking, gambling, and girls.

This was not how Dill was raised, how he conducted his life. His idea of entertaining his own bank's customers, his neighbors and friends back home, was to kill the fatted calf (literally) and have a backyard barbecue with wives and kids invited. Non-alcoholic drinks were in a big washtub filled with ice, bottled soft drinks or water. Period. Jo would go so far as to brew a big urn of coffee for those who wanted it.

Dill began working on his excuses for not going. In the end he knew he would have to cave in. He'd never been there, but surely he could find something at least slightly uplifting to do in Vegas to usefully fill his time.

He remembered someone had told him about Lake Mead nearby and how it had such great fishing—bass, channel catfish, stripers. He'd try to look up a tackle shop in Las Vegas and arrange to spend as much time as possible fishing, away from the happenings at Buckley's so-called seminar.

Then he thought of Jo. How would she react? Would she insist that he go? Or would he feel overwhelmed with guilt for leaving her and beg off?

Jo said he should go; she was in a better frame of mind after her recent meltdown over the loss of Corrie.

Executive Air Terminal, Denver

Dill found himself on Friday evening standing on the tarmac outside the Denver executive air terminal. He was dressed in Wranglers and scuffed cowboy boots with a duffel bag in hand, wondering how the heck he ever got in this situation. He had a tickle in his gut that was telling him nothing good was going to happen in Las Vegas. A couple times he almost turned around and left. It would be so easy to just miss the flight. Surely, they wouldn't wait for him.

In front of him were four private jets, three Gulfstreams and a Lear, engines warming, ready to leave. The big shot bank executives had been picked up earlier in the day from various cities across the continent.

He squared his shoulders and began walking toward the sky ladder hanging down from the Lear. A pretty flight attendant stood at the top to welcome him with a beverage. Alcoholic. He smiled but held up his hand, palm out. "No thanks."

Onboard, they had already started to party. It was approximately 630 air miles from Denver to Las Vegas, or about two hours flying time, but, in the first few minutes, Dill had already turned down several offered drinks and had ignored the suggestive looks from the young women and the too-friendly touch of one who ran her fingernails down his forearm as he made his way to his seat. Dill whispered a short prayer, *Parce mihi, Domine* (Spare me, Oh Lord).

As he settled into his seat and strapped on his seatbelt, Dill had a thought. He wondered if this was the used Lear they made the $3 million loan for? He couldn't remember the name of the buyer but smiled and promised himself he'd check on the registration numbers on the tail later. The plane smoothly taxied to the end of the runway for takeoff.

Gary Swope spent his last night in Denver typing up his report on the same Royal portable typewriter that had gotten him through college. It had been his high school graduation gift from his parents. Now, due to budget cuts, it was his agency typewriter.

His report was generally benign, stuff about how the bank was experiencing the normal growing pains of a new institution, working out the hiccups and bumps in the road, in order to obtain a desirable working relationship among management, bank employees and the public they served.

Much of this drivel he cribbed from the bank's glossy brochures. He'd been treated with courtesy, respect and businesslike deference by all the bank people. They seemed to be sincerely trying to work in a responsible and professional manner.

Then his report got down to the important stuff. Was the bank, in his opinion, engaging in the practice of safe and sound banking? Was Gary confident that they were, in fact, acting like a bank should act in taking the public's deposits and making loans?

Well … it was too early to tell, but the few loan files Mr. Dill Robertson, Chief Loan Officer, had shown him, all looked to be in order. Mr. Robertson had apologized that the files he had were for fairly small loans, explaining that all the paperwork for the larger loans was stored off-site.

Swope had highly recommended loan files be kept on premises. He also recommended that management seriously consider investing in new computer systems to better automate the bank's records and processing.

Bottom line of report: Larimer Square Bank bears close watching. Concern #1: Bank is taking on a large commitment with laying off loans to participating upstream correspondent banks WITH RECOURSE. Subject: bank keeps portion of loan to service for fee generation.

Concern is, if several large loans go bad at the same time, will bank have adequate capital to cover contingency? (See Concern #3, below.)

Concern #2: Bank is taking in many jumbo deposits ($100,000 government insured accounts), which agency considers to be "hot money" since intermediation of deposits seeks highest interest rate return. Subject bank is heavily loaded with such deposits.

Concern #3: Based on initial scrutiny of financial statements, will recommend that bank consider increasing its capital and reserve accounts by at least 20 percent over present level. Future Action: Will insist on scrutinizing loan portfolio, executive compensation, and loan committee notes, records and loan approvals and appropriate documentation on first formal audit by agency.

Footnote: Will also follow up on request made by examiner that bank increase its capital and reserve accounts.

It was twilight, almost dark, when the Lear left Denver Executive Airport, banked left, headed southwest and climbed over the Rockies. When he boarded, Dill hadn't noticed the three young women in the bench seat at the back of the cabin. Once they gained altitude the girls unbuckled and began moving about the cabin and serving drinks.

They wore form-fitting uniforms with short skirts. A lot of thigh and even flashes of underwear were exposed as they bent over to pass drinks to the passengers. Dill realized this was a planned move. He looked away in embarrassment as some of the passengers, senior executives in the country's top-tier banks, warmed to the attention.

Dill pulled out some files from his battered briefcase and began reading loan applications and documentation to take his mind off the spectacle.

One of the men got up to use the cramped restroom. He weaved his way, obviously smashed already. On the way back to his seat, he stopped and introduced himself to Dill, then beckoned to one of the girls to come over and meet his new friend, Dill Rockford.

The girl leaned down so her face was almost touching Dill's. He could smell her perfume: musk, the newest popular fragrance. Dill moved back slightly, but his new friend urged him to join the fun.

“You should get a little better acquainted with this little doll,” the man said loudly, breathing alcohol fumes into Dill’s face. His companions watched and laughed. The girl laid her hand on Dill’s left hand. He moved his hand enough so she could see his wedding ring.

“Oh, that’s okay,” she giggled, “I’ll bet all of these boys are married.” She turned and waved a dainty hand to the other passengers. They waved back, smiling and winking. “I’m not picky who I date,” she said as she put her hand back on his, stroking lightly.

Dill wasn’t totally naïve. He took it as a blatant invitation. He was stunned at the open way this girl talked about such intimate things. He and Jo had never discussed their private life with anyone. When they were married, they set a rule: what happens in our bedroom stays in our bedroom. It’s nobody else’s business.

Dill hesitated a second, trying to form just the right response, and said gently, “You know, maybe to you it doesn’t much matter. But I made a promise, a covenant with my wife when we were married that I would be faithful. And I have been. I don’t intend to change now. Thanks all the same.”

She responded with stony silence for a few seconds. The only sound was the muffled roar of the jets. All eyes were on Dill. He could see some shaking their heads. He knew they were probably thinking, “Party pooper.” He didn’t care.

The girl withdrew her hand from his and turned to serve someone else. She’s just doing what she was hired for, Dill thought charitably. He speculated on how many more similar offers he’d be faced with this weekend. He should have never come.

Las Vegas, Nevada

They chased the sun westward. It was just settling over some rugged mountains to the southwest of Las Vegas when they touched down smoothly at the executive airport. The western sky was streaked with vermillion from the setting sun and high, white cirrus clouds. A convoy of sleek black stretch-limos picked them up for the short ride down the Strip to the Aladdin Hotel and Casino. More of Buck’s careful planning.

"Why can't he take that much care about the loans he's approving?" Dill thought as he deplaned with the others. He managed a forced smile at the girl who'd hit on him aboard the Lear.

The revelers rolled out of their limos, looked around and stretched. A platoon of uniformed bell boys was waiting to carry their equipage to their assigned cabanas. Dill had an opportunity to size up his fellow party-goers who, in casual clothes, without their English brogues custom-made by the likes of John Lobb Bootmakers, looked quite ordinary, pretty much like a country club set headed for a Saturday morning of golf.

But once they started drinking and gambling and tasting the other enticements Sin City offered, he knew their demeanor and behavior would change. At the end of this junket would they be able to look each other in the eye with any honor? Or would there always be a shade of guilt and doubt about this weekend and how they behaved? Would they always be looking over their shoulder, worrying that someday, somewhere, one of their companions on this trip would pop up at a future social event to embarrass them in front of friends or business associates? Their wives?

Aladdin Hotel and Casino, Las Vegas

Dill started to pick up his one battered canvas overnight bag. A more nimble young bell boy beat him to it. The lad said, "This way." Dill was escorted along a winding pathway bordered by lush tropical and desert foliage, dwarf palms, stunted Loblolly pines, and bougainvillea.

They passed one of several swimming pools where lithe, tanned young women in tiny bikinis splashed and laughed together beneath the artificial lighting. Dill didn't bother to take a second look. But his bell boy did. "Pretty nice, don't you think, sir?" he casually asked. Dill didn't bother to reply.

They stopped in front of cabana number 17. The bellboy unlocked the door and ushered Dill inside. He showed Dill the bathroom, the minibar, how to operate the huge television set, and pointed out the telephone and the baffling numbers to call for anything he needed. Or wanted. The bell boy winked as he handed the room key to Dill, waited. Dill dug into his pocket and found a $5 bill, handed it over. The bellboy thanked him, touched the rim of his jaunty cap and left.

The room was dark and Dill felt closed in, stifled, so he pulled back the heavy drapes to let in some light. Satisfied, he looked around at his lodgings. The suite had been decorated in faux Flapper-era, art nouveau. Not his taste in décor, too phony.

He fussed with the thermostat, trying to adjust the air conditioning. He put his few belongings into the dresser: socks, change of underwear, extra shirts and a sweater. Just in case it was cool in the evenings.

He glanced at the itinerary he had been given when he boarded the jet in Denver. Dinner was scheduled for eight o'clock. He looked at his watch: six here in Las Vegas, an hour behind Denver.

He had time for a stroll so he pulled on the sweater, didn't bother to lock his door, and found his way through the casino where most of the bank's guests were already doing their best to burn through the complimentary stack of chips they'd been given as part of their courtesy package when they arrived.

He asked a doorman for directions to a certain shop he had in mind and found his way out the front to the Strip. He paused just long enough to get a lungful of the dry desert air, to clear out all the second-hand cigarette smoke he had been forced to inhale as he had wound his way through the casino.

Doves cooed mournfully in the tall palm trees that lined the sidewalk. Streams of traffic passed him by, tired tourists mostly from California, judging by the license plates. Convoys of tour buses with indecipherable Japanese Kanji painted on their flanks. Taxis, horns honking, all fighting for position in the choked thoroughfare.

He looked up at the bright lights, the huge cranes towering over several new hotel-casinos in the process of rising into the desert sky, each new one seemingly bigger, taller, grander than all the others. Monuments to the hordes of money-worshipers drawn to this gambling mecca. They all dreamed of hitting the big jackpot that would solve all their problems.

Dill turned right and started walking on the wide sidewalk north, weaving through crowds of strolling fun-seekers. He had never been in Las Vegas, but he needed to get out, be alone for a spell. And think. And find the shop that sold a piece of special electronic equipment he needed to buy.

TWENTY-NINE

Friday evening. Aladdin Hotel, Las Vegas

Dill returned in time to wash up and attend the dinner, which was held in a private dining room. He ordered a broiled filet, medium, with baked potato. His table mates were a different set than the ones he had flown with earlier. Introductions were made all around, they did the usual who-do-you-know routine, then settled down to trade talk and easy banter.

The discussion typically centered on the banking industry, gripes about the economy, unusually high interest rates, and the stupidity of the government.

Congress, in particular, was targeted as the source of all the bankers' woes. If only Congress would just leave their hands off the laws and regulations, they opined, life for them would be so much easier. Dill suspected this meant the mega-banks would be free to gouge the consumers even more while squeezing the small banks completely out of the market.

The talk then turned to taxes and how they were finding ways to legally lower their tax bills or avoid paying any taxes at all. Again, Congress was the culprit. If only they would leave the tax laws alone.

Dill raised a question: what did they think about the recent flood of oil and gas limited partnerships, tax shelters, hitting the market? Especially the leveraged ones, the ones financed with letters of credit? Opinions varied from: "We should avoid issuing letters of credit at all costs, as doing so would be courting disaster" to "Think of the fees we're getting that add to our bottom line."

"But," someone asked, "what if the bank issuing the LC failed, who was left holding the bag? Someone else interjected, "What if the driller doesn't find oil and the investor would then be obligated to make good on his letter of credit? Weren't there going to be a lot of ticked-off investors?"

Another banker jumped into the debate with, "Right. And those investors usually can afford high-priced lawyers to try and get them off the petard of their own greed and stupidity and sue everyone in sight. Including the bank that issued their LC and the bank financing the drilling program!"

The banker on his left turned to Dill and asked, "What do you think? Dill, isn't it?"

Dill weighed his words carefully and registered his thoughtful response. "I'm concerned that we, our country, have created a huge oil bubble that is fast becoming overheated and is someday going to burst. I've always been skeptical of speculation, and I see a lot of speculation, even among our banking fraternity." He looked around. Some were frowning. That's not exactly what they wanted to hear. Who is this Jeremiah, anyway? I hear he's just some obscure small-town banker who's on the make with this Larimer Square Bank crowd.

Dill went on. "I'm afraid we're making too many loans that may be unsafe."

A banker across the table challenged him. "Give me an example. We signed on to this scheme of yours."

Dill raised his hands in a defensive gesture and protested, "It's not *my* scheme. Let's make that really clear. I didn't dream up this program."

"Okay, your bank, then. Anyway, we think we're feeling pretty safe and secure with our position. Your bank has the final liability if any of those loans go bad that you're laying off on us."

Dill didn't hesitate. "Just yesterday I reviewed one of our loan files. Two million dollars for a drilling lease of a section, that's 640 acres. Ordinarily, in normal times, a prudent banker wouldn't touch a loan request based on a mineral lease. But this one was supported by a reputable petroleum engineering firm in Houston, I won't disclose the name."

"Oh, I think we know!" someone piped up. The others nodded and chuckled.

Dill continued: "Anyway, this reputable petroleum engineering firm went out on a limb and decided, in their expert opinion, that the lease was worth X dollars based on projected oil prices at $85 to $100 a barrel. $85 to $100!" He let that sink in.

He went on: "And … and, based on *probable* reserves in the ground of Y million barrels. Not proven, by the usual standard that somebody has drilled and tested various formations and made a well and it's now pumping zed barrels per day on a decline curve of etc., etc."

Dill folded his hands and went silent, gazing around the assembled faces. "How many of you boys have even peeked inside the loan portfolios that have been sent up to you to fund? Now answer honestly: Under normal conditions would you loan on the kind of lease I just described?" A few scratched their heads, others furrowed a brow. A couple looked away, they couldn't meet Dill's honest brown eyes.

For his part, Dill wondered if he'd made any sense to them. These fellows were seasoned bankers, charged with the duty to protect the public's deposits and apply prudent banking practices in using those deposits in the wisest and safest way possible.

The dessert menu came and, to avoid Dill's searching eyes, they all quickly scanned their menus. The rest ordered coffee or cappuccino and cognac; Dill ordered vanilla ice cream. He went wild and added, "With a dollop of chocolate syrup."

Cabana Seventeen, the Aladdin Hotel

Dill was in his pajamas, sheepskin slippers and bathrobe, just starting a new Tony Hillerman novel, when there was a soft knock on the door.

Dill had to strain to hear as a quiet voice on the other side of the door said, "Room service." A female voice.

Dill was puzzled; he hadn't ordered anything. He got up and went to the door.

As his eyes tried to adjust to the change in lighting Dill was surprised to see the young flight attendant who had hit on him earlier. She was dressed in a terry robe, that was pulled off her shoulders and open in the front, revealing only a very tiny bikini underneath.

She smiled and said, "Remember me?" as she reached up with both arms around his neck, quickly pulled him to her and, before he could push her away, planted the most voluptuous kiss he could remember. He pulled her arms down, trying to wipe her coral lipstick off his mouth. It tasted like peaches and cream.

She disengaged, backed away, pulled her robe onto her shoulders tied the sash. She gave a bubbly laugh and quickly retreated into the shadows. "Sorry, wrong room, I guess," she called over her shoulder from cover of darkness.

In the shadows, strategically positioned behind a dwarf palm, Lucky had been squatting in the perfect spot. He got the entire encounter on super-fast black and white film with the latest Nikon high-speed camera. He also carried highly sensitive recording device, the kind favored by police detectives and FBI agents. He had been squatting from a perfect angle and he got it all.

Dill stood dumbly in the doorway framed in the room's backlight, wondering just what in Hades happened? Back in his cabana, after he wiped off the lipstick with a tissue, he settled down again to read his novel but couldn't focus his mind. He put down the book and tried to reconstruct what had just happened.

Out of long habit he took out a notebook and pen and began to write. He wrote down a memo to himself with all the details he could recall while they were still fresh in his memory. This memo just might come in handy someday, if…

If what? Was this a setup? Was she really attracted to him, trying to tempt him into sinning? Or was the girl just trying to get back at him? He did embarrass her on the flight when he'd turned her down. In front of several people. Something in his gut was telling him this was dangerous and to be very careful. He couldn't put his finger on why he should be careful, or what he was to be careful of. The voice in his head was just saying be careful.

Saturday morning. Dill woke early from a restless night. He actually never got a deep restful sleep but had turned things over endlessly while trying to drift off. A couple of wakeful times during the night he considered calling JoEllen and unloading his doubts and frustrations on her but then thought better of it. She needed her rest more than he did. In the early hours before dawn he did come to one firm decision: no more client schmoozing trips like this; let Buck and Seth Summers play the party hosts. This high life wasn't for him.

Another partial decision crept into the front of his thoughts: he needed to find a graceful way to step out of this situation he was in and get some distance from it and himself. If all went well, Jo would soon be finished with her treatments. It was looking like she had licked this thing, was clean of the rotten cells and would get the okay to go home. There was really no longer any good reason to hang on at the bank.

Home. He ached right now to be back in their old solid, sandstone ranch house with its huge fireplace, pine plank flooring, mostly hairless cowhide rugs randomly thrown around. Elk antlers over the fireplace. He thought of Thanksgiving days past. After a rough competitive game of touch football Jo would call them indoors to dinner.

They would all gather around the huge dining room table groaning under a load of turkey and all the trimmings, joining hands as a family and saying thanks for their abundant blessings. It was less than a week until the holiday and he would move the earth to be there with Jo and their four lovely sons. Dill wiped at the moisture in his eyes with the back of his hand.

But how to leave without your backside exposed? He was more than concerned, knew deep inside that Larimer Square Bank was a train wreck waiting to happen. Train wrecks sometimes smashed innocent bystanders as well.

The dilemma for Dill was how to protect not only himself from being dragged down with it when it imploded, but to also protect the people he had come to love. The people he worked with, the little people who showed up every day and tried their best to do a good job.

The eager-faced kids in the Bullpen. After working with them all these months he realized he truly cared for them.

What was it that Jo had said when they had had this conversation just before he left on this disaster of a trip? He had said something like he always wanted to be found on the right side of this experience. And he'd wondered if there even was a right side.

And she had said, "Oh, yes, there's a right side; there's always a right side. You just have to look for it."

And he had asked, "Where's the right side in this fiasco? Tell me that."

And she had said something like, "The right side is where you are always kind to the people around you, no matter what happens to yourself. In the end that's the only sure test. And I know you. You're always kind to your people. That's why they sometimes take advantage of you."

Then she had read him a little poem written on a get-well card a friend had sent. It went something like this:

There are things you do because they are right.
They may make no sense
& they may make no money
& it may be the real reason we are here:
To love each other
& to eat each other's cooking
& say it was good.

And he had nodded, admitting she was right.

Their talk turned to strategies but didn't come to any firm plan because he ran out of time and had to leave for Las Vegas.

But in his wrestling with sleep, he had come to a few conclusions as to what JoEllen would advise him to do.

THIRTY

Breakfast, Aladdin Hotel

Dill showered, shaved, splashed some bay rum on his face and pulled a fresh shirt on and tucked it into his Wranglers. He sniffed his socks and decided they needed changing too. He felt somewhat rejuvenated as he stepped out into the early morning desert air, already warming.

This climate disoriented him. Late autumn and it should feel downright frigid, cold enough for frosted grass to crunch underfoot and a roughout sheepskin coat to keep you warm. Here, it was warm enough to swim, even at this early hour. What a place.

Yet, a lot of people found this was the perfect place to retire. He was told they were moving into the Las Vegas metro area by the hundreds daily.

Land speculators and developers were going crazy while getting rich. They couldn't build apartments, condos and single homes fast enough. Prices were going through the roof. Now this was where a bank could render a real service, making solid loans backed by mortgages. Not these shaky deals he had been party to. Dill shook his shoulders to ward off a sudden chill and pushed his guilt down to a hidden chamber inside and locked the door.

Dill made his way to the private dining room where a few early risers were already filling their plates with breakfast from steamers loaded on a long side table. Dill chose a plate of French toast, slathered it with butter and real Vermont maple syrup and spooned up a side of scrambled eggs with two strips of crisp bacon. At his place at the table he found a goblet of fresh-squeezed orange juice.

At his table were already seated a few men he hadn't met yet. He nodded to them and sat down to try and enjoy what he had decided was his last meal in Las Vegas. Right after breakfast he planned on taking a commercial flight back to Denver, hang the cost. They could all have their so-called fun on their private jets. He was through with that stuff.

He was just forking a large bite of French toast into his mouth when he felt a lusty slap on his back. He almost choked on the food. This was accompanied by Buck's booming voice.

"There you are, you rascal! How'd you like your little bedtime treat last night? She's a special little honey. I reserved her just for you!" The other men grinned and nodded knowingly. All eyes were on Dill waiting to see how he'd react.

Dill pushed his plate aside and slowly rose, turned to tower over Calvin Buckley. Their knees were almost touching. Buck took a step back when he saw a look in Dill's eyes he had never noticed before. There was danger there. Controlled danger, but danger still. He wasn't sure what was coming next. He waited.

Then he noticed Dill had his hands balled into fists. Buck fully expected this large cowpuncher to clock him right there in public. Buck's mouth felt dry and cottony. Dill relaxed, let his hands loosen and leaned close to Buck's ear. Dill's bay rum mixed with Buck's own tobacco-soaked sweat.

Dill whispered, "This is now a private matter and we'll settle it outside. Follow me. Now …"

Buck swallowed hard, followed—more like, jogged—after Dill as the big man strode angrily through the casino and out front onto the Strip. Even at 8:00 on a Saturday morning, traffic was choking all lanes, moving slowly, horns honking. Dill turned and faced Buck. He spoke so softly Buck had to lean in to hear over the traffic noise.

"So, it was you, Mr. Buckley. I should have guessed. That wasn't such a dirty thing you did to me, but I feel for that young lady. What does that make her? I'll tell you what. It makes her cheap, filthy. Turns her into a word I don't even want to use."

Buckley recoiled, raised both hands, palms out, defensive, and tried to protest. Dill waved him off, "I'm not finished yet. I haven't really started on you. You were probably going to say she was just a nice college girl working her way through school and needed the money, right?"

"Yeah, something like that, I guess," Buck demurred.

"I thought so. And what does that make you? You're no better than a sleazy panderer."

"Now wait a minute."

"No, you wait. I'm barely getting going with you." Dill stopped for a breath and punched Buck in the chest with a strong forefinger. "Here's the bottom line, Buckley: I'm done with you. Done with Seth Summers and all his grandiose plans and promises. I'm done with trying to follow you around and clean up your messes. I'm done with worrying about how many of those loans are going to come crashing back on this underfunded two-bit bank and mash all of you like cockroaches. I am done."

Buckley took a step back and tried charm. He smiled broadly and said, "Aw come on. What's wrong? Why can't you just loosen up and have a little harmless fun. You know what your problem is? You're too uptight to know fun when it hits you smack in the face."

Dill was momentarily stunned. Was his mouth gaping?

Buckley continued his monologue, "For once in your life, why don't you stop playin' the mock cowboy and take a real drink? Just lay back, get a full body massage from what's her name. Nobody's gonna know what happens here. It all stays behind closed doors, buddy."

Dill didn't know whether to laugh, be insulted or raise the level of his anger. He let it go. Back to the subject. "I'm not your buddy! We were talking about shaky loans. Recourse, Buck. Focus on that one word. Recourse!"

"Ain't nothin' wrong with those loans, all good collateral."

"I call bull! Oil leases with flaky engineering reports stating millions of barrels, probable reserves. Yes, probable, not proven. Is that what you call good solid collateral? Any prudent banker would toss that borrower out on the street! And another thing, how many of those loans you make are to your buddies who cut you in on some kind of shady deal?"

Buckley blinked, tried to swallow. He looked sideways for an escape from this madman. How much did Robertson know? He could become real dangerous. Already was.

Dill barely stopped for another breath. "I've done a little research and your name keeps popping up on quite a few little oilfield service companies. Like water hauling, fracking, chemicals, drill bits, work over rigs, pipe supply companies. The list goes on. Am I getting warm?"

For a split-second, Buckley looked stricken, then quickly tried resuming a deadpan expression.

Dill paused, realized he had a fleck of foamy spittle on his lip. He wiped at it.

Buckley was cornered but saw an opening. "Okay, okay, I get it." He grinned lopsidedly.

"Get what?"

"You want in on the action." He rubbed a forefinger and thumb together. "That's what this is all about, isn't it? You're fishing for a piece of the pie. Okay, what's it gonna take to make you happy? How much are you asking?"

Dill was stunned, confused, shook his head in wonder. What was this guy saying? Didn't make sense or seem to have anything to do with the conversation.

Buckley forged ahead. "Look, I'm prepared to make you a deal. I'll … we'll, that is, Seth and me, we'll cut you in for a share. How does 20 percent of what we get sound to you? Course we'll each keep our 40 percent. What do you say?"

This slimy little crook is trying to bribe me! Dill wasted no time turning him down flat. "If that's an offer of a bribe, which is how I took it, the answer is no. Nope. Not on your life. Not interested. I'm leaving. Thanks for a really good time." Dill turned and walked away.

"Oh, I get it, the old used car salesman's walk-away ploy. Think I'll up the offer, huh?" Buck shouted after him.

Dill didn't turn, just waved him off.

"You're gonna regret this, Richardson. You'll be really sorry. Someday you'll look back and wish you hadn't walked away from a fat hog deal!"

Dill didn't hear any more, as he disappeared back into the casino. He left an angry, frustrated Calvin Buckley standing alone on Las Vegas Boulevard in front of the Aladdin Hotel and Casino. Buck looked around to make sure none of his fat-cat banker guests hadn't heard any of this heated exchange

But somebody was listening. After Dill had gone down a long hallway and turned a corner and was sure Buckley wasn't following, he reached inside his Levi jacket and turned off the mini cassette recorder hidden in his shirt pocket.

Back in his room he clicked the little machine on and played back every word of the exchange. It was clear enough to hear and Dill was certain it would someday make good evidence.

He removed the little cassette, shoved it in his jeans pocket and tucked the new recorder into his canvas tote. He picked up his room phone and called the concierge for a taxi to McCarran International. He'd soon be aboard a commercial flight back to Denver. And he'd be glad to pay the fare out of his own pocket.

Once there, while waiting to board, Dill used a pay phone and dialed a number he'd written in his Day-Timer three years previous. He waited while he heard the call buzzing intermittently several times on the other end.

Finally, a voice answered, "FBI. Special Agent Nieve."

Seth Summers's Suite, the Aladdin Hotel

Calvin Buckley was panicked, terrified. He was desperate to track down Seth Summers. They had to talk. Buck found him walking alone through the casino, greeting their guests, chatting them up. Seth was dressed casually, but still in elegantly tailored clothes: gray flannel slacks, black cashmere turtleneck pullover, a light gray checked silk-and-wool sport jacket, black suede slip-ons with gold buckles.

Buckley rushed up to Summers, gripped his elbow. "We need to talk. Somewhere private. Right now."

Seth could see that Buckley was upset, agitated about something. Seth smelled trouble. "Let's go back to my room," he calmly said.

"Excuse us, gentlemen." Seth strolled casually while Buck fidgeted with his room key. Buck followed him to a luxurious penthouse suite.

Seth motioned for Buck to sit while he poured an inch of rare single-malt scotch into each of two cut-glass tumblers. "Ice?" he asked. Buck shook his head as he dropped heavily into a leather wing chair opposite Summers. Seth picked up two ice cubes with silver tongs and dropped them into his own glass. Then he added an ounce of bottled water, swished his glass and lifted it, sniffed the contents, breathed deeply, let out an audible sigh. He handed Buck his drink. They raised their glasses and touched the rims in a salute. Seth sat down in a plush easy chair opposite Buck and draped one long leg over the other, smoothed the crease in his pants. Their knees were almost touching. Buckley squirmed.

Summers sipped his drink slowly, savoring it, while Buckley gulped his down in one big swallow. Summers set his glass on a leather coaster, crossed an elegantly tailored leg over the other, leaned slightly forward and said, "What's on your mind, Calvin?" Summers rarely called Buckley by his Christian name.

He's acting cool and calm, but he knows something serious is up, Buckley thought. Seth refilled Buckley's drink and waited for Buckley to spill his guts. Buckley took another huge gulp of the expensive rare liquid, almost choked on it, noisily cleared his throat, and said, "We've got a huge problem." He held out his glass for a refill.

"And what might that be?" Seth refilled the glass and waited while Buckley took another big sip. A sloppy drinker, Seth mused.

"It's that jerk Rossman."

"Robertson," Seth corrected. Buck impatiently waved away the correction.

"Whatever. Well, that no-good turncoat, your carefully chosen chief loan officer, has turned chicken on us." Buck paused for breath.

"Explain."

Buck let it all out, including the part where he had tried to buy off Dill.

Seth couldn't believe what he was hearing. "You what? Do you have any idea the damage you've done? You stupid, freaking idiot!"

Now it was Seth's turn to fidget. He suddenly got up and began pacing around the room, prowling like a lion.

"I didn't think it would hurt, Seth. He had me cornered," Buck whined.

"So, instead of thinking, engaging your pea brain before you spoke, you took the coward's way out. You should always consult with me first. Always. I'm the brain trust, the strategist in this little operation. Not you, not anyone else. Me! Do you understand that?"

Buck nodded limply.

Seth paced for a few more minutes deep in thought. His shoulders sort of hunched forward, his chin was cupped in one hand. Then he seemed to cool down as he stopped, refreshed his drink and took a sip.

"Damage control. That's the first thing. Damage control."

Buck nodded but didn't have a clue what Summers had in mind.

Seth picked up the house phone and dialed a number. "Operator? Yes, I'd like an outside line please." He waited a few seconds, then, "Thank you."

Seth punched a button and the phone was suddenly on speaker. Buck recoiled as the intermittent buzzing on the other end woke him out of his self-pitying stupor. Someone on the other end picked up.

"Boss?"

"Hello, Lucky, I have a little job for you."

"Speak to me," a deep hoarse, smoker's voice replied with a nasty chuckle.

"Did you get the pictures developed?"

"Yes, Boss."

"Have them delivered to my room. Plain brown envelope. Then we'll discuss a little project I have in mind for you."

THIRTY-ONE

FDIC, Kansas City. Saturday

Even though it was the weekend, Gary Swope went in to his office. He punched in the door code and let himself in. Only the maintenance people were there, Latinos or Blacks—minimum wage folks—mopping, sweeping, dusting, emptying trash. Gary clicked on the light to his cramped space and sat down. He set his Coke and a bag of Fritos on his desk and pondered. Then he made a decision.

Something had been nagging at him on the drive home from Denver. All the way back he'd turned over in his mind the bizarre experience at Larimer Square Bank. Something was out of focus in the picture he saw. But he couldn't quite put his finger on what it was. He needed help from someone with more experience. Monday he'd ask Max if they could have a chat and go over his so-called audit. He'd confront the thing that was bothering him. He'd leave nothing out.

When Gary was a new trainee, Max Watts had once told him that the gathering of facts and data was the first and correct approach to his job, but that sometimes it pays to follow your gut, your hunches. "That's why we have eyes and ears," his boss had said. They help gather what he called the *other* facts and data, details that then get stored away in a part of our brain. They may be little, insignificant things to you, but our brain takes them in and stores them anyway.

The other part of our brain, the one that controls our hunches, then sometime later comes knocking on the closed data door and asks to come in and visit. The two parts of the brain then compare notes and the hunches part walks out with a clearer picture of what has been going on.

Gary hadn't expressed his doubts at the time about this wacky notion. Gary was an accountant. His life was facts and figures. He had minored in math, he loved math, relied on the cold logic of math, the purity of science. Hunches were foreign to Gary's way of thinking.

But that cracker barrel chat came back to him now and he thought: What would be the harm in following my hunches?

Denver International Airport

Dill's plane touched down in Denver at a little after noon Saturday. He had to take a shuttle bus over to the executive terminal where he'd left his truck. Nobody had bothered his fly rod in the back. He wasted no time getting to the hospital where he told JoEllen about his trip.

She was frankly surprised to see him back early but wasn't upset when he explained his reason. He told her everything. Well, almost everything. He left out the part about the surprise kiss at the cabana door. The peaches and cream kiss. Some things are better left unsaid. At least for now. He'd tell her later when the time was right. Except for that, and the episode involving the little cassette in his pocket, Dill let it all out.

"So … what do you think?" he asked.

"Wow. And you told them you were leaving? Does that mean now?"

Dill nodded.

"You know what? I'm feeling so much better today and I think they'll clear me to go home in a day or so. Won't it be wonderful to be back home for Thanksgiving?"

Dill agreed. Then he got up to leave.

"You have to go so soon?" she pleaded.

"I have an appointment with an old friend at two o'clock. He's doing me a big favor to meet on a Saturday afternoon."

"Old friend? Do I know him? Or her?" Jo smiled when Dill blushed. He hoped there was no lingering whiff on him of the girl's musk fragrance from the previous night's close encounter. Jo had a sensitive nose.

"Chris Nieve. FBI agent. You remember him from that attempted heist at our bank three years ago?" Jo nodded as a cloud came over her lovely countenance. Dill was so happy to see color in her face, the natural rosy hue returning to her cheeks, light and sparkle in her blue eyes. For a moment he'd spoiled that beauty by burdening her with his troubles. But soon it would be behind them. He sincerely hoped.

"Be careful," Jo pleaded as he kissed her goodbye and left for his appointment.

Saturday Afternoon. FBI Offices, Denver

Cristobal "Chris" Nieve was born in the USA. He was born into a Mexican family who lived in a little town on the Mexican side of the border, across from a sister town in Texas, a couple hours south of Corpus Christi. His parents had crossed for work into the United States and back to their home in Mexico so many times that the border people on each side no longer bothered to ask for identity cards. Mrs. Nieve, who claimed she was half-Irish, often gave the border guards fresh pork or chicken tamales she made especially for them. His father was Mexican. Nieve in Spanish meant *snow.*

The Nieve family sought work in the fields in the rich farming valley on the U.S. side. There was little or no work on the Mexican side, so they gratefully accepted the below-minimum wages they were paid. Always in cash. That was okay because it was easy to exchange dollars for pesos and vice versa. Depending on which side you were.

Why was Cristobal called "Chris" and why was he born in the USA? His mother, nine months pregnant at the time, was working on the U.S. side when she went into labor (no pun intended). There was no time to get back to Mexico. So, little Cristobal was a U.S. citizen by reason of his birth, the only one in his large family to claim that privileged status.

His mother favored calling him Chico, while his father favored the formal Cristobal. Growing up in a big family he answered to either or both. As he grew, they realized he was very athletic, a fast runner. He excelled in organized sports and lettered in three sports in high school. He came in second in the 440 on the regional level and earned a beautiful silver medal. Ever fiercely competitive, he so badly wanted the gold first place.

In high school, his jock buddies, mostly *gringos*, gave him the nickname that stuck: *Snowball.* It was an amalgam of two words: snow (his last name in English) and the last part of his Christian name: bal. He preferred Chris.

Chris Nieve enlisted in the Marines right out of high school and was sent to Vietnam where he served two tours. On the second tour he was transferred from being a grunt infantry rifleman into an MP unit. He quickly took to the law enforcement duties.

When he came out of the Marines he knew for certain where he was headed. First, college on the GI Bill, majoring in law enforcement, followed by the FBI academy. He graduated first in his class at Quantico and eventually ended up in the FBI's Denver office.

Chris embraced Dill like they were long lost friends while his partner, Agent Cecilia Beardsley, "just call me Sissy for short," looked on, bemused. So, it was the Chris and Sissy team. Whatever. Just so long as they lock up the bad guys, Summers and Buckley and that rotten gang of crooks.

Chris offered Dill coffee and quickly apologized. "I forgot you're a Mormon. Sorry." Dill shrugged like it happened all the time and he wasn't offended. He asked for bottled water. Agent Sissy left and soon returned with three bottles.

They quickly got down to business. Nieve mentioned that Agent Sissy was a Columbia Law grad. She flipped some pages on her yellow legal pad and poised her pen to take notes. Nieve asked if it was okay if they recorded their interview and Dill agreed. Nieve flipped the start switch on a highly sophisticated recording device.

"You have the tape?"

Dill handed it over.

"And you're sure he wasn't aware you were recording?"

"I hope it's legal," Dill said.

"We'll let the U.S. Attorney's office struggle with that one. Agent, your opinion?" Nieve turned to his partner.

Sissy had short sun-bleached blonde hair, gray eyes that were almost purple, an athlete's wiry body and a lot of freckles on her upturned nose and tanned face. She struck Dill as an outdoorsy type who probably hated to be cooped up inside. He could relate.

Agent Sissy quietly explained: "The law is pretty clear. A string of recent appellate court cases have confirmed that it's legal, that is, the evidence is usually admissible, if at least one party, that would be you, Mr. Robertson, is aware the conversation is being taped or electronically recorded. It seems to me we can count this as evidence. Depending …" She hesitated.

"Depending on what it contains," Nieve finished, "and if it has anything incriminating, we can build a case on."

Dill nodded his understanding.

"Well, let's listen in. Shall we?" Chris said as he inserted the little cassette tape into another port in his new government machine and pushed yet another start button. The audio was surprisingly clear. They listened intently as the tape ran. Agent Sissy took copious notes, scribbling furiously.

When it was done, Chris rewound the tape and they listened again. This time he stopped the tape at certain points to ask Dill questions that would clarify the conversation.

When they were finished listening, Agent Nieve got up and paced around the little interview room. He turned and faced Dill, waiting for him to speak.

"What do you think? Am I in any trouble?" Dill asked.

Chris chose his words carefully. "I'd say you're in danger, not trouble. We ran a search on both Seth Summers and Calvin Buckley before you came in. Based on what we found, which is confidential, ongoing investigation and all that. You know the drill …" Nieve let it just hang there. Dill waited.

"Let's just say we think this is serious enough stuff that we're going to assign an agent to shadow you. You probably won't see him or her, but they'll be close by. Just in case."

“Just in case,” Dill repeated.

“In the meantime, just act normal, business as usual, no dumb moves or snooping unless we ask you to help us retrieve information or documents, or …”

“Another clandestine recording.” Dill finished Chris’s sentence. Chris nodded. Dill swallowed hard.

Dill left their meeting with a sick feeling in the pit of his stomach.

Halfway back to the hospital it hit him: they hadn’t mentioned a shadow for JoEllen. He wasn’t too worried about himself. He could probably handle any threats by himself. But Jo was vulnerable, a sitting duck.

FBI Special Agent Chris Nieve and Agent Sissy Beardsley methodically opened a new case file with the title on the tab: LARIMER SQUARE BANK – 10/1980. They began to draw up a checklist and discussed names of agents they would bring into the investigation.

All the agents on their team were experienced in white collar crime investigations, but had little experience with inside bank fraud being committed by officers or directors. Nieve kept coming back to one agent he would surely ask for: Randy Simpson, a CPA presently seconded to the SEC. Simpson had the determination of a bulldog, the amazing ability to memorize facts and figures, an extraordinary recall. Most of all, he had a track record of being able to follow the money through the myriad offshore banks, corporations, nominees, fronts and cutouts until he located the poison fruits of the crime hiding in secret accounts.

Chris was confident the SEC would loan Simpson to them for the duration of the investigation and later as a grand jury witness. Simpson would also make a good witness if the case later ever went to trial.

But Nieve was counting on a quicker solution: he would make one of the Larimer-Summers-Buckley gang, as he now called them, sing and turn on the others. He knew they would if he offered them the right incentives. But first, he assigned an agent to shadow Dill Robertson.

THIRTY-TWO

Dill's Room, Denver

Later that same Saturday evening, Dill was stretched out on the sofa in his extended-stay hotel suite where he had been camping for a couple months. He was now trying to get some much-needed rest. And camping was the right word. He only slept there and occasionally spent a little time when he could no longer endure the frenzy of Larimer Square Bank or the cloistered misery of the hospital.

He rarely cooked, maybe made some hot chocolate, ramen, or instant soup. Mostly ate out. That is, when he even bothered to eat. He had lost weight, had cinched up his belt a couple notches to keep his pants up. He still kept the bed in Jo's room. Just in case. But in a few days, this would all be over. They could go home, and try to pick up the pieces of their nearly shattered lives.

He was mostly worried about his boys. He had managed to get home a few times for hastily snatched weekends. In the meantime, they had been watched over, fed and nurtured by one of Dill's sisters, the widowed one. But he knew it wasn't the same thing as having both parents there.

Mom should be there when they came home from school in the afternoon. Dad should be there at night when it was time to do homework and prepare for bed. He missed the little chats he had with each son when they were finally bedding down for the night.

He knew from their frequent phone calls that they missed their mom. "How's mom doing? When does she get to come home?" He hoped they missed him, too.

Dill was watching his alma mater, the University of Colorado Buffs playing their annual football grudge match with Nebraska. A home game. Right now, the Huskers were up by a field goal with less than three minutes to play.

Nebraska had just kicked off. The Buffs had managed to return the ball to nearly midfield. Dill saw a glimmer of hope. Maybe this was the year the Buffs would win, wouldn't experience the shame of being crushed again. If only Colorado had a better defense and a better quarterback. They had a fair offensive line and seemed to be opening some holes for their excellent running back. Now if he can just keep from being injured. "And hold onto the danged ball!" Dill shouted at the screen.

Right then, the phone rang. Only a couple people had his number. He picked it up and cautiously said, "Robertson."

The voice on the other end had a definite twang. "Mr. Robinson? You don't know me, but I'm Ricky Bob Peabody and I'd like to talk to you all about a loan. I was referred by my old bank The Tulsa Guaranty Trust. That's in Tulsa. Oklahoma."

Dill nodded. He knew where Tulsa was and he knew who the Tulsa Guaranty Bank was. The name Peabody rang some bells. Peabody, Peabody. Aha.

"Peabody Oil?"

"Yessir, that's me all right. When can I come and see you all?"

"Don't you already have a loan outstanding with us?" Dill reached for the rarely used pad and pen he kept close to the phone.

"Yessir, I believe that's right. I think I'm current with you all on that loan?" It was a question.

"Yes, I believe you are," said Dill from memory. "You want to increase your line of credit, is that what you're seeking to do?"

"Well, it's a totally different deal. See, I have this partnership with some fundraisers out of Salt Lake City, some Mormon guys. And we have a shot at some of that deep gas in the Anadarko. You familiar with the Anadarko, Mr. Robinson?"

Dill nodded at the phone.

Ricky Bob continued, "Well, I'm aiming to drill that deep sonnagun but I need funds. And a rig …"

"I see. Why do you need to buy one? Why not lease a rig? I know it's an article of faith among you Oilies that you're not much of a man if you don't have your own rig, but …"

Ricky Bob laughed. "You sure nailed that one, yessir! Well, here's the thing, maybe we should meet and I can explain it to you."

Dill was trying to watch the game. The sound was turned way down. "Hot dang! We won, we won! I can't believe it, we won!"

"You watchin' a football game? I thought I heard a TV in the background. I used to play for OU. Back in the day. Before I got injured. Who you cheerin' for?"

"The Buffs of course. We just beat the Huskers with a last second Hail Mary pass. To our running back. All alone in the corner of the end zone. Game over."

"Sounds like you know your football."

"My oldest son played linebacker for University of Wyoming. My second-youngest too. Second string running back. I haven't seen even one of his games this year. Too busy," Dill offered sadly.

"That's too bad," Ricky Bob responded. There was an awkward moment of silence. Then Ricky Bob tried to nail the appointment. "Well, what do ya say, can we meet and talk about my loan?"

"How much does a rig like that cost, around three million?"

Ricky Bob laughed. "Oh no, sir. This baby will cost above six million, seven all fitted out with proper valves, pumps, super heavy diesels, the whole enchilada."

Dill whistled softly. "What are you doing Monday afternoon? Can you fly up here for a meeting at about three?"

"Well sir, I already drove myself here. I'm in Denver. Stayin' at the Hilton."

Dill had a sudden inspiration. "What's your number there? I need to make a couple of calls and then I'll get back to you a bit later. That all right with you?"

"You bet. I'll be waiting for your call. And thanks, y'all."

After he hung up, Ricky Bob did a little victory dance and high fived the air in his hotel room.

Dill laughed to himself as he rang off. His next call was to FBI Special Agent Chris Nieve.

"Chris, Agent Nieve? Dill Robertson here. I have an idea. I think I've found some bait for the trap."

"Care to elaborate?"

After Dill unfolded his idea and they hung up, Nieve explained the plan to Agent Sissy. She began immediately typing into her computer: Ricky Bob Peabody. Peabody Oil. Tulsa Guaranty Bank.

Nieve called in his technology guys to begin setting up the wire they would conceal on Ricky Bob Peabody.

First Nieve needed to make a call to the U.S. Attorney on his private weekend line. Agent Nieve briefly explained the need for a wiretap warrant. The lawyers kicked the process into high gear.

Agent Sissy took a few minutes away from her computer to fax over a transcript to the U.S. Attorney of the recorded conversation Dill had made with Buckley, together with the FBI's transcript of their interview with Dill Robertson.

The government lawyers knew a friendly U.S. District Court judge who just happened to be on duty that weekend. The judge was a Colorado Law alum. Now that the Big Game was over, U.S. Attorney Ryan Henning was confident the judge would quickly sign the warrant. Hopefully with just a mere scintilla of questions.

On Sunday morning, Henning sent one of his assistant lawyers to get the signature. She was professionally dressed in a beige pantsuit and ankle-length suede boots with high heels. She found the judge partaking of Sunday brunch at his country club with his wife and several friends. He was friendly and in a fine mood. After inviting her to join their meal, which she graciously declined, the judge motioned for her to sit, which she did.

He wanted to know all about her. Where did she grow up? Where she did she go to law school? Did she like the practice of law. Having answered his questions, the judge beckoned for her to hand over the petition for the search warrant. He put on his half-moon reading glasses and began to read quietly. The young attorney waited patiently as the judge meticulously read the petition for the search warrant. "I want to be sure it's in compliance within the rules of criminal procedure and statutory guidelines." It had been.

His Honor loved playing the part of a law professor. To the curious faces of his wife and friends, he explained what the petition was and what they were doing there that morning. He was careful not to divulge any details of the case presented to him. He touched briefly on the principle of probable cause for the search and what that meant in the law.

The young assistant U.S. attorney managed to hide her concern over what seemed an undue scrutiny. The judge finally assured all listening that he was satisfied the search was warranted and asked for a pen. One of his friends loaned him a burgundy-and-gold Montblanc fountain pen. He made one interlineation, printing in the word *forthwith*, then signed the document with a flourish. He wished the young woman well in her career. "I look forward to seeing you in my courtroom someday soon." She thanked His Honor properly and scuttled out of the dining room, holding her breath.

She raced toward her yellow motor scooter parked outside. Reaching the parking lot, she exhaled a huge sigh of relief. She carefully put her leather messenger bag containing the signed search warrant in one of the scooter's saddlebags. Then hopped on, donned her helmet, and sat for a minute, letting her heartbeat slow down to normal. She kicked the scooter into action and buzzed back to the U.S. attorney's office, weaving skillfully in and out of the stream of Sunday drivers heading west for the mountains. The weather forecast had promised one last glorious autumn weekend before savage winter storms would assault the Front Range again.

The judge never said anything about one Ricky Bob Peabody, citizen-turned-FBI-informant, using a hidden body wire at the behest of the FBI, to try and catch a suspected bank fraud scammer named Calvin Buckley. All that information had been set forth in detail in the petition for the search warrant, together with the facts underlying the *probable cause*—the legal basis the FBI needed the wire on Ricky Bob.

Monday morning. Hilton Hotel, Golden, Colorado

Ricky Bob finished shaving, patted on some Brut cologne and turned on the TV to NBC Morning News. He listened while he dressed. He put on his best—his only—navy blazer, freshly pressed khakis, a blue button-down shirt and looked at the two ties he had brought along. Both had stains and were getting a little worn. Thinking that a necktie was a bit too much, he dispensed with wearing one.

He quickly tired of the news and turned off the TV. He switched on the clock radio by his bed, twisted some knobs and found a country station. Linda Ronstadt was singing "Blue Bayou." Ricky hummed along. In spite of his anxiety, he was feeling pretty good this morning as he stood in front of the bathroom mirror, practicing the pitch he wanted to deliver to Mr. Robertson.

A loud knock on the door interrupted his monologue. Who could that be? He went to the door, "Yeah, what is it?"

"Room service."

Ricky Bob had not ordered room service. He was planning to eat in the hotel coffee shop downstairs. He hesitated, then opened the door and peeked over the safety chain. Standing in the hall outside his door were two men dressed in dark suits, white shirts and conservative neckties.

The closest one to Ricky softly said "Mr. Peabody? Ricky Bob Peabody? FBI. May we have a word? Inside?"

He flashed a badge. Ricky noticed the bulge under his left armpit, obviously a shoulder holster.

Ricky Bob's mouth went dry. He tried to swallow but got cotton instead of moisture. He released the chain and safety catch, stepped back and motioned them in. His mind was racing. What had he done to warrant a visit from the FBI?

The agents introduced themselves and asked if they could all sit down for a little chat. Ricky motioned to the couch. The lead agent, whose name was Harold Ethington, sat and his partner stayed standing halfway to the door. Ricky took one of the easy chairs. His knees were almost touching the FBI agent seated directly across from him. Easy chair! What irony. He felt anything but easy.

"What's this about? I'm not in any trouble, am I? At least I don't know of anything I've done." The lead agent waved his hand to indicate they were on a different mission.

"Relax, Mr. Peabody. Or should we call you Ricky?"

"Everyone calls me Ricky Bob."

From the bedroom, Dolly Parton sang "Here You Come Again." The agent lifted his head and listened to the music for a few seconds, smiled. Then his face became serious. He fastened his eyes on Ricky's. Ricky Bob tried not to shift or look away. He told himself to relax. He suddenly needed to use the bathroom.

"Okay, Ricky Bob, here's the deal."

For the next few minutes, Ricky Bob listened intently as the lead agent laid out the plan. Basically, Ricky Bob would wear a wire and try to get an officer of the bank, someone named Buckley or Buck or whatever, to engage in some loose talk. Hopefully this Buck guy would say something to incriminate himself.

This guy Buckman, or whatever his name was, was suspected of engaging in some serious stuff. Like bank fraud. "His name's Buckley, Agent Ethington corrected. Ricky was supposed to get this guy to authorize the $10 million loan. And hopefully Buckley would hit up Ricky for some kind of payola. A kickback or bribe. That's what the Feds were really after: evidence.

Agent Ethington laid it all out, showed him a set of very good black and white photos of Buckley in various kinds of dress. The lead agent even put on a little performance imitating Buckley's mannerisms, complete with waving a black Sharpie between his fingers like a cigar. When he finished, the agent sat back and waited for Ricky Bob's reaction.

"Why would I want to do this? Sounds like I'm bait or something." The agent nodded. Ricky Bob studied their impassive faces, thought for a full minute. They waited. They were used to waiting

"What I want to know is, what's in it for me? What if he doesn't take the bait? And what is the bait, anyway? What if he discovers I'm wired and shuts up? Or does something worse?"

The agent patiently explained two aspects about the bait. First, the bait was really what they already knew: Buckley's greed. His unbounded greed. His recklessness would be his own undoing. Without divulging details, he gave Ricky a couple of actual examples of the kind of loans Buckley had made. This was documented evidence he said. They suspected that Buckley had a pattern of getting kickbacks. (The agent actually used the term *quid pro quo*, which Ricky thought he understood. Vaguely.)

The second part of the bait: Ricky Bob, himself.

"But you still haven't said what's in it for me. Other than you're assuming I'm just a good old boy who wants to do his duty as a citizen of this wonderful country." They could feel the sarcasm in Ricky's voice.

"Look, I came up here because I was promised a loan of about ten million bucks so I could buy a drill rig and get into that deep Anadarko stuff." He looked at the agent to see if any of this registered. The agent nodded.

Ricky got up, started pacing around the small sitting room then continued, "It sounds to this old country boy that if your guy Buckley spills his guts on tape and you get him and he goes to jail, ole Ricky Bob here is shoot outta luck on my loan. Why? Because the guy making the loan is arrested, and I'm just standin' there with my hand out with nothin' to show while you guys get what you want." He waited a beat. "Am I right, is that how this is gonna play out?"

The lead agent nodded to his partner, FBI Agent Mike Smith, a younger man. Until now, he hadn't said a word. Agent Smith politely asked Ricky to sit back down and listen while he made a proposal that he was sure Ricky would like. Ricky was all ears. This better be good, he thought, or I'm sayin' no dice.

This part of the deal was simple: A $10 million loan would be provided. Ricky Bob would get the drill rig. And the Feds had the power to make Peabody's promissory note for the loan go away. It would simply disappear at some later date.

"I know you guys have a lot of power, but how's that possible? You can just make a loan disappear? Where does the money for that come from?"

Agent Ethington smiled and let Ricky Bob in on a secret: The bribes and kickback money they planned to recover from the corrupt insiders would cover more than Ricky Bob's small loan. Welcome to the world of clandestine operational financing. It was so simple even Ricky Bob could do the math. A broad smile creased his face.

The FBI agents now owned Calvin Buckley.

Ricky thought for a minute while Anne Murray sang "You Needed Me" on the tinny radio in the background. Ricky laughed and tilted his head toward the music. Agent Ethington caught the reference and joined Ricky in laughing at the situation.

Ricky Bob then asked, "I think I'm supposed to get one phone call. Ain't that the routine?" Agent Ethington laughed again. He was beginning to really like this Ricky Bob guy. His instincts were telling him they had found just the right man for the job.

Ricky Bob dialed Darren Magelby's number from memory. He hoped his lawyer was in and would answer. "Hello Darren? Yeah, it's me, Ricky Bob. Look, I don't have a lot of time, so listen carefully to what I'm about to tell you." He paused. "Then I need some advice."

Ricky laid out the plan to Darren who then asked to speak to the lead agent. When Ethington took the phone, Darren asked for his badge number. The agent confirmed all that Ricky Bob had told Darren, even filled in a few blanks. The lead agent nodded at something the lawyer said, handed the phone back to Ricky Bob. He listened for a moment, said, "Thanks, Darren," then hung up.

"My lawyer says you guys will send him a written memo guaranteeing the rig and loan part. That right?"

"That's right," Ethington said. He looked at his partner, who hadn't waited for Ricky's answer when he asked, "May I use your phone?" and was already making a call.

Fifteen minutes later, during which time Ricky and the FBI agents had guzzled bottled water and talked Big Eight football, the phone rang. It was Darren confirming to Ricky Bob that he had received a fax of the requested memo from the FBI. Ricky was now okay to go ahead with it.

Ricky extended his hand and they shook. “Looks like we have a deal. What do we do next? When do you want me to do this?”

“I believe you have an appointment at three with a Mr. Dill Robertson?” Ricky nodded. How did they know that? Ricky had no idea that since he had checked into his hotel, they had been listening to his every word on his hotel telephone.

The agent checked his watch. “Almost ten. We need to get started. We don’t have a lot of time.”

THIRTY-THREE

Three o'clock Monday. Larimer Square Bank

A few minutes before three, Ricky Bob entered the bank and asked if he could see a Mr. Dill Robertson. He had an appointment. He waited for several minutes then Dill came down the stairs. They shook hands, and Dill ushered Ricky Bob upstairs to a 10-by-10-foot glassed office that looked out over the Bullpen. Dill was careful not to pat Ricky's back, but, at all times, to act like this customer had come in the normal course of business. Which it was anything but. Ricky wondered if this Mr. Robertson was in on the sting or was he also part of the corrupt banking conspiracy?

They engaged in a few minutes of chit-chat. Ricky was obviously nervous. Dill tried to calm him down. "Can I get you something to drink—coffee, water, soft drink? Snack? Anything?"

"I sure could use a Dr. Pepper if you have one." Dill picked up the interoffice phone and asked Marty to bring them two Dr. Peppers. She came with two sweating bottles. They thanked her then clinked their bottles in a friendly toast.

Special Agent Chris Nieve had told Dill that timing was extremely critical in this little undercover operation. Dill knew that Mr. Buckley was on his way back from Las Vegas. Expected any moment. Marty had been asked to ring Dill the minute Buckley was back on site. Dill stalled for time.

"Tell me a little about your company. Let's start with how you began in the oil business, your track record. I'd also like a little detail on the Anadarko. I've done some research, but I'm still trying to get up to speed on natural gas and how you fit into this costly new venture."

He turned the dialogue over to Ricky Bob who wasn't sure why this nice Mr. Robinson person wanted to know all that. Ricky was used to the banker handling things over the phone and depositing the requested funds into his company bank account. Oh well.

After Ricky Bob spent the next 20 minutes explaining the deal and answering Dill's questions, Dill asked him about his prior banking experience with Tulsa Guaranty. Anything to fill the time.

Dill glanced up at the Regulator clock on the wall. Three forty-one. Still no Buckley. Where is that guy? Dill could feel the sweat rings forming under his armpits. Ricky Bob was surprisingly cool. Their Dr. Peppers were empty. Dill thought of asking Marty to bring two more, but decided that wasn't such a good idea. What if Peabody had to suddenly use the bathroom at a very crucial moment in the sting?

Dill was aware Ricky was wired, but he hoped the FBI hadn't clued Ricky Bob in to the part Dill was playing. The guy seemed edgy enough without adding more stress. Keep him relaxed and focused.

Ricky gave Dill a brief history of his relationship with Kyle, college at OU, his long track record with TGB. Dill reminded Ricky that Larimer Square Bank had purchased Ricky's loan from TGB so this bank already had quite a bit of information in the file. But there were some blanks, boxes needing to be checked off.

Finally, Dill's phone buzzed, and he picked up quickly. Ricky noticed and wondered why this Dill guy was so jumpy. It was Marty. Mr. Buckley was on the premises.

"Could you ask him to come here as soon as possible? I'd like for him to meet Mr. Peabody. Thank you, Marty." Dill hung up.

"Our CEO would like to meet you. It's sort of his practice to meet our larger borrowers in person. Wants to make sure everything is going smoothly to the customer's satisfaction." Dill smiled and Ricky nodded, took in a deep breath.

Show time. The Regulator ticked off one minute, two minutes, three …

The door opened abruptly and Calvin Buckley filled the frame. He was wearing a western-cut corduroy jacket, a snap-button western shirt, bolo tie with a huge silver and turquoise cinch, Tony Llama ostrich boots, a huge white felt Stetson. A fresh Cuban cigar clamped in his jaw. He made a show of waving the hand that bore a watch, a huge chunk of gold ego. Dill wasn't sure which smelled worse: the cigar or Buckley's disgusting Aramis cologne he had obviously bathed in.

Buckley removed the cigar, blew a cloud of rancid smoke, stuck out his hand like a sword point and approached Ricky Bob. "Hi there, I'm Calvin Buckley, but I prefer to go by Buck! What can I do for y'all?" Dill noticed how quickly Buck had morphed into a good ole southern boy's accent. The guy was such a chameleon. And a fraud, Dill reminded himself.

Dill briefly outlined the elements of Ricky Bob's loan request and passed the baton to Buckley who quickly took charge. Dill could see the greed building in Buck's bloodshot eyes. This is going well so far, Dill thought. He hoped the FBI was picking up the voices loud and clear.

In the alley behind the bank, the FBI surveillance team were huddled in a windowless unmarked white Ford panel truck. Inside the van they were listening intently through earphones. The latest in listening technology was picking up every word, every sound. Their sensitive listening technology could even pick up the drumbeat sound of Ricky Bob's heart beating loudly and fast against his rib cage. Relax, slow down and breathe normally, they pleaded silently.

"Y'all have your financial statements?" This was show only for Dill's sake. He already knew that Buckley hardly ever asked for or bothered with financial statements.

"No sir. Sorry," Ricky Bob lied. This was step one, and just what the FBI had coached him to say during the set up.

"No matter. You can fill one out while I go have a little discussion with the cashier. She's the little cutie that cuts your check." He winked at Ricky Bob knowingly, like two men of the world. "And I'm the guy who approves your loan. Mr. Robinson here, well, his authority is only good up to five million. Mine is unlimited. Maybe someday we'll let him do more."

Buck didn't bother to look at Dill, who sat silently by during this humiliating put down. Dill took it calmly while he fought the urge to smack the guy with the back of his hand across his foul, fat mouth. Only a couple more hours, Buck, and we'll see who's really in charge.

"So, while I do that, why don't we have Mr. Robinson here rustle up a blank financial statement form and you can take a minute and fill it in by hand. That work for y'all?" Ricky nodded obediently. Buck left, trailing his cloud of overpowering cologne and rancid cigar smoke.

Dill pulled a blank statement out of a drawer under the conference table where they were always available. He handed it to Ricky with a pen embossed with the bank's logo. Ricky began thoughtfully filling in the many blank columns with the dollar signs. The listeners waited patiently. They could hear the sound of rustling paper, Ricky's pen scratching across the paper. They picked up Dill's breathing.

Inside the bank lobby were two more FBI agents. Posing as a young married couple there to open a new account, they discreetly followed Buck's every move in the glassed-in office next to them, where he was getting a large check issued. His cigar smoke leaked into their cubicle. It was as horrible as everyone had told them it would be. So was his dreadful cologne.

About 10 minutes later, Buck returned upstairs. He was waving a cashier's check. He made a dramatic show of drying wet ink. He held it up for all to see. "Whooee ain't that a pretty sight? Ten million big ones. 'Course you'll need to open a new account with us—standard procedure." Ricky Bob nodded obediently. Buck continued, "Then this here check goes into that new account."

He made a grand show of sniffing the check, kissed it, then, with a flourish, he slapped the pink banknote paper on the shiny mahogany conference table. The listeners smiled at each other.

The $10 million figure printed on the check's face loomed large over the proceedings.

"Now, let's take a look at your financials," Buck said.

Dill handed him the one-page document Ricky Bob had hastily completed. Buck made a show of seriously studying the document, nodding, grunting, pulling at his lower lip, shaking his head. He looked up and said, "You know what I'm thinkin'? Maybe Mr. Ricky Bob here could tell me a little more about his plans."

He turned to Dill, and, true to habit, said, "Dilbert, I think your good work is done here. We thank you for your help. I can take over now. I'm sure you have other more important things to tend to, right?" He shot daggers at Dill who humbly nodded and picked up his papers. "And you can leave that file here."

Ricky Bob stood and thanked Dill, who reached over and shook his hand, squeezing it gently. Ricky felt it and took some comfort. Encouragement? A good luck sign?

The trap had been set and baited. Now it was up to one person to carry it through. Dill left Ricky Bob to spring the trap.

During their Saturday night strategy session in Las Vegas, Seth had warned Buck, "I repeat, do NOT do any more of your dirty little kickback deals. Not one more until this thing blows over. Do I make myself clear? Buck, are we clear?"

Buck had dumbly nodded. His head said yes. But, in his heart, he was already scheming ways to get even more before this whole thing fell apart. Buck needed to get his hands on just a couple million more. Then he'd think about his next move. "Now let's get down to the *real* business." Ricky Bob picked up on the emphasis Buck laid on that single word. So did the listeners.

Buck turned to Ricky Bob, picked up the cashier's check, waved it under Ricky's nose, teasing. He pulled his chair closer to Ricky so their knees were actually touching. Buck leaned in and lowered his voice.

"Turn up the input," said an FBI special agent inside the unmarked white van parked outside the bank. Inside the bank were two more FBI agents in white coveralls posing as electrical contractors come to check on a supposed wiring problem. They were all part of the FBI's technical crew put in place earlier—and would provide extra muscle should it become necessary. For now, their job was to monitor the radio transmittal from Ricky Bob's hidden wire. With their hidden camera, they were able to get many clear pictures of Calvin Buckley carrying the cashier's check.

In the van, a technician with earphones turned a dial on a large recording device and gave a thumbs up. So far so good.

"Loud and still really clear," he reported in almost a whisper. The special agent, their team leader, nodded.

The transcript produced verbatim later by the FBI would reveal Calvin Buckley putting pressure on Ricky Bob Peabody, illegally asking for a bribe, the quid pro quo for the bank to make the loan. In the form of a sizeable kickback from the $10 million loan—$2 million, to be precise. Buck gave Ricky detailed instructions on how the kickback was to be wired from the new Peabody account to an offshore company apparently owned and controlled by Buckley and/or associates.

Buckley wrote a series of numbers on a scrap of paper and shoved it over to Peabody who nodded and placed it in an inside pocket of his blazer. Ricky Bob, as instructed by the FBI, repeated the information written on the paper aloud so the listeners could hear. The account information and numbers were rapidly forwarded to Agent Sissy, who started crunching the information into her desktop computer.

Buckley went further. He demanded verbal acknowledgement from Ricky Bob that Peabody Oil would engage the services of several oilfield service companies. Ricky asked the names and owners of the companies. Buck hesitated. He avoided giving the businessowners' names, but, ultimately, he did supply the names of the companies. Buck wrote them down. That was a start; more intelligence for Sissy's computer. Buckley then picked up the phone and buzzed Anita. She came in and he handed her the $10 million check made out to Peabody Oil Company. Ricky Bob added his endorsement. Buckley gave her instructions to put it in a new account for Ricky's company.

Buckley then said in conclusion, "I feel we're going to have a long and mutually profitable relationship together, son."

At no time was Mr. Dill Robertson in the room or party to this exchange.

The next verbal exchange surprised even the FBI agents listening in. It went something like this:

PEABODY: Pointing out the window of the small conference room to all the people working in the Bullpen area, "Mr. Buckley …"

BUCKLEY: "Buck, please."

PEABODY: "Sure. Uh, Buck, just curious, but who are all those people out there, these young gals and guys? They, uh, your employees?"

BUCKLEY: Sounds of snorting and stamping of booted foot on floor. "Oh, no, son! They don't work for me. Them's all employees of our upstream correspondent banks. See that group over there?" Pointing, "They work for Mt. Rainier Trust in Seattle. That bunch is from First Trust Bank of New York. That's a bank in Newport Beach. Those guys are from National First in Midland Texas. That bunch is from Houston, name escapes me just now. Then those cute little gals over in that corner there are all from Northern Trust of Chicago. Just naming all them banks makes me tired. Oh yeah, I almost forgot. We even have a bunch of boys from Tel Aviv but I can't even pronounce the name of their bank. El something, I think. They're the ones wearing those funny little beanie caps."

PEABODY: "My, my. That's a lot of banking firepower. What are they, uh, doin' here, all of 'em so far from, uh, home?"

BUCKLEY: Sounds of loudly blowing cigar smoke. "Money. Money's what drives us all, ain't it? But seriously… Well, uh, that loan I just made you, that ten million? In five minutes I'll throw your paperwork out there in the middle of the floor so to speak and then stand back 'cause they'll jump on it and fight over it like they was wild dogs attackin' a scrap of raw meat. It's a biddin' war." Buckley laughs. "By the time you get down to your car on the street, one lucky bank out of that bunch will own the bulk of your loan under a master loan participation arrangement we have with them. We just keep the servicing portion and they pay us fees to collect from you. See how it works? They just can't seem to get enough of that paper we lay off on them…"

PEABODY: "I never imagined…"

The FBI agents then heard the sound of paper rustling, some indistinct chatter that faded away—probably Buckley bidding Peabody farewell—and the distinct click of the door closing in its brass keeper mechanism.

In the van the FBI boys had heard enough and signed off the air. All the coverall-clad agents—inside and outside the bank—picked up their tools and the orange cones, piled into the white Ford utility van and quickly disappeared. The young married couple concluded their business with the mortgage loan officer, picked up the glossy brochures and copy of the application that would later become part of the US Attorney's evidence file, thanked the bank's mortgage loan officer and casually walked out chattering excitedly like a young married couple.

Another successful sting.

Afterward, Dill was feeling unusually ebullient. And relieved. The sting had gone exactly according to plan. Ricky Bob Peabody had been superb, everyone agreed. After his masterful performance, Ricky met FBI agents at a previously designated motel in the outskirts of Golden. There, he had been relieved of both the wire and a load of anxiety.

The FBI also wanted to make copies of the $10 million loan documents. They also relieved Ricky Bob of Peabody Oil's new account passbook and newly printed checks issued by Larimer Square Bank. Then with surgical-gloved hands, they accepted the scrap of paper with the string of numbers Buckley had written. It also contained the names of the service companies Ricky had faithfully written down exactly as Buckley had dictated. It would all become part of U.S. attorney Ryan Henning's evidence dossier.

Special Agent Chris Nieve assured Ricky Bob again that he would get his promised drill rig and loan for delivering on his part of the deal. Nieve told Ricky Bob that thanks to his fine performance the FBI now had enough hard evidence to start the proceedings against Buckley and all the other persons of interest in his conspiracy network.

But Nieve's tone became serious as he warned Ricky that all this had to be kept confidential. In fact, Nieve said, because Ricky's life and that of his family might be in danger, he should lie low for a few days. Ricky's stomach did flips at this warning. In the aftermath of the sting, he suddenly became ill. He ran for the toilet and emptied his stomach three times. He came back into the sitting room pale faced, wiping his mouth with a wet towel.

The FBI suggested he should resume his regular routine. Go visit his Dolly P well in Weatherford for a while, at least until they gave him the all clear. In the meantime, try not to worry. The FBI would assign at least two agents as shadows for Ricky at all times, everywhere he went. His thought came out in a cynical laugh. Oh sure, like that is going to happen.

Ricky left Golden that afternoon driving toward Weatherford, a little deflated. On his truck radio, Crystal Gayle was singing "Don't It Make My Brown Eyes Blue" on his truck radio. It fit perfectly with how he was feeling right then.

THIRTY-FOUR

Oncology Ward, Denver Hospital

So why was Dill Robertson feeling so ebullient? He wanted to visit again with Jo before she took her nightly sleeping pill. He wanted to share the recent developments with her, get her assurance that he knew what he was doing. He was confident he was finally, completely on the right side of this whole bizarre experience. No more toe-dipping in gray areas. The end of rationalizing that he was doing this, taking this crazy job, for his family. Admit it, Robertson, you were bored with life in sleepy little Craig, Colorado. You yearned for a change, wanted some excitement in your life.

Then he thought, no, it wasn't that. Maybe partly. What he realized, what suddenly humbled Dill Robertson, was that, in spite of his many talents, his people skills, his brains, his education and acumen as a banker, businessman, and rancher, he really had believed that he had been big and smart enough to handle this thing by himself. Instead, it had turned and almost crushed him.

But this *thing*, this oil bubble and all the flimsy banking tricks and sophistry—the justifications, the letters of credit, the deep gas incentives, flaky engineering reports, favorable accounting tax opinion letters by respected CPA and law firms, rising gas prices, oil drilling mania, tax shelter promoters and the generous tax incentives enacted by Congress, the jumbo CDs and changes in banking laws, high returns, government guarantees on deposits of huge accounts, the recent oil embargoes in the Middle East, the greed of the staid old mainline upstream banks—this whole miasma of everything and everyone involved in this crazy Mulligatawny stew called crude oil—Dill Robertson included—was a monster. It had become so big and so powerful nobody, not even the mighty United States government could control it.

Everyone—including Dill—had lost their focus, had lost sight, had forgotten one very basic economic imperative: bubbles burst. Stock markets go up. Stock markets come crashing down. Oil prices go up. Oil prices come down.

We ignored that basic economic law. Now look where it's gotten us, gotten me, Dill admitted. But he also sensed that his own nightmare was almost over. He and his beloved JoEllen would be going home soon.

Dill breathed in the crisp autumn air. He could taste a little humidity in the air. Snow coming soon. As he parked his truck in the hospital lot, got out, he checked the back for his fly rod. It was still there. Waiting.

Dill nodded to the night nurse and, out of habit, took off his sweat-stained Stetson. He quietly let himself into Jo's room. He needn't bother to be quiet because she was sitting up in bed staring straight ahead. In the dim light he could make out a stony, angry expression in her countenance. She flicked on the overhead light and flung a large manila envelope at him. He grabbed at it, but missed. Several 8"-x-10" black and white photos spilled onto the floor. What he saw made him almost throw up the Whopper he'd wolfed down for supper on the way.

The evidence was clear. Those pictures caught him in the act. The ambush at his cabana door in Las Vegas. The peaches and cream coral lipstick. The skimpy bikini. Her smiling face turned up to his just before she planted that wet kiss on him.

And him smiling back at her. Why wasn't there a surprised look on his face? It was all there. Anyone would assume with one look what was happening. Anyone would reach the same conclusion. Dill Robertson off the rails. And enjoying it.

He picked up the pictures and turned to face his wife. "This isn't what it looks like." She archly raised an eyebrow, smirked.

"I can explain." His voice had a hollow, tinny ring.

"This better be good." He hadn't often seen that kind of anger in Jo's eyes, but there was no question that she was furious. And disappointed., She folded her arms defiantly across her chest. She was obviously spoiling for a fight. He sucked in his breath and said a silent prayer.

Dill tried to take her hand. She jerked it away. He looked her evenly in the eyes, forcing himself not to blink or look away. He quietly and slowly spelled it all out for her as he paced back and forth. He had been ambushed. Bushwhacked. Surprised. Then he apologized in the humblest way he knew how. He had truly meant to tell her everything. Some day. At the appropriate time. "And when would that be?"

"Just as soon as we can put this … this monster of a mess out of its misery. You know I'm working with the FBI now and I think they have a handle on things. They don't really need my help any more, now that this case is quickly moving forward. It's only a matter of hours, minutes maybe, until they arrest Buckley and Summers."

He described how the sting had been a success, thanks to the courage and cool acting by Ricky Bob Peabody. It was finished. Dill was done with it. Just a few more days to wrap up a few loose threads and to cover his own back side. Then they could pack up and go back home.

He was finished, so he stopped chattering.

At the word "home," Jo teared up. He sat on the edge of the bed and took one of her hands in his. This time she didn't pull away. Then he added, "I'm convinced that whole episode, that girl, was some kind of set up. I don't know what it all means. We just have to trust the Lord that He'll protect us and see us through this. The good guys will win. I'm on the right side. Right where you have always wanted me to be."

"The right always does win," Jo added. "Come here and kiss me."

Dill kissed her tenderly and asked, "So, am I forgiven?"

She pushed him away and said, "I'll think about it. After all, I don't want you thinking I'm easy." They both laughed. "Now you better go so I can get some sleep."

He nodded, clamped on his Stetson and started to leave.

"Wait. You said something about being protected. You think we're in any kind of danger? You'd tell me if you thought we were, wouldn't you?" Dill nodded. He hadn't told her about their FBI shadow agents.

Dill walked down the dimly lit hallways toward his truck, passing an intern wearing green scrubs and a face mask covering his mouth and nose. He was carrying a tray with several syringes, medicine bottles and various bags of liquids, with tubes wound around them. Dill nodded respectfully to the young doctor on his rounds. The intern averted his eyes, appeared to check something on his clipboard.

Dill turned the corner of the first hallway and passed a man leaning against the desk at the nurses' station. He looked like he could play in the NFL as an interior defensive lineman; he was that big. Otherwise, he wasn't remarkable to look at. He was wearing a rumpled suit. It looked like he'd slept in it for a week. Dill didn't get a look at the man's face other than to note he was black. The man was talking to the night duty nurse in a low voice. He sounded concerned about something or someone. Maybe he was inquiring about a spouse, a relative? Dill continued walking toward the exit.

The man Dill had passed was FBI agent Don Worthen who had been assigned to shadow the Robertsons. Worthen wasn't sure he had the right room number. He wasn't even sure he had the right hospital. His orders had been given so quickly over the phone. Worthen's head had been down briefly when Dill passed. But Agent Worthen had noticed the young intern in green scrubs walk by in the opposite direction. Worthen's many years of training as an FBI agent told him something was just a little off about the intern. Something was not quite right. Worthen thanked the night duty nurse and trailed the intern at a distance. The intern led him to Jo's room.

Jo was using the toilet when the intern entered the darkened room. He waited nervously. Jo flushed the toilet, opened the bathroom door and stepped back into her room. A strange man was standing just outside the bathroom door. He was uncomfortably close to her. Jo flinched in surprise. "You scared me! "

The intern was wearing a surgical mask and scrubs, a stethoscope hung around his neck. He carried a tray with things on it. But she quickly noticed he had no name tag. He mumbled something that sounded like he was sorry. He was still standing very close to her, too close. Jo eased around him and slipped into bed and pulled the coverlet up around her chin. She kept her eyes on the young man in green scrubs. "What do you want?" she asked.

The young man didn't answer at first. He looked down at the chart hanging on the end of her bed. It was hard to read in the dark. He hesitantly read out her name, "Mrs. Rob … uh, Robinson?"

"Robertson," Jo corrected him.

"I need to draw some blood and then I need to give you a shot.

"They just drew blood an hour ago. What kind of shot?"

"It's okay, Ma'am, just please roll up your sleeve, okay?" He stepped close to the edge of her bed. She could hear him breathing heavily. Jo didn't like the tone in his voice: it was threatening. She started to roll up her sleeve as the intern moved the loaded syringe toward a vein. Then Jo sensed danger and hesitated.

When Worthen reached Jo's room the door was slightly ajar. He stood for a few seconds with his ear against the small opening the intern had left. He caught the nervousness and fear in Jo's question. Then it hit him: the intern had not been wearing any nametag.

About the same time, Dill reached the outer door. A strange feeling suddenly seized him. Something was wrong. He felt panic seize him. What was it? Something was out of place with that young intern. Then the lightbulb flashed on. Doctors don't walk around with protective masks on. And this doctor was not wearing a nametag! It's usually hanging around the neck. Especially when they are doing rounds. And, why was he carrying a tray of meds? That's a nurse's job!

Dill turned and quickly retraced his steps, increasing his speed as he went. He skidded around the corner of the hallway leading to Jo's room.

"Drop it!" said Worthen to the intern as he stepped into the room.

"What? Who?" said Jo, confused.

The intern made a lunge toward Jo, with the needle poised to strike. Worthen was big but he was quick. His iron grip closed around the intern's arm, and he jerked the deadly syringe away.

Dill, racing toward Jo's room, heard the metallic crash of something being suddenly dropped. Glass bottles breaking. A loud smack like someone being hit. Jo was screaming, yelling. He couldn't make out what she was saying. She screamed his name. Dill reached her room, breathing hard, cold fear in his gut. He pushed his way through the door and quickly surveyed the scene before him.

The young intern was face down on the floor. His face mask was askew. The very large black dude in the rumpled dark suit and white shirt with the dirty collar ring that Dill had passed a minute earlier. The man's tie was crooked, and his knee was firmly in the middle of the intern's back, pinning him down with brutal force. The intern's face, what Dill could see of it, was cut and bleeding badly. A lump over one eye was swelling fast, closing off his vision.

The intern was yelling, moaning, kicking wildly. Probably because the large black dude also had one of the intern's arms twisted behind his back almost to the breaking point.

Strewn across the floor were the tray, clipboard, broken bottles, a puddle of spilled liquid. And, against the wall, a very nasty-looking syringe with needle exposed.

Dill looked at Jo. Jo looked back. Her face was a mask of horror. She burst into tears as Dill took her into his arms, patted her, soothed her. "Oh, Dill it was awful. He, that guy, that doctor there. He tried to kill me with that!" She indicated the syringe.

"And, who are you?" Dill asked the large black dude.

Agent Worthen extended his one free hand, as big as a hubcap, and offered to shake. "Agent Don Worthen, FBI. At your service."

"So, what just happened, Agent Don Worthen FBI?"

The large black dude, aka Agent Don Worthen, FBI, at your service, roughly jerked the battered intern to his feet, cuffed his hands probably tighter than was necessary behind his back, pointed to a chair and said, "Sit and don't move an inch unless you want me to beat the crap out of you." Dill had no doubt that Agent Worthen would do just that, and worse, given any excuse.

Worthen produced his credentials and said, "To answer your question as best as I can, sir, this piece of crap, pardon me ma'am, tried to murder this lady here." He tipped his head toward Jo. "I'm assuming she's your wife?"

They both nodded in the affirmative. Dill could see the bulging outline beneath Worthen's suit coat and under his armpit, a shoulder holster, carrying a service revolver, no doubt.

Agent Worthen fished a pair of surgical gloves out of his suit pocket, snapped them on smoothly, and picked up the syringe. He lifted it carefully to his nose and sniffed. "I think it's cyanide, if I'm not mistaken. But the forensic boys will confirm that. I caught this … this piece of … this perp here in the act of raising his hand with said syringe as the murder weapon aiming it at her."

"Alleged murder weapon," the intern snarled. "I want a lawyer!"

"Shut up!" Agent Worthen whirled and raised his fist as the perp flinched. The big FBI agent planted the toe of one of size 12 shoes harshly in the middle of the intern's shin. "That better be the last out of you unless I ask you any questions at which time you better be truthful or you'll also be facing additional charges of lying to an agent in the process of an investigation. Clear?" The perp nodded and managed to croak out something inaudible that passed for a yes answer.

"I think he was really after you, Mr. Robertson. But when you had already left, I think your wife was the next available target."

Dill nodded. "But why try to kill Jo?"

"Dunno. Sending a warning maybe? You are a material witness, I'm told. But that's all for the lawyers to figure out. Anyway, I managed to stop him," Don Worthen said simply.

"So, you're my shadow?" Dill asked. Don nodded in the affirmative.

Jo turned Dill's head around so he was looking her in the eye. "Shadow? Care to explain?"

Dill threw up his hands. Just then a team of FBI agents noisily crowded their way into Jo's room. They had arrived as back-up pursuant to Agent Worthen's earlier call.

"Thank heavens the cavalry arrived to save the day. And just in the nick of time," Jo laughed.

"What took you guys so long?" Worthen asked.

"We went to the wrong hospital," one agent said sheepishly.

“Figures,” Worthen said. He roughly jerked the perp to his feet, handed him over to two of the new arrivals. They were even less gentle as they frog-marched the bogus intern out.

THIRTY-FIVE

In 1970 Congress passed a law, now known on the books as Racketeer Influenced and Corrupt Organizations Act. Better known by its acronym RICO. What is RICO and why was it passed into law? Good that you should ask.

For some time, law enforcement agencies—such as police, the FBI, the SEC, the Alcohol, Tobacco and Firearms people (ATF), immigration authorities, agencies fighting illegal gambling, prostitution, human trafficking, child pornography, illegal drugs and so on—had, until RICO, been extremely frustrated. The criminal elements were winning the war on crime.

The bad guys seemed to always be keeping one step ahead of law enforcement. They had better, faster, deadlier firearms; faster boats for smuggling; better networks of organized minions, snitches, and seemingly unlimited supplies of money for sophisticated electronic communications, high-priced criminal defense attorneys, etc.

RICO gave law enforcement a powerful new tool to combat crime. It hinged on charging and prosecuting a corrupt or unlawful *enterprise*. What constitutes an enterprise? The RICO law has been interpreted by the courts to be any group with members who are associated through a pattern of racketeering activity. This broad definition sweeps up not only individuals, but corporations, partnerships, limited partnerships, trusts, companies or other businesses, and secret societies (think Mafia), who engage in organized crime. It also has been interpreted to include informal organizations, such as drug cartels and street, prison or motorcycle gangs.

The law established severe penalties—both civil and criminal—for those who engage in an ongoing pattern of wrongdoing as a member of a criminal enterprise. One of the most hurtful penalties is forfeiture. Forfeiture of not only the fruits of the crime – ill-gotten gains – but *any and all* personal or business or other enterprise assets wherever located, in the territorial boundaries of the United Sates or otherwise. This forfeiture penalty is automatic.

In other words, the authorities now had worldwide jurisdiction over these criminal activities. And any assets involved. Most of the 50 states quickly followed suit and adopted their own Little RICO Acts.

Title 18, Section 1961 of the U.S. Code sets forth a long shopping list of racketeering activities, the repeated commission of which can form the basis of a RICO Act indictment. These underlying federal and state offenses exist independently of the act and include the crimes of homicide, kidnapping, extortion, bribery, and witness tampering or the obstruction of justice.

Racketeering activities also include property crimes, such as robbery and arson. A number of financial crimes are also listed such as embezzlement, money laundering, counterfeiting, securities law violations, as well as bank, mail and wire fraud.

Violations of the federal act are punishable by up to 20 years in prison, which can be increased based on the nature of the underlying crime. There is also a $250,000 fine, or double the amount of the proceeds earned from the activity.

The government prosecutors need not wait until a conviction is secured to ask the court to enforce the forfeiture provision. When the property is difficult to locate or the criminals are suspected of absconding or hiding the property, RICO allows the government to freeze the defendant's assets before the case ever goes to trial. That makes it very difficult if not impossible for the defendant(s) to hire and pay defense lawyers.

The burden of proof for a criminal case for the government to prove is guilt beyond all reasonable doubt, which is a higher burden to prove by the evidence. Individuals who may bring their own RICO civil claim against the racketeers have a lower burden of proof: the preponderance of the evidence standard applies—a mere 50.1 percent proof is adequate.

A victim, i.e., a damaged party, can potentially recover treble damages if they win. In other words, three times the amount of money they lost to the criminal enterprise. A pattern of continued criminal activity must also be shown and the activities must be related and continuous.

The most often-used defenses are invalid search and seizure: the police did not have a warrant or the warrant may be defective and, therefore, the fruits of the search are tainted and inadmissible into evidence. The other most commonly utilized defense is entrapment: the arresting police officer(s) enticed the defendant into engaging in an unlawful activity that he (or she) would not have otherwise engaged in. Clever defense lawyers are adept at explaining to juries the elements of these defenses.

FDIC offices, Kansas City

It took Gary Swope some time to finally pin down his boss, Max Watts, to talk about Larimer Square Bank. Max reluctantly agreed to meet at 4:30. In the meantime, Gary had made a copy of his audit report and left it in Max's inbox. He knew it was Max's habit to put off reading anything until the last possible moment. Max was less than a year away from his coveted, long-dreamed-of retirement.

It wasn't until Gary was sitting in his office at the appointed time that Max read Gary's draft report. He finished, laid it down and leaned back. He looked up at the ceiling and asked Swope, "So what do you want me to do about this?"

Gary cautiously answered, "It's really your call. But I think it's obvious that there were some serious concerns that the FDIC needs to be aware of."

Max looked at Gary, then quickly away. He seemed bored, or a little lost. Gary thought. "Thanks for the heads up. Go ahead and submit your report," Max said.

In due time it would be circulated among senior auditors.

None of whom bothered to read it.

Larimer Square Bank

Dill was in the process of actually clearing his desk. He and Jo had discussed his quitting. That was just after the FBI agents had escorted her would-be assassin away for questioning. They both agreed: there was no hesitation in quitting the bank. Dill—and Jo, too—felt they had endured enough. It was time to go home. Dill's so-called marriage with Larimer Square Bank was over, failed, dead and done. The only issue was how to give it a proper divorce.

He was putting his few personal items into a banker's box when Calvin Buckley pushed his way into Dill's cluttered corner office. "What're you doin'?" he snipped.

"It's fairly apparent I would think," Dill said, not looking up. "I've had it with this sad experiment. I won't go on pretending to be happy with the way things are done here. I'm through, Mr. Buckley."

Buckley was searching for a response. Dill continued.

"I miss my boys, my ranch, and my own bank. I'm checking my wife out of the hospital later today and we're going home."

"Job too much for you? Not up to it? Can't handle the stress? I always knew you were a coward at heart. I hate quitters, you know?"

Dill rolled his fists into tight balls, told himself to just let it go. He handed his written resignation to Buckley, who didn't bother to read it. Buckley dropped it on Dill's desk, turned around and left in a cloud of wretched air pollution. Dill fully expected to be escorted unceremoniously out of the building by security at any moment. But it didn't quite happen that way.

Federal Grand Jury, Denver

Ryan Henning had recently been appointed by the president as United States Attorney for the Judicial District of Colorado. He and his staff of dedicated, highly professional government lawyers had the responsibility of representing his only client, the government of the United States, for all of Colorado, its Federal District Courts, and the United States Court of Appeals. Colorado was located in the conservative

Tenth District, which took in Colorado, Kansas, Oklahoma, Utah and Wyoming. Its rulings were frequently compared to the notoriously liberal Ninth Circuit, which took in all the rest of the western states, most notably, California.

Henning was a graduate of Yale Law School, had earned a masters' degree in legal history with particular emphasis on the British-American jurisprudential tradition, awarded to him as a Rhodes Scholar from Oxford University. He had clerked for a federal appellate judge in Washington, D.C., for two years before serving as an assistant U.S. attorney in the District or six years. He had taken several Justice Department-sponsored courses in white collar crime and felt he was quite expert to deal with anything thrown at him. He could handle it.

Then the appointment to U.S. Attorney for Colorado came, and he jumped at the chance to go back home. Both he and his wife were Colorado-born and bred.

Ryan was a good administrator, had good people skills and enjoyed a strong personal relationship with his staff lawyers, clerks, interns, paralegals and secretaries. He was a brilliant trial practitioner, at ease in the court room, comfortable with juries, both trial and grand juries, easily winning them over by his easy-going, soft-spoken approach.

He also had a good rapport with most of the federal judges he worked with. After all, they drew their paychecks from the same employer, the U.S. Department of Justice. His own boss was the U.S. Attorney General. Ryan secretly modeled his courtroom style after his hero, Atticus Finch.

Ever since he read ancient British and American jurisprudence at Oxford, Henning had a love affair with the grand jury system. He couldn't explain his fascination with the secretive workings of this antiquated relic of the criminal process. He just loved it. And he was devastatingly good with grand juries. His track record in that chamber was nearly perfect. So far.

A federal grand jury sits at the request of the U.S. attorney. The jury is composed of members called from the district's list of registered voters, property ownership records, etc., and can have anywhere from 12 to 23 members sitting for the term of the call.

Its job is principally to investigate alleged criminal conduct to determine whether criminal charges should be brought. In this function of their duties they are a finder of fact, a pre-screener of criminal indictments. Grand jurors are sworn to hear evidence presented by the US attorney *ex parte*, that is, without advance suspicion or being persons of interest or involvement in the matter being presented. Their deliberations are in the strictest confidence.

Prosecutors are not bound to always use a grand jury for indictments. Most often the case will first be heard in a proceeding known as a preliminary hearing before a district court judge or a federal magistrate judge, sitting without a jury. The sole purpose of this hearing is to determine if enough evidence exists of a crime that the case should proceed to a criminal trial.

But where the subject matter of a criminal case, its scope or its size, or the identity of the defendants, whether indicted or still the targets of an ongoing investigation, or the gathering of evidence is still ongoing, then the prosecutor may opt for the confidentiality of the grand jury proceeding.

The grand jury may cause an indictment for a crime or crimes to be issued, based upon the evidence presented to it, and that there is probable cause to believe that a crime has been committed by a criminal suspect. The indictment, in antique legalese, is also known as *a true bill*. The true bill or indictment is often sealed. That is, its counts or charges are known only to the grand jury and the prosecutor and his staff for the time being. Indictments may be later amended or charges added to it, depending on how long the investigation goes on before, or even during trial.

Search warrants and warrants for arrest of a suspect are not issued by grand juries; that is under the judge's power to do. Such warrants may be, and often are, issued before evidence is submitted to the grand jury for an indictment, upon which the suspect may be taken into custody for questioning. Under the law, the suspect still has the benefit and right of the legal presumption that he—or she—be considered innocent until proven guilty.

The prosecutor is the only one who determines the evidence to be presented to the grand jury. It only hears one side of the story, the side most favorable to the prosecution. It's no wonder then, that prosecutors have such good track records with indictments, true bills, issued by their grand juries.

FBI Offices, Denver

FBI Special Agent Chris Nieve and his team had been working around the clock to pull together the evidence to refer this case to the U.S. attorney. Nieve wasted no time bringing in Randy Simpson, CPA, now on loan from the SEC. Randy's role: to help track down the money that was suspected to have been acquired and probably hidden by Summers and Buckley and/or anyone associated with their criminal enterprise. Nieve was angling for a good solid RICO case and he needed—was relying on—Simpson's uncanny ability, his unique expertise, and excellent track record of ferreting out hidden money. Simpson had found and recovered tons of hidden cash and other assets, ill-gotten gains, in his career as a government financial forensics specialist. Everyone working on the case was confident that Simpson would come through yet again.

In the meantime, there was enough initial evidence of a major federal financial crime based on Dill's secret tape obtained in Las Vegas, and the wiretap obtained by Ricky Bob Peabody on the bank's premises, that Nieve and his team felt supremely confident in referring the case to Henning. Both recordings disclosed incriminating admissions by Calvin Buckley. Buckley, while a critical part, was only part of the criminal enterprise. They were really after the bigger fish: Seth Summers.

In another part of the FBI offices, a team of investigators, skilled at getting perps to talk, had the fake medical intern in a small windowless room for questioning. They had kept him overnight in a small cell with no heat, the single bright overhead light burning all night, a hard bunk with no mattress or pillow, and one thin blanket. The only other slight protection he had from the cold was the raggedy orange prison jumpsuit that was three sizes too big and a pair of broken-down plastic crocs that were four sizes too small, no socks.

What little food he had been given was disgusting: a cold sandwich of suspicious-looking lunchmeat with a greenish tint, carelessly slapped between two stale slices of white Wonder bread. It was served with a half-filled paper cup of cold coffee, no sugar or cream.

The intern hadn't been able to sleep at all thanks to various agents banging on his cell door every half hour asking if he was okay, did he need anything? Each time, his reply invoked his favorite four-letter word, followed by a guttural growl.

At 5 in the morning, he was rolled out with a quick stop at a restroom to relieve himself. He was then frog-marched in very tight cuffs and leg irons that pinched painfully, by two well-muscled agents to the interview room. There he alternated between staring at his bruised and battered hands and glowering at the agents.

He also went back and forth between clamming up and demanding he be allowed to make a call to his lawyer. They seriously doubted he had a lawyer. The FBI knew they could legally keep him for up to 24 hours for questioning before they either had to charge him or release him from custody. In the meantime, there would be no lawyer until they absolutely had to let him call one.

"You'll get to call your lawyer in a while. But first we have a few questions we need you to answer." This was from Agent Harold Ethington. He assumed the role of the good guy in this good-cop bad-cop duo.

Their target spit and swore.

Ethington turned to his partner, Agent Mike Smith.

"I dunno Mike. Think we should waste any more time with this guy?" The intern impersonator lifted his head up. He was unsure what these two now had in mind for him. He glared at them.

Agent Mike Smith walked around the small table and took a chair facing the suspect. He placed both hands lightly on the table. "Look, here's how it works. You're in deep trouble. Serious doo doo. You were caught in the act of attempted murder in a federal case. I count about a dozen other federal charges the prosecutors could make stick. Charges are being prepared by the U.S. attorney as we speak. And, I know him to be really mean. He hates guys like you. He loves nothing more than to put them away for life in Leavenworth. Ever hear of Leavenworth?" The intern had. His sphincter twitched and his bowels rumbled.

Smith continued, "He also loves to go for the death penalty in cases like yours. You're probably facing the needle. You seem to like needles, don't you?" The intern almost fainted.

"The way we figure, if you get a smart lawyer and he somehow manages to get you a lighter sentence, one not involving the needle …" He looked searchingly at Ethington, who nodded his concurrence.

"…we still got enough on you to put you away for about 50 years. You have heard of Leavenworth, haven't you, Eugene? Or should we call you Marcus?"

There was that word again—Leavenworth—the most dreaded of all federal penal institutions. Filled with the worst criminals on the planet. Gangs. Rapes. Stabbings. People died in Leavenworth. Nobody ever escaped Leavenworth. Few ever came out alive. He heard his name through his near-dream state.

At the mention of his name the suspect jerked up his head again. How did they know his name? That meant that either someone had ratted him out, or they had been doing some deep research. How much did they know about him?

As a matter of fact, Agent Sissy had been on the computer much of the night. She ran his fingerprints and mugshots through the government's massive databases. She assiduously worked at tracking down his identity: who he was, did he have form, a criminal track record? Who were his known associates in crime? The sort of stuff that cases are built on, convictions made.

These two agents knew a lot about Eugene—one of many aliases he went by, not his real name. He was Marcus Kessimakis, a Greek citizen, usually going by Gus Kessimakis. When he wasn't using an alias.

Gus was in the United States on an expired student visa. Formerly enrolled at Rice University in Houston before being expelled for unproven serious assaults and near-rapes reported by several co-eds.

After that he became part of a notorious Midwestern drug gang. Busted in Memphis for possession with intent to sell. Somebody posted his $25,000 bail and got him a high-priced criminal lawyer to spring him from jail. He jumped bail and had been knocking around getting in various scrapes with the law—including assault, petty theft, DUI twice in Kansas, and credit card theft. Generally on the run. Until last night. Why he had slipped through the net numerous times until last night, nobody in the Denver FBI offices could figure.

Finally, Gus decided to talk. "Okay, what do ya want to know?"

"Everything," Ethington said.

"Start at the beginning, Marcus. Or would you prefer we call you Gus?" Mike Smith asked gently.

Gus Kessimakis shrugged. Like, did it really matter? He took a deep breath, and started spilling his guts. He seemed to want to be relieved of a great burden.

"You mean where was I born, my parents, all that stuff?"

"We already know all that. So, for a start, why don't you tell us how you came up with the plan to assassinate Mrs. Robertson? And by the way, Gus, this conversation is being recorded."

Gus began to spill it. He had met this guy named Lucky in a bar in Las Vegas several days ago and after the guy –Lucky …

Ethington interrupted, "When was it? Saturday? Sunday? Day or night?"

"It was Saturday. Yeah. Saturday night for sure."

"You're sure it was night?"

Gus nodded.

"Please answer verbally. For the record." He glanced at the recorder that was running, red light blinking intermittently.

"Yes," Gus said. "Night. Saturday night."

Mike Smith said, "Okay. So…"

"Did this Lucky guy have a last name?" Ethington cut in again.

Gus didn't get a last name. Agent Smith made a note and the questioning continued.

After Lucky bought him several rounds of Greek ouzo, Lucky had looked around the dark interior of the bar, leaned in close enough Gus could smell the rye whiskey on his breath. Lucky's voice was now lowered almost to a whisper. Gus had had a hard time hearing. Lucky had then made Gus a proposition. How would he like to make a quick $10,000 in cash? Gus was listening.

But first, he had to go to the men's room. He needed to think.

When Gus got back, he said, "Ten grand isn't enough." He countered with $20,000.

Lucky thought for a minute then agreed to $20,000. Half now and the other half when the job was done.

Gus then had said, "Sure, what do I have to do?"

Lucky, sparing a lot of details, explained what the job entailed. Gus Kessimakis wasn't born a killer with killer instincts, the cold-blooded ability to look into someone's eyes as you watched them die and then just walk away and forget. He hesitated a minute. "I dunno, that seems like a really hard way to make a few bucks."

Lucky said something about maybe he should get someone else. "It's not like you're loaded and don't need the money. We both know you're dead broke."

The guy was spot on. Gus really needed cash. For $20,000 Gus could almost kill his own brother.

The two men shook on it and this Lucky guy gave him $10 grand down on the spot, cash, with the other $10 grand to come when Gus finished the job.

Lucky gave him a round-trip plane ticket Las Vegas-Denver-Las Vegas, coach class (the unused half of which was now in the evidence file), with detailed handwritten instructions (also in the evidence file) of where to go, how to create the murder weapon. There was also a detailed description of the room Mrs. Robinson [sic] was in at the hospital. She had cancer and was probably dying anyway, so … it wouldn't really be a killing. Gus would just be helping her speed up the inevitable. Give her a faster send-off to her eternal reward, that sort of stuff.

Gus detailed how he'd purchased the cyanide, how he'd sneaked into the hospital, found some green scrubs in the laundry room, and located the tray of medicines he used as a stage prop. It had all been very easy to find in the hospital. Late at night, hospital security was rather loose. Nobody seemed to care who came or went.

He described how he had filled the syringe intended for Mrs. Robertson. Agent Mike Smith took more notes.

They pretty well knew the rest of the story. FBI forensic people had found a partial fingerprint on the handwritten instructions. It wasn't Gus's print. Agent Sissy and others were now busy running handwriting and fingerprint searches, trying to find matches for the mystery fingerprint in the billions of bits of data in the massive FBI databases. Sooner or later, they would find a match, and they sensed it would be this Lucky person.

But Leavenworth? Yeah, Gus had heard of it. From what he'd heard it was far worse than any jerkwater jail he'd spent a night or two in. At the mention of Leavenworth, his sphincter had puckered and he'd nearly wet his orange prison jumpsuit. The two agents had noted the color briefly drain from his tanned face at the mention of the infamous prison.

Sissy had turned the plane ticket and handwritten instructions over to the forensic boys. It had taken them less than an hour to track down who owned the other set of prints they were able to lift off the documents, now known as Government Exhibits A and B. The other prints belonged to a career criminal named Pete Curtis, aka Lucky.

The FBI and several other agencies had had Lucky on their radar for some time, watching, waiting. He was suspected of being sometimes in the employ of Mr. Seth Summers. But they needed hard proof. The FBI sent out an alert to watch for Pete Curtis aka Lucky and bring him in. Top priority.

Agent Ethington took over. "Okay, Gus, can we go over this again?" Gus lowered his head onto his chest, defeated, exhausted. When would this inquest end? He just wanted it over with. He was starving, tired and scared out of his wits.

Ethington saw fear in the young man's eyes. He was really quite handsome, in a hard-edged kind of way: olive skin, curly black hair, lean and buff, light brown eyes, a dimpled chin, straight white teeth. Prison would likely change a few of those matinee-idol features. It usually did. Those who had been incarcerated came out a lot older, more hardened. Most of them came out with bad prison tattoos. Sometimes they collected a few facial scars.

"Why don't you cooperate with us, give us a little more to go on. You should know how the game is played in America. You help us, we help you," Ethington said. He turned to Agent Mike for confirmation.

Mike cracked a slight smile and added, "Let's go over this again, with Agent Ethington, shall we?"

They waited while Gus wiggled a little. Then he cleared his throat and spoke in almost a whisper, "I don't know anything other than what I already told you."

"Tell us again, Gus. Humor us," Ethington said.

"I told you I really didn't know the guy. Lucky. We met in a bar in Vegas only a few nights ago. It all happened so fast I really didn't have time to think about what he was asking me to do. I guess the ouzo got the best of me." He looked at the two agents for sympathy, this tough little Greek who was on the verge of tears. They knew they owned him.

"There is one thing …" They waited. They were professionals at waiting. Waiting produced results from long interrogations. "He gave me the money and instructions in an envelope."

"What kind of envelope?"

"The usual kind."

"Describe it for us. Was it white, long, small, how many inches by how many? Did it have any writing on it? What did the writing say? What did you do with it?" They already knew the answers. The envelope was tucked in the manila folder, the evidence dossier lying on the table at their very fingertips.

"I think … No, I'm sure, it was white. The size utility bills usually come in."

"A business-size envelope?"

"Yes. Now I remember, it was from a hotel," He thought, pensive. Then, his face lighted up. "The Aladdin. That's it. Yes. It was the Aladdin." The two FBI agents looked knowingly at each other.

Gus's confirmation of the envelope's origin and journey from Lucky to his own hands would be a key piece of evidence linking Summers and Buckley to the first phase of their conspiracy to commit murder. It was hard evidence placing them at the hotel, the location where Dill had obtained the taped recording of Buckley.

The envelope of itself wasn't that significant. But, when placed alongside the other bits and pieces of evidence—the written instructions, the balance of the cash that had been found in Gus's possession, the plane ticket from Las Vegas to Denver—all identified patiently by the U.S. attorney through Gus on the witness stand, it would be very convincing to a jury should the case come to trial. Which these agents seriously doubted was going to happen. There would be no trial. This guy was going to cut a deal and plead out.

Mike Smith handed Gus a yellow legal pad and a Bic pen and said, "Start writing, Gus. Tell us again everything you can remember, every detail. This time in your own writing. Write it all down."

"First, I need to know what you guys are gonna do for me," pleaded Gus. "And I want a lawyer, too."

"You're asking for some kind of deal?" Gus nodded emphatically, too quickly. "It's not for us to do deals. That's for the U.S. attorney to consider," Agent Smith said.

"I want to be in your witness protection program, too."

"You're getting ahead of yourself, Gus. You really haven't given us anything that indicates you need protection. You saying these guys that hired you are hardened criminals?"

Gus nodded. "We don't see it that way, Gus. They look like a bunch of goofballs to us. Don't you think so, Ethington?"

Agent Ethington nodded his agreement. "*The Gang That Couldn't Shoot Straight* comes to mind." Both agents shared a good laugh.

Agent Smith continued, "If they were real professionals, they would have hired a trained assassin, not some low-level screw-up like you. The only danger you're in, Gus, is if you don't get writing, you'll be sorry, because our boss is going to come in here and work you over real bad. Then you're going to Leavenworth for sure when he gets done with you. He's nowhere near as nice as we are. He's always saying we're too soft. It hurts us to hear him say that. So, help us out here, Gus."

Gus looked defeated. Then his jaw became firmly set. He sat back in his chair and became very fascinated with his fingernails, which had already been chewed down to the quick.

"First I need a bathroom break," he said.

"Sure. Then you start writing."

"I'll give it some consideration while I'm gone. I'm also really hungry."

"We'll arrange something," Agent Ethington promised.

Agent Smith took Gus down the hall and stood watch over him while he did the deed. The door to the hallway stayed open the entire time. Gus shuffled his manacled feet back to the interrogation room and sat down. He stared at the yellow pad for a full minute. He had already made his decision: he would sing. He'd just have to trust his lawyer to cut a deal to keep him out of Leavenworth.

"Can you take these cuffs off so I can write?"

Ethington approved. They removed the cuffs and nodded for him to start writing.

THIRTY-SIX

Tuesday. Larimer Square Bank, Denver

Buck paced around in his office. He was furious, enraged beyond belief at this self-righteous Mormon, Robinson. The one with the flagpole stuck up his back side.

Buck had endured Dill's smugness, his superior I'm-better-than-you façade for too long. If he had it his way Dill Robinson would have been the target of that crazy Greek, the hit man Lucky found in Vegas. Not the wife. What good did one dead woman do? The husband was the real enemy.

Buck was also worried. Deep in his gut he sensed the wheels coming off the stage coach. He should have heard from Summers by now telling him what to do, what was their next move. Buck sensed big trouble was on the horizon.

He should have heard from Seth! Why didn't that vain jerk call him?

Buck kept a gun hidden in his desk, another in his car. The desk weapon was a little Beretta .32 automatic pistol. He was of a mind to take it down the hall right now and waste that Robinson punk.

He heard the distinctive ring of the private line he'd had installed. Only his three mistresses and Summers knew that number. Pray it's Seth. He picked up. "Yeah?"

"Listen carefully. We can't talk here, not with the whole world eavesdropping."

In fact, across town, an FBI technician was listening in. The technician signaled to Special Agent Nieve as he pushed a button on his hi-tech snooping equipment. The whole room of FBI agents heard

Buck and Seth loud and clear. Every word was being recorded. Nieve smiled.

"There's a bank of pay phones at the Greyhound bus depot. You know where that's located?

"The depot. Got it," Buck affirmed.

"Good. Use the one in the middle and call this number. Whoever answers will tell you what to do next."

Seth rang off, but not before the FBI had traced the location of where Seth was calling from.

FBI Offices, Denver

The entire might of the western division of the FBI had already been on high alert. Every agent was suddenly sent scrambling. It looked highly likely these two guys were going to do a runner and the FBI had to stop them before they slipped through the noose and flew away.

They had quickly pinpointed Seth's location. He was calling from the airport in a remote town in Canada—Penticton, British Columbia. How he got through the international border undetected was anybody's guess. Nieve blamed himself. He should have anticipated this would happen. He cursed himself that he hadn't alerted all the various police and authorities to be on the watch. It was a mistake—his mistake—not to have contacted the FBI office in Las Vegas and the Las Vegas police, among others.

A call was quickly made to the Royal Canadian Mounted Police in Canada with a request for their assistance. Would they please move with all due haste and apprehend and hold for them a Mr. Seth Summers, wanted in the United States for a laundry list of criminal offenses? He would also be charged with RICO. The RCMP needed no explanation of RICO. The arm of the law had reached across international borders and was doing its best to collar Seth Summers.

The FBI faxed a folio of pictures of Seth Summers to the Mounties with a description of the fugitive.

On the road, I-15 north of Las Vegas

Just a few days before, in fact, the Sunday morning of the Las Vegas frat party (as Seth called it), at Seth's bidding, Lucky had visited a sorry-looking, run-down used car lot way out on the north end of Las Vegas Boulevard. Just a couple blocks from the Nellis Air Force Base guard gate.

The lot was owned by a couple of brothers who specialized in buying used cars from desperate airmen in distress for dagger-at-the-throat prices, then reselling the wrecks at huge markups. Buyers could always haggle with them and get the price down to a reasonable level to make a deal and drive one off the lot. At least those that were drivable

Lucky picked out a fairly nice-looking late model Chevrolet Impala station wagon, dark green with fake wood side panels. Very inconspicuous, family-wagon looking. He took it for a test drive and discovered very little wrong with it, other than it needed an oil change. In addition to the cigarette smoke that saturated the upholstery, it had a strong sour smell, vomit from the previous owner who had obviously drunk too much tequila and couldn't pull over in time. Both of those problems would be fixed at a combination oil, lube and car wash place Lucky had passed on the corner of Lake Mead and Las Vegas Boulevards. He was sure it could survive a long trip.

Lucky paid the asked-for price without haggling, in cash, to the surprised dealer. Then, he used a false driver license, signed the paperwork, pocketed the title, handed over a wad of hundreds plus a generous tip, winked, accepted the keys and drove the estate wagon away.

The dealer shook his head, "Crazy gringos." He knew to keep quiet if the cops ever came around asking questions.

Seth and Lucky left Las Vegas that same Sunday night, with Lucky doing the driving. They headed north on I-15 through Salt Lake City. Then they continued northwest through Boise, Idaho, and Pendleton, Oregon. They crossed the Columbia River at Hermiston, Oregon.

Their objective was the remote town of Penticton, in British Columbia, Canada.

On the Washington side of the river they stopped to consider their options.

They essentially had two routes they could take. The main route that almost everyone took when going north to Canada was I-5 through Seattle, crossing into Canada at the Peace Arch a mile north of Blaine, Washington.

But there was a variation, an alternate to this route called the Blaine/Surrey Pacific Highway Crossing, essentially a truck crossing. The border control shacks were situated on the northern edge of the town of Blaine. Because trucks were not allowed to cross into Canada at the more busy Peace Arch on I-5, the big commercial carriers were routinely routed north on Washington state highway 543/BC highway 15 through the town of Blaine, coming out the other side of the border into Surrey, B.C.

Seth decided either of those two ways was just too fraught with risk.

Their map showed them a back way to get to Canada by taking a route up the Yakima Valley to the town of Ellensburg, situated on I-90. Then they could continue north through Wenatchee, and the remote northern Washington towns of Omak and Tonasket. They would cross the international boundary a few miles further on at the sleepy little border town of Oroville, Washington. Across the border a couple minutes north of Oroville was another little town named Osoyoos, B.C.

They turned toward Yakima and Ellensburg.

Their first sprint took them north across a vast plateau of rolling hills planted with wheat fields. The wheat was gone, recently harvested, stored in bulging aluminum grain holders standing in rows of threes and fours next to isolated farm houses. Only neat rows of shortened stalks remained in the endless fields. Smoke from burning wheat stubble hung in thin layers across the pale blue sky.

The lonely highway finally breached a cleft in the plateau and began the swift, steep descent down into the town of Toppenish, home of the Hanford Works, formerly a major site in the 1950s and '60s of atomic energy activity—turning uranium into enriched lethal weapons. Now the secret activity inside the works was for peaceful purposes. Or so it was believed.

They picked up the highway to Yakima and followed a beautiful still-verdant valley with many farms neighbored tightly against each other. They drove for an hour passing a checkerboard of apple, hops, and mint farms, all dormant now after the fall harvests. Mackenzie drift boats, spaced a respectful distance apart, bobbed along carrying eager, intent fly fishermen rhythmically casting their flies at pods of trout hidden under the brushy river banks.

Lucky cautiously drove through Yakima, careful not to attract law enforcement by breaching any traffic laws. Safely through the town, they stopped on the outskirts again for gas, a bathroom, leg stretch and badly burned coffee.

They continued northwest up a long grade of stark lava and sagebrush country. It could easily have passed for somewhere in Afghanistan. Near the summit they overtook a long convoy of heavy Army Reserve vehicles slogging slowly along. The other side of the summit took them rapidly down to the town of Ellensburg. There they crossed I-90 and turned deliberately north instead of following the string of trucks and cars taking the more traveled route west to Seattle.

It was late afternoon. The autumnal sun was starting to settle below the Cascades to the west when they passed through the worn-out towns of Omak, then Tonasket. Oroville and the international border were just a few more miles. Lucky tensed and turned toward Seth who had been peacefully napping.

"Almost there, boss." Seth stirred and sat up. He checked his watch and suggested Lucky crush out his cigarette.

Lucky rehearsed his memorized speech for Seth's benefit yet another time as they drove through Oroville. The border loomed ahead.

International Border, Oroville, Washington

"Purpose of your visit to Canada?" the uniformed border guard asked. He was the only person in the small guard shack. It was getting on toward sundown, almost dark. In an attempt to make the travelers' entry into Canada more authentic—or enjoyable, it was hoped—someone in authority had suggested planting a border of pine trees along the highway. Long shadows from the pines lay across their path north.

Lucky was in the driver's seat of the Chevy estate wagon. He had rolled down the window, smiled. "I'm bringing my friend for a farewell visit with family. He's in the last stages of cancer and wants to say his goodbyes."

Lucky tipped his head to indicate the elderly man seated in the passenger seat. The border guard briefly looked in through Lucky's open window.

Seth held his breath, but Lucky gave his lines beautifully and convincingly. Seth had coached him what to say for several hundred miles.

Seth wore an outfit Lucky had bought for him at a Las Vegas Goodwill store: worn buffalo plaid flannel shirt, rumpled khakis and a brown leather bomber jacket. He also wore dark aviator glasses and an old sweaty, flat golf cap pulled low over his brow. He was scrunched down in his seat. Seth waved his hand weakly, gave the Canadian guard a faint, sickly smile.

It worked. Without hesitating the guard said, "So sorry to hear that. Well, you folks have a nice stay, eh?" He waved them through and they slipped quietly into Oroville's sister town of Osoyoos. Out on Lake Osoyoos a lonely fisherman guided his small boat through the last glow of daylight back to the basin. Pinks and oranges from the setting sun tinged the crest of the boat's gentle wake.

Seth and Lucky drove on toward Penticton and a waiting plane. Only another 45 minutes. Their pilots were already climbing aboard the jet, stowing bags, settling in and going over their pre-flight checklist.

The engines would be warmed and the plane cleared for departure by the time their passengers arrived.

FBI Offices, Denver

Seth was a planner, always considering the contingencies, always looking ahead at the dangers and risks that could possibly pop up and surprise. It was always the little details, the unanticipated that got people with criminal intentions caught.

Several months before, Summers had carefully cultivated and groomed a low-level secretary within the Denver FBI offices. All she had to do was keep her eyes open and her ears dialed in for anything that might possibly impact Seth Summers.

And then to keep him informed.

Her name was Bertina, but to her FBI colleagues, to her friends, and to Seth Summers, she was just Tina. She was fairly attractive in a sad sort of way. She wasn't yet saddled with the onset of middle age and the ensuing weight gain that most women dread. Tina was slender but with nice curves. Her hair was short and blonde. She dressed stylishly but not anything flashy. She wore little jewelry and minimal makeup. What little fragrance she used was au courant, not overwhelming, just enough to confirm that she was a woman. She rarely turned heads but had a photogenic face with high cheekbones and sincere hazel eyes.

She had easily become one of Seth's mistresses. She was flattered by the attention Summers paid her, the little expensive surprise gifts. She thought she was the one and only love in his life. Tina also was under the mistaken impression that she would someday soon be Mrs. Summers.

Tina was in the room when the call went to the RCMP in Vancouver. She took a restroom break, slipped out unnoticed and went downstairs. Out on the street, she frantically looked around for a pay phone. Across the street and a half-block away was what she needed. She placed a call to Summers. Her message was brief, cryptic. Summers didn't reply except to say, "Got it." And the line went dead.

Penticton, B.C., Canada

The Mounties sped toward the Penticton regional airport with sirens blaring, red emergency lights flashing. They had to stop for several frustrating minutes while a muscular Kubota road scraper moved a length of concrete drain pipe into a deep cut under repair in the road. Two stout Mounties jumped out of the back of their tan Suburban and shouted at the line of vehicles behind them to back up. Shouts and insults were exchanged before the closest car behind them finally obeyed orders and backed up enough that the Suburban could turn around. The two officers jumped back in, the Suburban turned around and they sped off to try another route to the airport. Those precious minutes lost would prove costly to them.

The Mounties arrived at the airport just in time to see a silver-and-blue private jet, a Gulfstream III, streak down the asphalt runway and lift its nose in the air. They watched helplessly as the wheels tucked up neatly under the wings. It was a beautiful sight to watch. But it wasn't beautiful to them. It was a freaking disaster, eh? The Gulfstream quickly disappeared through the low cloud cover into inky darkness.

The pilot's filed flight plan had indicated a destination of Saskatoon, Saskatchewan. The RCMP quickly concluded that was bogus. They considered calling for the Royal Canadian Air Force to scramble fighter jets from Comox Royal Air Base on Vancouver Island, to track down the Gulfstream, do a regulation intercept maneuver, and try to force it to land.

The Mounties requested approval from their governor at the Ministry of Justice, but hit a dead-end. They were crisply informed that the Canadian Ministry of Defence had a strict policy that only the Premier or his deputy could approve such an action for fear of setting off an international kerfuffle. The Gulfstream bore U.S. registration ID on its tail. Hands off. Notify the FBI in the U.S. They can handle it. Not our problem. File closed.

Sir, the FBI *were* the ones who got us involved in the first place. Oh. Too bad, eh?

A dark green Chevy woody wagon sat abandoned behind the farthest hangar at the Penticton air field. It had temporary Nevada paper tags that indicated the owner as one Matt Beardshall, of East Sahara Ave. Las Vegas, Nevada. The inside of the wagon had the lingering stench of years of tobacco smoke with a top-note of rancid vomit. The inside had been carefully wiped down to remove any trace of fingerprints. They were dealing with a pro.

Lucky watched the Mounties from a safe distance as they combed through the wagon for scraps of evidence. Earlier that same evening he had sanitized the inside, wiping down for prints, carefully vacuuming to pick up stray hairs, fabric threads. But he forgot to empty the ashtray.

The RCMP put the three Lucky Strike cigarette butts into a plastic evidence bag and left the Chevy. The bag would eventually be buried in some file box in some obscure warehouse in Kamloops, and forgotten.

Lucky waited a few more minutes until night and total darkness had descended. He then drove away in a new silver Ford sedan with Washington plates. It had been rented for cash—Canadian dollars—to one Edgar Boyer of Kent, Washington. The girl at the Budget rental desk had easily succumbed to his flirting–designed to distract – and had asked only a couple questions: How long did he need it, and since it had Washington plates and registration, would he mind very much driving it back to Seattle, for them? He would be doing them a great favor. He assured her that he didn't mind one bit. He signed the rental agreement and accepted the keys. She said she would have to accompany him out to inspect the car and note any dents or scratches. They looked it over and both said their goodbyes.

Lucky slipped behind the wheel and drove away from Penticton. He backtracked to Osoyoos, where the friendly border guard thought he recognized him, squinted in the darkness and waved him through into the U.S. without any conversation or questions.

Lucky smiled and waved a thank you to the Border Patrolman, let out his breath and lit a cigarette. Another Lucky Strike. He traveled only at night, holing up in cheap motels in one-horse towns during the day. He made his way steadily south and east.

And so it was that a couple nights after he slipped back across the border from Canada, Lucky was stopped by a couple of boys who happened to be reservation police from the Wind River Indian Reservation (representing, respectively, Eastern Shoshone and Northern Arapaho tribes). He was halfway between Riverton and Lander, Wyoming. He had been wrestling with his old Zippo cigarette lighter. He had both hands resting atop the steering wheel, struggling with the cigarette in one hand, the Zippo in the other. All he got from the Zippo were sparks as his rented car drifted across the center line, barely missing an oncoming law enforcement vehicle, a new pickup truck occupied by two young reservation policemen.

The police made a quick U-turn, sped up to catch the Ford, and flipped the toggle switch under the dash that activated the siren and flashing emergency lights.

Lucky saw the red flashing lights in his rear-view mirror. His bowels almost failed him. He had a couple seconds to make a decision: he had two options, pull over or try to outrun the police. He pulled over. He rolled to a stop on the verge, killed the motor, and slumped down into his seat.

After he produced his fake ID, he was made to step out of the car and submit to a breathalyzer test. It proved negative. Meanwhile, one of the reservation cops probed his strong flashlight beam around the inside of the compact rental, sniffing the air inside for traces of alcohol or pot. The only thing he smelled was new car saturated with stale cigarette smoke.

The reservation cops asked Lucky why he had been weaving across the center line, why he had almost collided with them. He claimed he was trying to light a cigarette, faulty Zippo lighter, etc. He even handed it to them to test for themselves. They flicked the lighter a couple times and a steady flame shot skyward on the second try.

They didn't buy his excuse. They put him in their truck between them in the front seat and took him to the reservation police headquarters where he was made to spend the night. He didn't utter a word on the drive. The Ford sedan was towed to an impoundment yard.

Calls were made. The Riverton Police were brought in to help. They ran Lucky's fake ID plus his new mug shot photo through their new computers. They struck out with the fake ID, which they quickly deduced was bogus. But on the new mug shot from his arrest, they hit the jackpot. They scored a match.

THIRTY-SEVEN

A Gulfstream Jet, En Route

After making himself comfortable and accepting a tumbler of rare single malt from the pretty flight attendant in the cute light blue uniform skirt and jacket, Seth made use of the airplane's onboard satellite phone and placed a call to Morty Resnick. Seth enjoyed the luxury of flying alone.

"Plan B," was all Seth needed to say.

Morty's Office, Ft. Lauderdale, Florida

Morty knelt down under his desk with a letter opener. He pried loose and lifted a false floor tile. Nestled safely in the depression he had had excavated into the floor was a small safe. He flipped the dials quickly, feeling the numbers fall from the memory stored in his fingers. The tumblers gave their telltale click. He opened his safe, withdrew several large tightly packed bricks of currency from various countries, held together with large rubber bands. The money represented over $100,000 U.S. Then he withdrew a covey of counterfeit passports, stuffed his overnight bag to the limit with cash and a couple extra changes of clothing. Still lying in the safe was a weapon, two loaded clips, and two boxes of hollow-point bullets.

He considered for a minute bringing along his newly purchased Walther PPK .32 caliber automatic pistol. It was an exact replica of the one favored by James Bond, 007. He felt its heft, the smoothness of the action as he slid it back to expose the chamber. It was ready to slide in a clip and fire. It would only take two seconds to pull out of his waistband, aim and shoot. But Seth had been explicit about bringing weapons along. Seth knew people who could provide them. If and when.

Morty sighed, put the pistol back in the safe and closed the door. He spun the dial for the last time, picked up his bag and walked out. On the street a cab was waiting. He tossed his bag on the back seat, climbed in and tapped on the plexiglass divider. The cabbie pulled into traffic and headed west. They quickly made their way to the private executive terminal in Ft. Lauderdale.

It took Morty's pilot less than 10 minutes to reach cruising altitude. Morty's destination was the pre-arranged rendezvous point: Freeport, Bahamas. After landing, he walked two blocks and circled back to be sure he wasn't followed. When he saw he was clean, he doubled back toward to executive terminal and waited in a bar where he sat on a tall stool facing the entrance, nursing a cold beer, waiting for Seth to arrive. He felt naked without the Walther PPK.

Greyhound Bus Depot, Denver

Calvin Buckley stood in front of the bank of pay phones in the bus depot. He looked around to see if he was being watched, thinking, mumbling to himself: Seth knows what to do, Seth knows what to do, Seth knows. He always knows. Seth is a planner. Seth knows.

He fumbled in his pocket for a dime and succeeded in spilling loose change onto the tiled floor. A little black kid chased some coins on his hands and knees. The kid's mother flashed Buck a smile.

Buck zeroed in on the center phone, approached, lifted the receiver and dropped in the dime. He pulled the scrap of paper out of his shirt pocket, damp from his own nervous perspiration and dialed the number Seth had given him. His hands shook. He waited nervously as it rang and rang. Rang too many times. Too many.

He tried again. Same result. Something was wrong. Seth, or somebody, anybody, should have picked up by now and given him directions.

Cold panic gripped Calvin Buckley's guts. His mouth and throat were dry. He could really use a double vodka. On the rocks. What to do? It looked like he might have to engage his own exit strategy.

Buck hung up the receiver and was walking rapidly toward the exit onto the street when two men in dark suits suddenly materialized blocking his path. He turned to go back and was met by two more men in dark suits. None was smiling. One dark suit took a step toward Buck and produced a shiny metal badge.

"Mr. Calvin Buckley? FBI. You're under arrest in connection with bank fraud committed by you in the matter of Larimer Square Bank. Please step outside with us."

One FBI agent on each side firmly holding his arms at the elbows, he was escorted, nearly dragged, out onto the sidewalk to a waiting black Suburban parked curbside. There were three such vehicles in all.

One agent said to him, "Please turn around and place both your hands behind your back."

Instead, Buck raised his hands in a defensive gesture.

"Please, sir, please do as I say. Don't give us any trouble."

Buck dropped his hands, his head sank onto his chest, defeated. He was cuffed and read his rights. He was roughly shoved into one of the waiting Suburbans.

They sped away to the Denver FBI offices.

Freeport, Bahamas

Seth's charter touched down briefly to refuel on Santa Catalina Island, just a leisurely 26-mile boat ride from Los Angeles. They paused only for fuel and some sandwiches and a thermos of coffee, and were off again headed for Freeport, Bahamas, via a couple of friendly islands in the Caribbean. About four hours later, after scotch-hopping some more Caribbean islands, Seth's Gulfstream rolled to a stop in Freeport where he and Morty hooked up in the bar.

They left the bar five minutes apart and walked two blocks in another direction to a pre-arranged address. It was a bank building. Seth went inside to appear like he was conducting business while Morty stayed outside and window-shopped in front of a boutique next door. Morty discreetly watched in the glass to see if they were being followed. They were clean.

After a couple minutes, Seth came out and they caught a taxi and drove a half-hour to yet another address, where they booked into separate rooms for one night in a secluded luxury hotel down-island. Morty paid for the rooms in cash, U.S. dollars. Early the next morning, the two men had coffee and Danish at separate tables, backs to each other. This time, Seth watched the entrance while Morty became very engrossed in the financial pages of his copy of *The New York Times.*

When Seth was sure they weren't being watched, he laid down his own morning paper, picked up his overnight bag and walked out to find a cab. He had the driver make a couple detours around the vicinity of the hotel, using many right turns, to make sure he wasn't being followed. Five minutes later Morty climbed into a separate taxi. Both men had disposed of their canvas overnight bags and now had sets of expensive Coach travel luggage.

They were mostly unrecognizable from the two men who checked into the same hotel the night before. Morty now had short black hair and was wearing crisp khakis, a blue button-down shirt over which he had a sleeveless jacquard cotton sweater. On his feet he wore cream and tan saddle shoes. He was now a rich Preppy, complete with horn-rimmed glasses. His mustache and goatee had been shaved clean. Fake suntan cream had been rubbed on his shaven facial parts to blend with his normal tan. He actually looked 20 years younger. Seth almost didn't recognize him, walked right past him at the Freeport public airport.

Seth's former mane of silver hair had also been turned a darker shade. It was now brown, with just a touch of the natural gray at the temples and over the ears. It was trimmed much shorter and his head was covered with an expensive Borsalino Panama straw hat. He was decked out in a tan poplin suit, lightweight cotton, pink-striped shirt, open collar, no necktie. His eyes were shaded with expensive dark glasses.

Overnight, he had managed to acquire a thick mustache thanks to the high-priced makeup artist who slipped into the hotel un-noticed and made her way to their rooms by a back passageway. She stayed the night in Morty's room, no surprise to Seth.

They proceeded directly to the public airport in Freeport, checked in at the Eastern Airlines desk where Morty purchased two one-way first-class tickets to Antigua, also with cash. Their flight left less than an hour later.

St. John's, Antigua

The big jet bumped down in Antigua and they deplaned, looking around to make sure they weren't being watched. They failed to notice a petite brunette, wearing a fetching light cotton print sundress and wraparound sunglasses. She was seated primly on a jade green scooter, a hemp shopping bag over her shoulder. While appearing disinterested she was actually watching as passengers deplaned from the big commercial jet. She was curious about two gentlemen in particular, supposedly businessmen. She discreetly snapped pictures of Seth and Morty with a miniature Minox camera.

Seth and Morty took separate taxis into St. John's five minutes apart. The pretty brunette on the jade green motor scooter slipped into the stream of traffic, followed the second taxi at a safe distance of a hundred meters. She floated along between two rattle-trap island cabs, their windows open, blaring reggae music. A wind blew her skirt up mid-thigh. She didn't mind. In fact, looking sexy was part of her cover.

Morty's taxi stopped at a row of two-story offices along the High Road, known to house lawyers, solicitors and accountants. Standing on the curb waiting was the older gentleman. His taxi was just pulling away. She continued on past them and made a stop farther up the street. The men didn't speak to each other but turned and entered the light-yellow stucco building together.

The men had planned to be there only long enough to have a short meeting with a solicitor before stopping by one of many private banks on the island. Satisfied that things were set up as planned, Seth carefully scanned the street outside the bank. He noticed a suntanned petite blonde with Hollywood starlet dark glasses intently gazing into a shop window across the street. She was dressed in shorts and a skimpy halter top, a large Gucci bag over her shoulder. Coming out of the shop, a handsome young man joined her. He also was dressed in shorts and a loose island-print shirt. They seemed like any normal couple, a pair of honeymooning tourists.

Certain again that they were clean, Seth and Morty hailed down another passing taxi. They were headed back to the airport. But first, a side trip for an early dinner at a trendy restaurant their private banker had raved about, famous for its conch salad.

The petite blonde and her male companion had followed them, riding double on a Flamingo-pink motor scooter. They entered the restaurant, touching each other like newlyweds on honeymoon. She giggled and kissed him below his ear. He kissed her back. The couple was seated at a table near the two men. They ordered drinks and put their heads close together, seeming to be whispering words of endearment to each other. Onlookers would rightly suppose they were in love. Seth paid them no attention.

Morty, always ready for any drink containing alcohol, ordered up a pitcher of chilled daiquiris. Seth ordered fresh-caught prawns grilled in coconut and lime with a conch salad on the side. They ate slowly, unaware the blonde was taking their pictures with her miniature Minox, the kind favored by clandestine operatives of various government agencies. Agencies that supposedly didn't exist.

The two men finished their meal and passed on pudding. Instead, they ordered espressos with cognac for their dessert course. Their waiter offered them Cuban cigars, which they enjoyed with their aperitifs. They paid double the meal's price listed in the menu and left a tip large enough to raise eyebrows with disbelief.

The petite blonde would later note this in her written, coded report. She quickly went back into town, had the film developed and faxed copies to her bosses back at Langley. Then she and her boyfriend/partner went back to their cottage near the beach on a picturesque point of land. The boyfriend changed into traveling clothes and silently disappeared without kissing her. She let herself into the cottage, where she took off the wig and, as a natural brunette, wrote up her report. The coded report also went to the bosses in Langley.

There, the report was quickly scanned and tucked into a manila file. The photos were examined, run through the computers for a match, and, satisfied that the two men were not wanted, were not terrorists, posed no danger to American security or interests abroad, the bosses and their army of analysts filed the photos away in their archives, where they would soon be forgotten.

Seth made it in time for the next available flight out of Antigua, first-class one-way on Eastern Airlines, a route that would take him to Rio de Janeiro, Brazil.

Morty went by another airline that left that same evening to Buenos Aires, Argentina. Both their tickets were paid in cash, this time with British pounds.

Morty stayed in Buenos Aires for 24 hours to make sure he wasn't being followed. He then booked a flight to Panama City, Panama, first class, where he was to stay holed up under yet another assumed name for a couple days. From there, he would take another flight under yet a different passport issued to a Mr. Paul Reeder.

Morty again changed his physical appearance to match the stolen passport. He threw away the last passport he'd used in a rubbish bin outside his hotel.

Seth Summers stayed in a private hotel in Rio facing Ipanema Beach for three weeks, working on his tan and a real mustache, admiring the many gorgeous girls in string bikinis before traveling on to a private spa in Switzerland, where he was scheduled for a complete facial makeover. Plastic surgery by the world's best.

Then after a reasonable time, on a secluded Greek island recovering from the operations, he would finally feel able to relax a little, confident that he had given the Feds the slip. In time, he would be able to quit looking over his shoulder to see if he was being followed.

His first day in Brazil, Seth had made a phone call to Morty, now known as Paul Reeder to the owners of a little boutique hotel in the Portuguese seaside town of Azenhas do Mar. According to his newest passport—British—Mr. Reeder sported short graying hair, a mustache and goatee. Real this time. He was a photographer and author, researching and gathering photos for a slick coffee table book on Portuguese country cooking.

Seth gave Mr. Reeder a message worded in code that only the two men understood. Translated it said: Sell all our holdings in Stagecoach Energy, starting at the rate of 50 thousand shares a day at prevailing *ask* price. Mr. Reeder would increase the daily volume of shares being dumped into the market by 10 thousand, until all shares were disposed of.

Seth was no longer concerned about how this dumping would affect the market price; they needed ready cash. There was too much risk in accessing the large deposits sitting in his private bank accounts in Lugano, Hong Kong, Antigua and Malta. He could wait.

Stagecoach Energy, Dallas

Stagecoach Energy CEO Lorne Bagley saw the large blocks of Stagecoach stock being sold daily by a host of mysterious stockholders from various foreign brokerage firms. The volume was increasing by 10 thousand shares daily, which made no sense to him. Every day the increased volume drove the bid-ask quote down further. He sensed that Seth, who supposedly had vanished, was selling. Or, rather, dumping. Why? Was Seth angry at Lorne for some imagined slight and this was his revenge? Lorne had always enjoyed a good working rapport with Summers. The only answer that made sense was Seth needed cash.

Lorne continued to stand firm as they saw the stock price dropping rapidly in the course of just three days of trading. Finally, Lorne couldn't take any more, couldn't stand by any longer. He consulted with Stagecoach's securities lawyers in New York and, on their advice, determined the company should voluntarily halt trading.

The SEC also was watching Stagecoach closely and was just about to stop trading when word came that management had already pulled the plug. An informal investigation was launched.

THIRTY-EIGHT

On the road, I-70 west of Denver

The day after they celebrated the sting operation, on advice of the Denver FBI, Ricky Bob Peabody took a circuitous route driving back to Weatherford. He was shadowed a couple hundred yards behind by two agents in a very plain black sedan. The convoy headed west from Golden on Interstate-70. The agents maintained a steady speed and distance between vehicles for several hours, as far west as Grand Junction, Colorado. Ricky stopped for a bathroom break and to replenish his coffee and gas tank.

At Grand Junction, the two agents passed him off to another pair of FBI agents. His new escorts were dressed like a couple of ranch hands looking for work, driving an old Chevy pickup. These two followed Ricky Bob west at a discreet distance nearly to Green River, Utah, where he turned off I-70 and headed south toward Arches and Canyonlands through Moab, Utah. He stopped briefly in Moab, then continued on through Dove Creek to Cortez, Colorado. The FBI agents followed.

Ricky Bob stopped again in Cortez for another fill of gas, a coffee and burrito break. The huge chicken, cheese and bean burrito, with locally grown red peppers was the best he had ever tasted. He could only eat half. His lips burned for the next hour.

His route then took him south through the reservation at the butt-numbing speed limit of 50 mph. It was now dark and getting late.

Ricky Bob almost collided with an oncoming pickup load of Navajo Indians driving without headlights. He was shaken from the near-miss.

Ricky stopped for the night in Gallup, New Mexico, opting for a seedy motel next door to a trading post of sorts that sold cheap silver and turquoise Indian jewelry, blankets, pottery and the ubiquitous carved wooden Koki imps. Most of it came from Taiwan.

The two FBI agents would take two-hour turns alternately watching and sleeping in the Chevy pickup in the motel parking lot. They had parked so that they had a good view of Ricky Bob's room.

After Ricky Bob had registered and settled in his room, a few minutes later, at precisely 10:08 p.m. he came out of his room used the pay phone in the lobby. The first call he placed was to Nan, who was very relieved to hear his voice.

"Where have y'all been? I've been worried sick over you. It's like you disappeared off the face of the earth."

Ricky assured her he was all right, that everything was fine and yes, he'd had a very successful business trip. He would be home by tomorrow night to tell her everything. He planned to spend the night at home in his own bed before he had to scoot off to Weatherford again.

"Oh, got a date with your girlfriend, that Dolly P fancy gal?"

Ricky Bob laughed. There was an awkward silence before he spoke again.

"Nan, honey, until I get home tomorrow there's somethin' I need you to do. Now I don't want you to get upset. Promise me you won't get hysterical?"

"What's wrong? Somethin's wrong I can feel it. Oh, Ricky now you got me scared!"

Ricky Bob did his best to calm her down and reassure her that she and the kids would be all right. But … He asked her to lock the doors with the kids inside. Don't send them to school tomorrow, call in to the school tell them they're sick or somethin' like that.

And don't answer the door or the telephone and don't call the police unless you see somebody like a stranger hangin' around actin' creepy-weird.

Nan was now sobbing with big loud gulps in between. And hiccups. She always got the hiccups when she started crying. He missed her so bad he ached.

The next call Ricky Bob made was to Phillip Connoff. He didn't answer. So, Ricky dialed Jerry Jordan to give him the good news about the big rig that would soon be in their hands. "That's great news, Ricky. Really pleased. Really. Have you told Phillip?"

Ricky said he wasn't able to get ahold of their other partner.

Then Jerry asked, "Where in God's name have you been? We were starting to get worried that something bad had happened to you up in Denver. How'd it go with the bank?"

"Got the loan," Ricky lied. "Yeah, I sure got that loan. That's what I went there for and that's all that matters, isn't it? And real soon we'll have that big rig. I'll fill you in tomorrow when I get back home and get me some lovin' and some rest. Right now I'm bone tired. See ya later."

"Yeah, later, Ricky. And thanks."

10:49 p.m. The two FBI agents watched Ricky Bob Peabody go back to his room and they relaxed. "You hungry for anything? Want a donut? Coffee? Anything?" the lead agent asked his partner who declined. It was going to be a long night. But they were used to long nights. They'd been on many a stakeout together. They would take turns sleeping, two hours on and two hours off. They worked well together. As good partners do who love their jobs like these men did.

Larimer Square Bank, Denver

Dill returned to the bank for what he hoped would be the last time. He had already completed the ritual packing of his things, only a couple final matters of business to conclude. He went down the hallway from his office and looked out over the Bullpen. All those nice young people, kids really. This ship is taking on water fast and what will happen to them? Will they get sucked down with the ship, drowned by the undertow? Dill struggled with his conscience. What was his duty toward these young people? What was the right thing to do? What would JoEllen tell him to do?

These kids had full lives ahead of them. How would this looming disaster affect their careers? Would they survive, move on, chalk it all up to another experience and learn something from it?

He thought about how being a philosophy major in college hadn't really prepared him for the real world and the many conflicting choices one had to make daily. His favorite professor had called these choices *matters of conscience*. These choices seemed to have no happy endings. Somebody would draw the short straw. Somebody was bound to lose. Somebody always got hurt.

Dill wandered into the Bullpen and sensed something was different. The young professionals looked up at him with a new strange expression in their eyes. They were expecting something. They sensed something was up but didn't quite know what it was. Rumors had been flying and they somehow knew they were all going to be affected. Negatively.

Dill remembered something he had read, about so many of those young soldiers in WWI, boys really, who had been forced to sit in muddy, stinking trenches for sometimes weeks on end, thinking about death, their own deaths, and how it might come. Would it be a single bullet, a grenade, a cannon shell, mustard gas, enemy bayonet, a slow death strung up on barbed wire in No Man's Land, wounded, slowly dying without morphine, food, water or human companionship?

They sat and they waited, those young boys, and thought of death and despaired. Despaired because they had no control over their lives. They waited until some went crazy and would shoot themselves in the foot or a hand or a leg and hope to get sent back to a hospital far away from the front. Some slipped away under cover of darkness and tried to find their way home, lost boys in a strange land speaking a strange tongue, road signs they didn't understand, starving, wandering until they got caught, summarily court martialed and shot as traitors, cowards.

The generals made the decisions to live or die. Decisions made far away from the front, the shooting, the filth, the rats, the crap, the blood, the stink. The generals—German, French, Scots, Brits, Aussies, Kiwis, Canadian, American—they killed the boys, sent them out to die.

But philosophers aren't called on to make those life or death decisions. Philosophers and poets don't send young boys out to die. Philosophers and poets struggle to make meaning out of the madness of war, the rules and moral arguments that apply only to war, the justifications of why it was all right to kill those boys, boys on either side, but still boys. Boys who would never fully grow to reach manhood, know love of a wife, children. Boys who would never have the warmth of hearth and home in a place far away from war. A place where there's peace—and no guns, no mustard gas, no barbed wire. Where there wasn't this monstrous thing called No Man's Land.

Dill looked in their eyes, those eager young faces in the Bullpen. Didn't they deserve better? Didn't they deserve a bright future? And he had an idea.

Dill went back to his office, closed his door, and sorted through a stack of business cards until he found the one he was looking for. He picked up his phone and dialed. It rang several times, then a voice. "Mr. Swope? This is Dill Robertson. Maybe you remember me? I'm calling from the Larimer Square Bank in Denver. That's right, we met when you were here recently." Dill sucked in a breath, exhaled slowly, sat up straight and continued, "I think there are some really bad things about Larimer Square Bank that you need to know."

Okmulgee, Oklahoma

The next morning two weary FBI agents in an old Chevy pickup left Gallup and followed Ricky Bob east on I-40 until they reached Albuquerque, where they passed the baton to another team of agents. This latest team followed Ricky Bob all the way to his home in Okmulgee. Assuring themselves that he and his family were in no imminent danger, they settled down to watch over him.

Ricky parked his truck in his own driveway. He found, true to his instructions, his wife had locked the front door. He rang the doorbell. A curtain covering the sidelight parted slightly and a tow-headed boy with freckles and a wide gap where his two front teeth should have been peered cautiously out. The kid disappeared, and Ricky heard the sweetest sound.

"Daddy's home. Daddy's home. He's really home!"

The front door opened and there stood his wife. In spite of her bloodshot eyes, red nose and puffy face from crying all night, she was still beautiful to him. The kids spilled out and swirled around him, holding on to his legs, jumping up to grab his neck, squealing with laughter.

He staggered inside, dragging the pack of kids. He hugged Nan, squeezing the breath out of her. It felt good to be home, even if only for a few hours. Nan demanded that he sit down and tell her everything. He said he would after they had dinner and the kids were in bed.

Larimer Square Bank, Denver

While Dill was on the phone with Gary Swope of the FDIC in Kansas City, Dill's secretary, Martha Caswell, poked her head in through the door and handed him a note. It read: Agent Nieve FBI needs to talk to you ASAP. Urgent. With a phone number that Dill had already memorized.

"Mr. Swope, could I call you back in a few minutes? I have a little emergency I need to tend to. Sorry. Back to you in a few minutes. Thanks."

Dill called the FBI.

"Nieve."

"This is Dill Robertson. You called earlier?"

"Just thought you should know, we picked up Calvin Buckley a little while ago. He's now in custody. My agents are questioning—er interviewing—him, even as we speak." Dill thanked the agent and hung up.

Dill sat and thought. coming down on the Larimer Square Bank and he wasn't sure now what he should do. Should he do anything? Did he need to do anything? After all, he had handed his written resignation to Buckley just this morning. And at the time he really meant what he'd written in the letter.

He'd also done what he considered his duty by the FDIC, the FBI. What more was required of him?

Poets. Philosophers. Matters of conscience. But first he needed to call Gary Swope and finish what he'd started there.

After calling Swope, Dill put on his coat and headed for the back door to get in his pickup. He needed to talk things out with JoEllen. He knew in his heart what was the right thing to do, but he needed her confirmation, her steady calm reassurance that this philosopher had come down on the side of right.

Dill was surprised to be met at the back door by two FBI agents in dark suits. One of them was Agent Don Worthen. "Well, Mr. Worthen, we meet again." Dill tried to sound casual, relaxed. Was his tone just a little too forced, too hearty? Worthen wasn't grinning this time.

"Good day Mr. Robinson," Worthen nodded, indicated his partner. "Meet my partner, Agent Horvath." Horvath nodded curtly. Too curtly, Dill thought. They stood there blocking the doorway.

"Anything I can do for you fellows?" Dill inquired.

"No sir. We're here for security. Some other agents are down the hall going through Mr. Buckley's office. They have a warrant. Were you going somewhere?"

Dill suddenly felt like he was under suspicion. Did they suspect he was guilty of something? He couldn't blame them; he did work for the bank, a bank that now was tainted. Of course, there would be questions, suspicion, questions to be asked, people to be interviewed. That's what happened in situations like this. That's what their job was, the FBI.

"No… well, yes, actually. I thought I'd go check on my wife, at the hospital. I think they're going to give her a clean bill and we can get home in time for Thanksgiving." Dill waited as Worthen looked at him for a long minute. "Is that okay? Am I needed here? I mean for anything? You'll know where to find me."

Worthen nodded, they stepped aside and Dill made his escape. Out of habit he glanced in the back of his truck to make sure his fly rod was still there. It was.

Okmulgee, Oklahoma

After they had gone out for barbeque to celebrate Ricky's return and the kids were in bed asleep, Ricky told Nan all that had happened. When he finished, her eyes were wide with amazement. He tried to downplay the actual danger he might have been in had Buckley discovered he was wearing a wire. He left her with the impression that the funds from the loan were actually in his new account at the Larimer Square Bank in Denver. In actual fact he had yet to access any funds. That wasn't going to happen until the feds gave him the green light. Until then he was in a state of nervous limbo. They would be watching their household funds and expenditures very carefully.

According to the story Nan would spread to her network of girlfriends over coffee the next day, Ricky had scored a big one and would soon be drilling for deep gas in the Anadarko. She was already making plans for some home remodeling, new furniture, a new car – a sensible family van for herself. Maybe even a new home in the better part of town.

"And, is that all? You've told me everything?" she asked. Ricky looked down at his hands. His fingernails were dirty and needed trimming. "Ricky?"

"Well … there is one thing. I need to ask your opinion." She waited, and he proceeded to tell her about the falsified drilling logs he had found in Weatherford, the dry hole scam the Stagecoach people were pulling. "What do you think I should do?"

Nan had been raised in a fairly devout Baptist family. Her daddy was a deacon, had been ever since she could remember. Her momma had always sung in the choir and was usually the first to volunteer to take in a meal when there was a sickness in a family or a new baby. They said grace over every meal.

Nan had been taught to know the difference between right and wrong and if she was ever in doubt she could pray and the Good Lord would safely guide her to the right answers. Every time. Without fail. Those early teachings were still deeply imbedded in her being. She still said her prayers every night.

Ricky had been raised in a Methodist home. Sort of. He had gone to church with his family when it didn't interfere with hunting or fishing. It was a hit or miss affair. But his mother had encouraged him to always do the right thing. His dad had never sat him down for the birds and bees talk. Anything he thought he knew came from his friends. So, he and Nan had sort of fallen into the habit of checking things out for themselves.

After high school he'd gone off to play football at OU, leaving a tearful Nan behind to finish out her senior year in high school. He'd asked her why she was crying. She said it was because he was going off to college and she'd lose him to some cute sorority girl and he'd forget all about her. He promised to never forsake her.

That last night she invited him to go all the way. When he came home for Christmas, she told him she was pregnant. They got married over the holiday. In the living room of her parents' home. It was a private affair. They moved into a small apartment off-campus in Norman, and Ricky finished his one and only year at OU. He was also finished with football. He started working for his father in the oil business and that was that.

"You gotta do the right thing," Nan said.

"I'm not sure what the right thing is."

"What is your conscience saying?"

Ricky grinned. "Well, on one shoulder there's a good angel sayin' I should blow the whistle, whatever that means. On my other shoulder, the bad angel's sayin' forget that. Buy those leases out from under those crooks and finish them wells yourself."

"Isn't there someone you can talk to in private, get some advice?"

"Like a second opinion?" She nodded. Ricky smiled and his countenance brightened, the shadow was gone. "I think I know just the guy who can help." He took her in his arms and said, "Now I think we need some time together. Are the kids asleep?" Nan nodded as she started to undress.

They went to bed and caught up on some much-needed togetherness.

THIRTY-NINE

Oncology Ward, Denver Hospital

Dill was happy to see JoEllen up and busy gathering her things into her suitcase and the cardboard box the hospital had provided. She straightened up and smiled as Dill entered. "Well hello, stranger." They embraced and kissed. "I'm ready to go home," she said.

"They've cleared you? We can check you out?"

She nodded. "Today, if you can swing it. I got my discharge briefing this morning. I need to come back in 30 days for a routine checkup, but other than that …"

Dill knew she could do it, beat the Big C. She had always been a fighter and he loved her for her courage and toughness, her dogged determination to keep on keeping on and never quit. He wiped a small tear of joy from the corner of his eye. He sat her on the edge of the bed and told her he needed her advice on something. She nodded, listening, waiting.

Dill explained his dilemma: turn his back on Larimer Square Bank, cut and run, clear out of Dodge, declare victory and go home as they had discussed. Or did he have some kind of moral duty to stay and try to help clean up the mess? He was in no doubt that with all the recent happenings and the feds' involvement it wouldn't be long before the bank closed.

"It's that bad?" she asked. He nodded. Then he explained the process of how the banking regulators had the power to declare a bank insolvent, if, in their opinion, it was no longer a safe and sound financial institution. If it had failed, in layman's terms.

She indicated that she understood, and asked, "So, what happens next?"

"I've already placed the call to the FDIC people in Kansas City. They have their own team who have a ton of experience in dealing with bank failures. They're on their way as we speak."

"What will they do? And how would it involve you?"

Dill explained how the FDIC would make the formal declaration that the bank has failed and they'd take it over, since they have that authority granted by Congress. The FDIC would put out invitations for interested financial institutions to buy the failed bank's assets, and assume the responsibility of taking care of the depositors' accounts in a safe and prudent way. In his opinion, there wasn't much in the way of assets, only massive liabilities.

He explained how Buckley had been the key person involved in soliciting jumbo CDs, "hot" deposits, and how Buck had made a large number of loans—mostly to cronies—that would probably go bad very quickly. Probably as soon as the borrowers heard that Buckley had been arrested and the FDIC had taken over, they would run, try to hide, try to avoid the collection process.

There'd be lawsuits aplenty. The courts would be clogged with litigation for years to come. All on account of one greedy rogue banker on the take who hadn't any business to be called a banker. He was a garden variety crook.

There was another very important factor, Dill said, and that involved the many upstream correspondent banks that had purchased a large participating chunk of those flaky loans. They would quickly discover their massive financial exposure and would have to write off huge losses.

"Like, how much?"

"In losses?"

Jo nodded. "Hard to say, but if I had to guess we're talking many billions. Dollars."

JoEllen drew in a breath. Dill continued with his analysis.

Some participating banks would probably be sucked down with the undertow of the sinking ship known as the Larimer Square Bank of Denver. Heads would roll. Bank presidents and CEOs would get the axe, maybe even be facing some serious lawsuits by shareholders for malfeasance—even fraud—and class action suits by depositors. Boards of directors of these proud old institutions would be forced to resign in disgrace, a cloud of suspicion and doubt following them around forever.

Careers would be ruined. He could even envision suicides. Jo looked shocked when he said that. And, again, there'd be huge lawsuits.

"How'd you like to be a lawyer right now?" Jo laughed. "Think of all the business that's going to fall in their laps."

Dill shook his head sadly. "Right now I'm thinking of the bank employees, the little people who are going to get hurt. Collateral damage, they called it in the Vietnam war. And there are all those nice young people who worked for those correspondent banks. What's going to happen to them? How will they manage?"

"Poor Dill. Always trying to save all the wild ponies. Honey, you can't protect everyone, you know."

"Yes, I know. Only too well. What should I do? Tell me, Jo. What's my moral obligation here? What's the right thing that Dill Robertson should do? Where should he look for his lode star?"

"First I have a question? What's going to happen to you? Are you in danger of being sued over this? And I don't mean just civil suits. We're talking possible criminal."

Dill winced.

She went on: "Could we lose everything we've worked so hard to build up? We have a long heritage to live up to. What's going to happen to us, our boys, you and me? Our lovely home and the ranch? I can see this thing possibly tearing us apart as a family, destroying us."

"That's the moral dilemma, see? I know we have a heritage to live up to. And those ancestors' voices are saying loud and clear: Dill, do the right thing!" He looked at her, pleading. "I'm too close to this thing. I can't see my way out. I need your clear vision and your wonderful sense of truth. What do we do?"

"I have an idea of how to start. Let's pray about it." She began kneeling by the side of her bed. Dill looked around, hesitated.

"Here? Now?"

"Sure, c'mon." He knelt and Jo began a sweet, pleading prayer, asking the Lord to guide her husband to the right solution. He was a good man, she said, and needed His help.

When she was finished, Dill arose with a sense of calm and comfort. He knew what he had to do now. He kissed her goodbye, squared his shoulders and left.

As he walked to the parking lot, it began to snow, light flakes, pure and white.

He glanced in the back of his truck. His fly rod was missing. Someone had taken it. "You gotta be kiddin'," he mumbled to himself.

Then he relaxed and thought it was probably some poor, homeless vagrant who would pawn it for five bucks and buy a bag of marijuana. He hoped they'd buy something to eat first.

FBI Offices, Denver

The first thing Calvin Buckley had said on his ride downtown was he wanted to talk with his lawyer. Demanded, even. Nieve told him, "Sure you can talk to your lawyer, but first we have a few questions we'd like to ask. Buckley used his favorite four-letter word and told Nieve he wasn't answering any blankety-blank questions without his lawyer present. Nieve didn't respond. Buckley clammed up. Nobody spoke for the rest of the ride.

Buckley noticed the bulge under Nieve's left armpit. His piece. Buck wondered what kind of pistol it was. Were they now using the new Austrian Glock 9mm, or were they still back in the Stone Age carrying Smith & Wesson .38 caliber six-shot Police Special revolvers? Was it chrome plated or blued? Four-inch barrel or snub-nose? Had they started searching his office? Probably already there. He hoped they somehow wouldn't find the .32 Beretta hidden under his desk.

They put Buckley in a small 8' by 8' interview room without windows and very little ventilation. He was still cuffed with his hands uncomfortably behind his back. The Feds had also added leg restraints before they locked him in the interview room. He had an itchy nose that was driving him crazy, and he couldn't reach to scratch it!

Buck was hot, perspiring. He could smell his own sour sweat. He wished he could have a drink—vodka on the rocks, Dr. Pepper, coffee, water, anything. His mouth was filled with cotton. And he needed the men's room. Badly. He didn't think he could hold it in any longer. Next time he got arrested he'd remember to visit the bathroom first. He laughed at his own sense of irony.

Why did they make these stupid cuffs so tight? His neck and shoulders ached terribly from his arms being unnaturally pulled tight behind his back. He was seconds from letting loose on these guys. He had a string of choice names running through his mind.

Where's my worthless excuse for a lawyer? And why won't they let me use the head? Buck thought. They're trying to wear me down, make me talk. Well, they won't get crap out of me.

The reason Buck was sitting so long in the interview room was this: U.S. Attorney Ryan Henning had called together his Grand Jury and had presented what he considered enough evidence for them to issue out a true bill. He would then quickly finalize the draft indictment his staff had been working on, charging Seth Summers, Calvin Buckley, the board of directors of Larimer Square Bank, and several other lesser defendants, together with a list of John Does Numbers I through XX, one of which was Pete Curtis aka "Lucky." Names to be provided if and when the prosecutors discovered the true identity of all the other said unknown malefactors/defendants.

The indictment listed a cafeteria-style roll call of various federal laws that said defendants had violated. Among them were bank fraud, wire fraud, communications fraud; securities laws violations and fraud; tax evasion; misfeasance, malfeasance (doubtful those would stick); obstruction of justice; witness tampering.

There was also attempted homicide in a federal case, this one for Gus Kessimakis and John Doe number I (which was reserved for Pete Curtis, a person believed to go by the assumed name of "Lucky").

Gus's court-appointed lawyer was ineffective, lazy, nearly worthless, scared of the courtroom. He was pushing his client hard to make a plea deal. After which the client would be quickly deported by the immigration people.

Of course, the indictment also included RICO, for all of the named defendants.

The prosecution reserved the right to amend the indictment from time to time as evidence would require, adding or dropping charges, adding or deleting defendants as needed. It was almost two inches thick, double-spaced.

When Henning was satisfied with the draft, he handed it off to one of his assistants, who rushed it over to the FBI who had been waiting. They would slap it down dramatically on the table in front of Buckley. They'd order him to read it. They fully expected he would refuse until his lawyer was present to advise him.

Nieve would lose patience, smack the table with the flat of his hand and thrust his angry red face so close to Buck's that his flying spittle would hit Buck in the face as he shouted.

He would swear at Buck and say, "You can read English, can't you? Then you don't need a lousy lawyer to help you read it!" At which point, Buckley wouldn't be able to hold it in any longer and would wet himself. Tears would run down his face. Would you look at what he just did to those Tony Llama ostrich boots!

He would break soon and start singing to try and save himself. Cowards and bullies usually did. He would name names and make all kinds of outlandish allegations against the "perps" he named. He would fool himself into believing that he was actually cooperating. It would be a long process, going over his statements again and again, clarifying, cross-checking facts, until they were satisfied that they had squeezed everything they were going to get. At least for now. There would be more "interviews" in days and months to come. Many more.

There would be a deal, a plea.

But then they'd work him over on the details of the plea agreement. There would be no offer of witness protection. His life wasn't in danger. At least the FBI didn't think so at this stage. That could change. They were often surprised at what came crawling out of the sewer when they got started.

In the meantime, Buckley would request to be bailed out. The judge would deny that request because Henning would argue flight risk. Just look at his confederates who've already flown the coop, judge. Your honor.

Then Buckley would be remanded to the custody of the U.S. Marshalls, who would stick him in the local holding facility, the Denver county jail, where he would await trial while the wheels of justice slowly ground forward. Nasty place that jail. I hear a dog wouldn't even touch that food.

Weatherford, Texas

Ricky Bob Peabody checked in at the Dolly P the next day—the first time he'd been there for many days. Todd and the rest of the crew were glad to see him. Drilling had progressed almost without any problems, and Todd had been able to handle the few glitches they'd had. Another couple of days and they would reach the target formation. Ricky thought maybe he could afford to leave Todd on his own again for a couple more days.

He urgently needed to see Darren Magelby. He called the lawyer and arranged to meet him early the next morning. Magelby could shift his schedule around to accommodate the young oil man. If Ricky left Weatherford this afternoon he could drive at least as far as home again, catch another night with Nan, leave early and be in Skiatook for his meeting. The two FBI agents tailing him called Denver for instructions. They were relieved when Special Agent Nieve said, "We think he's in the clear now. Come on back home."

Skiatook, Oklahoma

"So, what's up, Mr. Peabody?"

"Everyone calls me Ricky Bob. "

"Ricky Bob it is. What can I help you with?"

"I been wrasslin' with a problem and I need your advice."

Darren was attentive.

Ricky went back over what happened in Denver to bring Darren up to speed. Then Ricky said, "But my problem, I think, is this, and I want you to tell me where I stand and what my options are."

He went on to explain how Jerry Jordan and Phillip had been raising drilling funds by telling the investors Peabody would be drilling a deep gas well in the Anadarko, on a prospect to be named later.

This technique of pre-selling was known as a "blind pool investment." Some wags renamed it a "blind fool" because only a fool would throw money into an oil deal without knowing anything about the prospect to be drilled. That was insinuating a lot of faith in the driller. Many folks got burned this way every year.

Darren was only too familiar with blind pools. In fact, he had cautioned Jerry and Phillip to go very carefully here, especially in how they pitched it to investors and closed the deals. Darren had insisted they put a lot of disclaimers and extensive disclosures in their private placement prospectus he helped them draft. He had vigorously insisted on it over their angry objections that he was killing their deal before they even got started. He spelled out in very clear terms that they risked investor lawsuits for fraud if things went bad and they had failed to cover their fannies with adequate disclosures. "That's the stuff that investor lawsuits are made of," he warned. They finally gave in to his advice.

Ricky went on, "Well, here's my other problem. I think those two guys may have represented that I owned my own drill rig that would be used to drill on that un-named Anadarko prospect. I don't have a rig, yet. As you well know. And I sure don't have any Anadarko prospect to drill on. I'm guessing, with the part I played in bringing down that Buckley shyster, there ain't no loan from that bank for Ricky Bob to buy a drill rig or slap money down for no Anadarko prospect. I doubt there will even be a Larimer Square Bank left pretty soon."

Ricky sat back deflated. "What should I do?"

Darren lit a fresh cigar. "Mind if I smoke?" Ricky didn't mind. In fact, he'd enjoy one himself. Darren helped him light up. Ricky choked just a little on the smoke. Darren then explained to Ricky the one viable option left to him: Get your hands on a drill rig somehow, find a prospect fast and amend the prospectus. They would also have to do an offer in rescission.

Ricky looked perplexed at this new term he'd never heard. Darren explained that it was a good faith offer to let the investors have their money back and tear up their investment contract. Most investors usually opted to stay in the deal.

"I'm guessin' those two high binders have already deducted their commissions and spent it. They both like to live high on the hog." Darren nodded his agreement as he knocked some ash off his cigar, examined it, plucked a crumb of tobacco from the tip of his tongue.

Darren examined his cigar like it was a new object he had recently encountered. "You know these things are contraband? Cohibas. Cuban. Makes them all the sweeter, wouldn't you say?" He grinned and Ricky agreed.

In the meantime, Darren promised that he'd run down Phil and Jerry and explain the problems and the solutions, give them his expert legal opinion. They won't be happy but the only alternative is to return the money to the investors and hope they didn't sue their collective behinds off.

"And don't forget one thing …" Darren said.

"What's that?"

"You *do* have a big rig. Well, not yet but as good as … Sort of. Don't forget, I have that written memo from the FBI that says they owe you one. And, by heck, I mean to make them stick to the deal. Even if I have to file lawsuits personally against ever' durned one of them."

He laughed and Ricky grinned. So, Agent Nieve had signed off on his agreement after all.

Ricky thanked Darren profusely and left with a bit more spring to his step. He was sure Nan would be proud that he'd done the right thing.

FORTY

FBI Offices, Denver

Buck had been in FBI custody for just 15 minutes short of 24 hours, the most they could hold him for questioning without being formally charged. Or providing him legal counsel.

Special Agent Nieve let him make his call to his lawyer, a high-priced defense attorney named Itzak Jablonsky. He was well-known to both the FBI and Ryan Henning.

Jablonsky blew into the FBI building like a Category IV hurricane, screaming police brutality, violation of his client's rights, police intimidation, entrapment, etc., etc. And he was darn sure going to sue their behinds, every one of them personally. Starting with the U.S. attorney and working his way down the list through the FBI and beyond and back.

Chris Nieve just stood there mute until the windbag had to stop for breath. He nodded to Jablonsky and said, "Izzie. Nice to see you, too." They shook hands and greeted each other like two old friends.

Out of earshot of his client, Jablonsky asked Nieve, "Okay Chris, don't hoodwink me here. Give it to me straight. How bad is it for this chump? What have you got on him?"

Nieve said it didn't look good for Buckley. He told Izzie about Dill's taped recording from Las Vegas, and the wire Ricky Bob Peabody had worn. In both recordings Buckley had clearly incriminated himself.

He'd play the tapes for Jablonsky and his client to hear. But first, Nieve ticked off the list of charges that Buckley would be charged with. So far, that is.

He handed Jablonsky a copy of the indictment. "Here, have a look-see for yourself."

While Jablonsky was quickly scanning a practiced eye through the dense legalese and flipping pages, Agent Cecilia Beardsley and another agent walked in, carrying a bankers' box between them.

They placed the box on a chair. Agent Sissy reached inside, fished out a plastic bag, held it up like a prize, then handed it to Nieve, who said, "Well, lookie this. What've we got here, I wonder? Why it looks like a gun. My gosh, it's a real one. Not a toy gun. Now where did you find this gun, Agent Sissy?"

"It was part of the fruits of our diligent and thorough search of the suspect's office."

Nieve tsk-tsked and shook his head sadly. He said, "Looks like we already got to amend that indictment to include an enhancement for use of a weapon during the commitment of the crimes."

"Alleged crimes!" shouted Jablonsky. Then, he turned to his client and yelled, "You flaming idiot!"

"Oh, crap!" Buckley said through his hands covering his face. He almost wet himself again.

Larimer Square Bank. Wednesday morning, one day before Thanksgiving

Dill went back to the bank and searched in vain for TJ Brimhall who hadn't been in the bank yet that morning, and probably wouldn't even bother to come in. Dill had planned to break the news that the FDIC would soon be there to shut down the bank. He also needed to tell the old gentleman he was planning to stay for a while longer to help the bank with a smooth transition in its insolvency.

He'd even offer to stay a little longer, maybe as long as reasonably necessary to assist the FDIC in going through the books, the various scattered accounts, the loan files, both his and the ones that Buckley had supposedly ordered to be stored "off premises." Dill felt it was the right thing for him to do. Jo had agreed. But they also agreed Dill needn't stay any longer than the first of the New Year.

Today, he'd just have to take charge since technically he still had the title of Senior Vice President. That made him the only ranking executive officer on the premises. Not even the Cashier was on site. Nobody had seen him since the FBI stormed in and ransacked Buckley's office.

Dill donned his navy blazer, cinched up his necktie and walked resolutely down the hallway toward the Bullpen. Marty and Anita followed him, each armed with legal pads to take notes and a box of facial tissues. That was Dill's idea. He had a strong feeling there would be tears. The tissues were going to be needed real soon.

Dill asked all young people in the Bullpen to please stop whatever they were doing, finish any phone calls, and hang up. This wouldn't take long. He'd appreciate their undivided attention.

"I'm not your boss, and I don't have any authority or jurisdiction over any of you." Several heads nodded agreement. "I'm afraid the lot has fallen to me to be the bearer of bad news."

Dill soldiered on, "I'm sorry to say, your time at this bank has come to an inglorious ending."

"What's that supposed to mean?" one young man asked, hands defiantly on his hips, challenging Dill, who searched for just the right words. The truth, he heard Jo's voice in his head. Tell them the truth. They can deal with the true facts. Just don't sugar coat it and please don't mislead them in any way. They're young, they can recover their lives and move on. It's not the end of the world.

"Just this. The bank is probably, well, it truly *is,* insolvent. By this time tomorrow bank regulatory authorities from the FDIC and probably the Colorado state banking commission, and who knows who else, will be crawling all over this place, taking control."

"Mr. Robertson?" A trim, well-dressed young lady gasped and broke into tears. She raised her hand and, her voice trembling, called,

"Mr. Roberson? What should we do? We have no idea. Please tell us what to do."

"I know this is a shock but try to remain calm. Above all, you're all professionals, so please act like professionals. Be professional. And dignified."

"Nice platitudes, nice performance," the belligerent young guy said and started clapping slowly. Two girls turned on him. They scowled at him, staring him into silence.

"I'm not trying to stroke you or feed you a line," Dill said. "I suggest you each make a call to your respective banks, talk to your bosses or supervisors. Try to explain the situation without embellishing or hysteria. Ask them for your marching orders. They will probably tell you to grab any paperwork and bring it with you. Not a good idea since the FDIC needs every scrap of paper they can find to try and figure things out. Don't obstruct, don't shred. Please. Professionals. I just want to add that I have the greatest respect for you and your awkward situation. You didn't cause this. I won't burden you with my opinion."

"Please don't," someone hidden in the back of the crowd yelled angrily.

Dill understood their frustration. What more could he say. "Thanks for all your hard work. I have been truly proud to work with all of you. Every one of you."

Half the girls and even a few boys started weeping. Anita and Marty were also weeping as they handed out tissues.

The kids began the grim task of throwing their personal effects into bags, boxes, purses, anything they could find to carry stuff. Dill asked Anita and Marty to stay and keep a close eye on things to make sure the others followed his request to leave papers intact. He had another duty to perform but he'd be back later to check on things.

Dill walked out to his truck. He didn't bother to look for his fly rod. It was long gone.

He wondered if he'd done the right thing, deciding to stick it out with the bank. Only time would tell. Jo had said everything would work out okay in the end. He hoped so, he truly did.

As he drove to the hospital, he was confident that by now all of the correspondent banks that had purchased participation in Larimer Square's loans were aware of the imminent closure. But, did they have any idea how really bad the situation was? He knew they were in for quite a jolt.

Wednesday. FBI offices, Denver

Izzie was allowed to consult privately with his client for a half-hour. Then in the lawyer's presence the FBI began the questioning: what did Buckley know? Could he describe his methods in making the loans? How many loans had he made? How were they documented? What was the average size? What was the biggest loan? Who was it made to? What kind of documentation did he require of the borrowers?

On it went like that for two hours with Buckley obviously stonewalling. Agent Nieve had led the questioning. His level of frustration was mounting in degrees by the minute. Finally, he called a break and asked to speak to Izzie.

"Iz. A word?" they stepped out into the hall.

FBI Special Agent Nieve looked his adversary in the eye and said, "Look, this isn't helping your client any. It's obvious he's lying, covering up. This business of him saying 'I can't remember,' and 'I don't have any recollection' stuff is pure smoke and mirrors. It's garbage, that's what it is. You know it, he knows it, and I know it. If I find out that you advised him to do this you'll be charged with obstruction, and I'll also go for disbarment. And he'll face additional counts for sure. Now I say we cut through to the quick. Talk to him. You've got two minutes to turn him around."

Both Nieve and Iz knew there wasn't a snowball's chance the lawyer would be charged with anything. Or disbarred. The lawyer was doing his best with a gifted liar, a difficult client. Given the circumstances, Izzie was doing everything he could.

But he got Nieve's signal. Loud and clear.

Izzie started to go back in, hesitated and said, "Look, Chris, I think maybe it's time we started thinking about cutting some kind of a deal, don't you? Something for me to go on to get him to cooperate? You owe me at least that much. Remember that big drug case where I gave you some joy?"

He's actually begging, Nieve thought.

What Jablonsky was referring to is an unwritten practice that sometimes occurred between prosecutors and the criminal defense bar:

you give me something on this case that I'm trying to solve and maybe we can cut your client a little slack on his case. Nudge wink. Nothing in writing. Nothing to pin on each other.

There may be some who suspect that the criminal bar sometimes works like that, that they sometimes throw a client under the bus in a walk-off case in order to get a break for another client on a bigger, tougher case. But nobody can really prove anything. Just a handshake. Deal closed.

Nieve shook his head. "Isn't it a bit early for that? He hasn't given us anything yet. What's he going to give us? That's how the game's played, Iz, you know that. Let's see what he gives us, then we'll think about talking."

Izzie nodded, but he knew Agent Nieve was role playing a bit; they both did. "I'll work on him. I'm with you. I think he knows a ton. I just have to find his hot button. Give me five minutes."

"Two minutes."

Izzie started to go back into the cloistered interview room. Then, stopped, turned. "But give me some assurance, something to convince him."

"Just tell him you've worked with me before and I'm really a good guy..." Izzie laughed. "Tell him whatever you want, but let's get this thing going up to speed."

Izzie went back in to have a word with his client, try to convince him it was in his best interest in the long haul to cooperate. They'll dig out the truth anyway so it's just best if you tell them what they want to know. Truthfully, if you can possibly do that. If you cooperate, they'll probably figure out a way to convince the U.S. attorney and the sentencing judge to cut you some slack. But no promises. That part comes later. Let's get this over with. For your sake. Okay?

Calvin Buckley was used to things always going *his* way. Nobody told Buck what to do; he called the shots. He told others what to do and they sure as heck better do it or pay the price for insubordination. It irked him no end to have this cocky punk, smart-mouthed little Latino guy and his granola-eating pot-smoking girlfriend leaning on him. Agent Sissy! What kind of name is that? I hate them all! Including my stupid, incompetent lawyer! Just because those FBI guys have the guns and the badges and they really get off on pushing tax-paying citizens around, scaring innocent people, making them pee their pants, I'm supposed to respect them? Okay, sure, I see how the game's played. I'll give them what they ask for. I'll give them more than they ask for, and they can deal with the stinky hornet's nest they stir up. I wonder if they know about that account in Guernsey Seth helped me set up? There should be about $10 million in there by now if Summers did what he promised. They're sayin' I'm facing 20 years in the slam, 10 at minimum. They'll cut that down after I spill my guts. Five years tops. In some federal country club place with no barbed wire. Three and a half for good behavior and keepin' my nose clean. Cakewalk. Can I do it you ask? Heck yeah, I can handle five years if I got a cool $10 million minus attorney's fees in the bank waitin' when I get out. That's probably all I'll have left for all my hard work. This RICO thing … Can they really take all my other stuff, cars, horses, condos, jewelry, my guns? I could care less about most of it but I really have become fond of My Doll. What a sweet horse. And that matched pair of Churchill 16 gauges I'd hate to part with those. And this so-called lawyer is soundin' like he wants to throw me under the bus just to collect a fat fee and get on with scammin' his next poor sucker client. A hundred grand just to do what? Work a deal with the feds and offer me up as the sacrificial goat? Or was it a heifer? Who gives a flying fart? Let's get this farce over with. Gosh, I could really use a vodka on the rocks right now. This coffee sucks. Stay cool Buck, stay cool. Here comes my sorry excuse for counsel.

It had been exactly two minutes, eight seconds, when Izzie opened the door and invited Nieve and Agent Sissy back in. "I think he's seen the light. His memory has vastly improved. But first he could use a bathroom break."

Nieve nodded and took off his jacket, exposing his sidearm in a shoulder holster. This caught Buck's eye. I was right, it is a Police Special, he thought.

A pair of agents escorted Buck down the hall to the gents. One stood by the open door while the other stood uncomfortably close behind him while he went. His hand trembled slightly.

The agents resumed the questioning which went on into the hours of early evening with occasional breaks. They brought him coffee and sandwiches. They were actually pretty good this time. The agents took turns questioning, trying to keep up with their note writing, as Buckley was gathering momentum, spilling his guts. He actually seemed to be enjoying this exercise. And his memory had sharply improved. Much more clear and detailed. More than the FBI had bargained for.

FORTY-ONE

Larimer Square Bank

While the FBI questioned Calvin Buckley, the FDIC—including Gary Swope—had parachuted into Denver. They were now behind enemy lines. But they were there in force. They climbed into a waiting convoy of black government SUVs with their briefcases, luggage and equipment and rode downtown to the Larimer Square Bank. They quickly set up shop. Dill counted at least ten people on their team as he welcomed them. He was glad to see Swope among them. They had a friendly reunion.

The FDIC team was well-trained for this exercise. Each person knew exactly what his or her assignment was. They scattered out to various parts of the bank and began the grim task. They were serious, focused. Not one of them cracked a smile. There's little or no joy in closing down a bank in this way. Akin to assisting a patient who has given up hope, there's a sickness with no possible cure, deep inside a failed bank. The only thing left to do is give the financial institution a decent Christian burial.

Dill assured the team leader that he was available to assist them in any way he could. The first thing they requested were the loan files.

Dill had anticipated this and had already sent a team of the few remaining bank employees to the off-site storage facility to haul the boxes back. Anticipating pushback from the facility manager, Dill had sought the assistance of Nieve, who called Henning, who sent one of his assistants scurrying back to the judge to fetch yet another search warrant.

Special Agent Nieve told Dill that he and his staff were already stretched thin, so he was having the U.S. Marshall's office assist the search. That was fine. Whatever. Let's just get the boxes. Dill shuddered to think what they contained. More likely what they did *not* contain.

The storage facility manager nearly fainted when she was served with a search warrant from two big government men wearing gold badges and navy-blue nylon windbreakers with "U.S. Marshall" in bold yellow lettering on the back. She couldn't take her eyes off the badges; they sparkled in the late autumn sunlight.

To Dill's surprise, and great concern, the bank employees returned an hour later, dusty and grim, with only four Bankers Boxes to show the FDIC folks. This didn't look good. The FDIC went to Plan B: Contact the upstream correspondent banks and demand they send copies—at their own expense, from their own files—of all loans that had originated from the Larimer Square Bank.

These banks were scattered throughout the United States, Canada, London, and Tel Aviv. Plus, four other banks—one each in France, Brazil, Hong Kong and Spain—held a portion of a portfolio of Larimer Square loans that had been "syndicated," bundled into a large package and partitioned off under subordinate participation agreements.

Those four banks would ultimately refuse to cooperate, hiding behind issues of sovereign immunity from U.S. government jurisdiction.

Dill would later marvel, upon learning of this arrangement, that there was no end to the devious creativity of the money geniuses. The financial world went to great lengths in devising new ways to use what they referred to as OPM—other people's money. He wouldn't be surprised if a little group of MBA graduates, working for some of the big investment banking houses on Wall Street had gotten together one night around iced vodkas and hatched up a new way for their firms to get in on the oil action and charge yet even more fees.

Late Wednesday afternoon, the day before Thanksgiving

Dill checked JoEllen out of the hospital to take her home. After tearful good-byes and many hugs with the staff, nurses, interns, and even the orderlies, they got underway. He had changed into traveling clothes: blue jeans, flannel shirt, his worn cowboy boots, and fleece-out sheepskin vest. He steered with his left hand while he held Jo's hand much of their drive home.

It was snowing lightly, corn snow patted against their windscreen, shattered into tiny fragments. Dill felt secure in his truck. And happy. He brought Jo up to speed on all the recent happenings. It took her breath away to think of how quickly this oil bubble thing, all this greed, had spun out of control. It was like some monster from a cheaply made foreign movie with English subtitles. The oil boom had destroyed everything in its path—people, livelihoods, families, careers, businesses, reputations. It seemed unstoppable. All in the name of pumping a resource out of the earth.

"It's all about money, greed, power," Dill told JoEllen. "In the end, it always came down to that."

She sadly shook her head. "Let's change the subject. Let's talk about happy things."

So, they did. They talked about their family and how badly they needed to repair the loss of closeness. They came up with a plan for family recovery, starting with tomorrow's festive dinner. Dill's older, widowed sister, Aunt Ida, had been staying in their home, caring for the boys in their absence. They certainly owed her more than just the conventional "thank you."

Jo had talked with them by phone every day when she felt strong enough. Dill had called often and had gone home at least two times. Or was it three? But the conversations, and even the visits, had been short and unsatisfying for everyone.

It seemed like the time had passed fast on those visits. Dill had dealt with ranch and business matters during the few hours he had been back in Craig. And, during those visits, his sons had seemed to be more interested in spending time hanging out with their friends than with him. He and the boys never seemed to connect in any meaningful way. He felt like they were on separate ice flows drifting apart, only able to shout and wave to each other from a fast-receding distance.

When he and JoEllen had had one of their many deep talks together, he had described all this to her, together with his frustration and worry. They had discussed ways to try to fix it, but hadn't come to any satisfying solution.

Until just the other night, that is. When Dill had decided to make his stand for the Right Way. Deep in his heart he knew the right way meant what would ultimately be the best for the long-term happiness of his family, Jo, himself. He lifted her hand to his lips, tenderly kissed it. He loved this girl, his wonderful wife, companion, spiritual partner. Although they were evenly matched in so many ways, they still each had strengths and gifts that complemented, completed each other, made each other whole.

Happy things. Thanksgiving. At home. Dill's heart swelled up with pure joy. He was so blessed. Together. Dill, JoEllen, the Four Apostles, together they were a force. They could conquer anything. Together. Their happiness, each individually and collectively as a family unit, was dependent on unity. And, united in love, they could conquer any of life's problems. Together.

They talked about their favorite Thanksgiving dishes. And their least favorites. "What's your least favorite?" Dill asked. He knew what her answer would be.

"I don't care for the roasted marshmallows on top of the yams!" They laughed.

"Now you tell me yours. I think I know what you're going to say, but go ahead."

"You remember a few years ago when Ephraim and Pearl hosted Thanksgiving dinner at their house?"

She did.

"You remember how Pearl was on some kind of self-improvement kick, which included a cooking class she took every week over in Steamboat? And how she was always trying out these new recipes on everyone?"

"Yeah, I think I even still have a few in my recipe box at home."

"Well," Dill continued, "do you remember what she laid on the table as a side dish?"

"There were a lot of side dishes that year. Get to the point. We'll be home before you finish," Jo teased.

“Okay, okay. But the particular one I’m remembering was that gosh-awful thing of roasted parsnips in tarragon cream or some such concoction. The smell was overwhelming and only Eph would touch it. But, do you remember how he tried to hide his surprise at how bad it was, and then he actually told her how good it was?”

Jo nodded.

“I think you later figured out she had put a half-cup of minced garlic in it when the recipe called for a half-teaspoon. The dogs wouldn’t even get near it. The barn cats ran the other way.”

“I seem to remember Eph faking a cough while he spit it out in his napkin!” Jo said.

“Poor Pearl.”

They both had a good laugh.

FORTY-TWO

Thanksgiving Day, Larimer Square Bank

There's a kind of unwritten contract between a bank and the regulatory agencies that are there to protect the public interest. The unwritten contract goes something like this: we'll let you be a bank, take deposits, make loans and other investments. But you have to act responsibly, prudently. You have to look out for the public's interest first and foremost. Never forget that you are in a stewardship role. You have a trust to protect. Good luck. And try to stay out of trouble!

How does a bank become "troubled"? And, in the eyes of the regulators, like the FDIC, what form does that trouble take? As entities operating in the public interest, banks—similar to public utilities—are tightly regulated by government agencies.

Banks operate under written regulations set forth in black, loose-leaf binders that fill several shelves to overflowing. They are taken down only periodically to insert an amendment or update sent out by the Feds. Do bank officers and directors read all the regs, their upgrades, their amendments? Probably not.

Still, some of those regs are basic "thou shalts" and "thou shalt nots" that most bankers know by heart. Or should know. This includes detailed regulations regarding loan-to-deposit ratios.

According to those regulations, banks cannot turn around and lend out 100 percent of the deposits they take in. That's not safe or prudent. What if all the customers wanted to take out all of their deposited money at the same time? Similar to what happened many times during the Great Depression, disaster quickly follows. So, by law, the bank can only lend, say, 90 percent of the deposits it has on hand. The other 10 percent must remain in the bank's reserve account.

Then there is the loan-to-asset ratio, meaning the underlying capital footing of the bank. This is the net value of the bank's own cash issued for shares in the bank, properties, receivables and so on versus the aggregate amount of all loans outstanding. Generally, loans representing 40 percent of assets is considered a good ratio; 60 percent would be considered poor, bordering on dangerous.

If a bank exceeds one of those ratios by lending too much money, the FDIC not only gets nervous, it will inform the bank to fix it. Fast.

But what if the bank is having problems collecting on the loans? What if the debtor defaults? And, what if a loan officer (think "Calvin Buckley") ignores those ratios and essentially goes crazy in handing out loans like candy to family, friends, and drinking or golfing buddies? And then, what if those buddies default on their loans? Usually, the bank has to eat the losses, write them off against the bank's assets, or ultimately, its capital—or, in banking parlance, its "footings." Capital is the amount of money the stockholders have contributed to start the bank in business.

Now, consider this scenario: FDIC demands that a bank write off a huge number of "bad" loans against assets and capital and the bad loans exceed the aggregate amount of assets and capital. What happens next? FDIC requires bank management to infuse more capital until the bank is safely within acceptable ratios.

Typically, the FDIC requires new capital stock be subscribed by its board of directors and executive officers, together with any original shareholders who are not board members or officers. If they don't pony up enough capital, the next step is for the bank to float a new stock offering, sell more stock to outsiders, new stockholders, through either a public or private offering.

If that effort fails, the FDIC has to consider its options.

Depending on the severity and nature of the trouble the bank appears to be in, the FDIC has several tools in its kit. Among those tools are a simple "deficiency" letter, a written warning to the bank's officers and directors, a sort of slap on the wrist. It's a signal to shape up or things will get rougher next time. It usually lists the problems or deficiencies the regulators have found that the bank is required to fix.

If the bank continues to engage in the proscribed practices, ignoring the deficiency letter, regulators can slap a cease-and-desist order on the troubled bank. Meaning: Stop what you're doing or we, the FDIC, will have to take more drastic measures. Often that cures the problems. There's usually a general cleanup imposed by the bank itself, changes in management are made, more capital is injected, more stringent policies are enforced. Delinquent loans are forcefully collected.

In more serious cases, where the bank has not been able, or even refused, to fix the problems, the FDIC can declare the bank failed and invite offers from other banks to purchase the failed bank. Or the FDIC can simply close down the bank and proceed to liquidate it.

Sometimes, other banks will step in, "purchase" the failed bank and reopen under the acquiring bank's name. The new bank will assume liabilities that have been carefully cherry-picked, acquire the outstanding loans as receivables, and service the accounts of the depositors. Also cherry-picked. That is the most positive outcome, and it depends on the condition of the failed bank, what ugly creatures crawl out from under the rocks the FDIC examiners turn over.

The FDIC examiners from Kansas City, under team leader Max Watts, soon discovered they were undermanned, woefully short-handed. Not only would they be working long hours, probably seven days a week for the foreseeable future, but there would only be a four-hour break to observe Thanksgiving. As it turned out, only two people took the offered time off. The rest stayed to work and had pizza and Cokes for their traditional feast.

Max Watts was an economist by education. Mid-fifties, nearing retirement, tall and lean. His nearly bald head was decorated with a few stray wisps of gray hairs that stuck out at all angles. He had a tick of running his hand through what was once a full head of hair. Max favored tweed jackets with suede elbow patches, bowties and horn-rimmed glasses which gave him a decidedly professorial look. He was soft spoken, thoughtful. His style was to carefully gather the facts, dig deep for missing information, sift, analyze, dig some more if necessary, and ask for opinions from his team. Together, they would take the most obvious or sensible action based on the facts.

Max Watts and his team would spend the first couple of days digging into the bank's books, computers, records and files to ferret out the facts. They would confer, select a course of action and assignments would be made based on the expertise of the individual team members.

The first and most obvious decision the team made was that more help was necessary.

Because most of the upstream banks were national banks, chartered under the supervision of the Comptroller of the Currency, calls went out to that sister agency for help. Another call was made to the Federal Reserve Bank, also located in Kansas City. They promptly sent a couple of their examiners to protect the Treasury Department's interests. Once the seriousness of the crisis became fully known, that number of Treasury examiners would quickly grow to a dozen, then two dozen.

What Max Watts and his team found was not very encouraging: over a thousand oil-related loans had been made, the bulk of them by Buckley, either personally or at his direction. Not only had he failed (or refused, in some cases) to get loan committee approval or to properly document the loan files, there was also a definite pattern of inadequate collateral, and, in half the cases, no collateral at all!

For the oil-related loans nominally backed with reserves, the reserves were grossly overstated in value. Or, in some cases, reserves were highly questionable, as the reserves categorized by supposed expert petroleum engineers as "probable." Meaning not proven yet.

To make matters worse, whereas everyone had been touting oil prices to top $100 a barrel and many transactions had been based on that shaky assumption, crude oil prices were now dropping. Steadily. Tuesday's spot price for West Texas sweet crude was down below the $30 mark. Yesterday—Wednesday—it had opened at $26.

By far, the majority of the loans Buckley made or authorized were in the non-performing category. Meaning they were either badly delinquent, had been rewritten to get them off the non-performing list, or in many cases only interest was being paid, there was no reduction in the principal whatsoever.

The next shock was to discover Buckley had used a fraudulent technique of creating "phantom" notes, supposedly made and executed by the borrower, when in fact the borrower never signed the note.

Buckley had once bragged within Dill's hearing that he, Buckley, had a big following of what he proudly called his "debt junkies." These were bank customers who had exceptionally large debt loads. They continued to expand their little empires by borrowing an ever-increasing load of debt. And Calvin Buckley was only too happy to accommodate their addictions. So long as they could keep borrowing money, leveraging their businesses, they were happy. So was Calvin Buckley.

Then there was the added element of the participating banks and their appetite for those lucrative oil loans. In order to keep feeding the seemingly inexhaustible demand for participating loans by the upstream banks—a demand Buckley had created by his own enthusiasm, energy, and hype—Buckley would create fraudulent paperwork to pile added debt on his junkies. And Larimer Square Bank would casually pass the fake loan papers to the unsuspecting upstream institutions.

Neither the junkies nor the upstream banks were any the wiser of the scam. The truth was that there was no real money added to the junkies' debts, it was all an illusion to keep the upstream banks happy.

Not all of these phony loans bore the names of the debt junkies. The examiners would discover several loans made to professional athletes and movie stars who had never heard of Larimer Square Bank, let alone done any business with it.

Calls by the bank examiners to these people, or to their agents or managers, were met with shock and surprise. That quickly turned to anger, followed by nasty threats to sue for fraud, defamation of character, invasion of privacy, etc., etc. The examiners quickly backed off.

By far, the majority of Larimer Square's loans had not been approved by either Buckley's hand-picked loan committee or Seth Summers's hand-picked board of directors. Approvals by either or both of those bodies was standard procedure among bankers applying accepted safe and prudent banking practices. But at Larimer Square, loans were made just on Buckley's say-so.

How did he get so many people to do his bidding? How did he manage to keep up this hoax for so long?

The next "uh-oh" the examiners encountered was the master loan participation agreements themselves. How a large number of highly respected banks had allowed themselves to enter into these agreements was baffling to the examiners.

Max and his team wondered if these banks had even bothered to pass the paperwork by their lawyers before signing. How and why did they get themselves into this mess? It appeared that these big banks were in for a shock in the form of huge losses. Why?

Greed. And hubris. The upstream banks considered themselves mostly risk-free. First, they were old, highly respected financial institutions with a great deal of money at their disposal. And, with lots of money comes lots of clout.

They were stewards over billions of the public's dollars. They were trusted to make wise decisions on how all that money was used. Nobody ever really questioned the decisions. It was just assumed that these banks were making good decisions. Nobody told them how to run their business. That makes for a lot of unchallenged power. And if they happened to make a nice profit out of the use of all those billions, why, they were entitled. And they were focused on the huge profits now to be made in these oil loans.

Greed. Hubris. Which can easily lead to risk-taking. These oil loans were virtually risk-free. Or so they thought.

After all, they reasoned, these loans from Larimer Square Bank are with *recourse*. Meaning, if the borrower defaults on the loan, Larimer Square Bank is contractually obligated to make the upstream bank whole on its potential loss. The upstream bank would simply send the loan back to Larimer Square Bank to reimburse them for the funds that had been advanced to the borrower.

Larimer Square was good for it, weren't they? Of course they were, based on Larimer's healthy financial statements. Duly certified by a respectable Denver firm of CPAs.

Financial statements were treated like sacred writ. But the dirty secret was that Larimer Square Bank, i.e., Buckley, or somebody under his control, had somehow managed to fiddle and bend those financial statements as well. Without the knowledge of the CPAs or of anyone else.

Also looming was the regulators' next big headache: Very soon the press would get wind of the bank failure. And very soon the entire world would know that Larimer Square Bank was a corrupt, pathetic bunch of hustlers, fraud artists. A big fat failure. You couldn't keep this disaster secret for very long. Too many people in on the loop. Somebody was sure to leak the disaster to the press. Then the investigative journalists would come asking uncomfortable questions. They would soon find out about the criminals who ran the Larimer Square Bank of Denver.

Of course, that epithet didn't apply to all of the officers and directors; only the few Seth Summers and Calvin Buckley had managed to corrupt either through intimidation or bribery, or both. In the course of its clean-up operation, the FDIC and other agencies would come to appreciate the help from those few good men and women in the bank who had managed to retain their integrity. People like Dill Robertson.

But Dill was sure his name would also be dragged through the mud. It was inevitable.

The FDIC and their fellow regulators from the other agencies also soon realized they had their own public relations problem: The headlines would scream: Where were the regulators? What were they doing while this corrupt little bank diddled the public out of billions?

Regulators Asleep on Their Watch! No bureaucrat wanted to wake up to see headlines across their morning newspaper accusing them of screwing up.

Congress and the White House soon would be pointing fingers, laying blame, screaming for investigations, hearings. Heads would roll.

All because of one bent banker named Calvin Buckley. His name and the bank he had manipulated would soon become household words.

In the meantime, it was time to break the bad news to the public. The depositors, borrowers, bank's creditors, and, most of all, the upstream banks needed to know.

The president of the Kansas City FDIC wasn't going to delegate this nasty job. She wasn't a shirker; she would take on the unpleasant task herself.

An investment contract is broadly defined by the SEC and the courts as, "… a contract, transaction, or scheme whereby a person invests his money in a common enterprise and is led to expect profits solely from the efforts of the promoter or a third party." The underlying principle, the basic requirement, for anyone selling an investment contract is that the seller or person or entity that offers the investment must make *full and fair disclosure*.

Full and fair disclosure has been interpreted by the SEC and the courts broadly as "… the level of disclosure that a reasonably prudent business person would exercise to have all of the facts and information necessary under the circumstances to make an informed decision before investing."

This has been further broadened to include not only the information or facts that are given to the potential investor, but also any information *not disclosed that could or should have been disclosed.* The burden is always on the promoter or sponsor of an investment scheme to make full disclosure. Severe penalties, criminal and civil, await the promoter who fails to make full disclosure. That failure is typically painted in bright colors by a prosecutor in front of a criminal jury as fraud.

FORTY-THREE

Skiatook, Oklahoma. Wednesday before Thanksgiving

Jerry Jordan and Phillip Connoff weren't happy when they left Darren's office in Skiatook the afternoon before Thanksgiving. They were eager to go their separate ways for a couple of days to enjoy the holiday break.

Darren had just given them the bad news: they needed to stop selling their Old Bay Drilling Fund limited partnership investment interests for a while until Darren could amend their prospectus and get it reprinted. He patiently explained to them the concepts of full and fair disclosure.

The bottom line was that Darren would write the pretty language for them. And the amendment would need to disclose the recent revelations from Ricky Bob that: 1) They didn't have a drill rig—yet. But they could disclose that "they were in negotiations to acquire the necessary equipment and would commence the anticipated drilling in the foreseeable future."

And, 2) they still didn't have a designated prospect to drill on—yet. But, that could be fixed by disclosing "they were in current negotiations to acquire a suitable drill site which, in the sole discretion of the General Partner [Old Bay, the Nevada corporation], would be designated and promptly disclosed to the investors when identified."

Only when they did what Darren advised would he pass off on the issue of full and fair disclosure in their offering documents. Phillip and Jerry weren't happy. But what choice did they really have?

The other item of bad news was that Darren insisted the amended prospectus also include an offer to the investors to allow them for a limited time—"five business days"—to back out and get their money back. This is known in the investment trade as "an offer in rescission."

Promoters hated rescissions. For the obvious reasons that they sometimes created a snowball effect. Investors often referred friends or family who also invested. Word gets around—quickly. And soon there's a bandwagon effect: everyone gets panicked and wants out.

Unspoken to Darren, but suspected by him, was that Phillip and Jerry had already spent the commission portions of the investments taken in to date. They were both big spenders and actually didn't have the funds on hand to make a full-scale refund. In a stretch, they could probably come up with enough for two or three investors to get their money back. If they went out and reeled in a couple new fish to take their place.

Darren didn't ask, but he suspected this was the situation here. Based on his prior experience representing oil and gas limited partnership promoters.

"What do you think?" Phillip asked Jerry, as they waited for their separate flights in the Tulsa International terminal.

"It might cause one or two investors to chicken out and want their money back."

"I think we need to get an update from Ricky Bob," Phillip suggested. "I'll do it as soon as I get back to Salt Lake."

Jerry's flight was called and they separated. They hadn't discussed the elephant in the room: giving money back that they didn't have. They'd worry about that later.

Darren looked at the faxed memo he'd received days earlier from the FBI in Denver, promising a drilling rig to Ricky Bob Peabody in return for his assistance in an undercover operation.

Darren was turning strategies over in his mind. The key to keeping Ricky Bob, Phillip and Jerry out of trouble lay with this piece of paper. On the one hand, Darren didn't wholly trust the Feds. He'd seen clients screwed by federal prosecutors going back on their word. That's why he insisted this time on a written memo. He wondered if he'd have a problem enforcing it in court. If it ever came to that.

Still, it was a wedge he could use for leverage on behalf of his clients.

He locked the memo away in his safe, lit up a fresh Cohiba, slipped into his Birkenstocks, threw his jacket over his shoulder, turned out the lights, and walked out to his antique Ferrari humming a new ABBA tune. "The Winner Takes It All."

He reminded himself that Friday he needed to call Ricky Bob to talk strategy.

Darren drove the few blocks to his parents' home, where Thanksgiving celebrations were starting to take shape.

FORTY-FOUR

Thanksgiving Holiday, The Robertson Ranch, Craig, Colorado

Dill and JoEllen had driven west at a careful speed on I-70 through lightly falling snow and reached the resort town of Keystone at 5:00 Wednesday afternoon. In another half-hour it would be dark. They got gas, bought some snacks and refilled their soft drink containers, and headed north through the town.

There were crowds of skiers pouring into the resort from all over the map for some Thanksgiving fun. Christmas lights were already up everywhere, twinkling from live, native spruce trees growing along the streets. They drove toward Steamboat, through Craig, and home to the ranch, relieved and happy to be going home.

In the late 1880s Dill's great-grandfather had staked claim to a 160-acre homestead a few miles north of the town of Craig. A good part of his homestead bordered Elkhead Creek, a tributary of the Yampa River.

Over the course of the next couple decades, and by a lot of back-breaking work, his great-grandfather, Elvan Robertson, had added to his spread. At the time of his death in the great influenza pandemic of 1917-18, he owned a section and a half, comprising a thousand acres. Give or take.

Elvan's son, Frank, inherited the ranch, the large sandstone house, the buildings, cultivating equipment and livestock, together with a tidy sum of cash in the one bank in Craig. In a fit of patriotism, Frank enlisted in the army and was sent overseas as a doughboy. He fought in a battle the second day he arrived at the front, too new to be scared. His buddies saw him blown to pieces by a German shell 20 yards out of the trenches. Frank didn't live long enough to expand the ranch holdings; that would be the work of the next generation.

Frank left one son and two daughters, plus a young widow. His only son, Parker, was Dill's father. At a time in life when he should have known the joy and fun of being a kid, Parker had to start helping work the ranch. By the time he was 10 he could drive a span of mules or horses, plowing all day with the best of any grown men. Parker's formal education was pretty well over at grade seven when he took over managing the ranch for good.

In 1936, Parker turned 22. He was making the ranch into a profit center, raising good crops of wheat, alfalfa, cattle and sheep. He was careful with the money he made and socked away as much as he could. He had a long-term plan. He was saving to make his plan work. He wanted to expand the ranch, double its size. His neighbors on either side had been a little reckless and gone into debt to finance their operations. Parker had no debt; and he had a lot of cash stashed away.

So, in 1937 when the Great Depression was at its lowest depths, Parker bought one and then the other ranch on either side of his. His neighbors were only too glad to sell to him just to get out from under the crushing debts they had incurred.

Parker made a deal with the bank: he would buy his neighbors' mortgages from the bank. For a deep discount. The bank wanted 50 cents on the dollar. Parker haggled, waiting them out. Finally, the bank caved. Parker got the two ranches for 25 cents on the dollar. His ranch doubled in size overnight. And he hadn't even had to blast out a single tree stump or move one boulder.

He leased out the two adjoining farms to a couple of young brothers, Basque sheepmen, anxious to become farmers. It was an ideal setup for everyone. The brothers moved into the already existing houses and started right out from day one using the perfectly good equipment the previous owners had walked away from.

It wasn't long before the one bank in town failed and Parker was instrumental in organizing a new one. He was the majority stockholder.

World War II came. Parker was now too old to serve, had several children and was exempted by the local draft board because he was needed to raise crops and livestock to assist the war effort. He always carried a bit of a heavy feeling in his heart that he should have done more. It had been a slight to his manhood that they hadn't needed him to fight.

Parker married and had a daughter and two sons: Ida, then Ephraim and Dilworth—Dill. In 1958, Parker suddenly died from a stroke. All three children inherited shares of Parker's brokerage and bank accounts, with Eph getting the lion's share. Ephraim also inherited the majority shares of bank stock and Parker's very valuable collection of original Western art.

Dill got the ranch, a minority share of bank stock, and the job running the bank because Eph had big political dreams. Dill's family had been lifelong Democrats, but Eph figured he would do better as a Republican. So he switched allegiances. More power to him, Dill muttered.

In the presidential election of 1960, Kennedy won and Nixon lost. Eph was elected to the state senate as a Republican.

Dill was just starting college at the University of Colorado in Boulder in 1960. He didn't know why, but he'd developed a fascination with philosophy. He loved trying to get his head around tough, thorny moral and ethical problems. He took to the writings of Plato, Aristotle, Hobbes, Locke, Thoreau, the great minds.

His mother worried that he would become adversely influenced by the university and its godless "worldly philosophy." She was concerned doubts about God and about his own religion would creep into his head. She was sure he would deny his devout faith and fall away from the Mormon church—the Church of Jesus Christ of Latter-day Saints—and away from the way he had been raised.

She shouldn't have worried. He came through stronger than ever and more convinced that his religious beliefs were true. His belief in Jesus Christ and the gospel he was taught as a child was only enhanced and made stronger by his philosophy studies. He went on a Church mission to New England then came back, married JoEllen. They spent their honeymoon en route to Hanover, New Hampshire, where he'd spent part of his mission. Hanover was the site of Dartmouth University, where Dill would do graduate work to earn his MBA. Their little VW Beetle was loaded to the brim.

Dill now owned three sections of land, free and clear. Half the land, almost a mile and a half, fronted on Elkhead Creek and sloped gracefully up into the forests. Parker had also acquired grazing rights on thousands of acres of BLM and Forest Service land. Dill's herds of cattle and sheep had grown and expanded, becoming a significant part of the ranch's annual income. Dill loved to ride over his ranch, surveying his orderly, beautiful spread. He and JoEllen settled comfortably into the big sandstone ranch house.

But most of all, he loved spending stolen hours fly-fishing the Elkhead for cutthroat trout that made the big creek their home. There must have been something special about the water, its pH factor that was favorable because the aquatic life trout fed on was plentiful. The cutthroat trout in his creek were fat, abundant, and fairly easy to fool with a well-presented fly.

It was late, nearing 10 o'clock Wednesday night, when Dill and Jo turned the last curve of the mile-long gravel approach road. They rounded the hill and saw their home below. While driving out of Keystone, the night and its wintry darkness had dropped suddenly on them like a play's final curtain.

The lights glowing from their home were a welcoming beacon. Dill got a lump in his throat. Jo made a small gasp. Atop the hill he stopped the truck on the verge. They held hands and stared for a full minute.

Below them they could make out the dark outline of the cluster of four tall Colorado Spruce trees that Dill had planted one at a time, each time a child was born to them. The trees had been named in honor of each of their four boys. They were planted in a diamond formation off to the windward side of their circular gravel driveway. Someone had strung Christmas lights around the front eaves of the house. "It's so lovely," Jo whispered. Her face shone with happiness. She was a little girl again. Excited by the holiday again. Happy to be home with loved ones. Again.

Dill put the truck in gear and they rolled downhill toward home.

FORTY-FIVE

Seattle, Thanksgiving Day

Wallace Bennett, aka *Wally*, president and CEO of Mt. Rainier Trust, headquarters in Tacoma, Washington, was not going to have a peaceful Thanksgiving. He had just received a conference call from Carly Flack, president of the FDIC in Kansas City. She had succinctly informed him that the Larimer Square Bank had just been declared as "failed," and had been taken over by the FDIC.

Also on the conference call had been a representative of the Comptroller of the Currency, because Mt. Rainier Trust was chartered as a national bank and the Comptroller was now involved in the process. More agencies would soon join the party.

"Failed? Are you sure? It can't be. That bank is as sound as a truck load of Krugerrands!"

"Afraid not. Not anymore," came Carly's cold reply. "We would advise you to call an emergency meeting of your board, your executive officers, loan officers, anyone who may have been involved in the process of handling the loans Larimer Square made. Make an inventory and then get back to us as soon as possible. I don't need to tell you that you probably want to bring your lawyers into that circle."

Bennett poured himself a double bourbon. Jack Daniels. Straight. He gulped it down. It burned his throat. He poured and sloshed down another.

It was a cloudless, sunny afternoon, rare for the northwest in November. He stood in front of a tall picture window staring out of his 25th-floor condo adjacent to the I-5. He was looking to the east at Mount Rainier, the famous mountain-volcano in the distance. Today it seemed to be towering close, a wisp of a cloud over its top. Or was that smoke? Was the crazy thing ready to erupt?

He laughed at the irony. A volcano called Larimer Square Bank had just erupted. And blown ash and filthy fallout all over the planet. And a huge load of it had just landed on his bank. Failed? How could that possibly have happened? There must be a mistake.

In his heart of hearts, Wally Bennett knew the Feds didn't make these statements recklessly, just for grins. There had to be some underlying problem, something the auditors had discovered.

He thought back to one particular day. It was sunny then, too, he recalled. Early spring. Just over two years ago. A flashy cowboy from Denver had walked into their lives and convinced them they could all make a boatload of money by sharing in the oil boom. No risk. Loans with recourse to Larimer Square Bank, the originators of the paper. Larimer had been good for it. Look at their financials.

It had all been smoke and mirrors. Expensive Cuban cigar smoke.

Wally Bennett picked up his phone and rang the chairman of his board of directors. He just happened to be far away, having a lovely holiday with his wife and grown kids cruising on a private yacht around the Caribbean island of St. Bart's. He would have to cut it short, take the bank's Lear jet back to Tacoma as fast as possible. He wasn't happy.

Wally, seeing another irony, shook his head: Some officers plus a couple directors, handpicked by him, had quietly formed this little company. Their own private little side deal. Title was in the name of the new private company. The company they hadn't bothered to tell the full board of directors about. It had all been cleared and set up by one of the director's private law firms.

Then the little private, secret side-deal company had leased the Lear back to Mt. Rainier Trust for a whopping monthly payment. The monthly lease payment more than covered the small monthly interest payment to Larimer Square Bank. The rest was pure profit to this little group of insiders. More money in their own pockets. When the plane wasn't being used by the bank, it was put in a pool and rented out to other users. This clever arrangement was managed by the folks who also ran the executive air terminal in Tacoma. Yet another source of additional income into their own pockets, not into the coffers of Mt. Rainier Trust. Sure, maybe they were skirting banking laws just a little bit. Undisclosed conflicts of interest and all those stupid rules. But the lawyers had assured them—

The irony? They had financed the used Lear jet for $3 million through Larimer Square Bank which in turn had sent the loan papers upstream to … Guess who …? Mt. Rainier Trust! Their own bank owned a 90 percent participation in that loan!

Would the FDIC repo the danged thing? It would probably have to be sold to try and pay off the loan and recover some of their losses.

Speaking of losses—how deep were they into this Larimer Square Bank sewer anyway? He dreaded the answer.

Wally Bennett, a quorum of his board of directors, and his top officers and junior loan officers, as many as could be brow-beaten and dragged away from their holiday reveling, met in the bank's newly remodeled conference room. That remodel job alone had cost them over $600,000. Plus, the original Picassos. Antique Persian rugs. Original bronze sculptures. The whole enchilada. Another $3.5 million "construction" loan. From where? Yep, Larimer Square Bank!

As the first order of business, Bennett offered his resignation. It was turned down flat. At least it was on the record that he had offered. He then asked his cashier to give a report on how many loans they had purchased from Larimer Square Bank. "Just how badly, how much are we exposed?"

They held their collective breaths.

Then, the cashier whispered, "Nearly 550 million. Dollars."

The aggregate exhalation made an audible "whoosh."

Good Heavens, how did we let that happen?

Do we have the resources to cover?

How many of those loans are good? Collectible? How many are bad? The amount of write-offs we're facing? Anyone know?

So many unknowns. So much fear. So much anger. Lying just under the surface. Ready to explode. But who to direct that anger at? Bennett? Mt. Rainier's own loan officers? Larimer Square Bank? A lot of good that would do. We are already up a creek. We're already going down anyway. Can we go after that sneaky little cigar-smoking, fast-talking Texan with a civil action? What was that slimy little jerk's name, anyway?

FBI Offices, Denver

After the FBI had arrested Buckley on Monday afternoon and brought him in, he had first of all been forced to sit and listen to his own tape-recorded voice making some pretty damaging admissions. Criminal in nature. No doubt about it. His voice had been recorded, caught in the act, offering to make or give bribes. He'd also heard his recorded voice admitting that Dill Robertson had been set up. With the intent of extorting him. Another criminal act he could be charged with.

Then Buck had been subjected to almost non-stop questioning. For hours. Over and over. Izzie what's-his name, his squirrely little lawyer, had convinced him it was in his own best interest to cooperate.

He was sure—Izzie was—that Buck would be given credit for his cooperation and the FBI and federal prosecutor would try to pick a judge known to be soft on white-collar defendants at sentencing. Buck could most likely count on a max of five years at some federal country club joke of a prison and be out in a little over three. Like a vacation at a resort. Weight room, walking track. Good food. Easy time. No hard time for Buck.

So, for the past three days, today, Thanksgiving Day included, Buckley had cooperated. He gave them names, dates, amounts, assets he'd acquired, where they were stashed or located. But he held back on that secret bank account in Guernsey. That was his stash for when he got out of the pen.

He was particularly fuzzy on the loan details. There were hundreds of them. How could he be expected to remember every detail? Except for the names he knew well, his buddies, his debt junkies. Buck served them up on a platter with garnish.

He also gave them Seth Summers.

They went over it again and again and again until he wasn't sure what he'd told them. He probably made up some it. Maybe a lot. And he was paying his lawyer what? Three hundred an hour to sit there half asleep saying nothing?

Buck was exhausted, drained, wrung out. They had really worked him over. They put him in a double holding cell in the basement of the county jail. He was cuffed hand and foot when they hauled him back and forth every day. At least he got to see some daylight, some real people walking on the sidewalks, as he was driven to and from.

The jail food was horrible. He turned down most of the so-called holiday slop they served. "You gonna eat that?" his cellmate, a meth-head tweaker with bad teeth had asked. Buck shoved the plastic plate over.

The noise was worse. If only he could shut out the racket, then maybe he could sleep. Maybe think straight.

He needed a drink. And a cigar.

He vehemently denied any knowledge of a goon named Pete Curtis, aka Lucky, or of a plot to hire an assassin to kill Mrs. Robertson. He was shocked, appalled at the very thought.

They had moved on to other things.

The FBI team also worked through the Thanksgiving holiday, Nieve, Sissy, Don Worthen, all the rest of them. Their families—those that still had families—were used to it by now.

"What we got so far?" FBI Special Agent Chris Nieve asked. All agreed they had probably gotten all they were going to get out of Buckley at this point. There was enough to convict. They'd talk with Izzie about making a plea deal.

They all concurred that Buckley had cooperated enough. They had a ton to work with.

Of course, half the stuff Buckley had told them was probably made up. Diversion tactics. Enough to keep them off his own back. They'd take what they could and use it. It was a good start. There would be a lot of follow up. They would work carefully, methodically until they caught, arrested, convicted and put away any of the other co-conspirators on the list Buckley gave them.

Number One on that wanted list was Seth Summers.

"Okay, where do we see the problems in this case?"

There were essentially three. First, they would need to verify, double-check the "facts" Buckley had given them. That was standard FBI stuff. Two pairs of agents were assigned that job.

Next, Dill Robertson. This gave Chris Nieve some concern. Based on his prior dealings with Robertson, and based on how he had conducted himself so far in assisting the FBI, the man was probably clean. Still …

Nieve decided to let Robertson have his weekend home with his family on his ranch in peace. He could call him Monday and ask if he minded driving down to Denver for a little chat. Just to clarify a few things. Softly, softly catches the monkey. Chris would talk with Robertson himself.

The final headache was the list of names, prominent people, that Buckley had given the FBI. In one way or another, either through being on the bank's board of directors (or related to a board member), a borrower, a big depositor of those jumbo CDs, or just one of Buck's drinking buddies, there were enough big shots, public figures, politicians (current and former), some professional athletes, a couple big-name movie stars, to cause some real headaches. The FBI would move very cautiously here.

The social, political and business network of many of those named was complicated. The relationships interlaced so tightly. At this point, they had no idea how entangled these connections were. Their job was to untangle the knot. Carefully. Very Carefully.

Did any of those named by Buckley have any knowledge of any of the crimes that had been committed? Did any of them participate in the scam—directly or otherwise? Might they also be charged with conspiracy? Aiding and abetting a crime? Would any of them try to hide or destroy evidence? Lie when questioned? Offer bribes? Flee? Or worse?

Nieve didn't even want to think about a couple of tragic past cases where people who were otherwise innocent, buckled under extreme or imagined pressure and killed themselves.

Pizza arrived. But, after turkey and stuffing with cranberry sauce, nobody was hungry for greasy pepperoni.

FDIC, Kansas City

Carly Flack, the FDIC president, worked through Thanksgiving, stopping only long enough to break bread with her husband and a few close friends at the country club they all belonged to. After coffee and brandies were served (she passed on the brandy, had to keep a clear head), her driver picked her up and ferried her back to the FDIC offices in Kansas City.

"Should I wait, ma'am?"

"I'll call you when I need you, Carl. Go home, be with your family. Thanks."

"Yes, ma'am. Thank you, ma'am."

President Flack plodded through her list of banks she needed to break the bad news to: "Larimer Square Bank has gone under and you're in trouble, too. Call your officers and directors into an emergency meeting and break the bad news to them. Look, I know it's a holiday, but this can't be helped. Sorry," she had repeated, closely following the little script she'd penned on a scrap of memo paper between courses at the country club.

She looked down at the scrap and had a thought: Money was printed on paper. The volumes of bank regulations. On paper, too. Promissory notes and participation agreements were written on paper. Default notices. Paper. Lawsuits. Paper. Jury verdicts. Paper. News headlines? Paper.

And here, on this little 3x5-inch scrap of paper is the obituary of a once good little bank. At least it had started out with all the right tools to succeed.

She shook her head grimly and picked up the phone for the next call. Other FDIC heads around the country were putting their Thanksgiving dinners on hold to go through the same unpleasant ritual.

FORTY-SIX

Thanksgiving Day, Robertson Ranch

Early Thanksgiving morning, John—Dill and Jo's youngest—had shrugged into layers of heavy clothes for warmth against the cold. He loaded a handful of #2 shotgun shells into his coat pocket, took his little Charles Daly, 20-gauge shotgun, out of the safe, whistled up his Brittany spaniel, Clipper, and headed out.

JJ, as his family and friends called him, had been watching several large flocks of Merriam's wild turkeys that inhabited the scrubby native oaks, the stands of pinion pine trees scattered in the hills and coulees above the ranch house. The Colorado fish and game people had recently introduced another wild strain, the Rio Grande turkeys. But they were way to the southern parts of the state.

JJ saddled his horse and set out before daylight. He had already built a blind next to a little clearing that gave him an unobstructed view of any birds that would come to his call. He tethered his horse to an aspen bare of any leaves and quietly hiked the last quarter mile to his blind. Clipper followed him shivering with excitement. The dog could smell the birds and sensed they were nearby eating fallen acorns and pine nuts.

JJ and Clipper got settled and waited for their nerves to calm down. JJ took out his turkey call and began singing a turkey love song. Nothing. He waited a few minutes and tried again. He heard the birds fussing and chuckling their weird turkey talk before he saw them. They just sort of shimmered into the edge of the clearing, appearing like wraiths. One minute nothing, the next, there they were.

JJ had set up his shotgun in the fork of a sturdy tree branch. Any movement like raising the gun could scare the jumpy birds before he could get off a shot. He had kept the call in his hand, close to his mouth. He offered up one more soft morsel of sound, to which the tom, patriarch of the family, fluffed up his chest, fanned out his beautiful tail feathers and did a little jig in JJ's direction. But JJ didn't want to shoot this magnificent bird. A tender, succulent young hen or tom would make much better eating. The patriarch would survive this day to fulfill his task of replenishing the rafter.

The old tom danced sideways just enough to give JJ a clear shot. He silently slipped off the safety, let out his breath as he took aim at the young tom's head and fired. At the crash of the shot from the little 20 gauge, the rafter vanished in a clamor, airborne in two seconds. The young bird fluttered madly in his death throes. Clipper bounded out of the blind to pin down the thrashing bird.

Aunt Ida helped a proud JJ pluck and clean the bird and ready it for the oven, complete with her secret cornbread stuffing recipe. The giblets would make a fine gravy. Within an hour, the plump bird was in the oven, filling the entire house with the fragrant aroma of sage, rosemary and baking bird. JJ saved the tail and wing feathers for fly tying later.

Matthew, now back home from his Church mission to Thailand, had invited a friend home to spend the holiday with his family. She was an exchange student from Spain, a lovely girl named Francesca Montoya, who would have been all alone for the holiday. Matthew was clearly smitten with her, not wanting to leave her side even, until his dad and brothers insisted he come and watch the Detroit Lions playing the Minnesota Vikings in the traditional Thanksgiving Day football game on TV.

Jo took the pretty, shy Francesca under her wing and asked all about her family, life in Spain, what was she majoring in, how did she and Matthew meet? The girl was quickly put at ease.

Dill glanced up from the TV and caught JoEllen's eyes for a brief minute. Hers were shining. She was happy and so was he. Family. Home. Life was good.

Okmulgee, Oklahoma

Ricky Bob, Nan and their four kids had Thanksgiving dinner with her parents in Muskogee. Ricky would have preferred his parents' because they always had a well-stocked liquor cabinet. Nan's didn't. They were tee-totaling Baptists. Their kids didn't object to Thanksgiving with Nan's parents. But Ricky knew they preferred his dad because he always played the pull-my-finger game and made them laugh.

They got through dinner somehow without talking politics. Ricky, Nan, and the kids even, managed to suffer through a Bible class taught to her captive audience by Nan's mom. The topic, of course, was gratitude. The meal, though, was delicious. Nan's mother was an excellent cook. She'd had enough practice over the years, cooking and taking in meals for other members of her church who were in need. Ricky had to admit that she did bake a mean peanut butter pie.

Ricky Bob was nervous, restless all through the meal and the ensuing Bible class. He had a hard time focusing on playing the game his mother-in-law had devised. She had challenged them to see who could be the first to chase down a scripture that told of God's grace in blessing His earthly children. They then were to read the scripture out loud and explain it in their own words.

The pink princess wall phone rang in the kitchen. Mrs. Norton excused herself to go answer it. Years ago, she had outfitted the phone with an extra-long cord so she could talk and still sweep, dust and vacuum at the same time. Now, it allowed her to step out of the kitchen and into the dining room to hand the phone to Ricky.

"It's for you. He wouldn't give me his name." She said this loud enough that she was sure to be clearly heard by the person on the other end of the call. The message was: It's polite to give your name. She handed the phone to Ricky.

He stepped back into the kitchen. Then, knowing that Nan's mother would be straining to hear every word, he stepped out onto the back porch, closed the door behind him. "Yeah, Ricky Bob here."

It was Darren Magelby. He wanted to report that he had met with Phillip and Jerry and explained the need to amend. They were unhappy when they left. "Too bad. We got to be straight, do things the right way," Ricky said.

Darren said that he had done the re-drafts and wanted to fax copies to the two promoters with a copy over to Ricky. Everyone was to read and approve the final draft. Ricky thought that would be fine. He asked Darren if he'd heard anything back from the FBI about his promised drill rig? Darren said it was a little too early, but he expected the Feds would soon be wrapping up their case against Buckley and could then likely be in a position to work with Ricky. Ricky thanked him for his work and was about to sign off, when Darren said he had one more thing.

"Actually, two things. I took the liberty of talking to a friend of mine in the SEC office in Ft. Worth. I told him I had a client who suspected some business associates of his were playing the old dry-hole game with their investors. He said to tell the whistleblower thank you and looked forward to discussing the facts with *him* in strictest confidence."

"How would I be sure they won't turn on me and prosecute? I've heard they suspect whistleblowers and their motives. I've heard of cases where the snitch gets nailed."

"I don't think you need to worry. He, my SEC friend, assured me they would work out an immunity deal in advance for you to sign."

Ricky breathed a huge sigh of relief. "Good. But, you said two things. What else?"

"I also placed a call to another good friend of mine, actually one of my biggest clients. He says he has an option on a lease for deep gas you-know-where and is looking to partner with someone who has a rig and some darned good drilling experience. He's got what's known as really deep pockets and is sitting on tons of cash. He can easily pay his half of the expenses. He just wants to be in first position to get his lease costs back out. Then it's 50-50 after that. What do you think?"

"That's the best Thanksgiving blessing I ever heard. Praise the Lord for tender mercies! And thanks."

"You're welcome. Best keep it under your hat until it's a done deal. Don't mention it to your two partners, Phil and Jerry?"

Ricky promised to keep it quiet. But he would tell Nan. Just before they went to bed.

Friday. Steamboat Springs, Colorado

Dill and his family drove over to Steamboat for their annual day-after-Thanksgiving ritual: a movie matinee followed by picking out one new ornament for their Christmas tree. There were three movies playing in town at the same time. JoEllen, Aunt Ida, and Francesca wanted to see *Endless Love* with Brooke Shields. Chick flick! The boys shouted the girls down. The guys wanted to see either Harrison Ford in *Raiders of the Lost Ark,* or the latest James Bond 007 flick, *For Your Eyes Only*.

"I say we compromise: you guys see your movie and we'll go see ours. Meet you back here in a couple hours?" JoEllen's peace treaty was agreed to. The guys then flipped a coin and tails won: Raiders it is!

"Cool," Mark said.

Luke chimed in with "Harrison Ford, he's so dang macho!"

Larimer Square Bank, Denver

By Friday morning after Thanksgiving, Randy Simpson, the CPA on loan from the SEC, together with his team had labored almost around the clock for several days and had come up with some preliminary figures for the FDIC and Comptroller's team of examiners. "You better sit down," Simpson warned. They sat.

The regulators were staggered. The bad loans, which translated into certain losses for the banks involved, would top three and a half billion. Dollars. Maybe more. This was just the preliminary accounting. The regulators had guessed the number would be in the neighborhood of maybe $2 billion. They missed it by a lot, almost half.

And to think they were sitting there in the middle of a shopping center in a little obscure Denver bank that nobody had ever heard of, wedged between a five-and-dime store and a shop that sold ladies' frilly and lacy things. The little bank that very soon everyone around the world would hear about and would bring down several giant financial institutions with it.

Was Simpson able to give them a breakdown of which upstream banks were exposed, and did he happen to break them out by amounts lost, by the most to the least?

Yes. It's all in his preliminary figures. Of course, those numbers are subject to change with more research.

Simpson had made some assumptions and forced some figures to give the examiners a rough estimate. They sensed there were still dozens of missing loan files from which they hoped to fill in the missing numbers. Several upstream banks, out of fear of what they would uncover, had yet to send a complete inventory of the loans they had bought participations in.

Based on these preliminary numbers, the regulators were already making plans to deal with several banks that would likely go under as a result of their involvement. They just didn't have the means, the capital, to absorb such staggering losses.

The regulators wished they could say it was all largely caused by one man. But they knew that argument to be disingenuous. Many people were to blame.

The unanswered question—the one nobody had the heart to ask yet—did Simpson have any inkling yet whether Summers and his cronies had actually managed to embezzle or steal any of the bank's funds? He would get to that issue in due time, together with his search for the dirty money that was most likely stashed offshore somewhere.

Meanwhile, oil prices dropped yet another $2 a barrel.

Stagecoach Energy, Dallas

When the stock exchanges opened for trading on the Friday after Thanksgiving, Stagecoach had received an initial approval from the SEC to resume trading. Within 15 minutes, Stagecoach Energy was battered again by tens of thousands of shares coming at them from a half-dozen different foreign brokerages located in the tax havens of

Hong Kong, Singapore, Zug, and Panama City, as well as London and Tokyo.

The SEC was also watching. They told Stagecoach to stop trading. Again.

Stagecoach immediately put out an announcement through its New York PR firm, which said nothing of substance, except some pablum about how management was carefully monitoring matters. Management had quietly also agreed that the SEC action taken was in the best interest of Stagecoach shareholders. Blah blah.

In Chicago, a large international law firm was drawing up a lawsuit against Stagecoach, its officers and directors. They would allege three kinds of fraud, misfeasance and malfeasance by management, plus insider trading.

And RICO. The civil variety.

The suit would ask for millions in damages, both real and imagined, punitive damages, and RICO treble damages, court costs, attorney fees, interest both before and after judgment, etc., etc.

When Stagecoach was hit with the suit first thing Monday morning, they were forced to immediately put out a press release. The news article denied any wrongdoing, of course. We'll defend vigorously, blah blah.

Within mere minutes, Stagecoach was clobbered with more shareholder lawsuits from law firms representing a host of aggrieved, damaged parties. The suits were filed in several jurisdictions across the United States—Atlanta, Cheyenne, San Diego—and some place called San Juan. As in Puerto Rico. The new actions were hasty cut-and-paste jobs, photocopies of the first one. Then they fired the missiles. The suits were almost exact duplicates of each other. Stagecoach's reception area became a revolving door for process servers.

"Another one, sir," said Lorne's secretary as she handed the latest sheaf of papers to him. He tossed it in a Banker's box with all the others.

Lorne and Ted agreed it was finally time to throw in the towel. "Call the lawyers," Lorne sighed.

Stagecoach filed for bankruptcy protection in the U.S. bankruptcy court for the Northern District of Texas.

Weatherford, Texas

Early Friday morning, relieved to be away from his mother-in-law, Ricky Bob, dressed in clean Wranglers and checkered flannel shirt, stood on the deck of the Dolly P drill rig. He and Todd were waiting for a truck from the huge fracking company, Schlumberger, to arrive. Today they would test the target formation about 5,000 feet down the hole. Everybody on the drilling crew was anxious, a bit jumpy. If they found oil, made a producing well, there would be happiness in the form of big cash bonuses in time for Christmas. If not …

The Schlumberger truck finally rolled in. Ricky and his boys all stood aside for the expert Schlumberger crew. They knew what to do. They went about their work efficiently, setting up the fracking tool, essentially a "gun," a metal cylinder that was fastened to a cable or "wire" and lowered very carefully, very slowly into the bore hole. It would be set off by an electrical signal sent from the truck above ground.

The fracking tool fired a host of 50 caliber metal-jacketed bullets set in a circular design inside the tool. The bullets pierced through the metal pipe that earlier had been sunk down the hole and cemented into place. The high-powered bullets blasted out into the formation, parallel to the ground above. Those bullets were loaded with explosive devices that were supposed to crack or fracture the sandstone, limestone, or other porous rocks, where the gazillions of microscopic oil molecules were trapped.

The fracking tool was then retrieved back up the hole and chemicals would be forced downhole under extreme pressure. The chemical mixture was infused with tons of sand. The theory of fracking relied on the sand wedging into the fractures created by the bullet-explosives. The sand held the fracture open and remained wedged in place (think of food caught in your teeth) as the liquids in the chemical mixture were pumped out. Natural gas deposits create a lot of pressure down the hole. The gas gets released through fracking, which helps push the oil molecules through the fracture and out and up the bore hole to the top of the new well.

Then, if all goes well, after a lot of careful testing down hole, a pump jack will be installed topside. The pump jack, plus the natural gas pressure, forces those gazillions of tiny oil molecules to congeal together into a happy stream of crude and to begin the trip up the metal casing-lined bore hole to the waiting holding tanks.

The production of new crude is watched carefully to determine how much is being produced. This production is expressed as a certain number of barrels per day (BPD).

A well at this depth—5,000 feet—would be considered a good, commercial well (meaning it would pay out its costs plus a healthy profit over a fairly short time), if it produced in the range of 300 BPD to start. After several days, the well would likely settle down to a steady average volume of around 150 BPD.

The Dolly P came in at just under 500 BPD, with tremendous pressure. That much pressure would have to be choked back when they actually began production.

Ricky Bob applied to the Texas Railroad Commission to allow daily production of 300 BPD. It was routinely approved.

This well was technically owned by the limited partnership that had put up the risk money to finance it. But their share of equity was also subject to—or, *burdened* in oilfield terminology—by various other interests. The first one in line being the landowner who leased the prospect to the drillers. He'd be paid first from any revenues. The landowner's interest could range anywhere from 5 percent to 20 percent of production.

Then there are a couple more participants in the cash flow. This can be one of two types of "interests." The first type is called a *working* interest. The owner of a working interest has the legal obligation to pay his, or its, pro-rata share of any drilling, completion or any ongoing or future costs of operation.

Then there are *carried* interests. Carried means that these interest owners don't have to share in the costs. They are literally "carried" on the backs of the other interest-owners.

All of these various interests are accounted for in a document called a *division order*. The division order tells the crude buyer who, among all the claimed interests, has the legal rights to get paid out of the production revenues. It clearly defines how much, and in what order of priority, the spoils are divided.

Taxes need to be deducted from monthly production. Costs of transportation of the crude have to be figured in, whether by pipeline or truck. There are also costs of operating the well: electricity to the well site, fuel for the pump jack, excess water hauling, etc.

And don't forget the completion costs. There are "soft" costs like fracking, and "hard" costs like well-head, valves and pumping equipment, and tank batteries for crude storage until it's shipped to the refinery.

By the time a new oil-and-gas investor sees any production checks they are usually shocked to see how little they are actually getting back for their substantial investment. Some wells pay out quickly. Some slowly. Some never.

The risk to the investor can be somewhat offset by the tax benefits. Somewhat. The IRS may audit the partnership and determine there's been an abuse in the number of deductions taken by the partners. The tax-favored allowances may be denied in whole or in part by the IRS, much to the dismay of the taxpayer.

If the Dolly P could sustain production at this rate, the average investor would likely get their investment back in a little over a year. Their letters of credit would be paid and retired. Any future paychecks would thereafter be unencumbered.

Sadly, the Dolly P would be tied up in litigation for several years by Stagecoach Energy's bankruptcy proceedings and lawyers constantly wrangling, running up their fees. Eventually, the courts would get the mess resolved. But not before the referee in bankruptcy had taken his healthy cut, and the lawyers on all sides had persuaded the courts they should be compensated out of production.

By then—1986—the Dolly P was down to a steady 13 barrels a day and slowly declining. The spot price for West Texas sweet crude had dropped under the $30 benchmark. It hovered around $22 for some time before starting to creep back up.

FORTY-SEVEN

FBI Offices, Denver

Dill left his home in Craig in the pre-dawn hours on the Monday morning after Thanksgiving. With luck, he would still make his 11 o'clock appointment with Special Agent Nieve. Chris had called him Saturday afternoon to ask if they could meet, go over a few questions the FBI had, clear up some things. Dill said, “Yeah, sure.” And asked what he should bring. Nieve said the bank examiners had provided the FBI with all the files that Dill had touched while he was Chief Loan Officer of the bank. But if Dill had anything they think might help the investigation, they’d like to see it.

Nieve had also informed Dill that the FBI had picked up the suspect known as Lucky. The one who had worked for Seth Summers and had arranged for and paid the alleged assassin-suspect—Gus Kessimakis—to kill JoEllen. Lucky’s real name was Pete Curtis.

After Dill signed off, he had a thought. He called Nieve back. “Am I a target of your investigation?” he asked.

Nieve hesitated several agonizing seconds. Then said, “Let’s just say that at this time you are considered a person of interest.”

“What’s the difference?”

“I think we should save that discussion for when you get here.”

“Should I be worried enough to bring my lawyer?”

Nieve laughed. “Mr. Robertson, Dill. We’ve known each other long enough to shoot straight. My opinion? I think you’re clean. But that could change, depending …” He let that comment hang.

“Tell me how you got involved with the Larimer Square Bank. Start from the beginning and tell me everything.”

Nieve had taken off his jacket and had invited Dill to take a seat. There was no recording machine, no pad of paper for notes on the small conference table. Just two friends trying to work through a giant puzzle. Trying to find the truth. Dill was determined to help Agent Nieve see that he had done the right thing. Always had. And, during his tenure with the bank, nothing had changed in his behavior to cause him to cross over the line to the dark side.

Dill searched back in the dark rooms of his mind, trying to decide just which door to open to be examined in the light of day. The truth? It was in there somewhere.

"I was first contacted about working for the Larimer Square Bank by a gentleman named Seth Summers,"

"When was that? How did he contact you? What did he say to you? What did you say to him?"

The sun set a little after 5 o'clock. Dill got up to stretch, work out some knots in his neck and shoulders. He looked out the window of the small FBI conference room. A fresh layer of snow had fallen during the day while he and Agent Nieve had talked. Down below, the commuters patiently worked their way out of the city to their various residences. They were used to driving in snow. It was a way of life that came with living here.

Dill and Nieve had looked at a few loan files. Dill patiently explained the way a prudent banker would work up a loan, build the file, assure that his bank was safe and secure, that the loan had enough security—collateral—to justify advancing public monies to the borrower. He listed the steps he usually went through before making a preliminary recommendation to a loan committee. If he had the lending authority and the loan was within that limit, he could make the decision himself. But his practice had always been to have another set of eyes look at his work.

"Just to be safe?" Nieve asked.

"Just to be sure the bank was making a good loan."

All the while Dill was answering the agent's questions, talking, explaining, Nieve used his investigative skills and experience to watch and observe. He was looking for little signs, subtle signals, tell-tale mannerisms that indicated to his trained eyes, ears, brain—and gut—whether the interviewee was lying, covering up, misleading, telling part of the truth but holding back something. Something that might incriminate him or her. Little ticks, tone of voice, whether he looked at you or looked away, pulling ears, scratching, wringing hands, shifting in the seat before answering. Little things.

Nieve stood up to join Dill at the big picture window. He did a couple stretching exercises himself, and finally said, "Well, I think our work here is through." He smiled and extended his hand. Dill took it in a firm grip of friendship.

"So, I'm okay?" Dill asked. He needed some comfort before he walked out that door.

"I think so. Everything you told me seems to check out. Of course, I'll have my agents confirm a few things to be sure. But a lot of the details you provided today will help move our investigation along. Yes. A great help."

He shrugged on his suit coat, covering up his new Glock 9mm.

"I see you have a new sidearm," Dill pointed.

"Yes. The Agency finally decided we needed to keep up with the bad guys. So, they had us turn in our .38 Police Specials and issued these. I'm still not used to the way it feels in my hand."

They started to walk out when Nieve turned to face Dill. "You sure you don't have a clue where we might find your Mr. Seth Summers?"

Dill shook his head. Nieve laughed and said, "Don't worry. We'll get him some day. The law is very patient, you know?"

Dill had no doubt he was right.

FORTY-EIGHT

March 4th. A New Year. Skiatook, Oklahoma

Darren called Ricky Bob to report that he had some excellent news. Buckley had finally appeared before a federal judge in Denver for sentencing. He and his lawyer had finally agreed to a sentence for his part in the Larimer Square Bank scam. He would serve 48 months in a Federal prison camp, with some of it shaved off for time already served. More, if he was a good boy. The judge approved the deal and passed sentence.

"He was ordered into the custody of the U.S. Marshalls and ended up in Florence," Darren said.

"I'm not sure I know Florence," Ricky said.

"Florence? It's a new facility way down in the southeast corner of Colorado. Anyway, the FBI wants you to take a look at a storage yard in Oklahoma City. There's a ton of drill rigs stacked there. Some of them, well most, are bankruptcy cases. Some are RICO forfeitures. You can take a look, have your pick of any one that fits your needs," Darren said. Then, added: "But they insist you pay for it."

"What the …?" This was shocking news. Ricky Bob was under the impression he would get the rig for free, for playing his part in that very dangerous sting operation the year before.

"Relax. They have to charge you something. For the sake of appearance. I negotiated hard and got them down to—get this—how's one dollar sound?"

Ricky let out a huge breath he'd been holding. "Awesome! Wow! That's great, Darren. You're the best. Thanks, I'll do that. It couldn't happen any sooner. Phil and Jerry are barely managing to hold their investors together. Everyone's nervous to get started drilling that deep gas lease out in the Anadarko. I'm pretty pleased with the deal your other client made for us. He's even offered to take a working interest. I said we would, too."

"Did Connoff and Jordan agree to be a working interest too?" Darren asked.

"I'll tell them. I doubt they know the difference between a working interest and a donut."

Darren laughed and Ricky Bob signed off. He had an appointment with Kyle in Tulsa. Now that Ricky Bob swung a big stick in the oil patch, The Tulsa Guaranty Bank had "graciously" offered to take Peabody Oil back as a prime customer.

They were going to celebrate Ricky's return back into the Tulsa Guaranty fold over lunch at the exclusive Tulsa Petroleum Club. The bank would pick up the tab. You bet your britches they will, Ricky Bob said to himself.

EPILOGUE

Spring, 2002. Dallas

Calvin Buckley drove his older model pink Cadillac through the evening rush hour traffic on Preston Road in North Dallas. He had the Caddie convertible top down to luxuriate in the lovely warm spring air. A set of Longhorn cattle horns stuck out the front of the grille. The car's horn loudly played "Dixie" when Buck pushed the red button. He liked to push the button often.

On his rear bumper was a sticker. It read: *Dear Lord, Please Give Me Just One More Oil Boom and I Promise I Won't Gamble It All Away This Time!*

While waiting for the light to turn green, Buck fiddled with the dial on his car radio trying to find the station that carried Rush Limbaugh. It was still a few minutes early for Rush, so Buck left it on an all-news station. He heard this piece of breaking news:

> *U. S. Marshalls have announced that they have arrested a fugitive they had been trying to find for almost 20 years. The Marshalls took the man into custody without incident earlier today. The fugitive was identified as Seth Summers, who is alleged to have been on the run all this time after he slipped through an international dragnet 20 years ago.*

Buck nearly choked. The light changed to green. Buck didn't notice. The driver behind him laid on his horn. Buck shook his fist, then lurched forward.

The newscast continued:

Summers was the prime suspect in the massive financial scam that caused the failure of a small bank in Denver, Colorado, known as the Larimer Square Bank.

Larimer Square had convinced a number of big-name financial institutions to participate in a colossal number of highly risky energy bank loans. Most of those loans went bad, causing a major financial meltdown. Several of those large banks, unable to cover their losses, went under along with the smaller Larimer Square Bank. Officials determined that at least $5 billion were lost through the scam, making it the largest financial crisis since the Great Depression.

Summers, now believed to be 71 years old, had apparently lived abroad for the last 20 years, where he had undergone plastic surgery on his face to change his identity, had assumed a new persona with a fake Irish passport under the name of Gil O'Brien. While on the run, Summers had married and divorced and married again. Name of his current wife has been withheld at her request for privacy.

Summers had been operating three fried chicken franchises in the college town of Conway, Arkansas, near Little Rock.

Investigators, acting on a tip from a confidential informant, had Summers under surveillance for nearly four months before confirming his identity and moving in to make the arrest. Federal investigators were able to make a positive ID after obtaining a DNA sample from Summers. Agents declined to say how they got the DNA sample.

Summers will be returned to face criminal charges in Denver in connection with his alleged role in the bank failure as the mastermind of the fraudulent scheme.

If convicted, he is facing a possible sentence of 10 to 20 years, and a fine of up to $250,000. Summers's lawyers have already filed motions to have their client released on bail. The court deemed him a flight risk and denied the motion.

Spring, 2002. Parma, Italy

Morty Resnick strolled out on the tiled terrace of his Italian townhome villa. It was a lovely spring morning, sunny and full of promise. He checked to make sure he wasn't being watched, then sat down to sip his cappuccino and read his morning paper, *Corriere della Sera*.

Morty read the brief article about Seth Summers buried in the business section. He smiled to himself and remembered the day a few years ago when he had cleverly persuaded Seth to give him the passwords to the secret bank accounts Seth had set up around the world.

Morty had traded account numbers with Seth on the premise that if something happened to either one of them, the other could still have access to the funds. There must be at least around $50 million lying there for the harvesting.

Randy Simpson and his team had tried valiantly to find the money stashed by Seth and Morty, as well as Buck's $10 million. But, in spite of Simpson's expertise at following tainted money, of trying to penetrate the many layers of offshore brass-plate banks and cut-out companies buried behind numerous other cut-out companies, the secrets had proven to be impervious, impossible to break. For the first time in his storied career, the job had proven to be impossible. The FDIC finally paid him his last retainer check, and they quietly folded up the case files and went on to other failed banks.

Recently, though, Seth mistakenly convinced himself that he could slip back into the States by way of Ireland without being detected. Morty, knowing it was sheer madness, tried to talk Seth out of it. That was just last year. Still, Seth had contacted Morty and let him know where he was hanging out in the United States. Somebody was listening.

Placing the anonymous call to the American embassy in Frankfurt with a disposable burner phone had been easy for Morty. It was just one of the many tools of his new trade that he was taught by a certain American agency. After hanging around Milan for a couple years the *Carabiniere*, the Italian police, who had kept a nervous eye on a certain *Mr. Paul Reeder*, brought Morty in to determine if he was of a criminal disposition. One of their seasoned interrogators ran the profile of Paul Reeder, aka Morty Resnick, through their new computers and spotted some dirty secrets buried in his checkered past.

He was then turned over to the *Sistema di informazione per la sicurezza della Repubblica,* or *AISI* for short, Italy's agency for internal security. After an exhausting two-day interrogation, the agent thought Morty might be of some use to the shadowy Americans operating out of Milan on Italian soil.

This man had all the elements of being a good spy: he was arrogant, confident, self-assured, self-centered, a consummate liar, and most of all, he was without conscience or remorse. In the right hands he could be molded. That was the collective thinking as the Italians handed him over to their American counterparts.

Morty was then recruited and trained by an attractive, petite brunette operative. American. She looked an awful lot like a certain pretty girl in a light cotton sundress he had once spotted riding a Flamingo pink motor scooter on a Caribbean island. Except this woman was now several years older. Still pretty, though. She reminded Morty to stop lusting and keep his mind focused on the business at hand. She did have lovely tan legs.

The deal the bosses in Langley offered Morty was too tempting to pass up: Work for us and your past involvement with Seth Summers will quietly go away. They assured him that the FBI no longer had an interest in a person named Morty Resnick. So, he signed on. He was given a new, foolproof identity that Langley had spent weeks creating, together with his newly minted British passport. It was filled with many strategically aged visa stamps that further authenticated his new persona. His new employers also provided him with the comfy little villa in Parma where he resided for now as Anthony Craddock.

Anthony smiled again, laid down the newspaper, took out his flip-phone and called his private banker in Lugano to check on his balances. He also placed a couple of stock trades. Although his new employers frowned on betting, his next call was to his bookie. Anthony Craddock placed a bet against his local football club, Parma Calcio, and in favor of the Torino club to win its match tonight. He placed the bet of $1,000 U.S. and took the over/under of two goals. Parma was next to last in Series A football standings and the odds were they would probably lose tonight. The only question being, by how much?

Two missionaries of the Church of Jesus Christ of Latter-day Saints emerged from the villa next door, dressed in dark gabardine trousers, short-sleeve white shirts, wearing sensible, clunky shoes and conservative dark ties. Their haircuts were short, almost military. They had light backpacks over their shoulders stuffed with Books of Mormon in Italian, big smiles on their shiny young faces. They waved to the man they knew as Anthony Craddock, Englishman, retired public school classics teacher. They each carried the front wheel of their bicycle that they expertly re-attached to their bikes.

With their bicycles ready to ride, they asked, "How are you today, Mr. Craddock?"

He said he was fine.

"When are you going to let us teach you the gospel?" they asked for the umpteenth time.

"You know I'm an Anglican. At this age in life, I doubt I'll change. Too much trouble" he laughed. "Besides, I've already told you I've done so many bad things in my lifetime that I doubt God would waste his time on a wretched sinner like me."

"You'd be surprised what he's capable of. Christ's Atonement was for everyone," one of the elders replied.

Anthony Craddock had his doubts. But he always teased them with, "Maybe someday."

The elders grinned, fastened on their helmets, adjusted chin straps, mounted their bikes and pedaled happily off to save the world.

His morning business now concluded, Anthony Craddock, formerly known as Morty Resnick, lit a slim Italian cigar with an expensive, slender gold propane lighter and blew a stream of smoke toward the orange tree overhead. Anthony went inside to change out of his bathrobe and sandals into more appropriate tennis togs. Fruit-scented smoke followed him inside.

Anthony took a long shower then examined himself in his bedroom mirror. Mid-fifties, he was still quite handsome, with the tanned, chiseled facial features of a matinee idol. He used his looks and charm as weapons in his new trade. He wondered if he would ever have to undergo plastic surgery to change his identity. He'd read about such things in spy novels.

Anthony Craddock had a date on the clay courts with a gorgeous, willowy blonde girl who had a great body and spoke four languages, Russian being her native tongue. She claimed she was a duchess. Or royalty something. She had been identified by his associates in the Milan embassy as an agent of the Russian Federation's FSB, formerly the KGB. He hoped to learn a few tidbits, something he could pass on to his handlers.

Anthony Craddock was now the classic honey trap in reverse. This time he was the bait. He thought about the Russian girl. She called him Tony. Other than his name, how much did she know about him? He suspected she knew a lot. It was all part of the game they played.

Maybe she is royalty, probably she isn't, thought Anthony Craddock. Who cares?

Don't we all assume personas—masks—to protect the real person hidden in a dark room inside? Don't we all tell lies?

Elkhead Creek, Robertson Ranch

It was the kind of spring day that would draw a man outside with high hopes. And so it was, that Dill Robertson found himself in his battered truck, fly rod and waders in the back. He nosed the rattling vehicle out of the graveled driveway, ignoring the piles of fat gray clouds pregnant with moisture looming on the purpling horizon. He was curious about the spring snow melt, the level of runoff in Elkhead Creek.

The water was rising slowly but still fairly clear. Dill finished tying on the dainty size 14 wet fly. It had a dark, slim profile, sparse hackles made of a single partridge breast feather, a small pinch of white calf tail hair for a wing, and a single small gold bead head for weight. This was one he'd tied himself. He thought he'd name it the Ricky Bob fly. If presented properly, a well-dissembled fly would fool even the wariest cutthroat trout into striking.

Dill made two false casts and rolled the fly down gently at the head of the riffle. It barely sank under the surface when the fly was engulfed in a savage swirl of water. It was a nice cutthroat, big and strong, muscled like an MMA cage fighter. The kind of trout its smaller neighbors avoided. He played the trout for five minutes before bringing it to the net. He gently held the fish, slipped the barbless hook out of its jaw. Then he took a few seconds to admire its spots, the brilliant striation of colors—olive back, rosy flanks and throat, red-orange gill slashes, creamy-yellow belly—before lowering it back into the icy stream.

Dill straightened, stretched his back muscles, and walked several yards upstream where he cast again with similar results. After an hour of successful fishing, he reeled in his line. He walked back to his truck with a decided limp, the result of an autumn elk hunting accident two years ago. His horse had shied at something, reared back on a narrow mountain trail, lost its footing and Dill had been thrown off into a stack of huge granite boulders.

He had suffered several broken ribs, a punctured lung, dislocated shoulder, hairline fracture in his elbow and a badly broken leg. The horse had bolted, disappeared into the dark green pine forest. So, Dill had grimly cut a crutch out of a pine limb and frog-hopped the three miles back to camp. The ribs and other parts healed nicely but the leg required several surgeries. It still wasn't right.

Dill carefully laid his new Winston fly rod into the back of his truck. It was the third one he had to buy to replace the earlier ones that had been stolen. First the Fenwick in Denver. Then it was a Sage, filched at a campground in Rocky Mountain National Park. Some things never change. How long before someone gives into the lustful urge to separate this one from him? Maybe it was time to put a rod rack in the cab. Time to start locking his truck?

As he drove back to his ranch house, he thought of JoEllen. After 10 good years in remission, the leukemia had returned and she had finally lost the fight. Dill was now all alone in that big, empty stack of sandstone blocks he called home. He was thinking seriously of turning the whole package, ranch and bank, over to his eldest son.

Then, maybe Dill would retire and stay on in the little guest house out back and spend more time fishing his beloved Elkhead.

Then again, maybe he wouldn't.

AUTHOR'S NOTE

OILIES is a work of fictional entertainment and should be read as nothing more. Consequently, the names, persons, characters, places, businesses, companies, locations and incidents portrayed in the story, unless otherwise indicated, are either the product of the author's own creation or have been used fictitiously. Any resemblance to actual persons, living or dead, names, companies or businesses, or places, is entirely coincidental. That said, I do need to provide further explanation:

When one tries to write an historical novel—and I guess this book falls into that niche—there are facts, and then there are *imagined* facts. The trick is to take the basic facts—a framework—and weave onto them a story composed of mostly imagined facts and make it sound convincing. It's my sincere hope that the following notes help clear up any confusion between the two kinds of facts.

The definition of *Oilies,* at the head of Chapter One, is made up. It's a fake dictionary definition. My apologies to all the dedicated Wordies of the world, but it seemed to serve my purposes.

Real facts: In the summer of 1980, I had the experience of accompanying a client and his partner on a business trip to Oklahoma. The purpose: request a $2.5 million bank loan to buy a drill rig. He and his partner were using limited partnerships to raise drilling funds. Somehow, we ended up at a small independent (downstream correspondent) bank known to be friendly to small-time oil operators. Very little documentation required, very few questions asked. This large loan was made in less than an hour together with two cashier checks of $1.25 million to each of my clients personally. Walking around money they laughingly called it, a total of $5 million. I left stunned at the casualness with which those loans had been made, the speed, the lack of due diligence or documentation by that little bank. A huge loan was made based solely on handwritten personal financial statements done on the premises at the time of the loan. We were also introduced to the flamboyant bank president.

Because of the sacred nature of the attorney-client privilege, I can't divulge the identity of the client or his partner. The small bank's name is also withheld, but for different reasons.

Before we left the bank, I asked the president, a loud, cigar smoker with strong cologne, about the many young professional people I had watched with great interest working in a large bullpen area adjacent to the small, glassed-in room next to us. They were not his bank's employees. All were employed by various well-known, large upstream correspondent banks, and he named them for us. He described in detail the correspondent-bank participation scheme he had engineered. A fact he was very proud of.

I left thinking this was another major house of cards, based on many questionable assumptions, the main one being that crude oil would soon reach $100 a barrel. Such were some of the underlying forces driving the oil bubble madness. I wondered how long before it would all come down.

So, no big surprise when a few short years later that little Oklahoma bank located in a strip mall went under. Big time. And took with it several of the nation's largest financial institutions, creating the largest-ever domestic banking debacle up to that time.

If you wander around Denver looking for the Larimer Square Bank, you won't find it. But there is a very real Larimer Square, a lively part of Denver, the area where the city was originally started back in the gold and silver-mining days. It's a fun destination filled with little shops, restaurants, boutiques, entertainment venues, parks, but very little parking. The old red brick buildings have been carefully preserved as part of a long-term restoration effort. The restoration is to be admired since our national tendency is to tear down, replace, and rebuild with ugly concrete, Kremlin-like structures.

My apologies to the Canadian RCMP. They really are a smart, tough, effective, dedicated group of public servants, and no slight was intended in my portrayal of them in this story. Apologies, also, to both the United States and Canadian border officials. They are truly dedicated public servants. No criticism was intended.

The names of the various banks in this story are all fictitious.

There truly was an Aladdin Hotel & Casino in Las Vegas at the time of this story, and there were, in fact, private cabanas located in the back. I know because I stayed there more than once. It was originally known as the Tally-Ho, from 1962-64 before it changed its name to the Aladdin Hotel, based on an Arabic theme. It finally closed in 1997 and was later demolished in a dramatic explosive-engineered implosion to make way for yet another huge casino complex.

There really was an Oscar's BBQ in Cisco, Texas. Unfortunately, it now appears to be permanently closed. But when it was open it served some of the finest BBQ in that part of the world. The labels on the Mason jars of sauce portrayed were authentic.

My apologies to Dolly Parton for using her name in connection with an oil well. No slight was intended. I admire her both as a great country singer and as a very smart, generous, and funny role model for girls and women worldwide. My thanks also to the other movie stars and the vocalists/recording artists mentioned; they all made great movies, and music, and provided colorful background of the period.

There does exist a regional office of the FDIC in Kansas City. My admiration for their dedicated hard work is unbounded. I don't believe for a minute they were asleep on the job during the great bank meltdown of the early 1980s. I admit I took some dramatic liberties there. But I'm confident they were also victims of a massive fraud and the ensuing attempt to cover it by the perpetrators.

Much of the background presented on the US Securities and Exchange Commission (SEC), is based on prior experience and expertise acquired when I was an attorney practicing in that very technical legal specialty. I'm well aware that our financial markets, and the regulations and policies impacting those laboring in that business, have changed a great deal since the time period in the story. What I tried to present was the regulatory policies and conditions on the statute books during that era; likewise, with anything touching on RICO or the federal rules and practices of criminal law and procedure.

There are many used car lots on Las Vegas Boulevard near Nellis AFB, Las Vegas; so, take your pick. Since the one in the story was totally made up, it didn't have a name. The use of the name *Coke* was not intended to promote *Coca Cola* products; it was included simply for the convenience of its short name and worldwide recognition. My apologies to drinkers of *Pepsi Cola* and other soft drink products.

There truly is a Petroleum Club in Denver. It was established in 1948. I have never eaten there or even been invited inside. Likewise, there was a Petroleum Club in Tulsa, established 1950. Sadly, it appears they closed their doors in 2011. I was never invited by my friends in Tulsa to eat there, either. I selfishly included both establishments for background and color; my apologies if any members take exception to anything about those clubs written in this story.

As far as I know, Elkhead Creek near Craig, Colorado, with many fat cutthroat trout, does exist. It's on my list of Fifty Places to Fly-Fish Before I Die.

There really is a very fine, modern regional airport in Penticton, B.C.

No possums or armadillos were hurt in the writing of this story.

ACKNOWLEDGEMENTS

Two good friends of mine provided me with valuable insights into the inner workings and field operations of first, the FBI, and second, a certain agency in the Washington, D.C. area, that for reasons of national security shall remain unnamed. My appreciation to my friends and the agencies they served is unbounded. They are both now retired, so they shall forever remain unnamed. But if they read this story, they will recognize themselves. I tried to present them as I know them.

Thanks must go to my daughter, Amy Jonkhart, The World's Greatest Juristic Mind, a terrific, smart, dedicated, hard-working lawyer and assistant Utah A.G, for her insights on some of the legal stuff herein.

My gratitude to my wife and editor, Janet, for her keen eye, sharp red pencil, and expert knowledge of Strunk & White's *Elements of Style* and the AP writing style. She packs a wallop and has the final say on questions of capitalization, commas, quotation marks, etc. I, however, have the last say on matters of prose and creativity in my writing. I also jealously guard the secrets of my characters.

Thanks to several friends and family who did me the favor of laboring through the early drafts of this book and provided valued suggestions: Amy Jonkhart (again), Paul Landerman (a top-notch writer in his own right), Limerick-specialist J. Brent Bluth; my former law partner and one of my best friends Lowell Snow; fishing partner and World's Foremost Expert of Jazz Trivia, Tom Williams; and to good friends Amy and Travis Banta.

Appreciation also goes to Cecily Condie for her incisive suggestions on revisions and her labors as final editor. Also, my undying thanks to our layout designer, Leslie Thompson, and to Jonas Harding for his clever cover design. Thanks also to my publisher, The Lahontan Press, for their patience in waiting for the final ouvre. If I inadvertently overlooked anyone, my sincere apologies. Wait until my next novel, you may just end up as one of the characters.

OTHER WORKS BY RICHARD LANDERMAN:

The Fly Rod Chronicles
A collection of essays on the quiet sport of fly-fishing

The Man Fisher
A novel

Kennedy's Kids
A novel

The Fly Rod Prospector
Another Collection of Essays on the Quiet Sport of Fly-Fishing

RECENTLY PUBLISHED:

The Fly Rod Schoolmaster
Lessons Learned While Fly-Fishing

www.ingramcontent.com/pod-product-compliance
Lightning Source LLC
Chambersburg PA
CBHW071408200726
48294CB00002B/321

9781735446806